From Ross – ___ ___ Johnston King. My hero,
my pal and my 'Pops'. Forever in my heart.

From Shari – For John. My love. Always.

And from us both, thanks to
Sidney Sheldon for lighting a spark.

And to Jackie Collins with love, respect
and gratitude for the inspiration.

People say that movie stars are really just like us.

They are.

They get up in the morning, go to the toilet, put on their pants one leg at a time . . . but after that it's all different.

TAKING HOLLYWOOD

When a budding radio DJ, and actor, met a young nightclub manager in Glasgow in the 1980s, little did they know that over twenty-five years and thousands of miles later they would still be friends.

Los Angeles-based Ross King is a four-time News Emmy award-winning TV and radio host, actor, producer, writer and performer. King has starred in London's West End, appeared in over ten movies and hosted TV shows in the UK, Europe, USA and Australia. He has also presented countless radio shows and has his own Sunday newspaper column.

UK-based Shari Low has published thirteen novels, including those penned under her pseudonyms, Ronni Cooper and Millie Conway. She is the writer of a newspaper column renowned for its biting humour and straight-talking opinions. Shari has written for television and is a regular radio contributor.

Visit Ross's website at www.rossking.com
Visit Shari's website at www.sharilow.com

TAKING HOLLYWOOD

Shari King

PAN BOOKS

First published 2014 by Pan Books
an imprint of Pan Macmillan, a division of Macmillan Publishers Limited
Pan Macmillan, 20 New Wharf Road, London N1 9RR
Basingstoke and Oxford
Associated companies throughout the world
www.panmacmillan.com

ISBN 978-1-4472-5500-0

1 3 5 7 9 8 6 4 2

A CIP catalogue record for this book is available from the British Library.

Typeset by Palimpsest Book Production Ltd, Falkirk, Stirlingshire
Printed and bound by CPI Group (UK) Ltd, Croydon CR0 4YY

Visit **www.panmacmillan.com** to read more about all our books
and to buy them. You will also find features, author interviews and
news of any author events, and you can sign up for e-newsletters
so that you're always first to hear about our new releases.

Prologue

The 65th Academy Awards,
Dorothy Chandler Pavilion, Los Angeles,
29 March 1993

Lights.

The heat of the lights is as oppressive as the thick cloak of insecurity and desperation that shrouds the audience.

Billy Crystal steps to the podium, his laconic grin a teasing, gentle rebuke to a collection of egos teetering on the edge of explosion.

His fourth time in the role, Crystal introduces the presenter of the next category with an ease born of confidence and familiarity.

Romcom queen Lana Delasso glides onto the stage, blonde hair an homage to her namesake and idol, Lana Turner. Her nomination in the category of Best Supporting Actress will be decided later and she's done everything possible to win. Everything. In her forties now, she doesn't look a day over thirty in her white, cobweb Versace gown, defying the rule that you should never show tits and ass at the same time. The physical reactions in the audience are instant and visceral: tight smiles of envy on bejewelled women coincide with ferocious hard-ons under the $1,000 tuxedos sitting next to them.

1

Her words are white noise until they reach the point:
'. . . Best Original Screenplay.'

Behind her, on a thirty-foot screen, the nominations roll.

Husbands and Wives *by Woody Allen. A smattering of applause, hesitations fuelled by the desire to come down on the right side of the moral judgement on Allen's affair with Mia Farrow's daughter. In Hollywood, picking sides has little to do with principles and everything to do with career enhancement.*

Lorenzo's Oil *by George Miller and Nick Enright. More applause. Camera zooms to a row in which the suits are overshadowed by Susan Sarandon's uncommon beauty.*

Passion Fish *by John Sayles. A movie that was released in only two theatres, grossing only a few tickets over $36,000 before its nomination.*

Unforgiven *by David Peoples. A crowd-pleaser. Directed and produced by Clint Eastwood, the audience of stars greets it with a show of worship reserved for work that has been touched by a deity.*

The Brutal Circle *by Davie Johnston, Zander Leith and Mirren McLean. An outsider. A harrowing story of a life born in violence, lived in violence, cut short by violence. The big screen spans several seats, but all eyes are on the ebullient form of the producer Wes Lomax, legendary head of Lomax Films, the studio responsible for more million-dollar-grossing movies in the last decade than any other.*

The image returns to Lana Delasso, revelling in her moment. The same fingers that held the cock of a studio mogul only an hour before now slide delicately along the folds of the gold envelope.

'And the winner is . . .'

The band kick into action with a cacophonous drum roll.

'The Brutal Circle by . . .'

Sycophantic cheers drown out the names; stars rise to their feet, determined to ensure that when Wes Lomax watches the playback, he will see them heralding his triumph.

In the chaos, the producer in the gallery is a fraction late in switching to the three bodies that move towards the stage, all of them almost as unrecognizable as the extras hired to fill the seats vacated by stars drawn to the restrooms by the call of nature or the need for a line snorted off the top of a toilet.

When the zoom lens on Camera 5 finally catches up with the winners, they are ascending the stairs to the stage. Davie Johnston, at twenty-two the youngest winner of an award in that category in Academy history, strides forward with the surety of a man with an unblinking eye on his destination.

Behind him, Mirren McLean, in the only haute-couture dress she has ever touched, her wild mane of Titian curls tamed to match the elegance of the midnight-blue Dior. Unaccustomed to heels, she steps with care, her expression a mix of concentration and disbelief.

Finally, with a demeanour that suggests reluctance, Zander Leith. For every woman who tried to ignore her partner's sexual interest in Lana Delasso, here is six feet two inches of payback. Wide shoulders, his square jaw set in a brooding grimace, he could be heading to a wake, not the spotlight of a winner.

When only a few feet separate them, Lana's eyes meet his and she instinctively flinches as she recognizes the scorn that is only partially masked by his thick, black lashes. Rebuffed.

While the outside remains a movie goddess, on the inside she is twelve again: the odd kid at school that even the trailer-park waifs avoid. The one that turned into the most beautiful woman in Hollywood, but still felt she had to respond to the summons to Wes Lomax's yacht and blow him to get her own nomination.

Davie Johnston takes the Oscar and moves forward to the microphone.

'I just want to say thank you . . .'

More applause. Most of the audience know of this trio, despite the fact that they are barely out of their teens. Wes Lomax has ensured that their story has saturated the Hollywood press in recent months. All three are credited as writers on the script, the two men playing leading parts in a movie that had killed at the box office. The success was due in part to a publicity and distribution campaign usually reserved for A-list releases, and in part to the fact that it was a damn fine piece of cinema. More than that. It was a raw, hardcore two hours of urban menace that had a generation of American teens queuing for their Saturday-night thriller kicks. It hit $15 million on the balance sheets after the first month, and was now close to double that.

This is the kind of American dream, the triumph of the underdog, the discovery of wonder that this city loves. Three friends from Scotland, the creative talents behind an outstanding script, discovered by Wes Lomax when he took his annual golfing trip to the UK. It was beyond surprising that these kids had managed to get their work in front of Lomax. Even more so that he'd taken enough time off from fucking high-class hookers in the presidential suites of the best hotels in the UK to read it.

Now the audience in the red velvet chairs furrow their brows as they try to decipher Davie Johnston's accent. This isn't the Scottish burr of Sean Connery. Nor does it come close to the accents they heard from Davie and Zander in the movie. It is harder. More guttural. Like bullets being sprayed from a gun in a scene from Reservoir Dogs, Tarantino's big hit of the previous year.

'Thank you to the Academy. Thank you to all of you for letting us be part of this incredible world. And most of all, thank you to the brilliant Wes Lomax. We owe him everything.'

Camera 3 zooms in on Lomax and millions of people watch him nod, eyes glistening, a godfather acknowledging gratitude from his chosen family.

Davie bows to signal the end of his speech, then punches the Oscar into the air. Neither Mirren nor Zander step forward. Recovered from the sting of Zander's rejection, Lana sweeps them off stage right, into the unbridled chaos of runners, technicians, gophers and make-up artists brandishing thick brushes at agitated stars.

They are propelled into a press room, cameras flashing, journos screeching questions, all of which they answer with naive honesty.

How are they enjoying Hollywood? Fine. Great. Aye, it's, erm, amazing.

Are they here to stay? Dunno yet. It depends. Nothing decided.

Is their next project already underway? No plans yet. Nothing concrete. Just ideas.

Davie answers most of the questions, with an occasional contribution from Mirren.

Lou Cole, a young, sparky journalist on the LA Times, changes the pattern.

'So, Zander, how does it feel to be called the new Hollywood heart-throb?'

His bashful grin is automatic, and conceals the fact that for the second time that night his eyes flicker with pure contempt.

'I don't think Tom Cruise has anything to worry about.'

Oblivious to the underlying sentiment, the press pack laugh, as Paula Leno, Lomax Films' hard-ass head of publicity, sweetly but firmly calls an end to the photocall, determined to minimize the risk of a fuck-up and all too aware that the next winners will soon be arriving on the conveyor belt of achievement.

Finally alone, there is a pause as each of them absorbs the last ten incredible minutes of their lives. Davie is the first to react, throwing his arms around Mirren and squeezing her.

'We did it. Shit, I don't believe it.'

She doesn't reply, because over his shoulder her gaze has locked with Zander's, dispelling all notion of celebration. Davie doesn't get the memo. His first burst of excitement over, he turns to the new Hollywood heart-throb. His lifelong friend. Two kids from the same street, bonded as youngsters by a shared recognition that no one really gave a fuck, their symbiotic pairing paying no heed to the reality that in the gene pool of life, Zander got height and physical perfection, while Davie got the kind of non-threatening appeal that made women want to ruffle his hair and tell him about their last broken heart.

'C'mon, man, that was incredible! Did you hear them? That was for us. That has to make everything worth it. C'mon, man . . .' The desperate repetition isn't lost on either of them.

Mirren's teeth clench together as she raises her chin in defiance. She knows there is no point looking for resolution and rapprochement there, and she refuses to show weakness by trying.

Her instincts are right.

For the last photograph, Zander was asked to hold the Oscar to give the picture editors a range of different images to choose from. Now he tosses it to Davie like it is a can of Bud taken from the fridge to wash down a burger.

'Take it.'

Davie's reflexes are just quick enough to save it from the floor.

'You got what you wanted.' Zander's words are barely louder than a whisper, yet drown out all other sounds. 'Now both of you can fuck off, and if I ever see you again, walk the other way.'

1.

'Young Americans' – David Bowie

Beverly Wilshire Hotel, 2013

By the pool, Davie Johnston has taken three cabanas – one for him, one on either side so he doesn't get overheard or interrupted. He's wearing linen trousers and shirt, open just low enough to reveal every perfect contour of his lasered torso. Clothes pale blue. Every time he wears blue, someone mentions that it brings out the colour in his eyes. Every time he replies, 'Oh really? I didn't realize.' Then he goes home and orders ten more shirts, same shade.

As always, he's combining business and pleasure, taking pitch meetings for the next big reality show. He already produces three of the top five in the ratings. He chose the Beverly Wilshire because it kills two birds with one stone. If a meeting goes exceptionally well, he's only an elevator away from a California-king-size bed.

A couple sit down for the three-o' clock slot. It's the first interview after lunch and he's had two glasses of Pinot Noir. In this postcode that qualifies him for AA.

She's a supermodel; he's an ageing rock god, best hits

behind him. They pitch the show. Fly on the wall. *Beauty and the Beats*. Great premise, shit title. They tell Davie every network has expressed interest in this show, but they want him to produce because he's 'the Man'. They're not lying about the second part.

The meeting goes well, like every other meeting in the industry. Both sides flatter the other. Both sides claim interest. Ninety-nine times out of a hundred, one side refuses to take the next call.

Davie listens. Definitely has potential. They shake hands; he tells them he'll be in touch. He will. His secretary will call on Monday and arrange a follow-up meeting. Only the supermodel. Room 567. With the California-king-size bed.

On the ground floor, at Wolfgang Puck's restaurant Cut, Mirren McLean is at her usual table, with her husband, producer-director Jack Gore, and their children, Chloe and Logan.

If anyone added up the value of the diners in the room, it would hit the billions. People have no problem paying $150 for a Japanese 100% Wagyu steak because this place is regarded as the best. And in Beverly Hills, it's only the best that matters.

Jack has been on location for a few weeks, so Mirren is thrilled he's back. Even happier because both her children are there. This is what life is about – family. Right now, she's a mum and a wife, and that's all she wants to be. Just a mum and a wife.

Paul Bonetti, the legendary producer, approaches her table. Shakes hands. She's polite because she has manners, but she wants him gone so she can get back to her family. She likes to keep the two separate. But hey, let's get real. In this town, there's no forgetting about business.

Bonetti smiles, like he's her best friend. 'I couldn't be more pleased for you – still number one at the box office after three weeks,' he says, attempting jovial and sincere, achieving latent fury and crippling envy. His leading men could act; he couldn't. 'Just hope I'm up against you next time around – make it a fair fight.'

'Oh, I'm sure you'll take that one. It must be your turn,' she says, wide grin, while the words 'over my dead body' explode in her head. She makes a mental note to bring forward the release date for the next Clansman movie to ensure it clashes with whatever action killfest he has coming out. Time to put him back in his place. If he wants to play that game, she'll take the challenge.

She'll win. Because she's the biggest and ballsiest player in Hollywood.

And everyone in the room knows it.

On the seventh floor, room 731, Zander Leith is sitting in a solid-mahogany high-back seat. He's already refused the director-style chair left by the company who organized the press junket, as this one forces him to sit up straight. It's all about the angles.

His new movie, the sixth in the Dunhill franchise, hits the cinemas in three weeks' time. He's now been in this airless room for seven hours, answering the same questions from TV and print journalists who all look different but act equally inane.

Cute young girls asking flirtatious questions. The enthu-siastic newbies who want to be your best mate. The older, jaded ones who try to catch you out and twist your words.

Very occasionally, there's someone who has well-researched questions that actually make you think – they're the only ones that hit the pause button on the eradication of your will to live.

Next door, his hair and make-up team, publicist and manager sit ready to pounce when they are required.

One of them is required now. The journo in front of him, wearing the shortest of skirts, is giving him a glimpse of her Victoria's Secret panties. He knows the brand because he shagged the model who was wearing them on the catwalk only a month before.

The interview is coming to a close. Once upon a time, he would get someone else to do his bidding. Now, he just cuts to the quick. It's speed-dating, movie-star 101.

He leans towards her. 'Warren Beatty Suite. Seven p.m.?' It's a question to which they both know the answer.

She leaves satisfied. He will be later. His publicist enters the room, turns to the sound guy.

'Make sure that last exchange is deleted?'

He nods.

Of course he does.

Because no one ever says no in Hollywood.

2.

'Got to Give It Up' – Marvin Gaye

Bel Air, Los Angeles, 2013
A few months later . . .

Davie Johnston

It never crossed Davie Johnston's mind to wonder when he'd stopped feeling lucky.

This life he'd created had nothing to do with luck and everything to do with smarts. Skill. Talent. It wasn't a perfect existence, but as he drove his Bugatti Veyron through the landscaped gardens to the door of his $40-million baroque mansion in the exclusive enclave of Bel Air, he knew it was pretty damn close.

Drego, the Ukrainian gardener, was hosing down the play equipment custom-built for the seven-year-old Johnston twins, Bella and Bray. In this town, his red-haired, fair-skinned twins were a rarity, and it had served them well. Since they were three years old, they'd been in the cast of the hit sitcom *Family Three*. A week didn't pass without a request for a family photo shoot from the celebrity mags, and every now and then he indulged them.

Not that he needed the publicity. He got enough of that

presenting *American Stars*. It was still number one in the ratings, knocking *America's Got Talent* and *American Idol* back to the also-ran positions they deserved.

He'd be signing this season's contract any day now, and that would, once again, put Seacrest in his place too. The last decade had been a tussle for supremacy between them, a battle Davie was winning. Thirty million dollars for his last *American Stars* contract had made sure of that, not to mention the success of the reality shows he produced. Global profit on those had put him in the financial 'fuck off' stratosphere. He never had to ask the price of anything. But he did. Not because he perpetuated the ridiculous myth that Scots were tight with cash – in his experience, generosity was in their cultural DNA. He asked the price because he was smart. Scots invented the telephone, television and the steam engine. Davie invented the most watched shows on the planet.

He had *American Stars*. He had *The Dream Machine*, a sentimental slushfest that made dreams come true and left no heartstring untugged. And his other baby, *Liking Lana* – a car-crash docu-soap featuring the fucked-up life and family of tarnished has-been Lana Delasso – had finally topped Seacrest's baby, *Keeping Up With the Kardashians*, last season.

He checked his limited-edition gold Panerai Kampf-schwimmer watch – the case designed and made by Panerai, the movement by Rolex. It didn't get any better, but it did cost $1 million. Two o' clock. The kids wouldn't be back from the set for another hour. Time for a shower and to put a couple of calls in to the East Coast. The second-season premiere of *New York Nixons*, his latest scripted reality hit, starring the extended family of rock legend Jax Nixon, was due to air next week and Sky, the wayward daughter of Jax's first wife, Rainbow, was due to stage an overdose in the next couple of days. Cue shock, outrage, sympathy and more free headlines than even the best publicist could drum up in a week. That was Davie's talent. He was adaptable. Saw opportunities. Ran with them. Strategized for success. When the acting jobs dried up a few years after the Oscar, he morphed, schmoozed, spotted the potential in TV. There was a whole new dawn of talent shows just waiting to happen. They'd already stormed the UK market. Davie sought out Simon Cowell, the man behind them, asked questions, listened, learned. Then he developed his own concept, a variation on the UK theme, and took it to the American networks. They commissioned it as a summer filler. To their surprise, it rocked the country. Massive ratings. Massive buzz.

Davie hitched a ride on that bus of wannabes and it had brought him as much fame, glory and cash as any A-list actor. And when the era of the reality shows dawned, he was in pole position again, using his own cash to bankroll pilots that became syndicated shows that added more zeros to his bank account.

As he opened the front door, he could hear Drego's wife, Ivanka, singing some unintelligible song in the kitchen. A Russian chick who dressed like a whore and loved country music. Thankfully, she cooked like a dream, and her OCD meant every corner of the house glistened.

Ignoring the temptation of the aromas emanating from the kitchen, he headed up the left-hand side of the sweeping double marble and glass staircase. No point eating now, especially when he'd skipped a gym session and headed home early. He'd pay for it tomorrow. Clay, his trainer, was an ex-middleweight champion on the US Olympic team who abided by the only two rules Davie had set at the outset of their partnership: don't hit the face and don't kill me.

Crossing the upper hallway of his palatial home, he lifted his Prada T-shirt – blue, of course – over his head in readiness for the shower. Still moving, he opened the top button of his jeans with one hand, turned the doorknob of his bedroom with the other.

The brush of the white shagpile carpet muffled the sound of the door opening, giving him a couple of seconds to take in the scene in front of him before the occupants of the room registered his presence.

The curve of her back caught his eye first. How many times had he seen his wife's silhouette on billboards and in magazines, and how many other men had jerked off over the perfection of her breasts or the exquisite beauty of her ass?

Or the deep raven hair, long and thick, that flowed down past her breasts, natural, high, the perfect size for her slender frame. Or the hazel eyes, with flecks of gold that changed colour in the light.

When he married Jenny Rico nearly ten years ago, he'd sometimes find himself lying awake at night just staring, almost unable to believe that he could touch that body whenever he wanted to.

Now, from his side view, he could see every contour of

her shape as she knelt on the bed, legs open, eyes closed, her head thrown back as her hands caressed her breasts.

Lying beneath her, another shape, one that would confuse the TV addicts of the nation. On the screen, in the hugely popular cable cop show *Streets of Power*, these two people were partners, their relationship purely platonic.

At no point in the show was his wife's clit being licked to orgasm by her slightly older, more experienced sidekick. Mixed race, her skin a luscious caramel, her hair a waist-length curtain of ebony gloss, Darcy Jay was second only to Jenny in her physical perfection.

A sound, once familiar, escaped from his wife's throat and he paused out of courtesy and curiosity, realizing that she was just seconds from coming.

When her gasps stopped, she fell to the side, reaching over to cradle the face that had been checking out her Brazilian grooming schedule only seconds before.

'I love you,' she whispered tenderly, and despite himself, Davie winced aloud.

The two heads on the bed snapped round, his wife's face creasing into something between quiet amusement and exasperation. Her companion preferred a more vocal demonstration of feeling.

'Jesus, Davie, have you never heard of knocking? Or were you so busy getting your rocks off you forgot your manners? I've told you, you're welcome to join in anytime.'

All three smiled, acknowledging the exaggeration in the statement. Davie threw his T-shirt in the direction of the bed as he crossed to his en suite, aware that there weren't many men on earth who wouldn't have accepted the offer.

A hot threesome with Jenny Rico and her co-star Darcy Jay. Numbers one and two, respectively, on *People Magazine*'s Most Beautiful Women list for the last three years in succession. In public, both straight, both gorgeous, both sexy as hell.

The irony was that this *arrangement* had been his idea. On the opening night of *Streets of Power* six years earlier, the three of them had ended up drinking late into the night in a bungalow at Chateau Marmont. Too many bottles of Dom Pérignon had led to clothes on the floor and a sexual experience that came pretty close to heaven. It wasn't the first time he and Jenny had played around with a new friend, but as the weeks passed, the two women developed a relationship that went far beyond getting fucked up and indulging in some girl-on-girl for fun. And he was no longer invited to the party.

The transition had been tough, but when it came down to a choice between accepting their relationship or divorce, he'd chosen to go with the flow. Adapt. Hustle. Just like always. To the outside world, he lived a charmed existence with a stunning wife, regularly socializing with her best friend and TV partner, the stellar Darcy Jay.

The world would say that a guy didn't get much luckier than that. It was all about perceptions. Illusions. Making the view look very different for those on the outside, looking in.

So, no, as the jerk-off wet dream taking place on his bed proved, life wasn't perfect. But as he told himself every day, it was pretty damn close.

All he had to do was keep it that way.

3.

'Make You Feel My Love' – Adele

Mirren McLean

The slam of Mirren's glass on the marble worktop made the assembled group of PR managers and lawyers blink.

'I was under the misapprehension that keeping my daughter out of trouble and out of jail was what I paid you for.' Her voice had dropped in tone to somewhere between serious and deadly, masking the inherent weariness that seeped through every fibre of her being. For a fleeting moment she wished that Jack were here, someone to have her back and share the worry, but that was just the exhaustion talking. He'd be on location in Istanbul for two more weeks, shooting a spy thriller with Mercedes Dance and Dan Powers, the hottest on-screen couple in Hollywood. Besides, after nineteen years of blissful marriage to Jack Gore, much of it spent separated by the demands of their careers, she could handle this. Didn't she always?

Chloe Gore, wild child, Hollywood brat, Californian beauty, her daughter, the one who shunned growth and development for repeating the mistakes of many yesterdays.

That's why Mirren knew that this meeting and the next few hours of activity were only delaying the inevitable. She was depressingly aware that later that day she'd sit in this kitchen again, in the home these people had contaminated time after time, and the questions would start swirling around her mind.

How had she let this happen? Where had she gone wrong? Was it something she'd done? A mistake she'd made? Had she not loved Chloe enough? Did her devotion to Jack somehow shut out her kids? Was she such a terrible mother? How could one child turn out so happy and another so damaged?

It happened so often it was becoming just another normal day, one that invariably started with the same 7 a.m. call.

'Honey, she's locked up again. Beverly Hills. DUI. Resisting arrest.' Mirren's best friend, Lou Cole, editor of the *Hollywood Post*, a stunning African American who looked like Iman, and – when it came to all things celebrity – had the encyclopedic intelligence of Einstein.

A doyenne of the gossip columns, a twenty-five-year veteran of the LA press circuit who had connections in every club, hotel concierge and gutter of the city.

'I'm sorry, hon,' Lou said sadly.

Mirren knew the sympathy was sincere. The two women had been friends for two decades, and right from the start their relationship had been a sisterhood in every sense of the word.

Besides, sometimes she thought Chloe's bond with her godmother was closer than the mother–daughter ties that had been shredded by years of disappointment and defiance.

Mirren McLean loved her daughter. But right now, she didn't like her much.

Two hours later, the depressingly regular war cabinet was in session in her kitchen, the anxieties of the publicists and lawyers clear in every nuance of their speech and actions. Chloe Gore had made them all plenty over the years. A dozen arrests, a couple of short-term sentences and more incidents requiring damage limitation than any of them could count.

Strategy agreed, they made their way to the courtroom for a 10 a.m. appearance. Mirren thought she caught a look of empathy as Judge Leighton Hamilton took his seat, and had a vague recollection of reading about a sting involving his teenage son, a tabloid magazine and a large bag of Colombian snow.

When Chloe shuffled in, she avoided eye contact, kept her gaze on the floor, her lids swollen and ringed with dark shadows. Mirren was desperate to reach out to her, to stroke her tangled hair, but there was little point. She'd tried the love-bomb approach and it had been every bit as unsuccessful as the harsh rejection of tough love she'd tried next.

As the case was set out by a couple of expensive lawyers in Armani, Mirren zoned out, wondering if the crowds had started to form outside yet. There would be the usual paps, and then there would be the idle curious with their camera phones at the ready. That was the problem. Everyone these days was a potential videographer. Telling stories all over town. Recording snapshots they might be able to flog for $100, or, if they got really lucky, $100,000. They would be out there. Waiting. Calling their friends.

Perhaps, just like last time, a rumour would already be sweeping the city, claiming that Chloe's brother, Logan Gore, was inside supporting his sister, and a thousand teenage boy-band fans would be outside right now chanting his name.

The noise of the gavel interrupted her thoughts and she listened as Lou leaned forward from the row behind. 'Mandatory rehab. Under the circumstances, that was the best verdict we could have hoped for, darling.'

Only when she was almost at the door that led to the bowels of the building did Chloe raise her eyes to meet Mirren's. The emptiness was harrowing. Nothing. Nothing there at all. Any sign of the little girl she'd adored had been snuffed out by her cocktail of choice: Xanax and coke.

'Want me to come home with you?' Lou offered.

Mirren shook her head, causing some of her curls to come free from the grip that held them in a loose chignon. Physically, twenty years in Hollywood had changed her very little. She was still as slender as she'd always been, with just a few crow's feet belying the passage of the years. She put it down to yoga, SilkPeel and OXYjet facials, and the skills of Dr Lancer, the dermatologist who was on speed dial for half the stars in town. No trout pouts or G-forced faces there. Just small tweaks, natural work that gently took the years off without leaving a trace of a needle or laser.

'Thanks, but I'm fine. I need to get organized. We start shooting next week on *Clansman 5*.'

Her other love. The Clansman. He'd come along right after the Oscar, when she realized that millions of American women got their rocks off at the thought of those mythical bare-chested, kilted heroes of historical fiction.

The Clansman had been her first novel, penned almost two decades before, as she cocooned herself in a tiny Santa Monica apartment in her first year in California. A bestseller, it demanded a sequel, then another. Ten years after it was written, Mirren wrote the screenplay and persuaded a small studio to back her directorial debut. That studio backed a winner. Clansman was now a brand that encompassed novels, merchandise and movies, all of them written and directed by Mirren.

She was one of the top female earners in the town, rich in everything except maternal satisfaction.

As the courtroom began to clear, Lou leaned in and whispered in her ear, 'Can I come and leer at Lex Callaghan's pecs? C'mon, throw an old broad a bone. I can be there any day you like.'

Mirren's eyes narrowed. 'Lou, that's a totally inappropriate thing to say. We're in a court, for God's sake. And he won't be half naked until week two.'

It was impossible to resist. The humour of their friendship had got her through so many tough moments in the last two decades.

'Miss McLean, there's quite a crowd outside. My men will see you to your car.' She smiled in thanks to the sergeant, a tall, handsome guy with the lean, muscular build of an NBA player, who looked much younger than his rank suggested. It wasn't lost on her that this was the type of man she would want for her daughter. Strong, streetwise, employed, focused. Was it too much to ask?

As good as his word, the sergeant got her out of the building. There, they were joined by another four officers.

There was a myth that every officer in Beverly Hills was also a member of the Screen Actors Guild. Looking at these guys, Mirren would hedge her bets that it was only the three with the buffed fingernails.

They almost got to the car. Almost.

Later, she wouldn't be able to remember the paparazzo's face, only the voice.

Sitting back at that kitchen table, whisky in her glass, watching the sun come up over the city, the familiar questions once again swirled around in her head.

How had she let this happen? Where had she gone wrong? Was it something she'd done?

A mistake she'd made? Had she not loved Chloe enough? Did her devotion to Jack somehow shut out her kids? Was she such a terrible mother? How could one child turn out so happy and another so damaged?

But almost immediately they were pushed to the side by the words she'd heard as she left court. 'Mirren!' a vaguely familiar photographer had shouted as she passed by. 'Do you have any comment on the rumours that Jack is fucking Mercedes Dance?'

She hadn't reacted, aware that it was a common ruse to get a reaction, one that would sell pictures to news desks across the country. An old trick. It meant nothing. Move on, people, nothing to see here.

But now, as dawn broke and she replaced the whisky with coffee, her gut clenched as the phone call she'd been expecting all night finally came.

'Honey, it's Lou . . .'

Chloe was locked up. Only an hour before, Logan had

sent a text saying he was just about to go on stage in Miami. So there were only two things that Lou could have discovered that would warrant an early morning call and inject such dread and despair into her friend's voice. One belonged in the past, had sat on her shoulder since long before Hollywood was her home, and could rip apart her life, her reputation, her career and everything she'd ever achieved. The other lived in the present and came with the prospect of slicing her heart in two. Every instinct told her heart to adopt the brace position.

'I know,' she replied. Calm. Serene. Resigned.

'It's Jack.'

'I know.'

'And Mercedes.'

'I know.'

'Mirren, she's pregnant.'

The pain exploded inside her. Her career, her reputation and her achievements remained untouched. This was much, much worse.

Her heart began to bleed.

Lou broke the silence. 'Do you know what you're going to do?'

Mirren could only manage a whisper. 'Yes.'

4.

'I Still Haven't Found
What I'm Looking For' – U2

Zander Leith

The plump nurse trundled towards him, brandishing a cup from the coffee house down the street. Zander knew it would contain a skinny latte with a vanilla twist and three extra espresso shots. His caffeine overdose of choice. He also knew that somehow his coffee-winning manner, combined with a perception that he was a lovely guy who always got the girl/ saved the day/won the war in the movies had given this woman a glimmer of hope that the top box-office draw in the country would respond to her daily gift by screwing her in a very expensive Malibu rehab clinic, sometime between group counselling and having his pee tested to ensure he hadn't discovered a way to smuggle in a bottle of JD.

It happened all the time. The groupie who got a friend at the alarm company to disable his house alarm so that she could sneak in, strip and lie spread-eagled on his kitchen table. The model who would upgrade on a flight so that she was sitting next to him and 'accidentally' roll her head onto his shoulder as he slept. He'd never found manipulation to be much of a turn-on, so while it was always a conversation-opener, it never ended in a relationship. A blow job, maybe. But ever since Clinton, that didn't count.

However, he accepted his coffee from Greta with his million-dollar smile and a wink that ensured the same scene would play out again tomorrow morning. It was Groundhog Day in here. Same walls, same people, same shit for weeks now. The expensive carpets, manicured gardens, the top-class therapists and the prime location on top of one of Malibu's most scenic clifftops didn't mask what this was – a collection of misfits and desperadoes who had everything yet couldn't deal with reality without a pill or a swig from a bottle. And he was one of them. Again.

He made his way along the corridor to the patient reception, where Lebron greeted him with a wide grin of perfect white teeth. 'Hey, man, big day today. You want me to, like, do a drum roll or something?'

Zander laughed. He liked the irreverence and the sarcasm. Reminded him of another place and time, many years and several thousand miles ago.

'Naw, just give it to me straight.' The strength of his Scottish accent surprised him a little. It had softened over twenty years in LA and rarely made a reappearance unless he was talking to someone from home.

Home. Strange that he still called it that when he hadn't been back in two decades. The memory of that night in 1993 when he was forced to attend the Oscars ceremony still made his perfect, professionally whitened back molars grind.

His thoughts were cut short by Lebron handing over a telephone with a flourish and a cheeky bow.

His weekly phone call. Zander thanked him and strolled out through a side door to the garden, punching in familiar numbers as he walked. Last week, he'd used it to call his PA, Hollie. This week, it was to the only other person in the world who gave a shit.

The call was answered immediately.

'Yeah?'

'Wes, it's me.'

'Hey, bud. How you doing?'

Zander could picture Wes Lomax reclining in his $10,000 calf-hide chair, cigar hanging from his mouth, much to the disgust of the anti-smoking lobby, who wanted an immediate death penalty for anyone who sparked up in this town.

'You tell me,' Zander replied, aware that the clinic management sent a daily report to the head of the studio and the insurance company that were underwriting the movie. It was standard practice for all productions to have a safety net. The policies were expensive, but they paid out for delays and shutdowns caused by freak weather, terrorism and actors going off grid.

Zander had become high risk. One more strike and they'd start withholding a percentage of his salary as collateral against another incident.

The next level above that was uninsurable. If that happened, his career was over. No one would touch him. When Robert Downey Jr. was in the depths of his chaos, the insurance companies refused to back him. His career was only saved when Mel Gibson stepped in and paid an insurance guarantee to allow him to work on *The Singing Detective*. Ironic. One hellraiser saves another.

'They say you're doing great, son. Spoke to the insurance company yesterday and they want one more week. Publicity are saying that public opinion is still with you – that *Entertainment Tonight* special really helped. Legal have made the charges go away and shooting starts in a fortnight, so we're looking good.'

Another week. He supposed he should be grateful. The blowout had been spectacular, a combination of Jack Daniel's, a reality-show prick who crossed the line and the kind of beating that no stunt coordinator could fake. Zander's hands had healed, and no doubt a large cheque from Lomax had helped the wounds to the Z-lister's body and ego heal real quick.

He was lucky he wasn't in jail. But the insurance company had been unequivocal in their insistence that he go to rehab before they'd back his next movie, the seventh in a spy series featuring Seb Dunhill, an MI6 operative who could kick Bond's ass. Bourne went to four movies. Die Hard was at five, but there was another in the works that would take it up to match Rocky's six. On number seven, Dunhill didn't quite match Bond in numbers but it blew the other action franchises away at the box office. That bought Zander Leith a whole lot of leverage and understanding.

So it was back to the five-star, all-inclusive package in Life Reborn, the finest rehab in town. He knew the drill. It wasn't like this was the first time.

Hanging up with a sigh, Zander lit a cigarette, the smell blending with the scent of the flowers that bloomed in shades of white all around him. It was like drying out in a fricking morgue.

It was only when he tossed the remnants of his smoke into the sand of a podium ashtray behind him that he noticed her. Sitting in the corner. Hugging her knees. Head down. Long red curls falling around her. The image kicked him in the chest, closing his airwaves. Mirren.

But no.

As if sensing his presence, she looked up. 'What the fuck are you looking at?'

His shrug clearly wasn't the answer she was looking for. A light of recognition switched on in her eyes.

'Zander Leith.'

It was a statement, not a question.

'I'm Chloe.'

'I know.'

Run. He should turn and run. For once in his life he should do the smart thing and walk away from trouble.

'You grew up with my mom.'

'I did,' he replied. Run. Just run.

'So you already know.'

'Know what?'

'Just what kind of bitch she is.'

5.

'Don't You (Forget About Me)'
– Simple Minds

Glasgow, 2013

The room smelt of death and a million futile wishes. Sarah McKenzie prided herself on having a strong stomach, but the stench was making her want to retch. Swallowing, she fought to keep down the bile. Nothing was going to get in the way of this story. She'd been working on it for months. Manny Murphy. Glasgow gangland crime lord. A giant of a man and a legend in this city.

But that was before the cancer started eating away at his organs until he was nothing but skin, bone and disease. Now in his seventies, he was bedbound and totally reliant on the nurse his sons paid for to assuage the guilt they knew they should feel for stepping into the old man's shoes and walking in the other direction. His young, gold-digging wife had left him, and none of his three boys had been near his home on the outskirts of Crofthill, the area he'd grown up in. Now, he wouldn't go any further afield until they took him there in a box.

His sons belonged to the new Glasgow. The side that left

the Mean City behind. The glittering shopping centres. The world-class restaurants. The architecture, there for hundreds of years, now appreciated for its historic splendour. The commerce, the culture, the fashion, the forward-thinking buzz. Glasgow was an extraordinary city. A remarkable green place. Somewhere to belong. A city of ambition, aspiration, humour and hope.

Not that his sons' desertion was a great loss. Manny was never slow in telling any audience what a disappointment his offspring were. All of them too impetuous, cardboard gangsters who thought they could throw their weight around without the intelligence to back it up. Where were their plans? Where was their class? Their long-term strategies? Not like it was in his day. Back then, the territories were marked and everyone knew where they stood. Now, it was all about a fast buck with no thought to the future. Coke. That's what his boys were into now. Running it up from Liverpool in the back of fruit trucks. Ironic. He'd heard the rumours that all three of his kids were using the drug as one of their five-a-day.

He'd told Sarah all of this on her last visit. Three times she'd sat here now and so far there was nothing she could use without ending up sued or dead. Patience. Wasn't that what her editor always told her she needed? Patience. Quick reactions on the daily stories, patience on the long shots. She'd spent months on this now, setting up the meetings, bribing the nurse, getting Manny to agree to speak to her, determined that he was going to give her the story that would make her career. Put her on the map. At twenty-five, it was time to prove she had the grit that was needed to make it in newspapers.

If only the old bastard would tell her something she could

use. For the last hour he'd been banging on about a post-office job he'd carried out in the early 1990s. None of what he was telling her was new.

He hacked up some phlegm and wiped his face with the sleeve of his black silk pyjamas before continuing.

'The whole crew got ten years, except me and Jono Leith.'

Sarah almost missed it. On the face of it, nothing in that last statement jumped out. Manny's ability to dodge justice was the stuff of urban legend. He'd already moved on to the next anecdote when something niggled. Perhaps it was the fact that in all her research she'd never come across Jono Leith. Perhaps it was the unusual surname, made famous by one of Glasgow's most-loved exports. Something made her stop Manny mid-flow.

'Jono Leith?'

Manny paused for a moment, as if rewound straight back to the memory of a long-ago time.

'Aye, Jono. Whit a guy. Bampot. Maddest bastard I ever knew.'

Coming from someone whose friendship circle comprised many mad bastards, that was quite an accolade.

A shot of adrenalin made Sarah's hand shake just a little.

'What happened to him?'

Another pause. 'Dunno. Disappeared off the face of the earth one day. Just never showed up again. Heard he fucked off with some bit on the side he was shagging. Christ knows there were many.'

The obvious question niggled at her. 'How come I've never heard of him?' If Sarah was ever to have a specialist subject, it would be Glasgow criminals, past and present. She'd spent years studying her subject, reading reports, searching old archives and she didn't remember ever coming across the name Jono Leith.

Manny's shaking hand lifted a mug half filled with dark, stewed tea to his cracked lips.

'That wis Jono's thing. A bit paranoid. Never bragged about the big stuff and never got busted for it either. Stayed oot the papers and there was nane o' that internet pish then. Naw, Jono kept it all quiet and tidy. The polis knew him, but they could never tie any of the major stuff to him. Fucking Tefal he was.'

That could have been the conversation-stopper if the journalist in Sarah, trained to keep asking questions until she got something she could use, hadn't gone for a stab in the dark.

'Don't suppose he was any relation to Zander Leith?' Her self-conscious laugh broadcast the message that she realized she was being ridiculous. Zander Leith was a local hero, one of the famous movie trio who'd left the local streets and conquered the world. Zander Leith, Mirren McLean, Davie Johnston. Megastars with more column inches and interviews than any other Scottish export. Hell, Gerry Butler and Ewan McGregor didn't even come close. If Zander was connected to a shady figure, surely it would have come out long ago? Nah, there was no way she was on to anything here.

'Zander . . .' Manny's tongue rolled the word around for a few moments. 'You mean the bloke in the films?'

Sarah was embarrassed. She'd known it was stupid. Too much of a leap. Manny would think she was a complete imbecile now and she wasn't rushing to disagree with him.

'Aye, hen, that's him. Back then he wis just Wee Sandy. And aye, Jono was his old man.'

6.

'Walk this Way' – Aerosmith

Davie made his regular morning pit stop at the Nespresso Boutique on Beverly Drive. It was the Rolls-Royce, the private jet, the Gucci of the coffee world. It was the only place to be seen to re-caffeinate. Davie bypassed the outdoor patio and went straight for the product. There were twenty-one choices of gourmet grand cru. His was strong, black and fast.

If it was true that the most beautiful people in the world lived in LA, the ones who loved coffee were here. Over the years, he'd been asked a hundred times how he could live in a society so fake. If the six-foot blonde drinking her iced macchiato in front of him was fake, then the realists of the world could cry him a river.

While he was waiting, he used his iPhone to scan the gossip websites. He'd already seen the news on TMZ the previous night, but somehow, seeing Chloe's mugshot just made it so much more vivid. His first reaction was irritation that it had knocked Sky Nixon's overdose off the front page. Shit. They were counting on that to send the ratings on the opening episode of the second series of *New York Nixons* through the roof.

His second reaction, more of an afterthought, was sympathy. Mirren must be going through hell with that kid of hers. Not that it was any of his business, and he knew she wouldn't thank him for the pity. Or would she? How long had it been? Fifteen years? More? The last time he'd spoken to Mirren McLean, she'd made it perfectly clear there wouldn't be a follow-up conversation.

Coffee delivered, he headed back to the car, shrugging off the memory. In the Bugatti, he made a call. It went straight to the answering machine of Sky's mother, a wacked-out heroin-chick-turned-organic-tree-saver called Rainbow, who kept it quiet that her much-publicized, minimalist crusade to be at one with the earth was secretly bankrolled by enough cash to buy her very own small island.

They were all the same, the Hollywood tree-huggers. Pontificated about saving the Amazon rainforest while hiring private jets to fly their favourite meal from one coast to the other.

'Rainbow, it's Davie. Problem at this end. Sky's situation didn't get as much airtime as we thought. Two choices: we need a repeat, another overdose, or else make a press statement saying she's not recovering. You know the drill. Tears. Prayers. Twitter. Facebook. Call me back to discuss.'

He'd just hung up when the phone rang again. This time, he flicked it to loudspeaker, channelling it through the sound system on the Bugatti.

'Hey, Al. How the devil are you?' Davie's tone switched immediately from pissed to positive. Hollywood didn't do negativity. Even if you were down to your last dollar and the critics had handed you your ass on a plate, you had to maintain the aura of a winner, one that sat somewhere in the middle of the scale between confident and Charlie Sheen crazy.

'Davie. News.'

The top agent at Creative Stars Agency, Al Woolfe was always succinct and straight to the point. That's why he was the most sought-after representative in town. Besides, Davie hadn't paid him 10 per cent for the last 10 years to be his buddy.

'Am on my way in, bro,' Davie replied, pre-empting the conversation. His *American Stars* contract had been discussed and their offer was due to hit the desk that morning.

'Listen, this is just a holding call. The paperwork isn't here yet. Pricks string it out every year. We should have added on an extra million just for their aggravating dick-tugging.'

As he hung up, Davie changed course. No point in heading to the CSA offices now. For a moment, he wasn't sure where to go. The sun was shining, it was 75 degrees, he had all the time and money in the world, and yet he couldn't think of a single thing he wanted to do.

At the bottom of Beverly, he made the decision. Instead of heading right, he hung a left. Fifteen minutes later, he was pulling up to the security checkpoint at Captis Studios, the home of *Family Three*.

The guard treated him like an old friend.

'Mr Johnston, we didn't have you on the list for today. Good to see you.'

'Thanks, Rick.' It was an old trick. He had an encyclopedic memory for the names of anyone who may ever be in a position to make his life easier. 'Just missing the kids and thought I'd pop in to see them.'

Rick gave him a high five as he waved him through. Laying out some love made life easier. Case in point.

Outside soundstage 23, he spotted Bella and Bray being herded from their trailer to the set and pulled over out of sight. As soon as they were gone, he parked up and made for the biggest trailer on the lot.

Opening the door, he congratulated himself on the decision. Vala Diaz, the twenty-five-year-old Mexican star of *Family Three*, was standing completely naked being spray-tanned by one of the huge entourage employed to keep her looking hotter than the midday sun in Tijuana.

A lazy smile played on her lips when she saw him and she immediately dismissed the acolyte. She didn't flinch from her position. Hands on hips. Shoulders back. Feet apart. Long, glossy black hair now unclipped and falling in two perfect sheets to her waist. Her golden skin oozing St Tropez and sheer sex.

'Something is wrong,' she said, her intoxicating Spanish accent changing the vowels.

'What's that?' It was a game Davie was all set to play.

'You have been here for a minute and I cannot see your cock yet,' she teased.

Davie responded by leaning over and biting down on one of her nipples, just the way he knew she liked it. He'd been screwing her for the last year and he'd never known a chick to like it as rough as she did. Sometimes he wasn't sure if it was passion or legal assault.

As he unleashed his dick and lifted her up, her legs automatically wrapped round his waist. Pushing up against the ivory silk fabric that lined the wall of the trailer, he slid inside her, grinding against her as she barked out orders. Harder. Faster. Her hands were in his hair, grabbing, pulling, as her lip bit down on his until it felt like it was bleeding. This one was a wildcat. Thankfully, he'd always been known for his support of wildlife causes.

The ringing of his cell interrupted his amusement. Taking one hand off her ass, he reached round to his back pocket and extracted the phone, immediately recognizing the tone that was allocated to Al's number.

Two things happened at once. He answered the call and Vala slapped him hard across the face. He grabbed her wrist, trying to speak as she climbed off his dick, still slapping and biting.

'Al, hey.'

'Switch on the TV.'

'What?'

'Switch on the TV. Sam Rubin. KTLA. Quick.'

Pushing Vala away, he grabbed the remote from the walnut table in the centre of the room and flicked it onto Channel 5.

Rainbow Nixon was standing in front of a press pack, dressed in a long, flowing white robe, a string of fricking daisies round her head, speaking to the crowd.

'My poor darling Sky is lying in hospital right now, close to death.'

Davie couldn't help a twitch of a smile. That was quick work. He'd only left the instructions an hour ago. Damn, she was playing the part well. If she'd acted as well as this back in the 1980s, she'd be a fucking megastar now.

'And I can no longer keep quiet and tolerate this situation. It's time people knew the truth about these so-called reality shows. The lies. The manipulations. We've fallen victim to the very worst kind of evil and now my beautiful girl lies in a hospital bed and I don't know if she will ever wake up.'

He froze. What? This wasn't in the script. She was supposed to spin them a line, whip up a few headlines. What the fuck was she doing? A cold chill rose from his toes, collapsing his erection as it passed on the way to his stomach.

'I discovered this morning that my daughter deliberately overdosed in order to get publicity for the Season Two premiere of our family's show, *New York Nixons*. I had absolutely no knowledge that my baby planned to do this.'

Lie. That was a lie. It had originally been her idea. Sure, he'd been happy to go along with it, but . . . shit, she was throwing him under the bus. Stop speaking. Stop. Speaking.

'Her actions were on the instructions of the producer of our show, Davie Johnston.'

The press went crazy, bulbs flashed, and dozens of voices shouted out questions at once. The suit standing next to Rainbow put his hand up to hush them, then pointed to a journalist on his left, who immediately reacted to his cue.

'Rainbow, these are very series accusations. Do you have any proof of this?'

'I do. Only minutes ago, I received this call from that vile man.' Rainbow held a recording device to the microphone and pressed play.

Davie froze. Paralysed. Mute. His entire brain hijacked by an internal voice screaming, 'No!'

'*Rainbow, it's Davie. Problem at this end. Sky's situation didn't get as much airtime as we thought. Two choices: we need a repeat, another overdose, or else make a press statement saying she's not recovering. You know the drill. Tears. Prayers. Twitter. Facebook. Call me back to discuss.*'

Holy. Fucking. Shit. Vomit rose from his stomach, making his oesophagus twist so tight it felt like he was being suffocated. No breath. No air. No strength in his legs.

He sank to his knees. This was bad. Really bad. A life-changer.

His phone fell to the floor and somewhere in the distance he could hear Al say his name. He grabbed the handset and pummelled it with his fist, intending to switch it off, smash it, anything to make this stop.

Instead, he heard the modulated tones of his answering machine: '*First new message.*'

His assistant's voice joined the cacophony of noise exploding in his head. '*Hi, Davie. This is Jorja. We've had an interview request from a journalist called Sarah McKenzie at the* Daily Scot. *I know you love to keep your profile up in the UK, so shall I set up a date? She wants the focus to be your life back in Scotland, growing up with Zander Leith and Mirren McLean. Oh, and she said something really weird, something about wanting to meet the families the three of you left behind.*'

Davie Johnston's world faded to black.

7.

'Fake' – Alexander O'Neal

'I never meant this to happen, Mirren.'

Oh, dear God, she was in cliché hell. Any minute now, he'd tell her he hadn't meant to hurt her.

'And I never meant to h—'

'Stop! Which bit did you not mean, Jack? The bit where you shagged her, or the bit where she accidentally got pregnant with your kid?'

Yes, she knew she'd switched from cliché to dialogue straight out of an afternoon soap opera, but she obviously hadn't read the manual on how to deal with a husband of nineteen years who had just ceremoniously shafted your life. They were standing in their indoor kitchen. There was an outdoor one too, but that was more functional. This was her dream room, every item hand-picked. The red lacquer La Cornue's Grand Palais range, copper sink, Hammacher juicer, Mugnaini pizza oven and the Meneghini Arredamenti fridge in solid oak, a contrast against the hand-painted scarlet solid-wood doors on the cupboards and drawers. The white marble worktops glistened under the rack of spotlights overhead. In the corner, a turret, her own addition, accommodation for a semicircular booth that had been the backdrop to years of family dinners, homework and long nights at the laptop.

They'd planned and built it with no expense spared because they'd wanted it to last a lifetime. Shame she'd had to find out that he didn't have the same view on monogamy.

Looking at him now, Mirren thought she'd never seen a man look so utterly pathetic. Jack Gore was from the Liam Neeson school of manhood. Tall, broad, with a naturally muscular, lean physique and a face that was undoubtedly attractive but stopped just a shade on the craggy side of movie-star handsome. It had always been obvious that Chloe took after her: same hair, same features, same smile. Logan had his father's blond hair, wide grin and deep blue eyes, yet somehow they were proportioned slightly differently, giving her son an all-American cuteness instead of his father's rugged appeal.

He was still speaking, but she wasn't listening.

For the first time in many, many years, she wanted to physically hurt someone, to smash his face until it was pulp. In all her married life, she could never have comprehended feeling this way about him. Jack. Her easy-going, macho husband, the one who could walk into any room and make her instantly feel at ease because he was there. That wasn't the guy who was standing in front of her now. This one was needy, weak, pitiful.

'You'd just been so busy and—'

'Don't you dare blame me.' Her voice was low and edged with pure ice. 'Don't you dare,' she repeated, stopping there, biting back the urge to justify herself, to rhyme off the contributions she'd made to this family. She'd brought up those children while he travelled the world working on movies; she'd run the home; she'd forged a career that made more damn money than him; she'd handled every single one of Chloe's incidents and problems; and she'd done it all while waiting for this lying, cheating prick to return home to her.

And she'd loved him. My God, she'd loved him.

'Help me, Mir. You've got to help me. I don't want this. I want us. You and me. I swear on the kids' lives it was nothing. Don't let it change us. You know I couldn't live—'

'Get out.'

He reacted like he'd been slapped. It didn't even come close to the physical pain she wanted him to feel, but it was a start.

'Get out, Jack. We're done.'

'Mirren, you can't throw away the best part of twenty years on one fling that didn't mean—'

'I didn't. You did. And it's not one fling, Jack. It's a lifetime. The baby is yours, I take it?'

He ran his fingers through his hair, the way he always did when he was stressed. A pang of pain shot through her as she realized that she used to think the gesture was endearing. She'd watched him do that as he waited for her answer when he proposed. When he watched her crease with pain when she was in labour. When a movie deal fell through or an actor was playing up. He'd done it the first time the police had brought Chloe home, and he did it now. Caught. Betraying everything they had for a midlife-crisis fling with a twenty-two-year-old.

'Yeah, well, you know. She says it is and we were . . .

together . . . but I don't know. I just don't know, Mir. It was only a couple of times.'

The twitch in his right eye confirmed he was lying. It was all lies. Even the fact that he was here proved a lie. Two more weeks in Istanbul he'd told her, yet here he was, saying they wrapped early. Lies. He'd probably had a couple of weeks end-of-shoot R&R with the mistress planned and now he'd cut it short to dig himself out of the huge crater his treachery had kicked him into. And still he was talking . . .

'Obviously we'll do a DNA test. It might not be mine. That's happened before. Look at Sly Stallone . . .'

Her hand gripped the edge of the marble worktop as a wave of dizziness kicked in. It was all so sordid. So cheap. If she stayed in this room a minute longer, it would destroy her.

Reaching over for the car keys that lay on the counter, she eyed him with such undisguised hatred that both hands went to his hair.

'Be gone by the time I get back,' she told him. 'And take your faithless dick with you.'

The slamming of the solid-mahogany door put the exclamation mark on the end of the sentence. Outside, she headed for his brand-new, bright red Maserati and jumped in. How predictable. How could she possibly have omitted to notice that he was swimming in the pool of the midlife crisis?

The engine roared as she powered out of the drive and turned right. Five hundred yards along the road, she stopped at the checkpoint that kept the residents of Malibu Colony protected from the scrutiny and threats of the outside world. These were some of the most expensive homes in the country, populated by people who spent half their lives earning enough money to live there, and the other half feeling paranoid that it could all be taken away.

What the hell was she doing here?

How had she gone from being a little girl in a Glasgow scheme to breathing the rarefied air of the chosen few?

At the next set of lights, she turned left onto the Pacific Coast Highway and started heading north, fighting feelings of envy towards the surfers who chased the waves on her left. Past Zuma, she caught a right and began heading up the narrow, twisting Trancas Canyon Road.

On a clifftop to her right, she could see the rehab clinic that held her daughter and for the first time tears sprang to the back of her eyes. All she'd ever wanted was the stability of a family and enough financial security to know that the fears of her childhood would never come back.

Well, that was lost now. Success had come almost too easy, in part due to her inherent ability to make good judgements when it came to building a team around her. Most of her people had been with her since the first Clansman movie – loyal, dedicated professionals who knew their jobs, did them well and never let her down. Professionally, she'd built something that worked incredibly well.

But her family?

She'd got that one about as wrong as it could get.

The car turned a sharp left and she pulled over into a lay-by on the edge of the cliff. It was the kind of place that teenagers came to make out – in the middle of nowhere, plenty of time to see someone approaching and with a breath-taking view of the ocean below them.

Standing against the metal of the barrier, she pulled her white cashmere cardigan around her to protect against the breeze. Her hair was loose and strands fell across her face as she hugged herself, desperate to feel a glimmer of warmth inside her soul.

Hundreds of feet away, the surfers were just dots, moving, chasing, riding the waves. An image, like a movie in her head, took her back just a few years. Jack was home between movies; Chloe would have been about fourteen, Logan a year younger. All four of them were out on the ocean, laughing as they surfed and paddled back and forth for hours. Chloe was a natural water baby, Logan the same, and she'd taken a snapshot that day with her mind. The perfect happy family.

What went wrong?

She tried to ignore the voice that said, 'Karma.'

Sins of the father? Nope, in this case it was sins of the mother. Was that it? Retribution for the sins of the past?

Another shudder. She realized that it came with a vibration in her cardigan pocket. Pulling out her phone, she stared at the text on the screen, trying to decipher the words, as if they were written in a foreign language.

'Mirren, it's Davie. Got your number from Al. Need to talk. Urgent.'

Karma. Coming back to get her. Suddenly, Jack and his betrayal paled into insignificance. This could be worse. Much, much worse. Davie belonged to another world. One she'd escaped from.

If the truth about her past came out, it would be over. Not just her marriage, but the life she had built.

Maybe it already was.

She would never return that call. Would never reopen that door. It was behind her and there was no going back. Only forward.

Mirren McLean returned to the Maserati. Started the engine. Rolled the car over the cliff.

8.

'Blurred Lines' – Robin Thicke
(ft. T.I. and Pharrell)

It was hard to know where Mirren started and Chloe stopped. Zander saw her every day, usually sitting in the gardens, sullen, uncommunicative, resistant to all attempts by any of the other inmates to speak to her. Of course, the staff didn't call them inmates, but that was how it felt. Ordered there by the courts. No time off for good behaviour.

They were hostages in a gilded cage. There were three kinds of people in rehab. The ones who seriously wanted to kick their habit and entered voluntarily with no fanfare or public declaration of intent. The ones who viewed it as a publicity stunt – hey, look at me, I'm sorting my life out – and invariably blamed their addiction on prescription pain-killers. They were inevitably out and back on crack by day four.

And then there were the Zanders and Chloes. Detained as a punishment in premises that were more luxurious than a five-star hotel, pampered, cosseted, but deprived of the one thing room service didn't sell – their next high.

It was no coincidence that the dreams had started again. Five years of 1990s therapy unravelled in a single week, a single glance. After that first conversation, he'd kept his distance and avoided further dialogue. It wasn't difficult. They had her so spaced out on drugs to help the detox that she was barely coherent.

She was there again now, and as he passed for the last time, he said a silent goodbye. She didn't hear.

'Hey, my baby boy, I'll be missing you. Who am I gonna spoil now that you're gone?' Nurse Plump enveloped him in a borderline inappropriate hug and blasted his ears with her gregarious goodbye.

Time to play the game.

He responded to her embrace, rewarding her with a wink when they finally pulled apart. 'I might just miss you so much I have to come back for you.'

'I'll be right here, sweetheart. Right here and waiting.'

He knew she'd be dining out on this conversation for months. Patient confidentiality would be screwed on the back of a tantalizing gossip after too many bottles of Two-Buck Chuck.

He signed his release forms, checked out and shook Lebron's hand after taking back possession of his wallet, his phone and his car keys. The material trappings of his life, handed back to him. Access to millions of dollars returned to a man they didn't trust to pee on his own last week.

A voice from behind him interrupted the goodbyes.

'You're going, Zander?'

His name. She said his name. Yet it wasn't her voice. The one in his dreams had his accent, was deeper, harder. And yet before he turned round, he knew it was her.

'Yeah, they're letting me out.'

'I'll miss you.'

It struck him as a strange thing to say. One conversation, that was all they'd ever had.

'I liked watching you here. Made me feel . . . safe.'

No, not again. No. No. No.

His palms began to sweat, a small distraction from the heart that was about to explode in his chest.

There wasn't a second of the last week that she hadn't been in his mind and now this.

His fight-or-flight instinct chose flight.

He took two steps towards the door, hoping Lebron didn't notice his trembling hand and the sheen on his forehead.

'Can I come find you when I get out?' The question was calm, almost dazed, with no trace of desperation or pleading.

No. No. No.

Yet somehow what came out was, 'Yes.'

The door banged behind him and he broke into a run to his car, the silver Aston Martin DB7 that sat in the space nearest the door. A few minutes later, his heart was still racing as two cop cars with sirens blaring screeched past him, heading in the direction of a helicopter that was circling overhead. Must have been an accident up near Trancas. Only when he was ten miles away, crossing the boundary line into Santa Monica, did his breathing return to anywhere near normal.

He dialled Wes's number using the buttons on the dash.

'Hey, how're you doing?' The familiar greeting.

'A free man,' Zander replied jovially, a display of acting worthy of his third Golden Globe.

'Great. Knew you'd do it, son. Listen, shooting has been

moved up and they want you tomorrow. Can you make that work?'

When it came to Wes, there was only ever one answer.

'Sure. I'll be there. Just ask someone to fire all the details over to my office.'

'It's done. And, son . . .'

'Yeah?'

'Are you sure you're ready for this?'

'No problem at all. I'm good, Wes. Really good.' Christ, he almost believed himself. What was he supposed to say? No, man, I'm completely fucking rattled and ready to implode. He had to get it together. His career was on the line here. Time to pull this back, get over this shit. Bring down the shutters on a teenager sitting in a Malibu clinic freaking him the fuck out.

Time to get back to real life. He'd go home, grab a shower, head to the beach, catch a few waves and then spend the night rereading the script for tomorrow. It was the best one yet. His character goes into Iraq and finally tracks down the WMDs that started the last war. A win-win for America. A financial injection into the movie industry and fictional justification for the conflict. Not that he gave a toss about the politics, but as a career move, it didn't come much better.

All he had to do was keep off the booze and the drugs and do his job. Right now, he was psyched up on all counts. What did they drum into him in rehab? Choices. He had choices. And he was going to choose to get positive, focused, keep it together.

The traffic was still heavy. It would be at least another twenty minutes until he made it to his Venice home.

More to pass the time than out of any interest in what he'd missed, he hit the voicemail button on his phone. With any luck, the MTV hottie he'd hooked up with the night of the brawl with the reality-show wanker had left a message.

'*You have thirty-seven new voicemails.*' And that was just today. His PA, Hollie, made a point of going through his messages and filtering them every morning, passing on the details of any that were important.

He hit the number one button.

'*First new message.*'

There was a pause, a crackle, before the voice filled the car.

'*Mr Leith, this is Sarah McKenzie from the* Daily Scot. *Apologies, I know this will come out of the blue, but I would very much like to speak to you. You see, I have a few questions about the disappearance of your father . . .*'

Zander Leith swerved his car into the side of the road, put his head on the steering wheel, tried to stop the fear that had just battered his natural high to death.

No use. It was growing. Churning. Taking control. Seeping under his skin. Overtaking his brain. Screaming.

Make it stop. Make it stop.

On the dashboard, a Seb Dunhill bobblehead stared at him, a gift from a fan, customized by Zander. He leaned over, snapped it at the neck and put out a hand to capture the fine white powder that flowed from its fractured skull.

Everyone had choices in life.

Right now, his was, clean or coke?

9.

'Relax' – Frankie Goes to Hollywood

Glasgow, 1984

She was there again. Sitting on the bench. Alone. Staring into space. Doing nothing. Yet he couldn't stop watching her.

If Davie's mum knew he was still up, he'd be in trouble, but he didn't care. Anyway, she worked three jobs, only Saturday night off. She'd already been dozing when he got back from the chippy with the fish suppers, so she was probably now crashed out downstairs on her brown Dralon armchair, bottle of her favourite American Cream Soda and discarded news-paper on the teak side table next to her.

She was all right, his mum. Strict, a wee bit bossy, but at least she wasn't stuck-up like Zander's mum, all 'Leave your shoes at the door and go to Mass every Sunday.'

His gaze flicked around to the other houses in the square. A party going on at number 2. Old Mrs Squinty McGinty at number 18 had her windows open and was singing those old songs at the top of her voice again. 'You'll take the high road and I'll take the low road . . .' He heard his neighbour shouting that he wished to fuck she would and then maybe they'd all get some sleep. That was the thing about living around here – there was only a window or a wall between you and everyone else's lives.

Four blocks of five grey pebble-dashed terrace houses, arranged in a square. Communal ground in the middle with benches and a play area. It was supposed to enhance community spirit. Instead it just meant every bugger knew everyone else's business.

The drift of smoke from the girl's cigarette dispersed into the night sky as she stubbed it out on the leg of the concrete bench she was sitting on. There had been wooden benches there once, but the council had replaced them after one of them had ended up in the garden of the weird bloke at number 6. He claimed he'd bought it in a pub. The council decided not to bring in the police, and instead just replaced the whole lot with concrete seating that hurt your arse, but at least it wasn't going to get flogged for a tenner down the King's Arms.

The council blokes were always round doing things to the scheme. They'd planted flower beds in the middle of the play area last year. All right to look at, he supposed, but the soil didn't half bugger your trainers when you were taking a penalty.

Frankie Goes to Hollywood's 'Relax' was silenced in the middle of the chorus by the stop button on his Walkman. He still couldn't believe he owned one. Zander had given it to him for his twelfth birthday. He'd overheard his mum saying it fell off the back of a lorry, but hey, Frankie Goes to Hollywood didn't seem to mind where it came from, so neither did he.

The catch on his window resisted his first attempt to push it open, but he succeeded on the second try. He slipped over the sill and walked towards her as casually as a twelve-year-old who'd just snagged the crotch of his jeans on a window catch could manage.

As he crossed the tiny lawn in front of his house and headed to the centre of the square, getting closer to her with every step, she didn't look up, didn't look in his direction, not even once.

'How's it going?' he said, his breath making clouds in the freezing night air.

Just when backing away slowly seemed like the only possible way to salvage a shred of dignity, she finally spoke. No eye contact. No smile. Just words.

'What do you want?'

'Nothing. Just, erm, I'm Davie. Live at number 15.'

'I know.'

'You just moved in?'

'Why?'

He shrugged. 'Oh, you know, erm . . .'

Why hadn't he just stayed in his bedroom with his Walkman on, ignoring the world? The answer was already in his head and there was no way he was saying it out loud.

Because he'd seen her out here every night this week. And she was gorgeous. Crazy mad dark red curly hair. Huge eyes. Really skinny, like that dancer chick from Flashdance.

Eventually, after what seemed like an hour and a half, she put him out of his misery with a bored 'Yes'.

This was too hard. OK, one more try and then he was giving up, heading back inside for a heat.

'So why are you out here, then?'

Another pause. His Adidas Bamba took a step backwards.

He'd wanted Sambas, but his mum said there was no point paying extra when you could hardly see the difference.

He paused, about to pivot, when her voice stopped him.

'Because she's in there with a bloke and I don't like hearing them.'

Wow. It took him a minute to catch up.

'So every night you're out here because . . . ?'

'In there with a bloke,' she repeated.

And again, wow. Davie's dad had pissed off before he was born and since then the closest his mum got to a conversation with a bloke was shouting out the answers to the questions on the general knowledge round of Mastermind.

His brain had no answer for this girl's quiet, blunt manner. Usually he could talk his way out of anything. His teachers said he talked too much. His mum said she couldn't hear herself think for him sometimes. Even his gran would deliberately take out her hearing aid when he'd been in her house for more than ten minutes. However, now his mind was racing, but his vocal cords were parked.

A noise behind him made him start. For a horrible moment he thought he was about to suffer the indignity of being dragged back inside and bollocked every step of the way by a mum that smelt of vinegar, American Cream Soda and Embassy Regal.

When he realized it was Zander, he muttered a strangled 'Yes!'

They'd lived on the same block their whole lives, Alexander Leith – Sandy to his mum and dad; Zander to his pals – on one end and Davie on the other, which put this new girl smack bang in the middle.

Zander's house may have been identical to his once, but

now it was completely different. His dad's mates had painted the front, put on a new door, added an extra room on the side and put a garage on the communal grass next to them. No one complained. A council officer came round once and hadn't been back since.

'How's it going, pal?' Davie greeted him, his trademark grin back in place for the first time since he'd dropped out of his window.

Zander countered the question with one of his own. 'What you doing out?'

'Just talking to . . . to . . .'

'Mirren,' she offered, and Davie noticed that for the first time her stare had left the space in front of her and was now fixed on Zander's face. Her reaction was nothing new. Half the girls in school fancied him. Even the posh ones who came to school in a car and lived up in the bought houses.

Zander barely glanced in her direction and Davie was unsure why that pleased him.

Davie checked his digital Casio. Eleven o' clock. For Zander, this was late. His mum usually had him under house arrest as soon as she came home from eight-o' clock Mass every night.

'Where you going?'

'King's Arms. Need to see if my da is in there. Polis have been round looking for him. Burst in the back door. My ma is going mental. Wanna come?'

Davie's hesitation was so slight Zander didn't notice. Stay here with the girl who was treating him like a dose of the measles or go with Zander to track down his dad? Zander won. And not just because his dad would give them a tenner for coming to warn him about the police.

As Zander shoved his hands into the pockets of his Fred Perry jacket and walked off, Davie fell into step behind him.

As he and Zander turned out of the square and headed in the direction of the pub, a movement caught his peripheral vision.

So hostile, angry girl had decided to tag along too.

10.

'Like a Prayer' – Madonna

Glasgow, 2013

Sarah's morning had started off well. Coffee and croissants in Princes Square, a Grade B-listed building on Buchanan Street, built as a merchant square in the centre of the city in 1841, now home to upmarket stores. It had been a delicious assault on her senses. The aromas from the restaurants on the ground floor infused the air, while the light streamed down from the glass atrium roof. Her partner, Simon, a lawyer, had dragged her there to buy new work shirts from Ted Baker. She'd resisted at first – shopping wasn't her thing – but later she was glad. It was a snapshot of tranquillity, of luxury, a cocoon of loveliness that protected the inhabitants from the world. As they'd chatted over brunch, they'd listened to an amazing choir sing gospel songs in the central performance area.

Now, just a few hours later, she was in a different building, listening to songs with the same theme, but without the God-given talent.

'The Lord's My Shepherd' was proving to be a challenge

for the organist, who played with elaborate flair and a blatant disregard for the Almighty's preferred musical arrangement.

Not that any of the amassed congregation in the crematorium would be filing an official complaint.

Sarah just hoped the *Daily Scot*'s photographer, perched in the window of a flat directly across from the crematorium, was getting good shots of the mourners as they filed in and out, otherwise the fifty quid she'd given the old bloke who owned the rotting tenement room would be wasted.

When the last bars of the hymn faded, the minister cleared his throat and welcomed the crowd to the service to celebrate the life of the dearly departed soul.

Another fifty quid said this bloke who was proclaiming that the Lord had called one of his beloved flock home had never met Manny Murphy in his life.

Looking down from her standpoint on the upper balcony of the hall, Sarah spotted Manny Murphy Junior in the front row, passing a tissue to his wailing stepmother, Manny's estranged wife Della. Another rat that had fled the sinking ship when Manny got sick.

Della (36): speciality act – removing flags from her vagina on the stage of the Crystal Gentlemen's Club. If the Scottish Independence lobby could get her onside, she'd add a unique new patriotic slant that would definitely grab the attention of at least 50 per cent of the voting public.

Was it Sarah's imagination or did Manny Junior's gaze linger just a little too long on his stepmother? Didn't matter. The editor wouldn't run speculation like that unless he walked in and caught them shagging on his desk in front of a judge, a lawyer, the irrefutable eye of a CCTV camera and several members of the SAS for protection.

As for the rest of the attendees, the only story here was a background Glasgow gangland piece, and it had been done a dozen times before. Every killer, crook and conman from the criminal world not currently banged up at Her Majesty's pleasure was here today. Jimmy Lowe: head of the biggest drugs family on the west coast. His lifelong rival Danny Dodds, sitting opposite surrounded by a network of relatives who made more from vice and smack than most mid-level corporations. Cass Miller: never to be underestimated, the matriarch of a family that boasted a national shoplifting operation and two of the most prolific gunmen available for hire. Franz Lowery: confessed to three murders in the 1980s, now out of Carstairs and married to a junior member of royalty who clearly wanted to fuck off her parents.

Generations of crime, corruption and fear, all of them gathered in the black clothes of hypocrisy to pay homage to a man they probably despised but who would be elevated to the status of gangland legend now that he was gone.

None of that interested Sarah. She'd leave that to the crime reporters and the out-of-work journos who made a fast buck by trotting out a true-crime exposé that bore little resemblance to the truth.

She was more interested in who wasn't there. The way Manny Murphy told it, he'd grown up with Jono Leith, shared women, wages and jobs. Manny's passing had made national news. Why wouldn't his old mate Jono come to pay his respects? And would Sarah spot him if he did?

Zander Leith was tall, over six foot. According to Manny,

he looked just like his dad: same stature, same dark blond hair, same green eyes. Even allowing for some age-related subsidence, there were very few sixty-something men here who topped that height.

Sarah counted three, before being interrupted by another wail from Della. Jesus, she should get an Oscar in the category of Most Hysterical Attention-Seeker in a Supporting Role.

Eyes back to the mourners. One of the possibilities had jet-black hair, greased back and auditioning for a role as spokesperson for Just for Men.

Another was bald, but sallow-skinned. There was a third, but his head was bowed, so she couldn't make out his features.

A subtle vibration against her hip compelled her to surreptitiously slip her phone from her pocket, and under the pretence of lowering her head in prayer, read the message on the screen.

'Tonight. 7 p.m. Rogano. Dress gorgeous. Sxx'

The elderly lady next to her mistook her sigh for an exhalation of sadness and gave her an empathetic smile. Sarah recognized her from a feature she'd done the year before on professional mourners, all of them perched up here day after day, vicariously sharing grief and hoping for the holy grail of an invitation back to the food- and drink-laden wake.

Not that she was in a position to judge, given that the only thing she was mourning right now was her planned night in front of the fire, laptop open while drinking wine to the TV backdrop of *Grey's Anatomy*.

Of course, she could say no to the text, but she wouldn't.

Sxx was Simon Anstruther, lawyer, activist, firm member of the establishment, key player in the SCCRC. The Scottish Criminal Cases Review Commission was the last source of appeal against miscarriages of justice in the Scottish legal system.

They'd met when she was covering the final stages of a judicial inquiry into the conviction of a serial rapist who maintained his innocence despite overwhelming evidence to the contrary. Sarah's theory was that dragging out the case, reliving it in court after court, was a sick distraction for the sick excuse for a man, another chance to toy with his victims, torturing every last shred of misery from them.

By the end of it, it was obvious to Sarah that Simon felt the same. Case closed. The rapist's sentence was increased and Sarah got an all-access pass to a bloke who knew the details of every high-profile case in Scotland since criminal records began.

Victory all round.

It helped that Simon was actually a nice guy, easy on the eye in a Harvey Specter-*Suits* league, with an understated arrogance that was backed up by the knowledge that he was damn good at what he did.

It was Simon who had given her the background to the life and times of Jono Leith. Small-time crook, promoted to mid-level suspicion after the Bank of Scotland in St Vincent Street lost two of its basement walls and almost £100,000. Back in 1984, Leith and five others were charged, but it didn't stick. Neither did the convictions for armed robbery, assault and a few domestics on which the charges were dropped when complaints were withdrawn.

Under a scratched surface, Sarah could see he was a scumbag, one who, it seemed, disappeared off the face of the earth right after a fraud charge was dropped due to several witnesses falling victim to an amnesia epidemic. It was a pattern. He'd been arrested many times, often held on remand, but never convicted. So on the face of it, Jono Leith was a man with a relatively unblemished record. No press cuttings, nothing online, the invisible man.

Sarah had read everything there was to read on Zander's history too and there was no mention of anything that would raise an eyebrow. According to every bio, he grew up with his mum, Maggie, and dad, John, and lived with them until he was discovered by Wes Lomax at nineteen. That's where any mention of his family ended. No interviews, no 'proud parent' pieces. Just a statement early in his career, around the time of the Oscar win, saying that his family were private people and had no wish to be in the limelight. Nowadays, there would be internet chatter, gossip-mag profiles and tweets from half of Glasgow declaring they knew the Leiths. But it seemed like a new chapter on Zander had opened when he headed to Hollywood and the previous one had been well and truly closed.

All Sarah needed was a crowbar. But in the meantime, a sighting of the elusive Jono Leith would be a start.

As the priest wound up proceedings, Della made a break from the front pew and threw herself across the coffin. The older members of the audience shuffled in discomfort, while the younger ones were no doubt itching to get their phones out and get this on YouTube.

Sarah took advantage of the spectacle to slip downstairs and head outside first, positioning herself to the left of the doors, where she would have a perfect view of the emerging faces.

A photograph she'd stared at for ten minutes this morning was pulled to the forefront of her mind. Simon had photocopied an image he'd 'borrowed' from the archives of Jono Leith, standing in a group shot at the funeral of Jono's mother.

He was flanked by women on both sides, his wife to his right, two others, perhaps his sisters, to his left. In front of them were three kids, and straight away the eye was drawn to the tallest. Even then, aged about twelve, Zander was a striking boy, already over five and a half feet, the hair dropped in front of his eyes unable to mask a haunted stare and the firm, angry set of his mouth.

Sarah pulled her coat tighter around her neck to try to block the icy breeze that was cutting her in two. Who could have known what was in front of that kid? Stardom. Success. Rehab. Fame. A sexual prowess that was legendary. He'd even fucked Lila Day, the showbiz reporter on her paper, during a press junket for his last movie. Thankfully, he didn't return her calls, which gave Lila an axe to grind and made her willing to share his contact details as soon as Sarah had bribed her with a bottle of champagne and a new D&G scarf.

It was a long shot that had the potential to leave her screwed professionally and in debt to Visa and Mastercard, but that wasn't stopping her. The calls she'd put in to Davie, Zander and Mirren had delivered only a tiny glimmer of hope. No answer or reply from Mirren's people, nothing from Zander, just a blanket acknowledgement from Davie's PA, Jorja, with a vague promise to get back to her.

The mourners were starting to file out now, the women dabbing at their eyes, the men itching for a drink, but first there was the serious business of being seen to pay respects to the dearly departed.

Della took her place, last in the line-up, the grand finale. Despite the freezing temperature, she discarded her coat, determined that something as trifling as hypothermia would not prevent her from giving her public an eyeful of the Hervé Léger bodycon that was struggling to constrain her assets. Sarah didn't know him well, but from their handful of meetings, she had a feeling Manny Murphy would have laughed his decrepit arse off at the spectacle.

So captivated was she by the soap opera unfolding in front of her that she didn't spot him at first. The man was standing back from the others, the tall, ageing frame she'd noticed in the church now straightened, head up. This guy was in his fifties, too young to be Jono Leith. There was no resemblance either: the nose too straight, the eyes further apart, the jawline too square.

But it was the woman by his side that had Sarah transfixed.

Mid-height, perhaps five foot five, her white hair swept back in a perfect elegant chignon, an expensive-looking coat, almost certainly cashmere. There was something in her bearing, a regal posture, a serene expression that made her stand a million miles of class and style apart from the others.

Sarah locked eyes on her and experienced an almost immediate wave of recognition.

Jono Leith may be long dead and gone. But Sarah would stake her career, her lawyer boyfriend and her colleague's new D&G scarf that she was looking at Zander Leith's mother.

Politeness and the wish to avoid drawing attention to herself cost valuable minutes as she worked through the crowd. Damn, if only she'd worn heels so she could keep the target in her sight every step of the way. By the time she got to the spot where the woman had been standing, she was gone. Frantically scanning the crowd again, it was a few seconds before she spotted the back of the white coiffure dipping as the woman climbed into the back of a black limo. Two choices: let it go or run across the grass and throw herself in front of the car. Even for Sarah, there was a limit

She watched until the back bumper disappeared through the ornate gates. Sarah cursed under her breath. She'd just lost her best lead so far. She wouldn't make that mistake again.

11.

'Superstition' – Stevie Wonder

'How the fuck could you let this happen? Do you know what this will do to our brand?' Jenny screamed.

Not their family. Or their marriage. Or his career. Their brand. Plural. God bless Hollywood.

Davie had thought that the fact that Jenny was shooting on location in Vancouver would have given her a bit of space to take on board what had happened, calm down and help him work out a plan to deal with all this in a mature, strategic manner.

The proof that he had never understood women was that he had clearly got that wrong on all counts. She and Darcy had arrived an hour ago, both of them all rock chick chic and long flowing hair, which did nothing to detract from the fact that his wife was incandescent with rage. And that was just a warm-up.

One of Davie's four cell phones, the solid-gold iPhone he reserved for the press, buzzed incessantly. Jenny picked it up from the antique Nepalese meditation table and threw it at the glass wall which gave a view over Hollywood that represented the fact that the golden couple reigned over the City of Angels.

Past tense.

He flicked the phone onto silent and attempted to deflect his wife's ire.

'I didn't see you worrying about our brand when you were fucking your pal over there,' he spat.

'Really? Is that the best you can do? Urgh, what a dick.' Jenny's poster-girl face was contorted in disgust. Over in the corner, Darcy Jay's lips held a hint of amusement. Davie fought not to react. A murder charge was the last thing he needed to add to his list of great decisions right now.

The fallout had been brutal. Forty-eight hours of solid abuse and bombardment on all fronts.

Three days ago, he'd been one of the biggest names in town; wannabes would beg, steal and blow-job to get five minutes in his presence. Since the scandal broke, his stylist had emailed to say he was no longer available, his trainer had quit, and even his assistant, Jorja, had taken her copy of their non-disclosure agreement and disappeared into the sunset. It was a bad day when the nobodies in this town cut off ties. Even the pizza delivery service wouldn't return his calls. He was toxic.

There had been a few who had hedged their bets, sending supportive texts and private messages, but not a single one had come out to defend him in public. Not that there was much to defend, but the gesture would have been nice. Traitorous fucks. Even the car crash that was Lana Delasso didn't use the drama as an excuse to suck up to him, and in this town she only just won a popularity contest with genital warts.

Ivanka teetered into the room. 'Mr Davie, that was the gatehouse – Mr Woolfe is here.' Her accent was so thick he had to concentrate to decipher her words. 'They've let him in and he's on his way up. And he's asking if you are watching *Hollywood Today*.'

Despite wanting to do nothing less, he flicked on the TV and went straight to his DVR. The lunchtime bulletin was on series link so that he never missed a mention of his name. Might be time to rethink that decision.

He fast-forwarded through the lead story – breaking news about a former NBA star getting dragged out of a crack den by a private SWAT team hired by his soap-star wife – then stopped breathing as his face filled the screen.

Was it wrong that even today he was instinctively insulted by the fact that he didn't get top billing? What did ten guys in blackout gear storming the gates of a Hollywood Hills mansion have that he didn't?

The shot cut back to the studio, to an anorexic presenter whose brilliant-white, veneered smile was wider than her thighs. Flicking a waist-length mane of jet-black hair that had only last month been on the head of a fourteen-year-old factory worker in Bangladesh, she delivered the segment in the manner of a pageant queen being asked her opinion on saving the rainforest.

'And here's what *Family Three* leading lady Vala Diaz had to say to those gorgeous ladies on *The View* today about the wide-reaching repercussions of this shocking situation.'

The image changed to one of Tilly Cantor sitting on the

couch of *The View*, speaking in her trademark tone: breathy with an edge of Republican superiority.

'Vala, I know you're not here to talk about this today, but I couldn't let you go without asking you about the latest controversy surrounding producer Davie Johnston and poor teenager Sky Nixon. We hear she's still in a coma, and obviously we've all seen those heartbreaking images of the fans holding a vigil outside the hospital where she lies fighting for her life, but what's been the impact on your show? How are Davie Johnston's children, Bella and Bray, holding up?'

Beads of sweat burst onto Davie's forehead. Holding up? *Holding up?* They're fricking seven! As long as they've got their iPads and a supply of candy, all's right in their world.

The thoughts ricocheting off the inside of his skull skidded to a halt as Vala opened her beautiful mouth.

'Well, I think it's just a tragic situation for everyone involved and my heart goes out to darling Sky.'

Davie's thoughts kick-started again. Darling Sky? The one and only time they'd been in the same room, Vala had threatened to impale her on an ice sculpture because she was all over Davie like a fungal infection.

'I don't know Davie very well, as obviously I only work with his children, who are adorable by the way . . .'

The audience murmured their approval of her sentiment.

'. . . but I do know that as a cast we are coming together to protect those innocent children and we will continue to do so for as long as they need us.'

Over in the corner, Darcy broke off from stroking Jenny's hair to speak to Davie for the first time. 'Next time you bang her, you might want to introduce the concept of a gag.'

Davie ignored her, about to flick the TV off when the next segment caused whole-body paralysis.

'And it's been a week for scandalous happenings among Hollywood royalty, as a name that will be very familiar to Mr Johnston steals some headlines of her own. We still have no word on the whereabouts of Mirren McLean, Johnston's former film-making partner and lifelong friend. As we reported two days ago, a car belonging to Ms McLean's husband, Jack Gore, was found wrecked at the bottom of Trancas Canyon. Police have reported that as far as they are aware, no crime has been committed; however, they are still searching the area. This morning, her husband refused to comment on rumours that his close relationship with co-star Mercedes Dance has been a source of marital problems.'

Oh fuck no. Mirren. He must have called her a hundred times in the last two days and mentally branded her every bitch under the sun for refusing to pick up or call back.

His mind went on overdrive as a dozen scenarios played out in his head, none of them good. His knees almost buckled and he had to grab the table to support him. This shit shouldn't happen, and if it did, he should be able to deal with it. He'd dealt with every situation in his life and survived. Every trauma. Every drama. He'd written every cliché into his shows. Go big or go home. Swing for the fences. If this was a movie, it would be his Braveheart moment. Conquer or die trying.

But right now, he needed someone else's oxygen.

He needed Mirren. Needed her.

Oh no. Oh no. Oh no.

The vibe in the room changed suddenly as Al strode in and threw his hands up in outrage.

'Are you fucking ready to deal with this?'

Al's voice. Every hitman in every blockbuster of the last twenty years had imitated Al Woolfe when they were delivering their final words to their victim. *Goodnight, sucker.* His voice was low and deadly, at odds with a stature that was whippet-thin and a pallor that belonged to an accountant who avoided daylight hours.

But it wasn't his voice that chilled Davie right now; it was what he was saying.

Was *he* ready to deal with this? For years they'd been a team. What happened to 'we'? What happened to 'us'? It was the way it worked in this business. Everyone claimed credit when the going was good, denied culpability when it all went to shit.

We had a hit show.

Your show tanked.

But for now, they were still in it together. They had to be.

'You need to pull this off,' Al told him. There it was again. Singular. But the warning was unnecessary. Twenty years in the business had left a muscle memory that caused a snap in Davie's psyche.

What was it they said? You found out who your friends were when the chips were down?

Right now they were scattered all over the floor and he was getting a harsh reality check.

Exit one friend, so fast the sparks were coming off his Gucci loafers. The ones purchased with Davie's 10 per cent.

Fuelled by desperation, demanding inspiration, Davie wasn't letting go.

'You have to help fix this, Al. We're a team, right?'

Al didn't even try to hide his discomfort or distaste. Oh, the irony. Yesterday, he'd have given his grandmother up for Davie Johnston, but now, he'd happily hand him over to any other agent in town. He peeled Davie off his torso and reclaimed his personal space.

'OK, the guys are outside, every reporter in town is there, and we've got them cordoned by the guest house. Camera crews are ready. Security is tight. Ready to be humble?'

'Yeah, Al, about that, I—'

'Your opinion ain't required, Davie. Just get out there and grovel.'

Davie nodded like a schoolkid trying to please the priest by telling him that he did three decades of the rosary every night.

But hang on.

Suddenly Al was giving him points on performance? Davie was the talent. He was Mr Public. Davie was the one who got 90 per cent because he was the one out there. When cameras were rolling, he called the shots.

And right now, his shots had to be on target.

Jenny and Darcy said nothing as he checked his hair in the Rennie Mackintosh mirror above the travertine mantel, dusted on some loose powder to counteract the shine and added a subtle coat of mascara. Waterproof. Just in case.

Walking behind Al, and followed by a tribe of publicists from CSA, they headed out of the glass doors and crossed the lawn, which was so vast Rod Stewart had once asked him why he hadn't remodelled it into a football pitch.

As they approached the ornamental meditation garden,

between the yoga deck and the maze, he could hear the buzz of expectation. It was unusual to hold a press conference at a star's home, but they were using every trick in the book to ensure a mass turnout. If the wolves didn't come out of journalistic interest, they'd come for a view of the sixteen-car garage that hosted some of the rarest specimens in the country.

The flashbulbs popped like strobe lights from the second he came into view, mounted the small stage that had been hurriedly purpose-built for this morning and took his place behind the microphone at centre stage.

Like a synchronized dance, the crowd hushed at once, each of them pressing record on their handheld audio devices and cameras.

'Ladies and gentlemen, thank you for coming.'

Watching the polished greeting, taking in the relaxed posture and the trademark cheeky grin, not a single person there would have guessed that fifteen minutes before, he'd almost been on his knees.

'Obviously, my name has been in the headlines over the last couple of days and for once I'm thinking that's not a good thing . . .'

The self-deprecating humour earned him an automatic murmur of amusement.

'I just want to set the record straight and let you know the truth behind what happened. That was me on that tape – I won't deny it. But what you didn't hear was that my words were being recorded as part of a cameo stunt we were going to set up, a satirical piece about the rumours that all reality shows are scripted. I'm sorry that Rainbow Nixon used that tape out of context. I'm sorry that she chose to release it at a time that was so sensitive for her daughter and her family. I have no idea why that happened. I can assure you, quite categorically and absolutely, that I did not have any part in Sky Nixon's decision to take drugs. I can only hope now that Rainbow, with her own extensive experience of addiction, will be there for her daughter and focus on the truth and – yes – *reality* of the situation.'

Silence. They were absolutely and completely in the palm of his perfectly manicured hand.

He owned that stage, called the shots, and his demeanour gave off a well-practised confidence perfected over twenty years in the business. He was Davie Johnston. America's favourite presenter. A good guy. Decent. Trustworthy. Dependable. They wanted to believe him. And there he was, giving them what they needed. Reassurance that was almost presidential.

His future would be decided by public perception. Was this the honesty and integrity of a commander in chief? Oh hey, I'm Davie Johnston. I did not have sex with that woman.

12.

'She's Gone' – Hall & Oates

Mirren Gore was dead. Dead. The wife of Jack Gore, the devoted mother of the famous Logan Gore and the infamous Chloe Gore was gone.

All that was left was Mirren McLean. Exhausted. Defeated. Speaking only to the two people on earth she could trust.

'Doll, you're going to have to say something soon,' Lou told her. 'They're scouring the fricking country for you. Let me put something out, take the heat off.'

'Fine. Whatever you think.' The voice was so devoid of emotion it could have been the utterances of an automated phone system.

Lou's sigh of relief was audible. 'How's Logan doing? You told him yet?'

'Nope. Haven't quite worked out how to share the news that his dad is screwing a girl whose poster was on Logan's wall last year.'

'Have you called Chloe?'

'No. Last time I tried, she still wasn't accepting my calls. Will try again later once I've picked up a new cell. Leaving my phone in the Maserati wasn't my best moment of forward-thinking. You can get me on this number until I do. How about that for a role reversal? Logan is complaining because I'm monopolizing his phone.'

There was a roar in the background: 107,000 screaming girls in the Estadio Azteca, Mexico City. Logan's world had been the obvious place for her to go. There was no better place to disappear than into the entourage of a boy band that had a security team rivalled by none. Twenty strong, all former members of Shabak, the Israeli Security Agency, these guys were as close to impenetrable as it got. After the Maserati hit the deck, she'd hitched a lift back to civilization and taken a cab to Santa Monica Airport. If only she'd done an Angelina, a Travolta, a Harrison Ford and got her own licence, it would have been so much quicker. No matter. Within the hour, her American Express account was $30,000 lighter, a private jet was on the runway, and she was heading south.

Might have been an idea to stop for supplies. She pulled her long cardigan around her, a sympathy gift from one of the girls in wardrobe when she arrived. The clothes she'd stood in – grey skinny 7 For All Mankind jeans, a white tank, Prada biker boots – weren't quite adequate for an unusually cool Mexican night.

The temperature had dropped to somewhere in the forties. Mildly chilly, yet she was shivering. She hated the cold. Reminded her of home.

Of her.

A snapshot of her childhood flickered to light in her mind. Mirren. About twelve. Sitting outside her house on a summer night. Then another. This time the leaves on the trees were brown and red. Another. Now bare branches towered over her. That was the overwhelming memory of her youngest years, shivering in the cold, sweating in the heat, always sitting outside because she couldn't face what happened on the other side of the walls of her home. The laughter. The screams. The smell of perfume and cigarettes. The words that no child should hear. Mirren knew them all. And she knew that she came way below the buzz of her mother's long nights of play.

And then there was the flip side. When he didn't show up and her mother was alone, drowning in tears of self-pity, pining until the moment that he walked back through the door, took her hand and led her upstairs.

Over the years dozens of TV interviewers and journalists had asked her what drove her infamous work ethic, what made her so determined to succeed, what the secret was behind her successful marriage. She had stock answers, meaningless platitudes for every question, but the truth was that there was only one explanation.

She was determined that she'd never end up like her mother.

Marilyn McLean was the reason that Mirren's whole life had been built on a craving for security. Certainty. Stability. Change freaked her out. The unknown scared her. And the only thing that took away the fear was success in every area of her life. Career. Money. Marriage.

She had been in love with two men in her life. The first time had ended so badly she thought that she'd never recover. This time . . . this time . . .

The phone in her hand vibrated and a familiar image

flashed on the screen. One that didn't belong there. Why would Lex Callaghan's number be in Logan's phone?

Accept.

'Hey.'

'Hey, boss. So, anything happening lately?'

It was impossible not to smile. Lex Callaghan was that rare thing in Hollywood: an actor who didn't take himself too seriously, who didn't look at everything from the point of view of what it meant for him. Mirren had always thought that it was because his success had come later. He'd been around Hollywood for a decade, racked up dozens of minor parts, acted in half a dozen pilots that hadn't been picked up. He had just hit thirty when he walked into the casting office for the first Clansman. For Mirren, it was like watching a character lift off her page and come to life. The collar-length, unruly black hair, the physique of a warrior and the blue eyes were straight out of her descriptive prose, but it was more than that. Every guy who'd auditioned so far looked like he'd stopped off on the way to have his nails buffed. Lex Callaghan looked rough, like he could climb mountains, swim lochs. He had a walk that exuded attitude with every step. But the deal-sealer was the accent. He spoke with a Highland lilt that was so authentic she couldn't make out a trace of his natural Montana drawl. A childhood spent in the company of an immigrant grandmother who never lost her Perthshire brogue had given him a voice that was flaw-less. This was her hero, the man who had the courage of his convictions and was willing to die fighting. The view-ing public felt the same. The four Clansman movies they'd worked on had made him a global star. The fifth was supposed to start in two days and would add another legion of fans to his adoring army.

'Hi. How did you get this number?' No irritation, just surprise.

'Last year's wrap party. Logan sorted out tickets for my niece, gave me his number. She will now visit me when I'm old. Didn't expect you to answer, though – was just going to interrogate him for information.'

'He'd never crack,' she said with a smile.

'You're right. So how you doing?'

'I'm OK.'

'Really?'

'No.'

'Want me to come down? My niece would love it.'

'Thanks but no. I'll be back soon. Just needed to get my head together, stay out of the spotlight.'

'We can push back the start date.'

'No.'

It was unthinkable. Even a day of delay would cost the studio hundreds of thousands, but it was more than that. It was what it said. That she'd fallen apart, couldn't handle it.

'Look, Mirren, I'm here for you. Whatever you need.'

She needed something, but not from Lex Callaghan. They were friends, end of story. He had lots to offer: he was handsome, talented, had a body that rocked. He also had a wife, Cara, his high-school sweetheart, who had stuck by him through rich and poor, good times and bad, a one-bedroom condo to a fifteen-hundred-acre ranch in Santa Barbara.

Right now, she needed things he couldn't give her. Reassurance. Strength. A rewind button. And something to take away the tsunami of dread that was making her block out Davie Johnston's text. She wasn't going back there. Not for anything.

The rising sensation of bile from her stomach made her gag and she struggled to pull it back together.

'Lex, I have to go. I'll see you Monday.'

Hanging up, she pressed her face against a steel support for the lighting rig. Hot. Cold. Hot. Cold. Terror and dread were making her temperature fluctuate from one end of the scale to the other.

And breathe. Dear God, please breathe. Years of ashtanga yoga kicked in and jump-started her cardiovascular system.

The voice in her head, the one that she'd trained over two decades to support her in everything she did, made a valiant attempt to do its job. Break it down, Mirren, break it down. You can deal with this. You can. All of it. You don't have the answers now, but you'll figure it out. You just need a bit more time. A bit more space. Lie low. Keep thinking. It'll come. Space. Contemplation. Privacy. Breathe.

Her internal monologue was interrupted by a chorus of screams and cheers that made the ground under her feet tremble.

Logan rushed off stage towards her and then two arms were around her, lifting her and swinging her round.

'Mom, come on – I want you to come on stage.'

'Logan, no.'

'C'mon, mom.'

Where were the Israeli bodyguards when she needed them?

Her 120 pounds were no match for a 6-foot boy who worked with a personal trainer 6 days a week.

The spotlights blinded her; the crowd roared; the rest of the band cheered as the lead singer pulled his resistant mother onto the stage.

'Mexico! I want you to meet my mom!'

As 107,000 camera phones captured the moment, she realized that the plan to hide out until she was ready to deal with all this shit had just hit a large, son-sized complication.

It was time to get back to the real world before the real world came to her. And somehow, for Chloe's sake, for Logan's sake, and for the sake of her sanity, she knew she had to find the strength inside her to kick its ass.

13.

'Riders On the Storm' – The Doors

His head was in a vice, and the wheel was turning tighter and tighter. Only a few more seconds now and his brain would explode, grey matter would splatter against the walls, and forensics would have to use tweezers to pick skull shrapnel off the carpet. Any second now. Any second.

'Zander, some, like, chick keeps calling, and she says if you don't speak to her now, she's going to break the fucking door down. She has, like, a serious attitude problem. Is she, like, your wife or something?'

Zander opened one eye, took the phone being dangled in front of him by Daisy . . . Donna . . . Deedee . . . fucked if he knew. Shit, he'd taken it too far last night. The bottle of Jack Daniel's he remembered; the coke he'd rather forget. If the pain in his head was a sign that he was about to die, let it be soon, here in . . .

He made a quick scan of the room. Yep, definitely his own apartment. How he'd got back here was a mystery to him right now, but at least he wasn't lying in some fleapit hotel off Sunset with unidentifiable bites trailing across his back.

That had been the night before last.

Ignoring his companion's unanswered question, he put the phone in the vicinity of his ear and grunted.

Her reply was instant. 'It's me.'

Zander automatically winced. Hollie only spoke two words, but they had all the impact of a double bullet shot to the centre of the forehead. Fierce, unrelenting and un-equivocally honest, for the last ten years she'd managed all the sane aspects of his life. Only two people had real meaning in his world: if Wes Lomax was his father figure, Hollie was the sister who would defend him to the world while kicking his butt behind closed doors. It was an unusual dynamic in the land of the sycophants, but he needed that kind of reality – just not today.

'What the fuck are you doing? No, don't answer that. On a messed-up scale of one to ten, give me a figure,' she said, her tone thick with irritation.

'Ten.'

'You are such an asshole. OK, open the door.'

'Why?'

'Cos I'm standing outside, you moron, and I'm not wasting these Manolo Blahniks on breaking down the fucking door.'

He hung up.

'Baby—'

'It's Dixie. Don't call me "baby". I'm, like, a feminist,' Dixie wailed, while pulling on the crotchless panties that matched her purple lace peephole bra.

He groaned on the inside.

'Can you open the door. Please. Dixie?'

With a petulant stomp, Dixie crossed the room and swung

the door open, making no effort whatsoever to conceal her partial nudity.

Hollie barely glanced in her direction, marching straight to the huge circular bed in the centre of the room. He took no credit or blame for the furnishings in the room. He'd bought the apartment in Venice with that first pay cheque and never got round to moving. There was no need to. On the third floor of the pale green timber-clad block, on the corner of Speedway, just over the invisible line that separated the wealth of Santa Monica from the eccentricities of its artisan neighbour.

The location suited him. On the edge of the sands, he could ride out on his paddle board at dawn, and when he opened the windows at night, he could hear other people laughing, talking, fighting, just being. Somehow, that mattered.

When he'd first moved in, he had a chair, a sofa and a bed. When Hollie joined him, she had a try at persuading him to move to a more affluent, secure neighbourhood. When that didn't work, she helped him buy the apartment next door and then remodelled the two into the kind of penthouse an A-list actor with simple tastes should call home. A vast, open-plan loft with a long glass wall that became opaque and inscrutable at the touch of a button. Dark-stained maple floors, white walls, grey leather sofas. A screen that could motor across the floor to separate the bedroom and living area at the touch of a button. On the walls, the two original artworks by Jack Vettriano were Hollie's idea too, a nod to his Scottish heritage.

The soft furnishings were cream, the bedding was 800-thread count, the cutlery and crockery expensive. As long as there was beer in the fridge, sport on the TV and his surfboard was by the door, he barely noticed.

'OK, hero, up.' She pulled back the Pratesi sheets.

'I can't.'

'Don't make me kill you.'

Hollie turned to Dixie. 'Nice outfit. Look, honey—'

'Don't call me "honey". I'm, like, a feminist,' Dixie announced for the second time in five minutes. Zander closed his eyes. He couldn't look. No one should witness blood being spilt at this time in the morning.

'OK, let me try that again, Hillary Clinton. Can you please do something for me?'

Not bad considering every word was spat out through clenched teeth.

'Can you, right now, take your skinny, half-covered ass and remove it from my sight?'

'But . . .'

Hollie was one step ahead of her. She pulled ten $100 bills from her wallet.

'For your lingerie fund. Stick with purple – it's your colour.'

It was difficult for the self-proclaimed feminist philosopher to work out whether that was a compliment or an insult.

Hollie pulled out another wad of notes.

'And here's another grand for your phone.'

'But—'

'It's that or I call the cops and say you're a stalker who broke in here. Your choice.'

Dixie flushed with rage, then realizing the futility of the situation, grabbed her clothes, pulled a Lycra minidress over her size-zero frame and stomped out carrying her shoes. She left her phone on the table.

Her parting words were, 'I'm at Sparkles every night. Drop by.'

Zander didn't reply. Just shut his eyes and braced himself for attack.

'Classy. I can see the attraction.'

Hollie's sarcasm barely dented his frazzled brain.

'OK, Mr Stud, what's going on? This is the third morning in a row I've had to drag your ass out of a naked situation. Zander, you're not helping me here.'

Zander couldn't reply, too busy trying to manoeuvre himself into an upright position. Didn't matter. What was going on? He could never explain it to her. When he stepped out of the clinic last week, he was so sure he could do this. Sober up. Make it right. Step out of the 'fuck up' lane. But . . .

'*Mr Leith, this is Sarah McKenzie from the* Daily Scot . . . *I have a few questions about the disappearance of your father . . .*'

How the fuck had that come up now, twenty years down the line? His family situation had been covered and put to bed two decades ago. Every reporter who had ever asked had been given a stock answer: 'Zander's family were private people and had no wish to be in the public eye.' In today's celebrity-obsessed, online culture, they wouldn't have stood a chance of retaining any privacy, but back then his home life didn't cause so much as a ripple of publicity. Since then, all requests for interviews or information about his family had been denied. All eyes turned to Zander's new Hollywood life, and over the years he'd provided them with so many headlines there had never been a reason for anyone to go raking up his past. End of story. Nothing to report. Until now. Nothing about this made sense.

Had something happened? Had he turned up? But no, that was never going to happen, was it? Yet . . . there was a reporter on the phone and her words kept playing in his head. And the only thing that made them stop was oblivion.

Hollie pulled the sheets off the bed and balled them in the corner, then picked up the glasses, bottles and discarded clothes and took them all into the kitchen. It was only on the way back that she noticed the detritus on the coffee table. 'Coke last night?'

The guilt that flashed across his face said it all.

'Jesus, Zander, they're testing you again in ten days. Right, detox until then. Man, can you just stick to being an alcoholic and give me less shit to deal with? Now come on. You're due on set in an hour and the 405 will be a bitch, even at this time. I don't need this. I could have been working for—'

'Matt Damon. I know.'

It was their personal joke. Hollie had interviewed for Damon on the same day as Zander. Zander had offered first.

'Clean-living. Married. Kids. No drama. Instead, I got you. Come on, Zander, don't screw this up. I need the pay cheque and it'll be a bitch to find another job if you turn up dead. No wonder I comfort-eat.'

Another private joke. Hollie was one of the few women in Hollywood who was not under a size four. In any other town, she'd be considered a healthy shape, but here, if her natural chocolate-brown hair and lack of cosmetic intervention didn't set her apart, the fact that she wore size-ten jeans made her as rare on the West Coast as a genuine blonde.

Over in the hung-over corner, her attempt at truthful cajoling only served to up the remorse.

What the fuck was wrong with him?

It was only day five on set and he'd been wasted for every one of them. Thankfully, he knew the role inside out and had managed to pull off the read-throughs, but he was on the edge of blowing it again and he knew it.

It was only because Hollie possessed the driving skills of a stunt racer that he made it to the Lomax lot in Century City for the 6 a.m. call time, showered, shaved and smelling like he'd just walked out of Tom Ford's boudoir. Two litres of black coffee and a Xanax had taken the edge off the pain; now the fresh orange juice was slowly transforming his complexion from grey to pink.

Hollie had already checked the schedule for the day. Morning in wardrobe. His character Seb Dunhill's suits had been custom-made by Burberry, but there was still work to be done on the rest of his outfits. Afternoon in rehearsals for the first scene, shooting the following day. Courtesy of the LA city chiefs, they'd closed down a section of Wilshire Boulevard for a car chase that was filming the next morning at five. Hooking up with Dixie at Sparkles just became a rain check.

The prep was his least favourite part of the process. A necessary evil. He just wanted to be out there, being someone else, not in here having his crotch position measured by Nessa, a very pleasant but noisy Texan grandmother who had mastered the art of speaking loudly while holding a spray of pins between her teeth and called him 'sweet cheeks'.

They were on their fourth costume adjustment and she had already served up more industry news than Deadline.com, when she paused for breath, before switching to the next subject. 'And ain't that great news that Mirren McLean is back in town? I was getting worried about that girl. Never liked Jack Gore. Eyes too close together.'

'Why? Where was she?' No amount of suave pretence could mask the sharpness of his tone.

'Why, sweet cheeks, her car went off a canyon. Rumour has it Gore is gonna be a daddy with that Mercedes Dance – my sister worked on her wardrobe last year, and thank the good Lord she's pretty cos she ain't gonna win any medals for bein' smart. Married man. What was she thinking?'

Hollie came in clutching a clipboard, square black glasses falling to the tip of her nose.

'OK, you've had a couple of calls. D'you want to go over them now while you're in Nessa's capable hands?'

'Hollie, what happened to Mirren McLean?'

Hollie thought for a moment, assimilating the facts and then relaying them in the correct order.

'Hit the press last week that Jack Gore and Mercedes Dance were doing the naked samba; she's first trimester with his kid; Mirren went off grid for a few days after trashing his Maserati over a cliff—'

'Amen!' Nessa interjected.

'And then she turned up in Mexico City. Now she's back and, according to *Entertainment Tonight*, started shooting on the set of *Clansman 5* today. You're welcome.'

She punctuated the sentence with an extended bow.

Zander's heart rate gradually returned to somewhere near normal. OK, it had nothing to do with what happened back then. Nothing to do with them.

'Hey, I meant to say, a journo called Sarah something from the UK has left you a couple of messages. Want me to reply?'

'Let me think about it.' Like it wasn't all he'd been doing for the last few days.

Nessa stood back and finally removed the pins from her mouth. 'OK, sweet cheeks, you're good to go and I'm a happy woman,' she said with a cackle of endearment.

Zander gave her a hug and then followed Hollie down a labyrinth of corridors. Over four decades Lomax Films had grown from one man with a flair for selling ideas to one of the biggest deals in town. Jerry Bruckheimer. Paul Bonetti. Kent Lang. Brian Grazer. Steven Spielberg. Harvey Weinstein. James Cameron. Wes Lomax had topped them all when his production company batted out of its league with *The Brutal Circle* and gave Lomax the dollars and the balls to set up his own studio. Lomax Films didn't have the vast reach of Sony or Time Warner, but they'd whipped Lionsgate and Miramax last year and were on course to do the same again.

The physical demands of the afternoon were a welcome relief after the mental stress of the morning. Nothing took your mind off your problems quite like the physical discomfort of having your scrotum crushed in a harness swinging ten feet in the air. Seb Dunhill had to jump from a helicopter and land on a tanker carrying toxic waste en route to downtown LA. There was a gift for the late-night talk-show hosts. That was a gag that wrote itself.

As soon as his character had saved LA, he was being shipped to the Middle East – balls intact – to save the world. In reality, most of the movie was being shot in Nevada.

'You go on – I just want to stop by Wes's office and check in.'

Hollie eyed him with cynicism. 'Or are you going to find a store cupboard and down a quart of bourbon?'

Zander gave her his most winning grin. 'That was the old me. The new me is teetotal.'

'Since this morning?'

For the first time in a week he laughed. 'It's fucking brilliant what you can achieve in one day.'

Hollie shook her head. 'Mood swings. Great. I swear Matt Damon would have been a lot easier than this shit.'

Zander rode the lift two levels to the executive floor, then ducked into the men's room and pulled a miniature of Jack Daniel's out of his jacket pocket. It was gone in seconds, the taste washed away by the miniature of mouthwash in his other pocket. After washing his hands, he took a bottle of Clive Christian 1872 from the vanity and gave a quick spray. Just enough to cover any lingering booze smell, not too much that Wes would be suspicious.

'Hey, Monica, is the boss in?'

Wes's secretary had been with him since he started out. She must be in her sixties by now, but the most generous secretarial package in the business kept her looking on the right side of forty-five.

'Sure. I'll let him know you're here.'

She'd barely pressed the button on her phone line when

Lomax came striding out of the office and greeted him with a bear hug.

'Great to see you, buddy. You're looking great.'

Wes led the way back through to his office and they both sat on the white buffalo-skin seats that bordered a sleek black Italian marble board table. A crack ran across the middle of it. Rumour had it that Wes had smashed it with a machete after a deal had gone wrong. The truth was that a four-way with three sturdy German film students had left its mark.

Wes didn't mind which story people believed.

'Feeling great,' Zander concurred.

Wes contemplated him for a moment. They'd been together in this business a lot of years and their relationship had long passed the need for niceties and platitudes.

'You sure, son?'

'I'm sure.'

They may not need niceties and platitudes, but sometimes a little dishonesty was called for. Wes chose to believe him. They batted about some stuff on the movie for a few minutes before Monica knocked on the door. The age-old sign that Wes's next appointment was waiting.

They shook hands and almost made it to the door before Wes put out a hand to stop him.

'Zander, the last one was close. It can't happen again.'

He didn't have to ask what that meant. If the public stays onside, an A-list star can survive one public meltdown. He couldn't survive two.

'I'm on top of it, Wes. Don't worry.' Zander wasn't sure who he was trying to convince.

'You have to be. Because we can't afford a fuck-up, Zander. There's too much riding on this.'

Wes's words lingered longer than the taste of the bourbon he'd downed in the washroom.

Driving home, Hollie realized after five minutes that Zander wasn't in the mood for conversation, so she'd settled for comfortable silence. The smell of the ocean flooded the car as they pulled up next to his block.

'Want to come in and order up some food?' he asked her.

There were two motivations. He felt like company that wouldn't get him robbed or arrested. And Wes's words had struck home. He had to pull himself out of this for all their sakes. It was time to sort himself out and get straight.

Hollie leaned over and kissed his cheek. 'Thanks for the offer, but unlike you, I have a life. And a date.' She caught his expression and hesitated, realization dawning. 'Look, I can change my plans – it's not a problem. Tell me you're not going to go in there and order two strippers and a Robert Downey Junior-sized speedball.'

He was already out of the car.

'Don't be crazy – it's fine. Think I'll go catch the last of the waves anyway.' He was gorgeous Zander Leith again – winning smile, confident, assured and back in charge.

He could do this. He just had to shut down the anxiety. Remove negativity.

'Holls, can you call that journo and tell her I'm not available for interview and my family life is private?' The end. Done.

'Sure.' She blew him a kiss. 'Look, any problems, call me, OK? I'll have my cell.'

'Will do.'

Walking to the door, he instinctively scanned for paparazzi. None. They all knew Hollie anyway, knew there was no story there. The two homeless guys perched outside his building's door raised their liquor bottles to him. He dropped a twenty and tried not to view them as a premonition of his future. 'G'night, guys.'

Inside, he pulled off his jacket, turned the water on in the tub and poured in some oils. Jesus, back home this would make him a few scented candles short of being a female. The thought caught him unawares. He'd spent years refusing to let his thoughts cross the Atlantic and now it seemed like he couldn't get it out of his mind.

When there was a knock on the door, the diversion was a relief. Typical Hollie. She got to the end of the road, called her date to cancel and came back for Thai. Or maybe sushi.

He didn't even bother to shove on a robe, just a towel round his waist. There was nothing she hadn't seen before.

'Hey, I . . .'

The door was wide open before his realization caught up.

'Hi,' she said. 'I brought a friend.' She held up a bottle of Grey Goose, then pushed herself off the door frame and walked past him. 'And no, before you ask, my mother doesn't know I'm here.'

As Chloe Gore kicked off her shoes and slumped onto his sofa, he was in no doubt at all that trouble had just wandered right back into his life.

14.

'Alive and Kicking' – Simple Minds

Glasgow, 1985

Simple Minds blared from the tape recorder on the wooden floor. Jim Kerr was 'alive and kicking'. Which was more than could be said for the three teenagers who were lying staring at the roof, blowing smoke rings in some kind of synchronized, lung-clogging competition.

Mirren broke her record of five hoops in a row and then extinguished her cigarette in the glass ashtray she'd smuggled from the house. They'd learned that lesson soon after they'd starting hanging out in the hut at the bottom of Davie's garden. She'd stubbed a cigarette out on the floor and they'd come back an hour later to find a void the size of a manhole, the edges still smouldering.

Davie covered it up with his mum's Flymo. If she ever decided to cut the grass, he was dead.

'A football player,' Davie announced, continuing the discussion they'd been having before their favourite song had come on. Mirren taped the Top Forty every Sunday night and it became their entertainment for the week.

Mirren pushed herself up onto one elbow. 'You want to be a football player?'

'Aye.'

'Well, can I point out the obvious?'

'What?'

'You might want to give up the fags.'

'Aye, stunts your growth,' Zander added. 'And at your height you might manage a game for Subbuteo.'

Their laughter could be heard right across all five back gardens in their block. Not that it mattered. Everyone was inside watching that new soap EastEnders or down the pub.

Besides, everyone was used to seeing them hanging around. Mirren knew that to everyone else it had seemed strange at first. Two boys and one girl, none of them members of any of the groups that hung out at the garages and shops around the scheme. Davie was the hyper, chatty one, always cheeky and looking for a laugh. Zander was quieter, with that laid-back thing that meant you never really knew what he was thinking. He didn't take any shit, though. Big Jim Anderson from the bottom end of the scheme had jumped Davie one night for his Walkman and Zander had gone straight down there, battered him and got it back.

Didn't say a word. Just did it. No one else had come near them since then.

It was a strange concept for her. Friends. She'd never had them. All through primary school she'd kept to herself, as the other kids had parties and sleepovers and day trips to Calderpark Zoo. She was never invited. Maybe if she'd made the first move, asked someone to come over to her house, they'd have done it

99

back, but her mum wouldn't allow it. Bad enough that she had one brat, she said.

So, naturally shy, Mirren just kept her head down. Went to the library after school. Filled her head with books. Snuck out some from the adult section when the old librarian wasn't looking.

Right now, she was reading Jackie Collins. Hollywood Wives. None of the characters in that was covering up a fag accident with a Flymo.

'What about you, then?' Davie asked.

'Dunno.'

Mirren tried to ignore the fact that he was staring at her now.

'You're lying. I can just tell. You look guilty.'

'Aye. All right then, Columbo,' she teased.

'Whatever. C'mon. Tell us. What do you want to do? A lollipop wumman so you don't need to start work till you're sixty-five?'

Mirren threw an empty can of Irn-Bru at his head. It missed.

'A writer.'

'A whit?'

'A writer.'

She should never have said it. They'd only take the piss. It's not as if she was even a swot at school. She liked English, but that was it. She still passed her exams right enough, even though everything else bored her rigid.

'What? Like write books?'

'No, colour them in. Of course I mean write books. Novels.'

With a twinkle in his eye that guaranteed he was about to continue the mutual slagging, Davie opened his mouth, but was cut short when Zander said seriously, 'You could do that. Be a writer, I mean.'

'You think?'

He shrugged. 'Don't see why not.'

It was about as talkative as Zander ever got and Mirren had learned not to push. When he had something to say, he spoke. That was it. And besides, he couldn't get a word in for Davie.

'Right then, come on, big shot. Tell us what you want to do,' Davie dared him. 'Only, they're looking for new priests doon the chapel. "Bless me, Father, for I have sinned: I've got off with three lassies in the last fortnight."'

'Shut it!' Zander kicked open the hut door with his foot and threw his cigarette butt outside.

Mirren felt the hairs on the back of her neck rise. She hated arguments and confrontations. Bloody Davie should have known better than to mention the chapel. It was bad enough that Zander's mum spent her whole life there without them talking about it here too.

She watched as he shook his head, then gave Davie's legs a nudge with the toe of his trainer. 'You don't half talk shite.'

'I know,' Davie replied, grinning.

Mirren felt herself relax. Tension over.

'You didn't answer the question,' she said, keen to move back to neutral territory.

Zander thought about it for a moment.

'Dunno. Rigs, maybe. Army. Anything that would get me the fuck away from here and him.'

There was no need to ask and it was as well they didn't because the hut door burst open and Jono Leith's frame filled the doorway. He was swaying from side to side, carrying a bag from the Co-op that clinked as he swung it in front of them.

Zander was the first to speak.

'Thought you were going to be locked up until trial.'

No happy welcome. No shaking of hands or pats on the back.

'Well, I'm out today, Sandy. Case dropped. I'm an innocent man and halle-fucking-lujah!' Jono roared. 'So up, the three of youse. Over to our house. The lads are on their way and there's gonna be a bit of a party. C'mon, you young 'uns. Switch that pish aff and come and hear some real music.' With that, he broke into a song Mirren recognized. The Rolling Stones. 'Satisfaction'.

'Come on, come on!' he repeated after the first verse. Move they lazy arses of yours and let's go.'

Davie was already on his feet, grinning at the prospect of yet another wild party at the Leiths', when Mirren caught Zander's eye and they exchanged a silent message of under-standing. He didn't want to go. Neither did she. But that didn't matter. Because when it came to the real world, they both knew that no one refused Jono Leith.

15.

'Labour of Love' – Hue & Cry

Glasgow, 2013

'Yes, I understand that he's now on a shoot, but I'd only need twenty minutes of his time. I was under the impression that his Scottish fans were important to him.'

Even as she went for the shameless emotional blackmail, Sarah knew it was futile. She was talking to some PA who was just carrying out orders, not in a position to be swayed by argument. The point was borne out by the click at the other end of the line as Zander Leith's PA shut her down.

'Buggering bollocks.'

She tossed her phone on the desk and then stretched back in her chair. The offices of the *Daily Scot* were in darkness, except for a couple of night-shift subs working in cubicles at the furthest corner of the room.

The rest of the staff were at Epicures, in the upmarket Hyndland, a former wine merchant's that had been transformed into a two-level cafe and bar for the trendies of the West End. It was a going-away party for a guy on the news desk who'd decided to toss in the dark side and head to

Australia to live life on a beach. Sarah could see why that would be an attraction. This wasn't an easy job, an easy life. But for her, there was something intoxicating about it. She told the news. Exposed the wrongs. Challenged the establishment.

But for now she was happy with challenging Zander Leith's PR people. So she'd left her colleagues dreaming of a better life and trudged through the torrential rain all the way back to the office.

The huge clock on the wall in front of her clicked to 9 p.m. Watching that happen had become a regular occurrence in her life since she'd become obsessed with this case. She spent hours trawling archives and the internet looking for something, anything that would help, and came up blank every time. Not a single interview or feature on the families of Johnston, McLean or Leith existed. Not one. Had anyone else ever noticed that was odd? Irritation was making it difficult to decide whether to head home or stay here and continue searching the Web until it was time to pick Simon up at midnight from some black-tie law thing at the Hilton.

'Would you stop swinging on those chairs? Health and safety will shut us down.' Sarah instinctively smiled at the sight of her boss. In his early sixties, with a grey complexion that suggested accurately that he had lived life under fluorescent lights, Ed McCallum had been the editor at the *Scot* for twenty years. He was considered old school. Traditional. Still rumoured to have a half-bottle in the filing cabinet. There weren't many of that ilk left these days. In an industry that had changed beyond recognition, evolving from ink to internet, most of the newspaper heads were dynamic media guys who talked about critical mass and click rates and had strategies for pulling back the readers that had been lost to the twenty-four-hour news channels and the instant gratification of the online update. They also couldn't smell a great story if it was served up with their morning skinny frappuccino, semi-skimmed, vanilla twist.

That wasn't to say he was fully on board with her latest line of enquiry. Cutbacks from London had left the paper so short of those little wheel cogs called journalists that she was covering it, with his knowledge, in her spare time.

'So where are you at?'

'The square root of nothing.' Her foot absent-mindedly tapped against the edge of her desk and she twirled a corkscrew of her deep auburn, shoulder-length hair round her index finger. Ed had watched her do that in times of stress since she joined the paper as a twenty-one-year-old rookie fresh out of Napier College.

Even then she'd stood out from the rest. The quiet ambition. The dogged determination. And the complete lack of awareness of the impact she had when she crossed a room. If she wasn't young enough to be his daughter, Ed might be just a little bit in lust with her.

'The only glimpse of progress was when Davie Johnston's PA acknowledged my request for an interview, but now she's not taking my calls. Not surprising given the shit he's in, right enough. The press conference the other day made my toes curl.'

Ed's trademark pause of contemplation lasted just a little longer than usual, before he – as always – cut right to the issue.

'Have you gone back to the start?'

Sarah nodded. 'They all grew up in the same street, all only children. Strange, huh?'

'Did you go chap on doors there?'

'Ed, it was twenty years ago and their kids are multi-millionaires. There's no way their parents are still going to be living in Crofthill council houses.'

One of his excessive eyebrows raised just a fraction.

Sarah caught on quick. 'You have got to be kidding me? You think they could still be there?'

Ed shrugged, knowing the effect it would have. With an irritated growl she was out of her seat and heading to the door before he could say another word.

Traffic was quiet, so it took her twenty minutes to get from the office on the Broomielaw to Crofthill, an area that commentators and council officials labelled 'urban deprived'. It took another two to locate the block that Hollywood's dream team had grown up in. It was difficult to say what it looked like back then, but now the buildings had been recently painted, the communal garden was tidy, and the only blot on the landscape was the squad of hoodies sitting on a wall next to a row of garages, sharing four bottles of Buckfast between eight.

With the synchronized movements of a tennis audience, they stared at her, looked at her Audi A3 and then back at her. Sarah pulled a wallet out of her pocket, opened it, flashed it in their direction and then closed it again. 'Police. If there's so much as a scratch on that when I come back, I'll hunt you down.'

She congratulated herself on the grit she'd managed to inject into her voice, while praying that at that distance they couldn't make out that they'd just been served with a membership card for her local health club.

Number 11 was at the nearest end of the block, and she knocked loudly at the door and then stood back, suddenly realizing that making unannounced visits at this time of night hadn't been a particularly well-thought-out plan.

Right on cue there was a scurry of activity inside, a bang at the back of the door and then a half-dozen teenage boys in tracksuits jumped over the side fence and ran off into the night. Safe to say that unless Zander Leith's sixty-year-old mother was harbouring a street crew of teenagers, then the house had been taken over by new owners.

There was no point even trying Mirren McLean's old house. The windows were boarded up, and each one had the telltale signs of smoke damage round the perimeter, natty accessories to a large hole in the roof that was covered with tarpaulin and wooden sheeting.

As she banged on the door of number 15, Davie Johnston's old house, she cursed herself for wasting time. She'd been right all along. Why would the mother of one of the biggest stars in Hollywood live in a scheme that had more burnt-out cars than employed adults?

'She's no' in.' One of the Buckfast Eight auditioned for the role of Neighbourhood Watch officer. 'Works on the soup bus at night.'

An even unlikelier scenario.

'Who are you talking about?' Sarah asked.

The helpful pillar of the community spat on the pavement before he answered. 'You should know – yer banging oan her door.'

His mates laughed, enjoying the show, but Sarah ignored the cheek. 'I'm looking for Mrs Johnston.'

'Aye. And she's no' in.' A half-pissed delinquent was talking to her like she was the one with coherence issues. 'She's on the soup bus,' he repeated.

'In town?'

'Aye. Nae wonder yer a detective,' the hoodie replied, to more hilarity from his gang.

Despite the piss-take, Sarah tossed them a tenner for the alcohol fund as she passed them, eliciting cheers of thanks. Subsidizing the destruction of a youth's liver wasn't normally on her charitable acts list, but this was the closest she'd come to a break since she'd begun.

Five minutes were shaved off her previous time as she raced back into Glasgow City Centre, careful to slow down at every one of the hated, cash-generating speed cameras.

The Thursday-night party squad were out in force as she drove along St Vincent Street and turned left, then right, onto West George Street. This was the young, wilder side of town at night, a sea of short skirts, bare legs and heels that started the night adding eight inches to their owner's height and ended the night being carried by a bare-footed clubber to a kebab shop. It was a stark contrast to the Merchant City half a mile across town, with its older, classier crowd and up-market bars and restaurants.

Sarah spotted a space right next to the white double-decker and pulled her Audi into it.

This wasn't the first time she'd been here. Only last month, the paper had run a series of features on the work done by the volunteers who ran and staffed the bus. It was a lifeline to those who used it: mainly homeless people in the early evening and street workers at night. As well as food, there were free toiletries and second-hand clothes, and practical help was available from a drugs and alcohol counsellor, a paramedic and a social worker who specialized in finding refuge for the seriously vulnerable or the ones who were committed to changing their lives. They all gave their time for free and they saw everything on this bus, every heart-breaking tale of desperation, every violent pimp determined to get his whore back on the street, every victory snatched by someone with the strength to accept help and turn their life around.

The driving force behind it was an incredible woman, Isabel Ross, who relentlessly badgered companies for donations, rallied volunteers for the cause and treated every customer with dignity and respect. On the night Sarah had spent there researching the feature, she had been blown away by Isabel's strength and conviction, and had decided this was the Glasgow that people should know about. This was the heart of the city. A piece about street vice had become a human-interest story of inspiration and courage. Ed had splashed it across the front page and donations had come in by the sack-load to the office.

Oh, the irony that this could be the place that could throw up a lead on the biggest case of her career. The whole way back, Sarah had recalled her memories from that night, pulling up mental photofits of everyone on the bus. Nope, no one even came close to the demographic of Ena Johnston. Not really surprising. The volunteers tended to work a maximum of one night a week, rationed because Isabel felt that a few hours per week spent swimming in this quagmire of desperation and pain was more than enough for anyone.

Two young girls who looked like they should be at home and in bed under posters of One Direction sat on the bottom step of the entrance, both smoking, one of them with a fierce blue bruise on her right cheek. Sarah's hackles instantly rose. Who the fuck would do that to a kid? Even one who sat there, in her miniskirt and hooker shoes, looking at her with such vicious defiance that it made Sarah want to take her home, talk to her, find out what had been done to her to make her hate the world that much.

Isabel had just put a plate of toast and two mugs of tea in front of a pair of women with hardened expressions that said they'd seen too much and now cared too little, when she spotted Sarah.

'Sarah, oh goodness, love, what brings you back out here?'

She wrapped her in a hug and pulled her over to a free bench. The seats that once ferried workers and travellers across Glasgow had been replaced by long padded benches that sat, train style, on either side of a Formica table.

'Just checking up on you, Isabel. Making sure you hadn't decided to swap this bus for a Saga tour and take off round the Highlands.'

Isabel's worn face crinkled when she laughed, but not a single strand of her peroxide beehive so much as trembled out of place. 'Chance would be a fine thing. Listen, thanks so much. Bloody van-loads of stuff has been arriving every week for our clients since you wrote that bit in the paper.'

Sarah reached over and put her hand on top of her friend's. 'Anytime. You deserve it.'

Isabel chuckled again. 'Aye, you're right. Ah deserve that George Clooney tae, but he's no' been dropped off yet.' More laughter, still not even an escaped wisp from the beehive.

'I'll see what I can do,' Sarah told her. Behind them, there was a flurry of activity as four new arrivals staggered on and shuffled into seats. Isabel's eyes scoped them and sussed them out immediately, and Sarah could see that this had to be wrapped up to let Isabel do her job.

'Look, I won't keep you, but can you tell me do you have anyone called Ena Johnston working here? A volunteer maybe?'

Isabel shook her head. 'Nope, sorry, love . . .'

Damn. So close. Sarah's fists clenched with disappointment. At exactly the same time one of the new arrivals screamed and Sarah turned to see her being dragged by the hair along the aisle by the young girl from the front step.

Isabel leaped to her feet and dived towards the altercation, with a loud 'Right, that's enough! Come on, Chelsea, put her doon.'

It was only when the screaming subsided that Sarah realized what she'd said as she sprang into action.

'But we've got an Ena Dawson who works a Sunday-night shift. Could that be her?'

16.

'Counting Stars' – OneRepublic

Jenny didn't even let the door hit her perfectly shaped ass on the way out. The only thing that might have slowed her down was the traffic jam in the driveway caused by the fleeing forms of Al, his team and everyone who'd participated in the sham of a press conference.

Every one of them gone now.

Jenny and Darcy had a month-long hiatus from *Streets of Power*, so they were heading over to Darcy's house to hang out there.

Al rounded up his team and cleared them out with the precision and cold efficiency of a serial killer leaving a dump site.

'Lie low for a few days and try to stay out of fucking trouble' had been his parting shot.

And then they were gone. All of them. It was just him, Davie Johnston, alone, sitting in the games room, like a spare prick at a wedding, contemplating places he'd like to slam the pool cue he was twirling between his trembling fingers.

Lie low. The only time he ever lay low was when the setting

included a twenty-one-year-old pageant winner and a five-star hotel suite on a Cabo beach.

For a man who was the ultimate chameleon, this situation was proving to be difficult to adapt to.

It was inconceivable that it could all fall apart. He was Davie Johnston. He was Golden Bollocks long before Beckham had tried to claim the title. It didn't go wrong for guys like him. They were untouchable.

Look at Zander Leith. The guy was a wasted, boozed-up, coked-out disaster and yet the public still loved him.

His shaking hands were sweating now too. Zander. In the early days after the Oscar, Davie had tried, really tried to get through to him, but Zander had cut him dead. It had devastated him, wounded, hurt, until Davie had just stopped trying. He'd bumped into him a few times over the years – in this town, that was unavoidable – but every time his old mate's eyes would blaze with warning and Davie would back off. It had been a lesson. Mirren. Zander. Both of them gone. Proof that friends fucked you over whenever it suited them. Davie had taken that on board and lived by it. Sure, he had acquaintances, drinking buddies, mates in a celebrity football team he turned out for on free Sundays, but that was as close as he got to friendship.

He thought again about the contact from the reporter on the *Scot*. The initial shock and panic had worn off and now he'd applied a layer of perspective and it seemed to have gone away. The interview request had been refused, end of story. Dear God, please make it the end of story. Desperate for an ally, looking for support, he'd reached out again to Mirren's people. Still no reply. For the first time he wondered if he should call Zander, give him a heads-up. But no. What was the point? It would probably all blow over, and right now he had bigger things to worry about.

He could hear his mum's voice in his head saying, 'It's all about family. Just me and you, David – that's all we need, isn't it?' Then she'd slip him a fiver for the chip shop and dispatch him down for the dinner. How long was it since they'd spoken? A year? Two? He'd brought her out to Los Angeles once, but she'd hated it. 'Can't walk anywhere. Too big. And why do you need a house with more bathrooms than bedrooms?' She'd wanted to spend the whole time in the garden playing with the kids, and got real upset when he pointed out that's what the nannies were for. 'Well, we didn't have nannies when you were a boy and we did OK, son,' she'd said. He'd been desperate to please her, to impress her with his home and life. Instead, she'd watched him bicker with Jenny, watched the way the kids were cared for by others and asked him where it had all gone wrong. At the time, he'd been furious. Now, he wondered if maybe she'd had a point.

He was Davie Johnston and he had nowhere to go. So he was sitting in a games room, with walls that were lined with frames containing every Scotland football top for the last forty years.

With the strength that came from a thousand workouts with a sadist ex-boxer, he launched the pool cue and then flinched as it smashed through the glass display cabinet on the wall. Some of the most valuable sports memorabilia in the country tumbled out. A jersey worn by Babe Ruth. Muhammad Ali's shorts. Home-run balls from a dozen baseball legends. A bat from the first World Series. NFL balls from ten Super Bowls.

And his prized possession – a jersey signed by Michael Jordan, LeBron James, Kobe Bryant and Shaq. He'd met them all at a charity dinner and bought the top for $1 million. Because he was Davie Johnston and he could do that.

Bollocks to lying low.

He was in the car in ten minutes and pulling up outside the Staples Center half an hour later.

A $100 tip to the expectant valet, then through the VIP entrance and he was in his regular courtside seat. Tip-off in ten – no time to stop at the bar. Usually his appearance got a cheer from the crowd, but there was nothing tonight. That was OK. His baseball cap was pulled low, and all eyes were on court, where the teams were finishing their warm-up. The Brooklyn Nets had a swagger about them since Jay-Z took over and renamed the club, and the Lakers were on home turf, so they had something to prove.

This is what he needed. A battle. A couple of hours of sweat and pain, and the bonus was that none of it was his.

The buzz from the crowd got his adrenalin going. Yes! This felt good. Nineteen thousand people in the stadium and he was courtside, one of the chosen few. Across from him, he could see Jack Nicholson deep in conversation with a stunning blonde. A few seats along, Mila Kunis was resting her head on Ashton Kutcher's shoulder. Just half a dozen seats to his left, David Beckham's brow was frowning with concentration as he explained something on court to one of his kids, breaking off to shake Jay-Z's hand as the team owner passed him on the way to his own seat. The seats on either side of him belonged to the boss of a record company and tonight they were occupied by a couple of rap kings Davie recognized from MTV, wearing more bling than the window at Harry Winston.

A beer appeared in front of him, served as a matter of course by a hostess who knew his preferences. The tip-off went the Lakers' way, and Kobe Bryant scored a lay-up off the first drive.

The game was fast, aggressive and fairly evenly matched, but most of all, it was a distraction. This wasn't about him. Or about the fact that his life had gone to shit. Here, he was anonymous. Just a guy watching a game.

A slow roar of disapproval started in the crowd and his attention snapped back to the court. Hang on, what had he missed? The teams were on a timeout and yet the crowd's disapproval was ascending like a furious ringtone, thundering now, with thousands of feet stomping the floor to add to the sheer ferocity of the noise.

What was this? What the hell was going on? Had he missed a foul? Or an injury? Or . . .

His eyes flicked to the big screen up to his left and a wave of ice sliced through his body.

There he was. On the big screen. Caught on the stadium camera. And the boos of the crowd, the disgust on their faces – that was all for him.

This was the modern-day Colosseum of Rome. And the crowd had just made it clear that he was going to have to fight or die.

17.

'Bang Bang' – will.i.am

Three a.m. was no stranger to her. Mirren couldn't remember the last time she'd gone a full night without a visit from her frenemy Insomnia. There were advantages to surviving on a couple of hours' sleep. When work pressure was on, she could achieve the impossible: rewrite a scene, work on her next novel, clear her inbox, plan her month, tackle the stack of outstanding tasks that came with running a home, a company, a family and a production.

But on nights like tonight, when even the distraction of work couldn't rouse her from a deep trough of melancholy, insomnia became a slow torture. Every minute lasted an hour. Every hour lasted a week.

Throwing back the duvet, she padded over to the seating area of her bedroom and flicked a switch to spark up the flames that rose from crystals behind the glass of the fire built into the wall. The Venetian mirrored door to the side of the fire concealed a wine rack holding ten bottles of their favourite Pinot Noir. The mini fridge below it had soft drinks, smoothies and a couple of bottles of Jack's favourite Krug, Clos d'Ambonnay 1998. Until last week the champagne was only liberated in times of celebration or passion. Tonight was neither, but somehow the fact that she'd just popped open a bottle of his $3,000 liquor and poured it into a coffee mug made her feel like she was achieving a small dig at the faithless dickhead. Petty, of course. Even more so when the first sip evoked so many memories that it made her want to retch.

Shivering, despite the heat from the fire, she swapped it for a bottle of water and folded her legs beneath her on the sofa, pulling a cashmere rug over her in the hope of getting some heat into her bones.

Beside her, her phone bleeped and she picked it up to check it, already smiling. It would be Logan. He had absolutely no concept of time difference and he texted her every night before he went to bed and every morning. Not very rock and roll, but it was one of the conditions of him going on the road. Not that she could have stopped him, but he was sweet enough to humour her and play by her rules. Two daily texts and a phone call every other day. Logan never stuck to that one: there was so much hanging around at airports and soundchecks that he rarely went a day without a chat.

A quick mental run-through of his itinerary reminded her that they were playing in Brazil last night. Six hours ahead. So 9 a.m. there. His breakfast text.

'Morning, Mom. Love ya! Hug Chlo for me. Xx'

If there had been any point, she would have wept. Not for that asshole Jack – she'd parked her grief over that one until she could think straight on how to move forward.

Right now, her sadness was all for Chloe. But what would regret achieve? It wasn't going to bring Chloe back or straighten her out. This was her doing. Her fault. She'd handled Chloe's life badly, pushed her away. Yet at the time, she honestly thought she was doing the right thing. Maybe still did. How many times was she going to go over that morning in her head and change her actions? Sliding doors. If she'd made a different decision anywhere along that fateful day, would the outcome have been any different?

Mirren closed her eyes. Pressed rewind.

A year ago. Almost to the day.

The sound of an incoming text on Chloe's phone.

Mirren was no longer sitting on her bedroom sofa. Her mind was back there, back in Chloe's bedroom twelve months ago, on the morning that changed everything.

Chloe was in the shower and Mirren had used the time to search her room. There was no doubt she was using again. They'd done rehab twice, they'd done four separate overnight stints in the cells, but nothing had shocked her straight.

Mirren was beginning to wonder if anything would.

They had a drugs specialist in the spare room, a lock on the door, and they were on the third sober companion this month. Two had quit for fear of their own sobriety, and the other one was back in rehab. Chloe's influence was nothing if not persuasive.

Beep. Beep.

Mirren's head jerked to the left, to the slight illumination that was radiating from a Louboutin sneaker on the floor. Chloe was obsessive about her phone. Kept it hidden. Never left it anywhere that it could be hijacked by a parent or a cop. It was probably a sign of how spaced out she was that she hadn't taken it into the bathroom with her.

Looking at it would be an invasion of her daughter's privacy. It would be crossing a line. But at that moment, Mirren didn't care. She was in the market for answers. Where was Chloe getting her drugs? Who was dealing? Where was the money coming from? How was it happening? And how could she make it stop?

Putting her hand into the shoe, the first thing she touched was hard, the second soft. Sighing, Mirren put the phone on the bed and put the bag of white powder next to it.

Evidence for the prosecution? Shit Mother, guilty as charged. How had she let her baby get to the state that she was hiding drugs in her shoes?

The phone demanded a password. Mirren paused, then typed in a word, one of the only two things in life that mattered to Chloe. Logan. Ping. Correct answer. The second guess had been coke.

The text was now on the home screen. A movie clip. And a message.

Mirren pressed play.

The image wasn't the best quality, but good enough to make it quite clear what was happening. A bedroom. High class. Expensive. A hotel. Brochures sitting on the black slate coffee table, in front of an angular black leather sofa. Behind it, a bed, glossy ebony frame, silver bedding. Rich. Opulent. Chris Brown's 'Don't Wake Me Up' playing in the background.

On the bed, Chloe, just a tiny vest and panties, her red curls matted and wild, her eyes alive, wide, giggling as she snorted a line off a ten-inch-square mirror that she held up to her nose.

The camera jerked as it scanned the room, then went still, as a guy came round in front of it. 'OK, baby, it's on,' he told her.

Back to the bed, to Chloe, beckoning him towards her. The guy – Mirren could only see him from the neck down – came into shot as he stepped towards the bed, the muscles on his naked torso rippling as he moved.

The voices in Mirren's head screamed, Don't touch my baby. Don't you fucking dare touch my baby. He wasn't listening.

Chloe pushed herself downwards until she was lying flat, then sprinkled a line of white powder in a straight line from the middle of her breasts down to where her G-string began.

'Come down here, baby,' the girl on the bed begged, her voice whiny and insistent. It wasn't Chloe anymore. It was someone else, someone who looked like her. It had to be. The same face, the same body, the same birthmark, a little brown circle at the top of her right thigh. But that couldn't be her baby. It couldn't be.

Only the back of the guy's head was in view as he leaned down, produced a rolled-up note from the palm of his hand and snorted all the way from the top to the bottom.

Chloe grabbed his hair and pulled him back up towards her, kissing him, laughing.

Then she pushed him back, flicked open the front of her bra, took another pile of powder from the bedside table and rubbed it round her nipples. He paid attention to each one in turn, Chloe moaning with pleasure as he licked them clean.

His hand was on Chloe's belly now, then moving downwards until he slid it inside her knickers.

No. Oh God, no. Mirren was whimpering now, rocking

back and forwards, desperate to turn it off, yet absolutely unable to.

Chloe's moans became even more insistent, demanding, ordering him to never stop. Oh no, never stop. He retracted his hand now, ignoring her wails of protest, then moved to the bottom of the bed, his back to the camera, but sadly not blocking out the sight of Chloe's salacious grin as he pulled off her panties.

It didn't matter. Mirren knew exactly who it was. She recognized the hair, the broad shoulders, the laugh, the voice, and most of all she recognized the expression on her daughter's face, the one that she saved just for him. She recognized the voice her daughter was using, the same one she used when she was calling him for the tenth time in a day. The one that she was using now to call the shots.

'Fuck me now,' Chloe ordered, spreading her legs wide, as he . . .

Cut to black.

At exactly the same moment as Mirren died inside. The message that accompanied the clip was almost irrelevant: $100k.

That was all it said.

It didn't matter. No amount of money was going to make that go away. No amount of money was going to save her girl.

Only she could do that. Or die trying.

Trembling, she slipped the phone into her pocket. She'd worry about Chloe's reaction later.

As she passed the rehab specialist in the other room, she popped her head in. Long grey hair, tied back, a shirt and tie under his medical jacket, he was a survivor of the 1970s rock scene, reinvented as a substance-abuse expert and had come highly recommended as one of the best in town. Mirren couldn't help thinking he wasn't that good if he hadn't discovered Chloe's stash. She tossed the bag of powder to him, saying nothing.

He nodded as if it was exactly what he'd expected.

'They're addicts, Mrs Gore. They find ways.'

'And I'm paying you ten thousand dollars a day to make sure you're better at finding them than she is at concealing them.'

He had the temerity to look offended. Mirren had never cared less.

'I'm putting some more security downstairs. I've taken her phone and she's going to kick off . . .'

'Mrs Gore, I'd strongly recommend against that. It demonstrates a lack of trust and could be detrimental to—'

'I don't give a damn. I'll be back in an hour. Call me if you can't cope.'

In the kitchen, she grabbed her phone and pressed number one on the speed dial.

'Hey, my doll face, what's going on?'

'I need help, Lou.'

Her friend didn't even pause to ask why.

'Shoot.'

'Jordan Lang.'

'Son of a bitch. Is Chloe still hanging out with that vile piece of crap? I was hoping he'd disappear after his daddy cut off the cash supply.'

'When did that happen?'

Lou immediately switched into information mode.

'Last weekend. Word is, he emptied his trust fund of half

a mill and sold one of Granny's rocks. Kent Lang went nuts, threw him out, told him to fuck off, disinherited him.'

The demand for cash suddenly made sense.

'I know it's a long shot, but any idea where he is today?'

'Give me five minutes.'

The phone clicked and Mirren used the wait to get prepared. In her study, she flipped open the panel behind the portrait of the kids, taken at the beach when they were about five and six. It was her favourite image of them, excitement and love radiating from them as they ran back to her, the surf in the background.

They'd thrown themselves upon her, sand kicking up everywhere, and they'd all shrieked with glee as she'd tickled them until they couldn't breathe.

It took less than a second to punch in the code; then the steel door opened and she extracted what she needed.

She was already in the car, completely confident in Lou's ability to deliver, when her phone rang. 'He's at the Combrian, room 456.'

The Combrian. Made sense. Five star, but famous for its long history of rock stars ejecting the contents of their room via the windows, including, last year, a high-class escort who died on impact when she landed on the roof of a Rolls-Royce Phantom down below.

The lead singer of the band was out on bail before her mother in Nebraska knew she was dead.

The door was answered on the second knock, right after she shouted, 'Room service.' Idiots didn't even have the sense to check the peephole.

A guy she didn't recognize eyed her quizzically, but she burst *past him, giving no time for his wasted brain to catch up. As soon as she was inside, she recognized it as the room from the video. If she had any doubt about what she was about to do, she had none now.*

Jordan Lang lay on the bed, his tanned, athletic body adorned with nothing more than a pair of tight white boxers, his thumbs flicking the buttons on the Xbox controller he held with two hands. To his left, a square mirror on the bedside table sat next to a bag and a tiny silver spoon.

Two cronies she didn't recognize lounged on the sofa, eyes fixed on the screen, watching two cars race while gunshots crackled from the sidelines.

Lang didn't even flinch or take his eyes from the TV screen when she entered. Hard to say if that was because he was high or an arrogant prick. Actually, there was no debate. He was both.

No reaction from the sidekicks either. The one that had answered the door just ambled over and joined his two buddies on the couch. It struck Mirren that they looked like clones: all early twenties, all in jeans that dipped beneath their asses, vests, chains round their necks, baseball caps. What the fuck were grown adults doing wearing baseball caps backwards and trousers that showed their underwear? Pathetic, yet something in their screwed-up DNA made them think it was cool.

Time to take their dangling crotches somewhere else. Mirren calmly crossed to the TV and flicked the off switch.

'Hey . . .'

'Glad I've got your attention.'

For a second there was a glimmer of confusion on Lang's face, before it switched straight to anger.

'What the fuck . . . ?'

'You three, time to go.'

'Fuck off.' Ah, the power of educated speech.

She held up her phone, demonstrating that it was on a video call . . . 'Right now I'm connected to a very nice friend of mine at LAPD.' She scanned the room with the phone, ensuring it captured each of their faces, before saying, 'Combrian, room 456,' into the speaker.

One of the three looked at Lang for guidance. 'Don't look at him, look at me,' Mirren told him, with absolutely no emotion in her voice. 'And I'm the one saying that it'll probably be best for your future criminal record if you didn't say a word on your way out the door.'

Over on the bed, Jordan Lang nodded slightly and the three were through the door before being told for a third time. Mirren disconnected her phone and put it in her back pocket.

'I'm Chloe Gore's mother.'

'I know who you are.'

The bravado and arrogance made her teeth grind. Oh, Chloe, how could you choose this one? For a second she wavered, desperate to go, to get his face out of her brain and make it stop polluting her thoughts. But an image of him with his hands on her daughter's stomach, touching her . . .

She opened her purse, took out the clear bag of wrapped notes and threw it on the bed.

'A hundred grand,' she told him. 'Just in case you can't count that high.'

No fear, no concern on his face, just a smile of satisfaction there now.

'Good to know that Chloe's got a mother who's onside.'

'Where's the original?'

'On my phone.'

'Give it to me.'

He grinned as he leaned forward, picked up the cash and whistled.

'That's not the deal. The deal is that you give me this, I make sure it never hits the tabloids. They'd pay a hundred grand for it, but this way no one finds out what your girl likes to do when she's having fun.'

'The deal is that you give me the original. Right now. End of story.'

His hands pushed back through his shoulder-length black hair as he made his amusement clear. 'Like I said, that's not how it works.'

Only once before in her life, a long, long time ago, had she been this desperate to remove a smug smile from someone's face.

But this time she knew how.

Her actions were almost matter of fact as she opened her Chanel tote, extracted her fully licensed handgun and pointed it at his face.

That got his attention.

'You wouldn't,' he said. Almost dared her.

'Oh, I so would,' she answered, voice absolutely calm and absolutely deadly.

18.

'Nothing' – The Script

On the scale of disturbing experiences, this night had been somewhere between the time Zander had left Elton John's Oscar party, spent three hours in a nightclub snorting coke from the cleavage of a supermodel and then wrapped his Aston Martin round a lamp post on Beverly Drive, and the time he spent the night in LA County after the altercation with the reality-TV tosser. And he couldn't even remember that prick's name.

'How did you find me?' he'd asked as she'd strutted past him into his apartment, arrogance exploding from every pore, only the fact that she couldn't walk in a straight line giving her a layer of vulnerability.

'I'm Mirren McLean's daughter. There's nothing I can't find out.' Her slur was barely decipherable. There was no arguing with her logic, though. It would only take one call to a publicist, who'd call another publicist, who'd call a secretary in an agency, who'd call a friend who worked at a car service, and the address would be delivered via text in minutes.

It was difficult to say whether Chloe plumped down onto the sofa or her legs gave way and it was just good fortune that there was a soft landing. Her skin was grey, her eyes barely open. Life Reborn might want to consider their strike rate. So far, in this room alone, they were zero for two.

Zander had closed the door, headed to the kitchen and grabbed a basin from under the sink. Hollie had put it there after she'd replaced the rug in the bedroom for the third time. Chloe had barely noticed when he'd slipped it in front of her.

'Hey, Zander Leith,' she purred. 'Zander Leith. Za-n-der Leith.'

Each syllable of his name was more protracted with each repetition. This seemed to amuse her. Difficult to believe that this was the eighteen-year-old daughter of one of the most important power couples in the industry. Spielbergs. Hanks. Gores.

Now she was sitting here, in denim cut-offs, Diesel boots and a white vest that fell off one pale white shoulder, looking like she was twelve.

Still he added nothing to the conversation.

'So tell me, Za-n-der Leith, what's the story?'

'The story?'

'About my mother. I hate her, y'know. So perfect. She's so fricking perfect. She took everything away from me. Do you know that? Fucking everything.'

Zander closed his eyes. Never had he needed a drink more than now. He reached over to the unit under the TV, pulled out a stack of screeners from the bottom shelf and liberated a bottle of Southern Comfort that was hidden behind them.

'C'mon, Chloe . . .' He sat on the coffee table in front of her, ready to catch her if she fell forward.

'Hey, you know my name,' she said with a giggle. 'Zander Leith knows my name.'

Her gesticulating hand landed on his thigh, then teasingly crept towards his crotch.

He removed it.

'Doncha wanna fuck me?' she slurred, a childish lilt creeping into her voice, followed by a mischievous snigger as she pulled her top over her head, exposing her small, pert, tanned breasts.

'Chloe, put that back on. Now.' He was on his feet. Pacing. Face turned away. 'Please, come on. Put your vest back on.'

Jesus, this was excruciating. He turned to see if she'd complied, just as she licked her left index finger and rolled it round one nipple.

'Chloe, come on. Stop.' He winced.

The old, stoned Zander would never knowingly pass up a sexual encounter with a half-naked female who was making it clear she wanted him, but this was different. So different it hurt somewhere deep down in his guts.

She was Mirren McLean's daughter. She had no idea what had happened between him and her mother. She could never know. What they'd had belonged in the past and—

'So did you fuck her, then?' Chloe interrupted his panic. 'My mother. Did you fuck her?'

Taking a slug of Southern Comfort saved him from answering. God bless the bottle.

'Did you?' Chloe repeated. 'I think you did. She won't

130

watch a movie if you're in it. I think you fucked her.' Another giggle.

He had nothing. Nothing to say, nowhere to go with this. This was pain. Gut-wrenching pain.

How hard had he worked to forget? How many years had he blocked it out, denied it? And now it was back. There were so many thoughts in his head that the trauma, not the Southern Comfort, had taken his speech.

The sensible thing would be to get her out of here. How could he ever explain her being here to Mirren? Would she believe him? After everything?

Even if he wanted to tell her mother, he didn't have Mirren's number, and calling Life Reborn was out of the question. Her detention was court-ordered, and if she'd blown that off, he wasn't going to be the one to turn her in.

But he couldn't let her stay here. Anyone could have seen her come in. There could be a crowd of paps outside right now timing their meeting, waiting to catch a walk-of-shame shot when they left the next morning. Or there could be one on the beach with a long lens. That one took a minute to percolate before he jumped up, closed the balcony door and pressed the button that made the windows opaque.

Then he grabbed a throw from the back of the sofa and wrapped it around her topless torso. She was too wasted to complain.

'Chloe, is there somewhere you can go?'

'Not goin' back.'

'I know. But the cops will come for you if you don't.'

'Nooooo.' It was almost animalistic. 'Not going back there. Hate them all.'

He drained his glass. Southern Comfort wasn't going to solve this, but it couldn't make it any worse.

Just at that moment, she lurched forward and Zander grabbed the bucket. Not a scene he'd ever anticipated dealing with. He was one of the biggest box-office stars in the world and he was here, at night, with a half-naked girl, fully expecting to be vomited on at any second.

There must have been some seriously scary shit decisions to get him to this point in his life.

'Need to pee.'

Oh Christ.

He helped her up, supported her to the bathroom and then guided her in. Etiquette? He had no idea, so backing out and closing the door seemed like the best option.

The thought of calling Hollie crossed his mind, but he knew exactly what she'd do. She'd call the cops, have Chloe taken back to rehab and then give him a lecture about the ramifications of letting wasted teenage socialites into his apartment late at night.

How long had she been in there? Ten minutes? Fifteen?

'Chloe?'

No answer.

'Chloe?'

Nothing. Damn. Tentative, dreading what he'd find, he pushed open the door. There she was, passed out, still breathing. He checked again. Definitely still breathing.

As far as he could see, he was out of options. He lifted her up, carried her over to the bed, covered her with a blanket.

It was difficult to tell if it was the situation, the Southern Comfort or the flashback that made him queasy. Mirren.

Around the same age. Sleeping on his bed. There was a party in his house. His dad had got out of prison that day and invited all his mates round for the usual freedom ceremony. Police had come to the door a couple of times to tell them to keep the noise down, but it didn't make a difference. The celebrations had gone on long into the night and . . . No. Not now. Hadn't he already decided this wasn't the time for memories?

The shutters came down on the past, and his hands started to shake. The inside of his skull started banging, so he went back into the other room. He lay on the sofa, then checked every twenty minutes to make sure she hadn't choked on her own vomit.

That was one headline he never wanted to read: 'Chloe Gore Found Dead in Zander Leith's Apartment'. The very thought made him shudder.

When the darkness behind the opaque windows became a shade lighter, Zander knew sunrise was close. He also knew he was only left with two choices.

He took another shot of the Southern Comfort and the rest of it was sitting on the table in front of him, calling his name. That was option one. Get wasted. Worry about the Chloe situation later. Just surrender to the fucked-up hand that karma had played him and let the whole sorry mess play out whatever way the Gods of Fucked-Up Situations decided.

Or . . . shit, he must be crazy.

Chloe was still sleeping like the dead when he wrapped her in the blanket, put her over his shoulder as gently as he could and silently made his way downstairs to his car. It was still the dark side of 5 a.m., so he didn't expect to see his neighbours up and about. As he passed his two homeless buddies, he realized that one of them was awake. Crap. This wasn't good. For twenty bucks he'd give a full report to the *National Enquirer* and Zander would be done.

Again.

But when their gaze met, his buddy on the street simply took in the sight in front of him, nodded, then closed his eyes. On the one hand, he was relieved. And on the other, he chose not to be concerned that the transportation of what looked like a dead body didn't command intervention.

After remotely opening the door locks, Zander man-oeuvred Chloe off his shoulder and balanced her against the car, while he fumbled to get the passenger door open. Success.

Several long, awkward minutes of manipulation later, Chloe was in the passenger seat and Zander was now aware that Aston Martins shouldn't be the car of choice when transporting a comatose human.

On the road, he made a call. Hands-free. Less danger of getting stopped by the cops with a crashed teenager in his front seat.

The rest of the journey, he stayed five miles under the speed limit and tried to ignore the palpitations that were making his breath come in short rasps.

When he pulled into his destination, he waited. This could all go so wrong. So, so wrong.

He'd set himself up for a fall and right now he was teetering on the edge of a cliff.

He was putting his trust in an untried source, one that had every reason not to help him.

A light went on in the window in front of him. The door opened.

Zander was out of the car and round to the passenger side, meeting the new arrival there.

Zander put his hand out and Lebron shook it.

'Thanks, man. I can't tell you how much I appreciate this.'

Lebron slipped an arm under Chloe's legs, one behind her back and used his huge bulk to lift her out as if she weighed nothing at all.

'No worries, bud. Thanks for bringing her back. She must have left after lights out because no one noticed she'd gone.'

Lebron had only taken a couple of steps away when Chloe's head jerked up and she let out a low wail as she realized what was happening. A piece of Zander's gut twisted as she looked over Lebron's shoulder at him, her eyes still hooded with sleep.

'Come back and get me, Zander Leith. Do you promise? Do you?'

Zander knew he had to be truthful. You can't lie to an addict. It only messes them up when they find out the truth. The last thing he should do is see her again. He was newly sober. She was still in the depths of her addiction. He shouldn't be around her. It would be a killer for him. Dangerous. Risky. Crazy. Foolish. Destructive. But hey, didn't he love all those things?

'I promise,' he told her.

19.

'Dream to Sleep' – H2O

Glasgow, 1986

His mum was crying again. Not the full-scale sobbing that he saw on the TV. In some ways he wished it was. No, this was silent crying, with pursed lips, eyes closed and only the tears that streamed down her face betraying her pain.

Zander wanted to punch a hole in the wall. How many times? How often would he watch her break her heart over a man that they all knew was a fucking arse?

Not that she shared that viewpoint. Not ever.

It didn't matter how many times Jono Leith didn't come home, or how many times he was dragged from his bed in the middle of the night by the police. It didn't matter what he was accused of, or how outrageous it seemed that they had a false wall in the cupboard under the stairs that concealed an arsenal of weapons. It didn't matter that he'd taken to carrying a knife with him whether he was just nipping to the bookie's or going out to 'work'.

It really didn't matter. All she cared about was that he was her husband, vows taken in front of God, never to be broken.

Even when the tears ran down her cheeks and made her bruises look like dark puddles in the rain.

Zander took her a mug of tea and sat it on top of the fire-place in front of where she knelt, praying to the picture of Jesus on the wall above it. Tomorrow, she would go to 8 a.m. Mass and by 9 a.m. she would be at peace again, after asking God for support in return for a promise to forgive the man she'd married in his name.

Jono would look at the bruises on her face and he'd swear he was sorry, promise to change, while telling her it was her own fault.

And then it would start all over again.

There was usually some warning – a loss on the horses, a job that had gone wrong, a couple of nights in the cells – but that afternoon, it had come out of nowhere. Jono had had a couple of the boys round, Jimmy and Hugh, his long-time cohorts. They congregated at the kitchen table, their low tones screaming that they were up to something.

At fourteen, Zander already knew to stay out of the way. His mother didn't. She made teas, looked for biscuits, asked after their wives.

'On you go now, Maggie,' Jono had said.

Maggie was about to do as he asked when she remembered that her rosary beads were on top of the fridge. She turned back to get them and walked right into Jono's fist.

It was short. Sharp. Brutal.

At the door, Zander gasped, then dived to catch her as she staggered. Jimmy and Hugh continued to stare at the box of caramel wafers on the table in front of them.

'Get her out of here, boy,' Jono warned, in a voice that made it clear arguing wasn't an option.

Rage ate at Zander's guts as he put his arm around his mum's waist and supported her as she staggered out of the room.

She didn't say a word until the door closed behind them.

'Sandy, he doesn't mean it, son. He's just under a lot of pressure. I'm fine. Honestly, it's nothing.'

The blood that dripped from her nose ran down her chin and stained the crucifix at her neck bright red.

Nothing?

It took twenty minutes of first aid and prayer for the bleeding to stop completely, by which time the banging of the door and the silence told them that the men had adjourned to the pub.

That was five hours ago.

Now his mother was on her knees in prayer and Zander realized the rage that was chewing his guts wasn't going anywhere.

'I'm going out, Mum,' he told her. Her response was to increase the volume on the next couple of lines of her Hail Mary.

He stopped by the cupboard in the hall, then grabbed his leather jacket from the hook on the door and headed out into the night. Only 6 p.m. and already it was pitch dark. He turned right and took the long way round so he didn't pass Mirren or Davie's houses. This wasn't the time for seeing them. There was no way anyone else was getting dragged into his battle.

Down at the King's Arms, he opened the door an inch and immediately spotted his dad, holding court at the bar, life and soul of the party. In a minute he would break into song *and the rest of his cronies would join in. Then maybe he'd turn on the charm for a woman who caught his eye. Zander had seen it so many times before it made him feel physically sick.*

He backed out and left the pub door swinging on its hinges, then walked to the end of the building and dipped into the alley at the side.

Waiting was the easy part. The hardest was the timing. It took instinct to get it right.

He heard Jono before he saw him, belting out 'The Wonder of You' as he staggered through the doors. Zander watched him come in his direction, an arm around a red-headed woman Zander didn't recognize. She wasn't even a patch on his mother. Not a patch. Yet she looked at Jono with that same adoration that was so familiar. If only she knew that the flip side of that gregarious charisma was cruelty.

Closer. Jono stopped, pulled her in for a kiss, sang another couple of lines of the song with their faces just inches apart.

Closer. She was giggling now, looking up at him with wide eyes as his hand went inside her jacket.

Closer. 'Wait! Sorry, Jono, but I've left my bag. Oh my God, how did I manage that? Let me just run back and grab it.'

'On ye go, doll, and make it swift. I'll be right here.'

She kissed him again, giving him time to give her arse a quick grope. She giggled and ran back inside.

Closer. Only a few feet away from where Zander stood, Jono turned to face the wall, unzipped his fly, took his cock out and started to pee, now whistling the chorus of 'Love Me Tender'.

'. . . Love me true. All my—'

Bang.

The spray of piss stopped instantly as the baseball bat made contact with the back of his head and he fell forward, banging his forehead against the wet patch on the wall and sliding downwards. Zander was fifty yards away, concealed by the darkness, when he heard a woman's screams.

He ran the rest of the way, washed the blood off the baseball bat in the stream that ran behind the gardens on his street, replaced it in the hall cupboard and checked the house. Empty. His mother would be at Mass again, her bruises concealed by make-up and lies that she'd ask the Lord to forgive.

Heading to the kitchen sink, he leaned over it and begged his body to vomit, to purge him of the feelings of disgust, both for the man who spawned him and for what he'd just done.

To the right, the bottle of whisky the men had shared earlier sat half full. Zander unscrewed the top and drank straight from the bottle. The nausea came first, but then . . . No sickness. Just a warmth, and later, a reassurance. Everything was fine. Fine. It was all OK. And his optimism grew with every drop that reached his bloodstream, until he finally stumbled up to bed and fell into a deep, contented sleep.

When the police came to the door, he didn't even stir.

20.

'Sweet Little Mystery' – Wet Wet Wet

Glasgow, 2013

Saturday night in the Grill On the Corner was like a winter wonderland. The sheets of tiny white lights that covered every window were like the separation between real life and Narnia. Outside, a cold, dark, Glasgow city centre night. Inside, laughter, beautiful clothes, subtle music and the aromas of expensive perfume and incredible food.

But that wasn't why it was Sarah's favourite restaurant. She loved the dark wood floor and the leather booths and the stunning chandeliers that dropped from the ceiling. It was the perfect mixture of class and comfort: gorgeous yet unpretentious, chic but simple.

'Red or white?' Simon asked, his hand perched above two bottles.

Sarah smiled. 'Neither. Just coffee, thanks.'

Wine would perhaps come later, but even though they'd just arrived, right now she wanted a hot drink to warm her bones and some caffeine to give her a jolt of energy. She didn't even want to count up how many hours' sleep she'd had this week, but she wouldn't need to work it out on a calculator.

She watched Simon as he immediately took charge, making everyone feel at ease, being charming as always. Sometimes it was such a relief being with him, knowing that he would be the driving force, arrange every detail of their lives. At work, she had that dogmatic determination to achieve, so when she came home, she was happy to relinquish the social control to him. And he did it so well. Incredible holidays to Dubai, the Maldives, New York in winter. Spontaneous weekends in Perthshire lodges. Nights out like this one, with their friends: great food and conversation. It left all her caffeine-suffused energy for work.

His brown hair, swept back in a Forties movie-star vibe, was a little longer than usual, but it was working for him. To his right, Pippa, girlfriend of his best mate, Rob, had been giving Simon twinkly eyes since they'd arrived. Rob and Simon had met on their first day at university and been friends ever since. Rob was a lawyer in the most profitable company in the city, had already made partner and had little time for a serious relationship. Pippa had been around for a few months – a remarkable achievement given that his girlfriends usually had a higher recycle rate than the paper bin in his office. He seemed unusually keen, and thankfully oblivious to the fact that she appeared to be doing some serious subtle flirting with his mate.

Simon handled the attention with impeccable grace, while Sarah didn't give it a second thought. As he often reminded her, she had been born without a jealousy gene. Zero on the territorial tantrums. Let Pippa flirt – it might keep Simon occupied while she popped out to have a quick chat with Ena Dawson. It had to be Davie's mother, didn't it?

Much as the neds up at the scheme were hardly on a par with Reuters, she had a feeling they knew exactly what was going on. And it wasn't like Ena was a common name these days.

There were just a few sips left of her coffee when the others' starters arrived and she took that as the perfect moment to make her excuses.

Leaning over, she kissed Simon on the cheek. 'Be back in half an hour, darling.'

Rob leaned back to allow the waitress to place his rock oysters in front of him. 'You leaving us already, sweetie?'

'Just for half an hour. Sorry, it's a work thing. Arranged before I knew we were meeting tonight.'

It was a small white lie. Simon didn't react. When she'd told him about it earlier, he hadn't been happy, but she wasn't going to wait another week to speak to Ena. Everything else had ground to a halt and Ena had become her last straw to grasp.

The slush lapped the sides of her black suede stiletto boots as she walked briskly up the incline on Wellington Street, turned left onto West George Street and got the bus in her sights. It was only a few streets but a million miles between where she'd left and her destination. Like all major cities, Glasgow had two sides: the wealth, culture, architecture and rich history lived right alongside the poverty and deprivation.

The bus looked quiet tonight, no stragglers around the entrance, only a few faces in the windows. As she climbed on, Isabel greeted her with a smile. 'Hey, love. Twice in one week. We'll be giving you your own seat on here.'

Sarah replied with a hug, scoping the long galley of battered leather seats as she did so. A few old men sat in silence as they ate their soup, their gazes fixed on the Formica table in front of them. Up at the front, Dan, one of the regular volunteer paramedics, was speaking to two others whom Sarah didn't recognize. Neither fitted the profile for Ena Johnston.

'Good to see you, Isabel. Here, I brought this.' Sarah wrestled a Boots carrier containing twenty miniature bottles of shampoo from her handbag, handed it over and was rewarded with a beaming smile.

'Thanks, love. Staying for a cuppa? Only you're a bit overdressed.' She gestured to the hem of the black sequinned tunic peeking out from under Sarah's coat, complementing the leather-look jeans and over-knee suede boots.

'No, thanks. I just wanted a quick chat with Ena Dawson. Is she around?'

Isabel gesticulated heavenwards. 'Upstairs. She's just giving it a quick tidy before the rush starts.'

The winding stairway was narrow and treacherous to navigate in six-inch heels. When Sarah reached the upper deck, her exhalation of relief caused a tiny cloud to form in the freezing air in front of her.

The woman sweeping between the chairs looked up. 'Can I help you?'

'Ena Dawson?'

Wariness and hesitation flickered across her face. 'Yes?'

Bingo. Sarah could see immediately that she'd got the right woman.

144

The resemblance to her son was uncannily obvious. The same dark, wavy hair. The brown eyes. Something in the shape of her face . . .

'I'm Sarah McKenzie. I'm a reporter with the *Daily Scot* and a friend of Isabel.'

'Och, if you're doing another one of those reports on the work Isabel does here, you're better talking to Dan downstairs. Lovely boy, so he is.'

Her smile was warm now, with just an edge of embarrassment. Sarah decided to go with open confidence and hope for the best.

'Actually, it was you I wanted to talk to, Mrs Dawson. I'm actually working on a story about your son, Davie. It did used to be Ena Johnston, didn't it?'

21.

'Losing My Religion' – R.E.M

'So what's the verdict? Give it to me one fucking disaster at a time.'

Al stared at the screen in front of him for so long Davie had time to contemplate what would happen if the heat of the blood coursing through his veins caused a spontaneous combustion. He just hoped the fire caught Al's $10,000 silk wallpaper and burned the whole fucking place down.

'*American Stars* have dropped you. They're offering it to Seacrest now that *Idol* has slumped. They had no choice – Pepsi and Nike threatened to pull sponsorship. The talk show with E! has been put on indefinite hold. Obviously filming of *New York Nixons* has been canned: Sky is out of the coma, but no other details yet, and Jax Nixon has announced that he's taken a contract out on you if you come within a hundred miles of the Eastern Seaboard. The Hugo Boss campaign is cancelled, Ferrari have taken you off their ad, and you've been politely informed that your services are no longer required for the Kids Kick Cancer Telethon.'

Al stopped with a sigh when he realized that Davie was no longer breathing.

'Look, it's not as bad as it sounds.'

'It's fucking worse.'

Al sighed again and rubbed his temples with his index fingers.

'I can see why you're thinking that. But look, Davie, there's still hope. Your productions are still killing it – *Liking Lana* got its best ever ratings last week, and *Dream Machine* is doing great. Even if you're not presenting it, you'll still get production credit on *American Stars* so you'll still be banking three of the top-rating shows in the country.'

It wasn't much of a consolation. Sure, the money, to a lesser extent, was still coming in, but for how long? These shows rarely went past five seasons before they ran out of storylines and the public got bored with them. Only the Kardashians had managed to hang on, and that's because he wasn't the only one who thought they were the most fucked-up people on the planet.

He might be at the top of that tree now, but it wouldn't be long until some bastard came along with a chainsaw. He slid out of the white leather Corbusier chair and started pacing, his white McQueen Puma sneakers leaving indentations on the thick black rug.

What did the ratings matter anyway if the whole world thought he was scum? The press conference had halted the damage only temporarily. There was at least a seed of doubt that he had the moral values of the average serial killer, but then Rainbow had hit back the following day denying his story, calling him a liar and announcing she was launching legal action. It was an entirely predictable move, but according to Al, popularity was a numbers game. Prior to the press call and the debacle that night at the Lakers game, 100 per cent of people thought he was guilty. The entertainment round-ups and daytime shows had all run his explanation slash apology the next day. Now 30 per cent thought he was guilty, 30 per cent thought Rainbow was making it up, and the remainder had forgotten about it because their attention had been entirely captivated by Miley Cyrus twerking at the VMAs last night.

Davie made a mental note to send flowers as a thank you for taking the heat off. Not that the pressure from the paps had cooled any. The tossers were outside his house, following his car, staking out the CSA offices. They'd even formed a welcoming guard at Nespresso on Beverly to deprive him of his morning shot of caffeine.

They were like vultures, circling, knowing that their biggest feed ever had just been given last rites.

Al clicked onto a new page on the screen. 'We've had requests from Leno, Letterman, Ferguson, Kimmel, Fallon, Ellen, Brianna Nicole, *The View*, *The Talk*, *Chelsea Lately*. And you know, Davie, we could do an *Oprah* special.'

Davie stopped mid-pace. 'I'm not doing *Oprah*. Lance Armstrong does *Oprah* to announce he doped. Lohan gets all repentant on *Oprah*. Cruise makes a dick of himself on *Oprah*. I'm desperate, mate, not fucking suicidal.'

Al's massage of his temples was now beginning to look like he was attempting to drill through his skull. 'We've got a meeting at four p.m. – full team, damage control. In the meantime, I've leaked your schedule today.'

'What schedule?'

'You're picking the kids up from set and taking them to

the playground at Coldwater Canyon at noon. The shots will be on long lens, so make sure they don't get you scratching your balls or ignoring the kids.'

Davie stopped and stared at him like he was insane. 'My kids. The park. Noon. Al, have you met my kids? They're fucking redheads. They don't do midday sun. Forget it, Al. Change of plan. I'll be back at four for the war room.'

'Look, Davie, do you want me to bring Harvey back in?'

Davie shook his head. Harvey Jones was his former manager of over a decade, fired a year ago because Davie decided he'd been giving away 10 per cent of his income to someone who added nothing to his career. Jenny had said at the time that he was being a control freak. She was probably right. But he was a control freak who had a couple of million a year more in the bank. The managerial stuff now got handled by CSA, alongside every other aspect of his career. It used to seem like wise strategic planning. Now, for the first time, Davie wondered if it was too many eggs in one overloaded basket. The peg that held Al's Zegna blazer was looking shakier by the second.

As Davie headed out of the underground car park, a squad of motorbikes and SUVs fell into a convoy behind him, one dick on a Ducati actually riding up alongside him and shooting off shots through the window. Davie had never been more tempted to swerve the car. It would make sense to go home, batten down the storm doors and keep a low profile for a few days, but the thought of being stuck out in Bel Air while his life crumbled around him drove him insane. He had to be busy. Had to be doing something. Even if it was just screaming at Al and manipulating those bastard paps.

He needed a plan, one that didn't involve bloody *Oprah*. In the meantime, he'd go get the kids, take them for ice cream in their lunch break and let the paps get their shots. Dad of the Year.

Twenty minutes later, the chase ended when he slid into the entrance lane at Captis Studios.

'Hey, Mr Johnston, good to see you.'

The beaming smile and courteous nod was proof that Rick the security guard was either a convincing actor who'd missed his calling or he didn't keep up with celebrity news. Or perhaps he just knew that in this town, it paid to stay onside with everyone.

It was a sad frigging day when he was grateful for the kindness of someone who earned less than he spent on gas every year.

The wave of white fear that had been slamming against him since this whole fiasco broke took over again, making his hands shake against the walnut steering wheel as he drove through the gate.

He checked his watch. Half an hour to kill. Usually he'd slip into Vala's trailer, let her amuse him in the only way she could, but not today. That bitch had trashed him on national television. Not a shred of defence. Not an iota of praise of his many talents. Just the tremble of that salacious pout and the shudder of those glorious tits. Those glorious tits. Gorgeous . . .

Acting on pure testosterone, he doubled back, turned right, stopped and sprang out of the car, checking first to make sure he wasn't being watched. Security was tight in here, but all it took was one maintenance guy with a mobile phone looking to make a quick buck from Radar Online.

No one.

He knocked the door and then went straight in without waiting for a reply.

Vala was lying on her chaise longue, in a tank and G-string, watching the last Seb Dunhill movie. You have got to be shitting me. There was no way he was getting a hard-on now.

'Hey, are you ever gonna stop bursting in here?' Her accent was staccato, her voice high-pitched – the latter due to the fact that Zander Leith was kicking the crap out of someone on her fifty-inch plasma.

Libido crashed, Davie went into the fridge and took out a Bud, screwing off the top and tossing it in the sink. She kept a stock for him and her deadbeat brother, who showed up once a week looking for cash.

'What time are you due on set?' he asked. No pleasantries. No subtlety. He didn't care. No way he could shag her now.

'One hour,' she said, opening her legs wide, licking her finger, then letting it trail downwards.

It was amazing how a personal invitation could bypass brain and go straight to cock.

'I'll only need half of that,' he said as he walked towards her. Beer bottle still in one hand, he used the other to flip open the button of his AG jeans, slide down the zipper and pull out his erect dick.

Vala lifted the TV remote and pressed pause, leaving a huge image of Zander on the screen, looking down on them. Davie wanted to grab the remote and switch it off, but he could see she was in the mood for a fight and there wasn't enough time to humour her. Instead, he turned his back to the TV and walked towards her. Still looking over his shoulder at the screen, she put a foot out in front of her to stop him.

He played along. Eyes locked on his, she whipped off the tank and tossed it to the side, exposing her tight, high tits. Then she pulled hard at the tiny G-string so it barely resisted as the side band snapped and the flimsy triangle of lace came clean off, revealing perfectly smooth, hair-free skin underneath.

His erection was starting to throb as he reached past her outstretched leg.

'C'mere,' he said, his voice a couple of octaves lower than normal.

Vala hit his hand away and slouched down on the chaise, then opened her legs wide, revealing her perfect snatch.

His groan was as desperate as it was irrepressible.

'Kneel down,' she ordered.

Right now she could have told him to sign over his worldly goods and he'd have done it. He sunk to his knees, then shuffled in closer, ready to enter her and relieve the unbearable pressure in his dick.

Once again, she stopped him.

'No, no, *amigo*, not today. Today, it's all about me. Now eat.'

She leaned forward, grabbed his head and pulled it down towards her pulsating clit. As he got to work, even the roaring in his head couldn't block out the fact that she had restarted the movie and was watching it over his head. He blocked out the voices, Zander's guttural roar.

In just a couple of minutes, the rasping of her breath, the heat of her limbs, the shudder of her ass told him that she was coming.

'Oh yes, baby. Oh yes. Oh yes. Oh . . . oh . . . Zander!'

Something both inside – and outside – died.

What would, by most men's standards, be considered the zenith of their life experiences became the moment that Davie Johnston knew for sure that his time at the top was over.

22.

'How Can You Mend a Broken Heart?'
– Al Green

There was something comforting about being back in the office. Every single thing in here had been picked by Mirren, set up when she'd won the development deal with Pictor Films to make the first Clansman movie. The two pale cream jacquard sofas sat on either side of a tile coffee table she'd brought back from Mexico on the back of a pickup truck ten years ago. Her desk was worn and much loved, found at the Fairfax flea market and previously installed at the tiny Santa Monica house she'd lived in when she first moved here, the one in which she'd written the first Clansman movie. Simple. Basic. Warm. Some thought it too low key and cheap for a woman of her status in this city, but for Mirren, it said the opposite. She didn't need a $10,000 marble desk to reflect the size of her dick.

She knew who she was. It was all there, on the soft caramel walls, punctuated by huge dark oak frames displaying promo posters for each of the Clansman movies, and smaller frames showing pictures of the people she loved. Logan on his first album cover with the band. Chloe when she modelled for Hilfiger in a 'kids of celebrities' campaign. Snaps of them both when they were younger – running in the sand, throwing snowballs in Aspen, riding horses in the Napa Valley.

The McLean Productions HQ was in a quiet corner of the huge Pictor lot, past the sets of two hit sitcoms, turn right at the street that was built for a drama about five suburban housewives gone wild, turn left at the replica of the White House and through the mock-up of the fountain area in Central Park. The building behind hers was purpose-built and staged the location shots for Clansman's house and village. Sixteenth-century Scotland brought to life in modern-day Century City, LA.

It looked exactly as Mirren had imagined it would when she wrote the first book. Haunting. Beautiful. Atmospheric. Historic. There had been an impressive budget for sets and Mirren had repaid the studio's faith in her production and directorial debut by ensuring that every cent was used wisely.

That diligence and work ethic had never wavered.

Already this morning she'd had meetings with accountants, engineers and costume, and now she just wanted a half-hour at her desk to take stock. Think.

The click as her door opened was the first sign that thinking would have to wait.

'Hi.' Sheepish. Apologetic. Weak.

Mirren put down her pen and reluctantly looked at the new arrival.

'Really, Jack? Here?'

He shrugged. 'Didn't have any choice. Seems the locks

have been changed at home and the staff are under instructions to keep me out.'

'Correct. It's not such a challenge. Half of them hardly know you given that you've barely been there for nineteen years.'

She mentally kicked herself for going there. Classy and dignified, that was how she had decided to handle this. Somehow, right now, those emotions were being batted out of the park by bitterness and fury.

Mirren watched him as he slouched in the doorway, holding two coffees and a brown bag that she would bet her last dollar contained an apple and cinnamon tart from the French patisserie on Santa Monica Boulevard.

Dear wife, sorry I fucked another woman. Can I take the pain away by offering you a wildly indulgent yet delicious high-sugar snack?

Sighing, she got up, came round to the front of the desk and took one of the coffees. They both took them the same way. Black and strong.

'Outside,' she said, knowing he would follow. She cut into the replica of the Central Park square and sat on the grass in front of the fountain. It was one of her favourite lunch spots. There was every possibility the next half an hour would taint that forever.

'So speak.' Her tone was calm again. Back on track with the dignity strategy.

'I've fucked it all up, Mirren.' His voice was hoarse. Too many Marlboro Lights, with an overtone of sleep deprivation.

'Indeed you have.'

Although staring straight ahead, she could just catch his silhouette in her peripheral vision. Was it wishful thinking or did he seem older? Tired? Jack was fifty-two, but he'd always looked a decade younger. Now, not so much. A week ago, that would have concerned her, made her resolve to persuade him to take time out, head off for a holiday. Now, she felt nothing at all. Nothing.

The only twinge of pain was when she realized that he'd accessorized his black T-shirt and charcoal jeans with the black cowboy boots she'd bought for him when they sneaked off to Vegas to watch the ACM Awards last year. They'd danced all night to the best country music outside Nashville, drank tequila shots at the Hard Rock Cafe, made love overlooking the city in a glass suite at the Palms and Mirren had thanked God for making her happier than any person deserved to be. God clearly decided that too much of a good thing couldn't be allowed to continue.

'I'm staying at Casa del Mar.'

'I didn't ask.'

'I know. But just in case, you know, you thought I was staying . . . there. At her . . .'

'You don't need to spell it out for me,' Mirren snapped, before curiosity got the better of her and she asked, 'Why aren't you?'

'Because we're not together. Shit, Mirren, she's barely older than Chloe.'

'That was going to be *my* next line.' The inside of her gum was starting to hurt, but she couldn't stop chewing it because if she did, she knew she'd cry. And there would be no crying in front of Jack Gore today.

'Mirren, I'm so sorry. It was a fuck-up. A couple of times. I was just—'

'Don't dare make an excuse, Jack.'

He put his hands up. 'I know. You're right. But what can I do to fix this, Mirren? We can't walk away from our family. We've got something great . . .'

'Not great enough.'

'OK, I deserved that. But, Mir, come on. I don't want the kids to have the kind of home that we had.'

His words delivered a thud to her stomach that took the wind out of her lungs and made her wince with pain. He knew where her weak spot was and he'd gone straight for it.

He'd been brought up by a single dad in South LA after his mother died when he was three. A succession of his father's companions had come in and out of his life. It was an area of instant recognition and compatibility when they met, both of them determined not to repeat the sins of the parents.

'Until death, only you' was engraved on the inside of their wedding rings. Until last week, Mirren had believed it. It took her a while to regain enough composure to speak. Calm. Dignity. Even though right now she could happily stab him through the heart.

'Jack, I know how we were brought up. I know how that felt, and I know what it did. And when I met you, I knew that I'd finally found the man who would make sure that no child of ours ever went through that. And they didn't. But it's not me who changed it. It's not me who's taken a wrecking ball to our family, Jack. It's you.'

'I know, Mirren, and hell, believe me I'd do anything to change it. Please, honey. We have to get past this.' He was right. They did. And there were only two options for moving on. Either they put it behind them, forgave and found a way to forget, or they called it a day and let Jack do what they'd set out to do all those years ago.

'Your new baby needs stability, Jack. What about it?'

There was a long pause. 'I don't even know if it's mine.'

'But if it is?'

'It doesn't matter.' The flash of anger that crossed her face made him back-pedal immediately. 'I mean, the baby matters, of course it does. I'll take care of it financially and I'll take responsibility, do my share. But I can't lose you and the kids for it, Mir, I just can't.'

God, he was so sincere, so heartbreakingly earnest and it was impossible not to feel for him.

'I don't know, Jack. I just don't. So if you're looking for an answer right now, I can't give it to you.'

He put his hands up in surrender again. 'That's fair, Mir. I get it. I know this is huge and I know it'll take time. I'm just asking for another chance.'

They both knew the conversation was over for now. Jack was first to his feet and he offered his hand to pull her up. She took it, ignoring the urge to use it as leverage to fold herself into his arms and make the stabbing pain in her stomach go away.

Jack walked her back to the office, pausing in the reception area, where her assistant, Devlin, had his head buried in his iMac. It was a sure sign of distaste, given that the tall, buff twenty-five-year-old from New York generally balanced relentless chattiness with a relaxed confidence that let everyone know that there was nothing he couldn't handle.

'Hi, Jack,' he muttered, before immediately returning his focused gaze to his work.

Nope, Mirren noticed, he couldn't keep the edge out of his tone there. Gotta love loyalty.

'Anything urgent?' Mirren asked, hoping Jack would take it as a cue to leave.

Devlin looked from Mirren to Jack, clearly unsure as to whether to divulge anything in front of the enemy. 'Just a message about Chloe from Life Reborn. I've left it on your desk.'

Task delivered, indiscretion avoided, but Mirren was too anxious to delay.

'And it says?'

'Sorry, but she's asked that you don't come up to family therapy today.'

Mirren nodded slowly. She'd half expected it, but there had been a tiny bit of hope there.

Jack reached out and touched her arm. 'Honey, she'll be fine. She'll be OK. We'll get her sorted.'

Too much. Too, too much.

'*We'll* get her sorted? We? Are you kidding me? All these years and not once have you been here when Chloe has gone and got in a mess, got arrested, gone missing. Who's sorted everything out every time, Jack? Me. So don't you dare talk about how you are going to swoop in and save the bloody day.'

'Mirren, I—' He didn't even get the words out before her right fist, working entirely independently of the rest of her body, harnessed years of kick-boxing training by swinging round, connecting with the target and cracking him square across the jaw.

With a mutter of 'Asshole', she swept past him and marched

through to her office. She had never been a victim. Never. And she wasn't going to start now.

Slamming the door behind her, she picked up her phone. 'Is he gone yet?' she asked Devlin.

'Yes. And remind me never to ask for a raise.'

'Excellent. Can you get Brad Bernson on the line, please?'

Seconds later, Mirren picked up the receiver, pressed the button next to the one illuminated light and greeted Bernson, a PI she'd called on to help her with Chloe's many disappearances and misdemeanours over the years.

'Brad? . . . Good. Listen, my husband tells me he's staying at the Casa del Mar and no longer screwing Mercedes Dance. Find out if it's true.'

23.

'Let Me Go' – Gary Barlow

It was so close to the conflicting emotions he got when he knew he was going to drink. The gnawing feeling in his gut that he shouldn't do it. The depressing knowledge that it couldn't lead to anything good. Yet the certainty that nothing and no one could stop him.

Zander had to see Chloe. He had to. She was drowning and he could feel every twist of pain and every void of emptiness inside her. He had to help her. Somewhere in the whole scheme of karma and fate, Chloe's life was linked with his. If he hadn't done what he'd done, if he and Mirren hadn't made the mistakes they'd made, then Chloe's life could have been so much different.

He owed her.

But more than that, he wanted to know her.

Dr LeComber, Chloe's case leader at Life Reborn, was frank in his disapproval of Zander's visits, but Chloe had agreed to actively commit to the therapy if she was allowed to see him. Zander knew more than anyone that the manipulation was classic addict behaviour, but Dr LeComber had decided to give her the benefit of the doubt because nothing else was working. Chloe still refused to work with the therapists one to one or in a group.

So far the gamble was paying off. The mute, sullen girl he'd seen when he was a fellow inmate had been replaced by someone who would at least occasionally make eye contact and utter the odd grunt. He'd been three times this week so far. The first time, she'd said nothing. The second and third, she'd answered basic questions but clammed up on anything personal and volunteered nothing deeper than demands for cigarettes. That was fine with Zander. No pushing. No stress. If they just sat there and said nothing every day for a month, that would be fine with him. When she wanted to talk, he was ready.

That afternoon, she'd barely acknowledged him when the residents were ushered out into the garden, just sat in the chair opposite him at a table for two in between the meditation area and the yoga space and stared at the ground. But now, after working her way through two Marlboros, her audio setting kicked in.

'They all hate me in here,' she spat, throwing her cigarette stub into the greenery.

He leaned over and shoved an ashtray in her direction. 'No, they don't. They'd probably just prefer it if you didn't risk a bush fire every time you had a cigarette.'

Defiance shot from her eyes as she finally lifted her head to meet his glare.

That was fine. Defiance was good. So were anger, irritation and spite. Sense and politeness were a bonus, but for now he'd go with anything that made her engage.

Her gaze went to the leather bracelet on her arm and she rubbed at the surface compulsively.

'Can I ask you something?'

Zander nodded.

'Why do you come? What's in this for you?' she challenged.

Hello, Anger, Irritation and Spite.

Zander grinned and sat back, leisurely shrugging his shoulders. Every acting bone in his body conspired to ape casual nonchalance. It was important not to rise to her, to give her an excuse to retreat back into her world of self-pity and isolation.

'Maybe I just like this place,' he told her, grinning, as if they were two buddies sharing a joke. 'Or maybe I get what you're feeling. Maybe I've decided I like hanging out with someone who fucks up as much as I do.'

The edges of her mouth twitched as she fought to suppress a smile and Zander's heart melted. Underneath all that shit, she was really just a kid. A lost kid.

He decided to test the water, see how far he could go.

'You know, sometimes it helps if you work with your family here, Chloe.'

'Fuck that.'

OK, too far. Reel it back. Nope, too late. Chloe took a deep breath and launched.

'My dad will only fuck off halfway through to go film in Morocco or Ibiza or somewhere else he can screw around. He's never been here for us. Never. Do you know he's fucking Mercedes Dance? Bastard. My whole life he would come home, be Daddy of the Year for a month, maybe two, then disappear again for a year. Asshole.'

OK, abandonment issues. Got that loud and clear. Now a choice. Quit while he was ahead or pick the scab? Nobody ever got sober by avoiding pain.

'And your mum?'

He braced for a tirade of abuse, but instead he got silence. Sadness.

'She took him away.'

'Who? Your dad?'

Chloe shook her head and shrugged. 'No. Just someone. Someone I loved. That's what she does. He loved me and she couldn't stand it. No wonder my dad fucked someone else.'

A bell rang to signal the end of visiting and Zander cursed. He'd been getting somewhere there and he knew it was more than she'd revealed since she got here.

'Do you want me to come back tomorrow?' he asked. 'I'm in the studio in the day, but I can come for the second visit.'

The pause was so long he thought she was working out how to say no.

Eventually she spoke so quietly it was almost a whisper.

'I feel safe when you're here.'

He took that as a yes.

The temperature inside the Aston was hitting sauna level when he jumped in, so he sat with the door open and had a cigarette, hand trembling. This was like the comedown after a blowout. The self-doubt. The guilt. The anguish. What was he doing? For twenty years he'd avoided anything that was connected to his past and now he was visiting Mirren's kid?

This was insane. Mirren would have his balls if she knew. Only the fact that Chloe was over eighteen and insisted her parents weren't told about his visits was saving him right now. This was playing with fire after a gasoline shower.

The journey home was a blur, each mile adding another level of need for that bottle of Southern Comfort that had been re-stashed after he'd succumbed the week before. Back in the apartment, he didn't even stop for a glass. How hypocritical was this? He was trying to straighten someone out and yet here he was chugging back the liquor to deal with his feelings. Getting wasted so he didn't have to deal with the situation. Pattern. Repeat. Pattern. Repeat.

He only knew he'd fallen asleep when the ringing of his phone woke him. Hollie! Crap, he'd overslept. Man, she was going to kick his ass. He answered without even looking at the screen. 'Hollie, I . . .'

'It's Chloe.' Like he didn't recognize the voice.

He squinted at his watch and saw that it was 3 a.m. Oh no, not again. They really had to tighten up their security. How the hell had she managed to get out?

'I'm still here. Don't, like, freak out. Got a phone off a dude that smuggled it in. You don't wanna know . . .'

He didn't.

'Are you OK?' he asked, his words thick with sleep and Southern Comfort.

'Man, you sound wasted,' she countered.

'No! No, I was just sleeping. Sorry. Been a long day. Crashed out as soon as I got home.'

The pause was so long he wondered if she'd hung up.

'I'm gonna do it this time. I just wanted to tell you that.'

Zander lit a cigarette – anything to distract him from the

sound of the promise in her voice. Hadn't he heard it all before? Hadn't he said the very same thing?

'I know you are, Chloe. We both are. We're both on the road to good things here.'

She thought about that for a moment. 'Yeah, good things. I believe that.'

Two dreamers. Two addicts. Zander knew he was lying. He wondered if she was too.

24.

'Raintown' – Deacon Blue

Glasgow, 1986

Jono Leith rubbed at his temples with calloused fingers. Bastarding headaches. Ever since some cunt banjoed him with a baseball bat, the migraines had been crippling. The doc said there was nothing that could be done about it. The sneering arrogance he said it with made Jono want to take a baseball bat to the back of his head and see if the snidey wanker could come up with a solution then.

It gnawed at him that he didn't see it coming, didn't see who had the kind of death wish that would make them take a shot at Jono Leith. He had a fair idea, though. Couple of the neds around here would do anything when they were smacked out of their nuts. Manny Murphy had warned him that there were a few names that weren't happy about Jono muscling in on a couple of jobs last month. The jewellers on Byres Road. The building society in Paisley. He'd heard they were going to be hit and how it was going to happen, so he'd stepped in and done the job first both times. Tasty spoils. Worth doing, even if it did piss off a couple of idiots. The way Jono saw it, he was doing them a favour, alerting them to the fact that someone in their crew couldn't keep their bloody mouth shut.

Yeah, he reckoned that's what was behind it. That or he'd shagged the wrong bird somewhere along the line. He felt no guilt for that either. If some pathetic specimen couldn't service his missus, it was only right that Jono step in and make the poor cow happy.

Not that he needed the aggro of a one-night stand. He had a couple of regulars who kept him more than horny and hard. Any more than that was just hassle. There was only so much skirt a bloke could tolerate in his life.

Anyway, the ambush wouldn't happen again.

No way. He'd be taking precautions from now on. Keeping his back covered.

'Tea, love. And I've put a biscuit on there. Garibaldi. I know you like those.'

Jesus wept, what was she wittering on about now? Could the stupid slag not just put a cup of tea down without War *and* bloody *Peace? What the fuck had he been thinking marrying her? Sure, she'd been a looker, but that was it. Nothing between the ears. And all that holy pish? If he'd known that was ahead of him, he'd have dumped her right after he screwed her up the back of the Barras. He couldn't even remember what gig he'd been at, but she hadn't taken much persuasion, just a few large vodkas from the bar and her legs were wide open.*

The pregnancy. The prayers. And the kicking from his da' had come next. Mortified he was, the old bastard. It was a council house and a registry office and a purvey in the front room before he knew what was happening.

Still, at least she knew when to take a telling. It wasn't his fault that he had to knock her about a bit to make the point. If she'd just cop on the first time and stop her infernal wittering, he wouldn't have to raise a hand to her. And she did keep a clean house. Aye, he'd keep her around for a while longer. Cheaper than a cleaner and she knew how he liked his mince.

Not that he'd be on the cheap cuts for much longer. He had a move planned. The one he'd been waiting for. Removing another idiot from the picture and taking over his operation. It was time. Jono Leith had been playing in Division Two for too long. Time for promotion. It wouldn't be quick and it wouldn't be painless, but he had no doubt he'd pull it off.

'Hi, Mr Leith. How's it going?' Davie boy strolled into the room, all cheek and cocky swagger. Jono liked that. Better than the sullen shit he got from his Sandy. Moody wee shite. He'd always thought that Sandy would follow him into the family business, but now he reckoned the boy didn't have the stomach for it. Too soft. He had the build for it – would be the man to collect in a few debts, put the fears on the diddies that thought they could get wide and pay late or change a price for a bit of gear. He'd had a bit of hope when he'd heard Sandy had leathered a nyaff from the bottom of the scheme for taking something off Davie, but it seemed like that had been a one-off. Shame.

Jono reached into the inside pocket of the jacket that was over the chair behind him, took out a hip flask and added it to his tea. That would chase the sore head. Not that there was much of it left. Must have drunk more of it than he realized last night.

'Whit are you looking at?' he challenged Sandy's stare. There was something wrong with that boy. What was his problem? Christ, the way he looked at him sometimes, he'd swear that the wee shit wanted him deid.

25.

'Pride' – Amy Macdonald

Glasgow, 2013

Sarah stood her ground as Ena's eyes flared. This wasn't going well. Time for damage limitation. 'Look, I promise I'm not here to cause trouble. I think Davie's great. Brilliant. He's my favourite actor.' It was door-stepping 101. Reassure. Cajole. Calm. Flatter.

This wasn't going to be easy, but Sarah had faced worse. And as long as she kept her head and found the right trigger, she usually managed to get what she'd come for. Granted, Ena Dawson was proving to be a considerable challenge. Her stance remained defensive, her gaze suspicious.

'Aye, well, I appreciate you've got a job to do, but I don't talk about my boy to the press. He's told me about that before. He's got one of those PR people and you have to talk to them if you want to know anything. I'll not be saying a word about him, dear. Sorry.'

The response wasn't what Sarah had hoped for, but at least it was confirmation that she was talking to the right woman. Ena went back to sweeping, conversation clearly over. Sarah decided there was nothing to lose by throwing in a little more bait and hoping for a bite.

'But don't you want to tell the world how proud you are of him?'

Ena didn't fall for it.

'The only person who needs to know how proud of him I am is Davie. I've no desire to be in the papers or out there looking for attention. That's why I took my mother's maiden name when the fame started. Davie might like that celebrity stuff, everyone knowing yer business, but it's no' for me. Leave me alone, lass – I won't change my mind.'

Head down, more sweeping.

Sarah gave it one last shot.

'Then perhaps you can help me with something else. Back in the 1980s, Davie's best pal was Zander Leith. I'm trying to track down Zander's father, Jono Leith.'

The bite was both sudden and fierce, with the thudding impact of a steel door banging shut.

Ena's head snapped up, and for a moment, Sarah actually thought the broom was going to double as a weapon.

'Then you're speaking to the wrong person again.' The apologetic tone had been replaced with high-grade hostility. 'Now if you don't mind, I've already said I don't speak to the press and I have work to do here. I'm saying nothing more, so stop wasting my time and yours.'

The turn of her back put a full stop on the conversation.

Sarah the woman knew it was time to call it a day and go back to the rainbow trout that was waiting for her at her favourite restaurant. Sarah the reporter couldn't stop herself from pushing just a little bit more.

'I'm not going to give up on this. I think something happened to Jono Leith and I'm not going to give up until I find out what it was.'

Ena stopped, sighed and cast her eyes back to meet Sarah's.

'Then you're a very stupid lassie who is making a huge mistake. There's no point in looking for Jono Leith. You'll never find him. And trust me, hen, that's one cage you don't want to rattle. For your own good.'

The warning was clear. The danger was implicit. Yet as Sarah trudged back to the warmth and safety of the restaurant, she knew that just like those who crossed the threshold to Narnia, she'd gone way too far to back out now.

Simon stood and pulled out her chair as she reached the table. 'Everything OK, darling?'

'Fine,' she told him, before asking a passing waiter to rustle up another coffee. These bones were going to take a while to defrost again.

Over his sumptuous feast of Kobe beef, Rob eyed her eagerly.

'I hear you've got a few days off next week.'

Sarah nodded. She had loads of holiday days banked because she rarely actually took time off. She'd planned to spend the week at the Mitchell Library, digging into the archives, until . . .

Simon was speaking now. 'Rob and I were just discussing caseloads and we can both get a couple of days off. We were thinking Paris. Maybe Rome?'

Sarah flushed – and not because the indoor temperature was finally raising her body temperature.

'I can't. I've got something on.'

Simon tried and failed to conceal his irritation. 'Honey, you can hang out at the Mitchell when we get back.'

'No, it's not that. There's been a change of plan. I need to . . . I'm, erm, going to . . .'

Her mind struggled to keep up with her spontaneous impulse.

'I'm . . . I'm going to LA.'

26.

'Talk Dirty' – Jason Derulo

This was the first time in weeks he'd come even close to silence. Yet he was surrounded by people. Surrounded. Lunch on the patio at the Ivy in LA was an eclectic hive of wealthy tourists, reality-TV stars and A-listers with a point to prove. It was the place to be seen and be papped. Where stars ate with directors to generate publicity for their latest movie. It was where famous couples dined together to show their marriage was doing great, or where they dined alone to show it was over.

To his left was an actress, one of the biggest box-office draws on the planet, dining with her new fiancé, sharing her happiness with the masses. Davie and the rest of Hollywood knew she had a seventy-five-year-old investor who bankrolled her movies and gave her top billing just as long as she fucked him on demand.

Over in the far corner, a global star sat with his wife, while his driver slouched against his limo further down the street. The same twenty-one-year-old driver who had been the actor's lover since he was an eighteen-year-old just off the bus from Arkansas and desperate to be the next Brad Pitt.

He didn't have the looks or the talent, but thankfully he had a driving licence and a raw ambition that made him determined to make it by any means. Right now, that meant servicing an action star who had given him three walk-on parts in movies that made over $100 million each. When his benefactor came to his room in the pool house every night, he told himself it was worth it.

Yep, the terrace at the Ivy was where Hollywood dreams seemed real, yet it was where Davie Johnston now sat, being bypassed by every name in town, all of them too afraid to be snapped shaking his hand in case his downfall was contagious. The fact that Sky Nixon was out of danger and recovering didn't make an iota of difference. He'd had Al's people keep daily tabs on the situation and she was now recovering well – no damage done. Thank God. Not that news of her recovery had been made public yet. The kids keeping a vigil outside the hospital may have got bored and gone back to school, but her mother was still issuing pleas for prayers. #prayforsky. Right now, he'd never hated anyone more. Rainbow was determined to keep milking it, absolutely loving the attention, and according to Al's people, she was already in talks with MTV about moving their show there, kicking off with Sky's triumphant release from hospital. What a load of shit. But then, if he was honest, he probably wouldn't have done it much differently himself.

That didn't mean he deserved the shit-storm that had come his way, though. Hell, every person in this town had made a living on smokescreens, mirrors and manipulation. The gay actors living with wives, having happy-family snaps before taking their male tennis pros to Cabo for practice with their swing. New balls, please. The A-list heroin addict who went to church every Sunday, then left five minutes before the end because he couldn't last any longer without a score. The twenty-five-year-old model turned actress who sent an occasional cheque to the ten-year-old twins she'd left in a trailer as babies when she got scouted while shop-lifting at a mall. The ageing talk-show host who installed a hidden camera in the guests' dressing rooms so he could jerk off while he watched them change before the show.

All twisted. All immoral. None of it any further up the messed-up scale than Davie's behaviour. The only difference was that Davie had made the fatal mistake of getting caught.

For the first time in years he felt vulnerable. On the outside of the in-crowd. A trickle of sweat ran down his neck and into the collar of his pale blue Stefano Ricci shirt despite the fact that the mercury had barely passed 70 degrees.

A month ago, he'd interviewed Mercedes Dance for an 'at home' special. She'd offered to blow him in the Jacuzzi. Now, wearing a floaty smock and Havaianas, the slut had just walked right past him like he didn't exist.

Davie stretched his neck to see who she was meeting inside. Jack Gore. He was doing a number on Mirren right enough. What a dick. No wonder Mirren still hadn't called him back. Not that he wanted her to now. With the benefit of hindsight, he'd probably overreacted after that journo had contacted him. He'd heard nothing more since he'd snub-bed the request. The bitch had probably gone on to some other story. Threat over. Done. Thank God.

The tension that was making his $50,000 veneers grind

was replaced by relief as a limo drew up and the driver opened the door to allow Lana Delasso to greet her public. Pushing seventy now, she looked a couple of decades younger, pausing as she alighted to let the paps get a few shots off. She wasn't big news, but her reality show had put her in the same nostalgic bracket of affection as Betty White and Joan Rivers. Dressed all in white, calf-length bodycon and a huge boa, her hair borrowed from the Jayne Mansfield-meets-Barbie shelf in the wig store, she teetered towards him, bestowing waves and air kisses on everyone in her path.

Choking as her cloud of Miss Dior reached his respiratory system, Davie managed to kiss her on each cheek and then hold out her chair as she sat down with all the flair and circumstance of a reigning monarch. Queen of the Has-Beens.

The waiter was at their side in a split second – early twenties, short, with a beaming smile and buckets of charm as he took the order for two waters and two Caesar salads, dressing on the side, neither of which would be eaten. No one who was anyone actually ingested real food in restaurants at lunchtime – only the calorie-reduced, nutritionally balanced, vitamin-enhanced creations of their personal chefs ever made it as far as their gullets.

Pouting her ruby-red lips, she leaned over and cupped his chin. 'Oh, my darling, who's been a naughty boy, then? I couldn't believe it,' Lana purred. 'Not my Davie. He wouldn't do something so underhand and manipulative. In all the time we've been doing our wonderful show together, he's never suggested such a thing. Of course, our show has Lana, so why would we need to?'

It was a struggle to keep the look of incredulity off his

face. It wasn't the fake laugh or the fact she was talking in the third person – that was pretty standard stuff. It was the fact that she seemed to be airbrushing more than her wrinkled tits. Since he'd rescued Lana from a soon-to-be-repossessed home in Brentwood, where she'd been doped up to her thrice-lifted neck with diazepam, they'd staged at least a dozen stunts to raise her profile and get this generation of viewers interested in her. There had been a near-death emergency hospitalization – great cover for her latest cosmetic work. The life-threatening car crash that was actually staged by a stunt mate of Davie's before Lana slipped into the driver's seat just before the emergency services arrived. No one thought to ask how she could wreck a Porsche without smudging her lipstick. There was the leaked hysterical call to 911. There were the rumours of an affair with a middle-aged action star, who was so outraged he'd threatened to kick Davie's ass up and down Sunset. The weeping on Sinatra's star on the Walk of Fame. The revelations about an affair with JFK. The threesome with Marilyn. The feud with Doris Day. None of it true, all of it great for the hype. Davie's personal favourite was the boy band, led by her grandson, that was currently living in her guest house. The story was that she was supporting them while they tried to get a record deal. The truth was that they couldn't hold a note in a bucket, but were picked from the books of a modelling agency and put in the show because they looked incredible, partied like the rock stars they'd never be and were there to have the teenage girls tuning in and turning on.

Lana had taken to reality-show manipulation like the pro

that she was and yet now she was coming out with some strange shit.

The all too recently familiar sensation of acid eating at his guts kicked off again. Either she was off her meds or up to something. Meds. He made a mental note to speak to her doctor and see if the old broad needed to up her dosage. He decided to go with it. Humour the old dear.

'You're right, baby,' he said, leaning towards her, his hand over hers, best smile at work. 'We don't need any of that stuff when we have you. So let's talk about the next series. I'm thinking Cannes. The film festival. You can take the boys over and we'll set up some gigs. Get them some European exposure. I'm thinking romance for you – an ageing but entitled prince from some shit-ass country we've never heard of. I'm thinking—'

'I don't think so.'

Davie stopped, tried to read her expression, but it was impossible given that she was so lifted and Botoxed that nothing moved below or above eyebrows that were tattooed in a perfect arch à la Joan Crawford, circa *Mildred Pierce* era.

'What was that?' he asked, another sweat bead slipping into his collar.

She sighed with unconvincing emotion. That pissed Davie off even more. Lana had been a fairly passable actress once. She and Goldie Hawn had been the chick-flick heroines of their generation, the quirky blondes that everyone loved. Goldie made the transition into older roles and kept her dignity and career. Lana lost it all on the back of too many bad decisions and too many surgeries, yet now he'd given it all back to her and she couldn't even muster up a decent performance for him.

'Darling, I'm sorry, but I think it's time this beautiful journey came to an end. I don't think you're the right brand for me any longer. I've been made an offer to move to another network and it's too good to pass. But I'll always love you, my little Davie doll.' Leaning over, she gave his cheek another squeeze of pure patronization.

No. Just no. How dare she do this?

A past master of the schmooze, he put his hand back on hers. 'Lana, baby, don't be crazy. You know we're perfect for each other.'

'Not anymore, Davie.' For the first time, her tone had a steely edge and he saw her body tense as she started to rise to her feet.

His hand flew to her arm, stopping her. 'You bitch,' he hissed. Her smile was the only reply, as she stood, spun on her eight-inch steel stiletto heels and flounced towards her waiting car. It was only then he noticed it. The raised square inside the back of her dress, just a few inches tall and wide. A battery pack. She was miked up.

He frantically scanned the street. There it was. Almost completely concealed by a large black van parked on the other side of the road, a guy with a camera, pointed his way. He'd seen him earlier, assumed it was just another chancer from TMZ. Now he realized he'd been set up. Punked. And he'd just been filmed and recorded calling Lana Delasso a bitch.

Davie Johnston decided that at this juncture in his life he had only three feasible choices: he could just slide off his chair and go ahead and crawl right into the gutter; he could take a hostage and hope for death by cop; or he could head into the back restaurant area and punch Jack Gore. The latter would serve no purpose, but hell, at least it would draw attention to the fact that there was another useless prick in the room.

27.

'Say Something, I'm Giving Up On You' – A Great Big World & Christina Aguilera

Mirren drummed her fingers on her desk, itching to call Brad Bernson for an update. Every time she reached for the phone, she stopped herself. It was pointless. If Bernson had anything to report, she'd know about it. Calling him just felt needy and desperate and more than a little pathetic – all emotions that were tussling with blind bloody fury for supremacy in her head. Putting her palms face down on the desk, she took a deep breath. Focus. Calm. OK, move on to something else. Distraction. Spreadsheets, there was a distraction. She clicked open the production accounts file that had arrived in her inbox a couple of hours ago and scanned the summary sheet. No surprises there. This movie was coming in at just under $56 million, but if it matched its predecessors, it would take four times that at the box office. No time to be complacent, though. Just because this was a major franchise with a stellar track record didn't mean that would continue. The movie business was fickle. Unpredictable. One wrong move and you could lose the audience in a heartbeat. The novel on which this one was based had spent months on the *New York Times* bestseller list, but now the challenge was to bring that enjoyment to the screen. It was a huge pressure, but Mirren thrived on it. Until now. Right now, it seemed like the least of her worries. All she cared about was getting Chloe well and home. Even Jack slipped below that on the list.

The urge to call Bernson flared again and she counteracted it by clicking open a couple more files. Salaries. Overheads. She should go home.

Location costs. Distribution.

She should go home.

Marketing. Sales. Promotion.

But she'd be going home to an empty house and she just couldn't bear it.

'I thought being the boss meant you got to go home and leave the overtime for us underlings.'

The figure in the shadows of the doorway made her jolt, then automatically smile.

Lex Callaghan, the Clansman, wasn't looking particularly historical in his beat-up jeans and black T-shirt. He sauntered over to the couch under the window to her right, took a seat, and as always Mirren wondered at the incredible act of casting that had brought him to her world. He *was* the Clansman – exactly as she had written him, exactly as she pictured him when she wrote. Blue eyes, a jaw that could have been shaped from steel, black wavy hair that was pulled back tonight into a ponytail. On other guys, it would look clichéd, or sleazy, or naff, but Lex's rippling masculinity made it sexy as hell. His wife was a lucky woman.

'What are you still doing here? Must be after ten,' she said, a quick glance at the time in the right-hand corner of her computer screen telling her she was correct.

'Working with the language coach. The Gaelic is going to sound great.'

'I don't doubt it,' Mirren smiled. It had been a risk in the first Clansman to have the dialogue in some scenes in Gaelic, with subtitles, but the trade-off of authenticity made it work. Right from the start the audiences had loved it.

'Anyway, how are you doing?' His voice oozed concern.

'OK,' Mirren replied with a hesitant smile, then immediately corrected her stock answer. 'Actually, shit. Really shit. Chloe's back in rehab.'

'Can I help? Is there anything we can do? You know, Cara would be happy to go see her, or Chloe could go out to the ranch.'

Cara, Lex's wife since they were sixteen. The ultimate happy ever after. Cara was a counsellor, worked with addicts on equine therapy out on their Santa Barbara ranch.

'Thanks. If we ever get her out of there, I might take you up on that.'

There was a comfortable silence for a few moments. They'd worked together long enough, been friends for enough years to know that they didn't have to fill every second with chat. Lex was a man of relatively few words who didn't do small talk or meaningless gossip.

'Do you wanna go for a beer?' he asked when he finally broke the quiet.

Mirren shook her head, stretching back in her seat and

yawning as she did so. 'Thanks but no. You know, the situation with Jack . . . The press would be all over it.'

'Yeah, I get that.'

Lex was out of his seat, out of the room, and Mirren stared at his retreating form, then the void, then his craggy grin as he returned with a bottle of Bud in each hand. 'Keep these in the trunk for emergencies. Might not be too cold, but I don't figure you'll care.'

Taking the beer, Mirren grinned. 'Wouldn't matter if it was the temperature of soup. Thanks, Lex.'

He slouched back on the couch again and she went over to join him, her standard work uniform of smart black shirt and black tailored capri pants a sharp contrast against her bare feet, with red nails and toe rings on three of her toes. Jack had had them made for her in Bali on their last holiday before the children. Eighteen years later, she'd still never taken them off. Her back against the arm of the sofa, she folded her legs underneath her, her face illuminated by the arc lamp that reached from the floor and curved round behind her. This was her favourite spot to read, to edit scripts and to take five minutes of peace at the end of a day. A red corkscrew tendril escaped from the clip that held her hair out of her face and she unconsciously pushed it away.

'I'm worried about you,' he told her gently.

Mirren took a slug of the beer and shook her head. 'Don't. Please. I can handle this. I promise.'

'So that's why you're still at work at ten o' clock at night outside of shooting schedule?'

Working sixteen-hour days was normal in production, but more unusual before the cameras started rolling. Mirren acknowledged the truth of his comment with a shrug. 'Just keeping busy. Less time to think.'

'Jack's an asshole.'

The vehemence in his voice made it clear this was an opinion he held with some conviction.

'Indeed he is,' Mirren eventually replied. Another pause. 'You know, even that feels weird,' she told him. 'I've never said a bad word about Jack to anyone else in all these years. Never. We defended each other. Stuck together. A team, you know?'

They both knew he did. His marriage to Cara was legendary for its devotion and longevity, and unlike most Hollywood unions, it wasn't faked for the cameras or the press.

'How could I have got it so wrong?'

Lex twisted round, one arm over the back of the sofa now, one leather boot across his other knee.

'Way I see it, it wasn't you who got it wrong.'

That elicited a grateful smile. Friends. That's what they did. Had your back and defended you against faithless bastards. Only her fierce insistence on restraint had persuaded Lou not to track Jack down and inflict some kind of pain on his body, mind or soul. But that wasn't Mirren's style. A long time ago, she'd learned that you had to fight your own battles.

'But I didn't see it coming, Lex. I thought I was smarter than that.'

Only when it was out did she realize how true that was. How could she not have known he was cheating? Not a single suspicion, not a single concern. How naive was that? What a fool. It wouldn't happen again. And yet . . .

'You trusted him. Doesn't mean you were in the wrong.'

His attempts to console her made her smile. This was so not Lex Callaghan. He didn't do hand-holding and deepest feelings. He did strong, silent and protective. The fact that he was trying made her love him even more than she already did.

'Are you gonna work it out with him?'

'I thought we'd be together until we died,' was her only reply, because she still didn't know the answer to his question. Could they work it out? Right now, she'd say no. But could she spend the rest of her life without him? Again, no.

It was just a case of working out which prospect terrified her more. At the moment, they were running equal.

Lex drained his bottle and set it down on the coffee table. 'Another one?' he asked.

Mirren shook her head, laughed. 'No way. Cara will have my ass if I keep you here any longer.'

'Don't worry about it. I'm back in early again tomorrow morning, so I'm staying at the shack tonight.'

It was typical Lex. Any other actor of his status staying in the city would go for the Chateau or the Four Seasons or one of the other five-star hotels, but Lex had bought a wooden cabin in the hills above Topanga Canyon. 'Shack' was a slight understatement, but only slight. There was hot and cold running water, a kitted-out kitchen and a fifty-inch plasma on the wall, but that aside, it was rustic, isolated and simple. Right now, that sounded just about perfect.

'Another beer sounds good, then. I've got nowhere I need to be.'

As he headed out to his truck to get the second round,

Mirren closed her eyes. This was the first time in weeks that she didn't feel that she was on the verge of disintegrating. 'Normal' was still a long way away, but at this point she'd settle for steady. Safe. It was like a timeout from the world.

Lex's footsteps interrupted her thoughts and she opened her eyes and reached for the outstretched bottle. He'd already opened it. Probably with his teeth, she decided.

'What's funny?' he asked.

'Ah, didn't realize I was smiling,' she replied. 'Was just wondering if you took the bottle tops off with your teeth.'

His laughter filled the room. 'Yes, ma'am. Right after I rustled up a herd of cattle and spat on the campfire.' They were both laughing now, the volume increasing when he added, 'Actually, I've got a bottle opener in the glovebox.'

Mirren was doubled over now, her laughter sending tears streaming down her cheeks, her emotions somewhere between hilarity and hysteria. All the pent-up emotion, all the stress, all the holy fucking terror that she'd suppressed and controlled now taking over and being released. Man, it felt good. Letting all that misery go felt fucking great.

She was so out of control that she missed the first couple of rings of her cell phone. The ascending tone rose another notch until it permeated her altered state.

It wasn't the ringtone that was assigned to Jack, Chloe, Logan or Lou, so her first thought was that it had to be Brad Bernson. In which case, he'd found something. Something important that couldn't wait until morning.

Snapped back to reality, suddenly icy calm, she uncurled her legs and was across the room in a second. The screen told her the number was withheld. Always a risk. Crank call?

Anonymous tip-off? Someone from the press, about to ambush her with more shit news that could ruin what was left of her life? There was a temptation to ignore it, but she would only torture herself with curiosity about who it could have been.

Accept.

'Hello?'

'Hi. Is that Ms McLean?'

A voice she didn't recognize.

'Yes.'

'This is Dr Le Comber, clinical director at Life Reborn.'

Mirren immediately put the face to the name. She'd met him a couple of times – the first time Chloe was admitted and then once on a previous stay during a family visit. A cold wave of dread and fear replaced the glimmer of warmth left by the beer.

'How can I help you?' she asked, knowing that her excruciating fear was probably making her come off like a cold bitch.

'Ms McLean, I'm really sorry to have to tell you this, but one of our nurses just checked on Chloe and I'm afraid she's gone.'

'What do you mean, "gone"?' It was an automatic question, out before she realized it served no purpose.

'I'm sorry, Ms McLean. We've done a full search of the premises and she's not here. I need to inform you that we've notified the police and a warrant will be issued. I can't apologize enough. I can assure you this is a rare—'

Mirren didn't wait to hear the rest. She clicked 'end', then immediately dialled a number stored in her contacts.

It rang once.

Come on. Come on.

Twice.

Where the hell was he?

It rang again.

An explosion of anxiety made her heart thunder and sent her nerve endings to the outside of her skin.

'Mirren? Hi.'

'Brad, I don't care where you are or what you're doing. Chloe's gone. You need to find her and you need to bring her home.'

28.

'Lose Yourself' – Eminem

At first he thought it must be morning and he'd slept in. The banging on the door had the same incessant rhythm of Hollie when she was seriously pissed. Through the haze of sleep, Zander did a quick mental checklist. Sober? Tick. In his own apartment? Tick. Naked stripper in bed with him? He groped around with his left arm. Nope. Thank Christ. He was already ahead of the game.

Leaning over, he grabbed a pair of black Calvins off the floor, pulled them on and headed for the door. Even through the fugue he could see something wasn't making sense. It was still dark and yet Hollie was here and . . .

He had the sense to look through the spyhole; then, situation suddenly clear, he opened the door to his returning visitor, who he caught just in time as she fell off a pair of ten-inch heels. Shit, she was wasted.

'Za-a-a-nder,' she giggled. 'I missed you. Did you miss me? Did you?'

This wasn't good. He'd so hoped she was ready to get sober. But then he knew how this worked. Didn't he swear he'd stay clean after every bender? And didn't it all go to shit in a vat of bourbon every time? Right now, all that mattered was that he got her off his doorstep before she woke the neighbours and someone called the cops.

'Oh, Chloe, come on, love . . .' He lifted her up and took her over to the bed he'd just left.

OK, a plan was needed. He picked up his phone and noticed the time was 4 a.m., before dialling the clinic. It answered on the second ring. 'Life Reborn. How can I help you?' A guy's voice, but not Lebron.

'Hey, can I speak to Lebron?' He slipped into a New York accent, aware that if he used his own, there were few people in the movie-going free world who wouldn't recognize it.

'I'm sorry, Lebron isn't working tonight. Can I help you?'

His answer was to hang up. A new plan. He couldn't take her back there and just knock on the door. Her escape would be reported to the courts, and besides, she was completely wasted. They'd move her down to County before she'd even sobered up. OK, think.

She was out cold, but by her breathing and her pulse, he knew that she just needed to sleep it off.

Choices. Take her back to rehab and she'd face the penalty. Or take her to Mirren. Or leave her here. The first was a definite no, the second made him want to throw up, and the third was out of the question. He headed over to the kitchen and got a bucket and a bottle of water. This was becoming all too familiar, but he had to help her. *Wanted* to. Man, he suddenly needed a drink.

'Zander?' Her eyes barely opened.

'Yeah. Hey.'

'Hey.' There was a hint of contentment in her voice as her

hand found his. The pause that followed was so long he thought that she'd fallen asleep again.

'Zander, let me stay here.'

'Honey, you know I can't . . .'

Her tone flipped. 'If you take me back, I'll leave again. No matter where you take me, I'm not staying there. And next time, I won't come here – I'll go find my guys.' And hello, defensive Chloe – abrasive, defiant and absolutely set on getting her own way. This kid was hard work. She was trademark addict. It was all about the manipulation and the self-obsession. Lies and emotional blackmail came as standard. It was his specialist subject.

But the mention of 'her guys' made his mind up. The low-life scum of rich kids and drug-dealing wannabes who would give her anything she wanted.

There was no way he was letting her loose with them.

The ding of his alarm told him he had fifty minutes before Hollie was here to collect him for his 5.30 a.m. call time.

If she saw Chloe, there would be no negotiation – the teen would be back at Life Reborn within the hour.

That couldn't happen. Chloe would find another way to get out and she'd be in a gutter before they knew she was gone.

Fuck it. He almost felt sorry for her. It was a tough gig when the only person who looked like even being in with a chance of helping her was a guy who had it so together he kept coke in a bobblehead on his dashboard.

'I'm staying here, Zander Leith. Staying with you.'

Damn it. Decision made. Keep her here. Let her sober up. Talk to her when he got back from work. Put together a strategy to get her sober permanently. He'd support her and help her make it happen.

When Hollie drew up outside at 5 a.m., he'd showered, brushed his teeth, gone through two inches of mouthwash and drunk a gallon of coffee. He checked on Chloe one last time – still sleeping, still breathing – left a note with his cell and asked her to call him when she woke.

If Hollie noticed he was distracted on the way to the studio, she probably put it down to alcohol withdrawal and tiredness. When he arrived on set, there was a bonus waiting – his new trailer, a gift from Wes to congratulate him on his sobriety. Usually he worked out of a standard star wagon, but this one was a whole other level. Fifteen hundred square feet, two storeys, expanding wall, hydraulic roof, full-size gym, full-service kitchen, arched windows, Italian cabinetry, brown leather sofas, a games room, roll-down movie screen, lounge, bar, boardroom, a spiral staircase to the three upstairs bedrooms. It cost $2.5 million.

The row of terraced houses he'd lived in as a kid could fit inside.

And he didn't give a flying. All he cared about was what was going on in the 1,000 square feet of his minimalist Venice apartment.

Every hour he called home. The first few times, there was no answer. By lunchtime, he'd convinced himself she was dead, and knocked back a few shots of Jack to try to mellow out. By 2 p.m. he had a feeling of dread that was eroding his guts quicker than cheap tequila, when she finally answered sleepily and assured him she was fine. He called again a couple of hours later and that time round she sounded irritable and snappy. He could hear the TV blaring in the background, but he didn't care. She was there, she was safe, and right now that was all that mattered.

The rest of the afternoon was taken up with the final rehearsal of a fight scene, one that gave his body a pounding because he refused to use a stunt double for the hand-to-hand combat. It was written in the Hollywood rules that no one ever, ever hurt the star, but Zander had pushed it, raged at the stunt director, demanded that he make it authentic and provoked him until he did. Today he enjoyed the pain. It gave him something else to focus on, a reason to think about anything other than the fact that Chloe could be lying in his apartment in a pool of her own vomit.

'You OK?' Hollie asked when they got in the car to head home at 6 p.m.

'Yeah, just . . . you know . . . tired.'

She didn't look convinced until her expression changed to one of irritation.

'Tell me the feminist stripper wasn't back for a second visit last night. Damn! She was. Man, I'm going to have to dip your dick in disinfectant.'

It was so blunt he actually laughed. 'No stripper, and I don't think dick hygiene falls within your remit.'

'Thank God. I tell you, working for you is going to scare me celibate.'

They stopped outside his block and went through their regular ritual.

'Want me to come in? Last week's date didn't work out. I'm back to being a dried-up single husk with the real prospect of dying surrounded by my cats in a house that gives the neighbourhood kids nightmares.'

Zander leaned over and kissed her on the cheek.

'Rain check? I'm slammed. Need sleep.'

'No stripper?' she checked suspiciously.

'No stripper,' he assured her as he climbed out.

'OK,' she told him through the open window, 'but I'm bringing Dettox in the morning as a precaution.'

He could still hear her laughing when he dropped $10 into the hat of his homeless mate outside the door.

Upstairs, as he put his key in the lock, he made a deal with himself and the Almighty. If she was still there, he was going to thank God and vow never to touch the drink again. If she was gone, he'd need a drink to get through the night. If she was dead, all bets were off.

Tentatively, he walked inside, gently closing the door behind him and wearily dropping his keys in the bowl on the console table to his left.

Other than the clinking of the keys against glass, there was silence.

The room looked like it had been the venue for a frat party. Food cartons littered tables, beer bottles were strewn across the floor, the blanket from his bed had been thrown over the sofa, and if he wasn't mistaken, the trousers from his Tom Ford tux were dangling from the handle of the balcony door.

But still there was silence.

This wasn't good. Really wasn't good. There was no way she'd made this mess on her own. Other people had been here, a few by the looks of it.

In past times, he'd have dealt with this level of anxiety

with coke, but he was expecting to be tested anyday now. Alcohol he could explain away as wine with lunch – coke was indefensible. Production would be shut down and there was too much riding on it to go Charlie Sheen.

His teeth clenched as his gaze moved to the bed. When he'd left this morning, she'd been in there, crashed out; now she was gone.

With the stealth of a SWAT team, he swung open the bathroom door. Nothing. He checked the balcony. Nothing. She was gone. Shit.

He was about to concede defeat and call the cops when he saw the note.

'Hey, sorry about mess – a friend came to collect me and we hung out. Have gone back to rehab. Promise. Will make you proud. Thanks for last night. Will call u tomoz. Cxoxox'

The relief was instant, sheer gratitude that she wasn't lying in a gutter with a crack pipe by her side, rigor mortis slowly claiming her body. Sure, there was a niggling doubt that she could be lying. Again he called the clinic, asked for Lebron, and again he was told that Lebron wasn't available. He hung up before they asked him for details. No point. The clinic wouldn't disclose any information to him. He was going to have to trust her. He weighed up the probabilities. If she'd gone on a bender, it was doubtful that she'd bother leaving a note. However, this place looked like shit, so unless she'd called a clean, sober but highly untidy friend, there was every possibility that she was off the wagon. He knew more than anyone that addicts lied, but he also knew that sometimes they beat the odds and cleaned up. Trust didn't come easy, but right now he was going to have to have some faith in her.

The tangle of emotions possessed him, taking control of his impulses. He pulled out the sofa and checked behind it, relieved to see that the quart of JD he stored there was untouched. He poured two fingers, peeled off his top, threw it in the laundry and then cleared the place up. Even in his darkest, most wasted days, he couldn't bring himself to live in squalor. An upbringing in a house that was cleaned daily from top to bottom, with a mother who demanded that her surroundings be as immaculate as her soul, had instilled some habits in his DNA.

He put the food containers in the trash, the clothes and blankets in the laundry cupboard, opened the balcony door to let the sea air neutralize the smell of stale smoke and excess. In the bathroom, he cleared away the wet towels and rinsed down the walls and glass screen. She'd had a shower. He supposed that was a good sign, added weight to the honesty of her note. If she was truly on a bender, then the little things like eating and personal hygiene would have been forgotten.

When the apartment was back to something resembling normality, he lit a cigarette and carried his drink and ashtray over to the sofa. Half an hour of TV, then bed. He had a 6 a.m. call and was back in training all morning with a stunt coordinator with a voice that belonged on a Navy Seal PT instructor.

He flicked through the channels. Football. *CSI Somewhere*. Talk shows that all said the same. He flicked past those immediately. Last thing he needed to hear was some arrogant asshole earning his million-dollar salary by having a swipe at him.

Flick. Flick. TMZ. Stay. Given that it was an altercation filmed by a pap that had landed him in rehab – again – he should hate those guys. When he'd had a drink, he did. They'd put him under the spotlight so many times, fighting, falling out of clubs drunk, snogging models in alleys, and once – in a particular moment of dignity – pissing in a pot plant at the door of a particularly upmarket Beverly Hills restaurant.

He hadn't gone back to check if he was barred.

But he had enough self-awareness to realize that if he didn't behave like an ass, they'd have nothing to report.

Case in point, Davie Johnston, whose image was now at the centre of the screen. What the hell was he doing? The cameras had caught him in full focus, screaming at a paparazzo at the entrance to the CSA building that afternoon. Jesus, the guy had lost it.

Zander downed his drink in one. They could live another lifetime and still his fists would clench at the sight of Davie Johnston's face.

His finger moved to the programme button to change the channel when the action switched to the entrance to Lix, the hottest club in town. Davie's wife, Jenny Rico, and her screen partner, Darcy Jay, were leaving, both of them smoking hot, with that whole rock-chick look going on. Tight jeans, tanks, tailored jackets. Zander smiled. He'd heard the rumours about their off-screen relationship. Now there was a mental image he could live with.

The thought had him so distracted that he almost missed it. Almost.

If the shot had been at a different angle. If the lights had been dimmer. If the cameraman had cut away just a moment sooner.

But no, there it was, in the background. On a female, approximately five foot eight, long black hair that had the synthetic sheen of a wig, his Tom Ford tuxedo jacket was walking into the club.

Fuck.

He realized immediately that this was one of those times when it would be so easy to make a shit decision. A month ago, he would have. But now, with everything riding on this movie, he had to be smarter. He was wrecked. Not drunk enough to fall apart, but too wasted to drive. He picked up his cell and pressed one digit.

'It's me. Don't ask, but I need you to come get me and take me to Lix to pick someone up.'

Silence.

For several moments.

Then . . .

'It's midnight.'

'I know.'

Silence. Until Hollie announced, 'I so need to get a new job. Give me twenty minutes and I'll be there. Is it gonna get messy?'

'Almost definitely.'

As usual, Hollie handled everything. She found Chloe passed out in the toilets at the club, bribed the security to get her out the fire exit and into her car, and then picked up the guy with the low baseball cap who'd watched the whole thing from a doorway across the street.

Zander tossed the cap in the back as they pulled off.

'Where to?' Hollie asked, trying not to sound too pissed off and failing.

Zander stared straight ahead. 'Malibu.'

29.

'Never Can Say Goodbye'
– the Communards

Glasgow, 1987

They were freezing, so they both jumped under the pale pink candlewick bedspread and then huddled into the middle of the bed. They often did this. Not because there was anything dodgy going on but because the house was bloody Baltic and this was the only way to get warm.

The council had been threatening to install central heating for years but had never come up with the goods.

'Hang on, hang on.' Mirren leaned over and pressed play on her tape recorder, then immediately turned up the volume. 'I love this song.' Jimmy Somerville was just reaching the chorus of 'Never Can Say Goodbye'. The Communards album had been his present to her on her sixteenth birthday the week before and she'd taped it onto a cassette so they could listen to it anytime.

For a couple of minutes, neither of them spoke.

There had never been any awkwardness between them, but lately he'd noticed that there was sometimes a weird silence.

Maybe she was just bored. Maybe she just wanted to listen to the words of the song. She was like that sometimes.

She turned to look at him, started to say something, then stopped.

'What?'

'Nothing.'

'You were going to say something. What is it? And no, I'm not going downstairs for a bottle of ginger, and no, you look nothing like that burd from T'Pau.'

She hit him in the face with her pillow, then put it back under her head. 'No danger – she's ancient.'

The two of them laughed and he felt his temperature rise to somewhere around normal. 'Thank fuck. Got the feeling back in ma toes.'

He pulled back the cover, ready to move over to the beanbag he always sat on when they hung out up here, then realized that her hand was on his arm, stopping him from moving.

'What the . . . ?'

Turning back, he saw that she was staring at him, but not in any way he'd seen before.

This was the way that Carol Cassidy stared at him right before he got off with her round the back of the school disco.

'It's OK if you want to,' she said.

He wanted to. He'd wanted to for years, but he'd always thought this was out of bounds. They were pals. She'd had boyfriends and he'd had girlfriends, but they'd never so much as kissed each other after a bottle of cider on a Saturday night.

Did she fancy him? If she did, she'd always done a magic job of hiding it. Or maybe he'd just been too scared to hope.

He leaned over and put his mouth on hers, tasting the strawberry lip gloss she reapplied every five minutes.

Her hand wound round his neck and then stopped on his face, and that's when an erection filled his jeans. He flushed with embarrassment. There was no way she wouldn't notice. Please go down. Down. Come on.

He waited for the punch, for her to pull back and have a berzy at him. It was one thing having a bit of a winch, but a hard-on was . . . well, a pure beamer. This was Mirren. This wasn't what they did together. They hung out. They spent nights talking shite in the hut. And now she was going to have a mad fit because his hard-on was pressing into her stomach and he couldn't stop it.

What a nightmare.

What a total nightmare.

'Mirren, I . . .'

If he said sorry now, maybe she'd pretend she hadn't noticed and they could forget it. He'd say he was pished and they'd laugh about it tomorrow. He'd had two bottles of Grolsch after the cinema, so she'd believe him.

'Sssshhh.'

It took a few seconds to realize that the sensation on the front of his crotch was her hand and it was rubbing against him. Touching his zip. Pulling it down slowly. Slowly.

He opened his eyes to see that she was staring at him.

'Are you sure?' he asked, whispering, as if raising his voice would change something, make her snap out of it and tell him to bugger off.

'Yes,' she said softly. 'I want to.'

Her eyes looked even more huge than they normally did

and he just wanted to stop, to look at her, to remember what this felt like.

Leaning over, he kissed her again. This time his tongue pushed her mouth open wider, and an involuntary groan escaped as her hand moved inside his jeans.

Gently, he felt for the bottom of her jumper and – still terrified that she was going to stop at any second – slid it upwards and cupped her left boob.

'Are you sure?' he asked again.

'I'm sure.' Her voice sounded different again. Like she was crying. The thought terrified him. Mirren never cried. Panic made him pause. Was he doing something wrong? Something she didn't like? She'd said it was OK, but maybe she didn't mean it. Maybe she . . .

'I love you,' she whispered.

And that's when he groaned again and then kissed her even harder, before slowly taking off her clothes and touching every part of her.

Because he'd loved Mirren McLean for as long as he could remember.

30.

'In a Big Country' – Big Country

Glasgow to LA

Sarah didn't know what she'd been expecting, but her introduction to LA wasn't it. After a fourteen-hour flight via London, she'd been forced to stand in a queue for two hours before reaching an obviously bored, shaven-headed man at the immigration desk. He'd grilled her on her reason for entry, any US work plans and return flight (holiday, none, one week later) before waving her through with such a disdainful manner she decided he was clearly disappointed that she hadn't brightened up his day by being an illegal immigrant, a drugs mule or Catherine Zeta-Jones.

She'd contemplated coming over on a press visa, but the application process was too long and convoluted, so she'd decided a tourist visa was the way to go. It wasn't as if this was an official *Daily Scot* story. Yet.

In her imagination, landing in LAX would be almost cinematic, with a futuristic airport and the occasional passing movie star. But no. It was a collection of low, somewhat tatty buildings that were the equivalent of an ageing actor who could no longer deliver the goods.

However, going by the amount of construction, it was getting a facelift. She was definitely in the right city.

No one offered to help as she wrestled her bag off the conveyor belt. It was a Carlton case, in silver, with her initials monogrammed next to the handle. Simon had given it to her yesterday in a bid to show that he was a post-millennium modern man who didn't care at all that his girlfriend had decided to up sticks and head to LA on what he considered a wild goose chase. They both knew it was a lie. He minded intensely, but knew that resistance was futile.

She tried to call him as she walked for what seemed like miles, following the signs for taxis.

Straight to answering service every time. Either he was in court or still in a huff. She really hoped it was the former. They were a great team and this had been the first stumbling block in an otherwise smooth relationship. Until now they'd rumbled along, their complementary personalities and mutual dedication to their work making their relationship easy. None of the petty squabbles that she heard the other girls talking about in the *Daily Scot* kitchen on a Monday morning. Just mutual support, great times and wholly satisfactory sex.

The leather on her black biker boots squeaked as she marched along a labyrinth of corridors, finally emerging into a large hall punctuated by sliding glass doors.

The heat hit her as she joined another long line, this time for a cab. By the time she reached the front, sweat was rolling down her back.

An Armenian cab driver took her case from her and loaded it in the boot.

For the first time, Sarah consciously stood, inhaled and scanned the hustle of four lanes of cars weaving in and out in front of the terminal building.

It seemed utterly incredible that she was finally in LA and yet here she was.

'Where to?' the driver asked her as they both climbed in.

'Le Parc Suite Hotel, West Hollywood.' Within her budget, with a rooftop lounge. Sold.

The driver nodded, then pulled out to a cacophony of blaring horns.

As her head fell back on the plastic seats, she felt like the cowboy coming into Dodge.

And a smile played on her lips as she realized that if this was an old-time cowboy movie, a lone rider would have stormed off into the night to warn Leith, Johnston and McLean that she was in town and she was coming for them.

31.

'Fuck You' – CeeLo Green

Davie's fingers were itching, desperate to hit the keyboard on his laptop. He decided this must be what it felt like when celebrities picked up a hooker on Sunset. They knew it was a really bad idea, but sometimes it was impossible to resist, despite the fact that they had to know it wouldn't end well.

Hookers had never been his thing. No need. And besides, he'd always been too aware that it was blackmail waiting to happen.

That's what made this current situation so unbearable. He'd been careful. Taken few risks. Only screwed people with as much to lose as him. And years of cultivating the guy-next-door niceness had been blown apart by one crazy bitch and her lust for fame.

Now, he was sitting at the island in his kitchen, where Ivanka had left a table setting for one, sandwich ignored, fingers at the ready, fighting a primal urge to . . .

'www.twitter.com'

'Davie Johnston'

'Search'

Oh dear God.

There were thousands of tweets and a quick scan revealed that most of them included wishes or threats that would limit his life expectancy.

Yes, there were a few positives too, but he suspected most of them were written in Bangladesh, where CSA kept a factory of fake clickers on retainer. Within seconds of the order being given, thousands of underpaid workers, all with multiple profiles on every social network site, could vote, trend or drown out opposition by writing their own pre-scripted tweets. On Al's command, they'd already bombarded Davie's Facebook page with messages of support and encouragement, in the hope of rallying the same message in the US. After reading some of the abusive arguments blasted at the favourable comments, Davie wasn't sure the strategy was working.

Oprah was beginning to look like the best of a bunch of bad options.

Like a masochist in a gimp mask who refused to utter the safe word, he decided he needed more pain. Back up in the browser bar, he typed in 'Davie Johnston Lana Delasso'. Bingo. A video upload from today, on a website linked to a celebrity-scandal channel. He pressed play and then immediately stopped. He already knew the script. It was the scene from the Ivy and they were running it with a tag-line promo promoting her new show, *With Love From Lana*. There was a fucking stunning stretch of creative imagination. Idiots.

Wearily he closed it down, then put a call in to Al. Straight to voicemail. That was becoming depressingly standard these days. He left a message telling Al about the video and asking him to get the lawyers on it. Just another layer on this great big onion of crap.

The buzz of his phone was a welcome distraction from thoughts of taking the knife from his table and pounding it straight into his jugular. His first assumption was that it was Al, but the screen told him differently. Surprised, he answered it with almost pathetic gratitude.

'Hey, Mum, how's it going?' His accent automatically reverted to a west of Scotland brogue as he did a quick calculation. It must be 4 a.m. in Glasgow. She'd probably just got back from that ridiculous bloody bus she worked on. He had no idea why she worked there. He sent her enough money to give her an incredible life and she never touched it, just left it sitting in the bank while she lived in the same house and spent her nights with hookers and homeless people.

'Fine, son. But it's just a quick call . . .' She always said that. It struck him that if he had a needle sticking out of his arm, she might have time for more than a two-minute chat. His attention was gone now, back on that manipulative, conniving bitch Lana.

'. . . but I just wanted to let you know that some lassie came onto the bus the other night. Asking questions, all sorts of questions. Said she's from one of the papers. Hang on, whit one was it? Aye, the *Daily Scot*.'

A brutal meeting between the knife and his jugular suddenly seemed like a welcome reprieve.

32.

'Won't Get Fooled Again' – The Who

Dinner with Lou at Ago, Robert De Niro and Agostino Sciandri's restaurant on Melrose, was a weekly fixture. They always sat at the same table, on the outdoor patio, an area embellished with greenery, recreating the vibe of a Tuscan garden. The larger parties knew to request a round table, otherwise they'd be seen and not heard. And no one went there to fade into the background. On any given night, the room would ooze power: producers, directors, stars that didn't get out of bed for less than $1 million or the promise of an incredible lay.

Despite the fact that the last thing Mirren felt like doing was donning high heels and getting out there, Lou, showing her hard-ass gossip-columnist genes, had refused to let her cancel.

'Screw that,' Lou blasted, when Mirren had hesitated over plans on the phone. 'Mirren McLean, don't you dare stand me up. Don't let this town think you've got something to hide from and don't leave me without a date on a Thursday night. Besides, it's work for me, sweetheart. I hear Clooney and the gang are gonna be there and I've got nothing for tomorrow's column.'

Mirren sighed. Having Hollywood's top scandal hound as a friend had many advantages – great insider info, fast news and a network of spies that could rival the CIA during the Cold War.

But the one disadvantage was that she had to be seen to be out mingling with – as Lou so eloquently put it – the great and the fan-fucking-tastic. And she was determined to drag Mirren along whether she liked it or not.

'Stop pursing your lips – it'll give you wrinkles that not even Dr Lancer can fix,' Lou shot down the line.

'How do you know what my lips are doing?'

'Babe, you're a creature of habit.' They both were.

Now, in the same restaurant they visited every week, having eaten the same dishes they always chose – rigatoni alla contadina for Mirren, linguine vongole for Lou – Mirren felt a welcome sense of comfort as Lou returned after having a chat with George and his buddies.

'God, I love that man,' Lou whispered. 'Gave me an exclusive on his next movie. If only he demanded sexual favours in return for information, I'd be a happy woman.'

For the first time all week Mirren laughed.

'So. What's the latest with that traitorous prick you married?'

Tactful transitions had never been Lou's strong point.

Mirren took a sip of espresso to buy time to formulate an answer that would hopefully cut the subject dead.

'Brad's looked into it for me. He's been staying at a hotel like he said. He just needs time. So do I. End of story for now.'

Lou's train of interference wasn't so easily halted.

'Time for what? Are you seriously thinking of taking him back? Come on, Mirren, you can't be.'

Mirren decided to go ahead and pull that Band-Aid right off. 'I am, Lou, and don't judge me for it. According to Brad Bernson, he's not spent the night with her this week. They met for lunch at the Ivy last weekend, but that was it. Obviously they'll need to talk, so if it's in a public place, it tells me there's nothing going on anymore.'

'Or Mercedes Dance is milking this for all the publicity she can get.'

Mirren exhaled and braced herself to share her decision. She'd agonized over it for days. Changed her mind a dozen times. But in the end, she knew it was what was best for her family. And they were all that mattered.

'Look, Lou, I need to take him back. We had nineteen years; he screwed up once. Sure, it was a huge screw-up, but I need to get over it for the kids' sake and mine. I need him to come back, make changes, get Chloe sorted out. The court is going to throw the book at her if she leaves rehab again without permission. She needs us. This is my family, Lou. I'm not losing it now or letting it become one of those tragic Hollywood fuck-up stories.'

There was a pause as Lou digested the pertinent points. 'Found out who took her back to the clinic yet?'

'Nope. They literally rang the bell and left her at the door. And she's not saying.'

Lou's glee over the Clooney exclusive was long gone now. 'I do get it, Mirren. And if you want him back, I won't say a single negative thing about it. Not one.'

'You're kidding.'

'Nope, not one. Although there's a good chance the only way I'll keep my promise is by stapling my lips together. Or suctioning myself to Mr Clooney's frigging gorgeous face.'

Their laughter was interrupted by the vibration of Lou's blinged-out iPhone in the middle of the table.

They could both see the message that flashed on the screen. 'JG. MD. CDM. 262.'

'My God, Lou, you're like a real-life spy chick.'

Lou didn't smile as her eyes rose to meet Mirren's.

'What? What is it?'

'You really serious about taking Jack back?'

'Yeah . . .'

'Well, you'd better get your ass in gear, because right now he's at the Casa del Mar, room 262, with Mercedes Dance, and in about half an hour every pap in town will be outside there.'

For a few seconds Mirren was torn. All she'd thought about all week was what she needed to do for the long-term salvation of her family and now that she'd made the decision that stupid bastard was threatening it again already. And worse, they were at the Casa del Mar. Their favourite bolt-hole, a haven of luxury on the sands of Santa Monica Beach.

'Maybe they're just talking. Sorting things out. That's our room, the one we keep on retainer for weekends and visitors. He told me he was staying. I assumed he meant alone. My bad.'

'You got a key?'

'Yep.'

'Then let's go see.'

Mirren knew it was as much of a challenge as an attempt to help, but if she was going into enemy territory, there was no one she'd rather have behind her. There was only one good way out of this and it had to start with letting Jack come home to kick off the healing process.

Lou put the pedal of her Mercedes coupé down to the metal as they crossed town in record time, pulling up at the Casa twenty minutes later. She tossed the keys to the valet parking attendant and scoped the streets for paps. None in sight. This wasn't a usual hang-out for them – too far out of the way of the usual haunts. She paid her source well for a one-hour heads-up ahead of any other media outlets being tipped off and it looked like this time he'd made it worthwhile.

The heels of two pairs of Louboutins clicked across the floor of the marble foyer, then faded to silence as they rose in the lift. Outside the room, Mirren took a deep breath.

'You ready?' Lou whispered.

Mirren nodded and reached towards the door. Lou put an arm up to stop her. 'We don't have to do this, you know. We can just leave now. Forget him. Act like this never happened.'

Mirren's reply was to click the key into the lock and swing the door open to see . . .

She scanned the room.

Nothing. Empty. The only sign of habitation was a room-service tray on the table by the window. One plate. One ice bucket. One empty bottle of champagne upside down in the middle of it.

It was one of Jack's things. He'd done that since the very

first night they'd ordered a bottle of Moët to toast their first real date.

Since then there had been hundreds of upside-down bottles in ice buckets – but none of them had made her feel the blind rage she felt right now.

The carpet muffled her approach as she crossed the room and opened the bathroom door.

She'd known he'd be there. The first thing he always did when he got home at night was to take a bath. But back in their house on the Colony, he had warm water, candles, oils, and managed to relax without a twenty-two-year-old movie star sitting on his dick in the middle of the tub.

For a moment Mirren was strangely fixated on the soft curve of her rival's stomach and the swollen beauty of Mercedes' breasts, shiny with moisture as they rose and fell. Her hands were in her hair, her head thrown back, her breathing thick and fast. Jack's eyes were closed tight, his face in the sexed-up, just-about-to-come expression Mirren had seen countless times before.

'Busy?'

It was all she could say, but it was enough. Mercedes screeched; Jack wailed.

'Holy fuck!'

Mirren snatched a small victory from the fact that he'd now have one orgasm less in his lifetime. Calm. Dignified. She had to overrule her urge to scream and kill by repeating this mantra in her head.

Unfortunately, it wasn't loud enough for Lou to hear. Mirren was bumped out of the way by her friend's charge towards the tub. There, she slapped Jack across the face with a hastily grabbed towel and then sneered at Mercedes, 'Right, slut-features, time to dismount. Get the fuck off your pay-cock and get out of here.'

'Jack, are you gonna do something?' Mercedes' whiny drawl notched the atmosphere up from dramatic to homicidal.

'Yes, he's gonna do something, you traitorous bitch,' Lou calmly informed her. 'He's gonna remove his limp penis from your body; then he's gonna beg his wife for forgiveness, otherwise I'm gonna drown the fucker right here and now. Any more questions?'

Mercedes shook her head, grabbed a towel and – trying desperately to recover some shred of decorum – covered herself up and marched to the other room, stopping as she passed Mirren.

'He said you two were getting a divorce.' Her tone made it clear it was an excuse.

'Maybe,' Mirren replied. 'But after it hit the press, you knew that wasn't true.'

'Well, I'm havin' his kid, so you're gonna have to get used to me being around.'

To Mirren's surprise, she felt a stirring of sympathy. This woman was not much older than Chloe. What did she know about anything?

Lou was still on a wavelength of fury and disdain.

'Yo, easy lay, did I say you could talk to my friend? You should stick to lines that are written in a script, honey, because at least then there's a chance of someone thinking there's a brain in there. Now get the hell out of here.'

Even Mercedes Dance, rising starlet, knew better than to argue with one of the most influential women in Hollywood.

Jack went on the offence. 'Mirren, for Christ's sake—'

'Get ready,' Mirren told him, cutting him dead. 'I'll be at home. If you're not there in an hour, don't bother coming back. Not ever.'

33.

'Amazing' – Kanye West (ft. Young Jeezy)

The driveway at the Beverly Hilton looked like a luxury car lot as the limos waited in line to discharge their esteemed passengers. The positions of the vehicles reflected the billing status on a movie – the closer to the front, the bigger the star. And the better the car.

This was the same driveway that morphed into the red-carpet area when the hotel hosted the Golden Globes every year. But not tonight.

Tonight, the cream of the movie industry was here to honour Wes Lomax, forty years in the business, still at the top and showing no sign of losing his touch.

Zander watched Sandra Bullock alight from the limo in front of them and pause for the photographers to get their shots. There was a woman who was in his definite top five of beautiful Hollywood women. They'd never worked together, but Wes had just optioned the movie rights of a true story about a couple who had survived a terrorist attack in Kenya and had Zander and Sandra in mind for the leads. Zander was up for it. Sandra's people would be contacted in the next week or two.

Zander popped a couple of paper-thin sheets of breath freshener. Extra strength. Not that he was covering anything. Turning up here wasted would have been such a career-limiting decision that he'd managed to refrain from anything stronger than mouthwash all day.

He'd been drug-tested by the studio yesterday and had breathed a Jack Daniel's-infused sigh of relief when it came back clean. Chloe was still at the clinic, although she was refusing to take his calls. He got it. She was mad as hell, and he would be too. But he knew he'd done the right thing. He had to believe she'd beat this. And when she did, he wanted to show he'd done it too. At least, that was what he kept telling himself in between waves of desperation for a drink. What kind of mentor was he when he still wanted to get wasted almost every minute of the day?

It felt like this was a defining moment. It really was time to clean up his act. He'd got away with it so far, but it wasn't going to last forever. The only way his current path ended was on the same crazy chapter of Hollywood history as Sheen and Sizemore. Or worse, the tragic finale of Cory Monteith or Philip Seymour Hoffman.

Time for change. Time for sobriety.

Time to forget the past, leave the demons behind him and move forward in a straight, balanced, sober line.

'You OK there, Zander?'

Leandro, his usual driver, checked him out in the rear-view mirror. Zander leaned over, slapped his shoulder and slipped him a $100 bill.

'You know it, man. Look, don't hang around here. I'll call you when I'm ready to head home.'

'You sure?'

'It's Saturday night. Can't have you missing the game. You'll get a few hands in if you head home now.'

Leandro's Saturday-night poker with his bowling buddies was a regular fixture back in his neighbourhood of condos at the foot of the Hills.

Zander almost wished he could go with him and swerve the party. The industry stuff wasn't his thing. But tonight was different. Tonight was for Wes Lomax, and he wouldn't miss it for anything.

Shit, he needed a drink. A large one.

Deep breath. Smile. Sobriety. Go.

The flashbulbs went crazy when he stepped onto the red carpet and the predominately female crowd that had formed around the door instantly went from silent to scream.

Zander gave them his trademark grin: square jaw, well-trimmed stubble, perfect white teeth. One hand in his impeccably cut Dolce & Gabbana suit trousers: confident, sexy, with just a hint of bashful. Zander Leith was on.

At the door, a runner, a 20-something 120-pound girl who wouldn't have looked out of place on a Vegas stage with the Pussycat Dolls, held a clipboard and mike in one hand and stretched out her other hand towards him.

'Hi, Mr Leith. I'm Cindy. Let me show you through. Reception drinks are on the International Terrace, and then you're on Mr Lomax's table for dinner in the ballroom.'

'Thanks, Cindy. I'm all yours.'

Cindy rewarded the charm with a flush and a coy smile that made it clear she wasn't averse to that idea.

'And I'm all yours,' she sparred, enjoying the flirtation.

Through on the International Terrace, waiters greeted him with trays of champagne and cranberry juice. He chose the latter, knowing that if he took just one sip of alcohol, it would be on Twitter within seconds. Every member of staff in Hollywood was an aspiring actor, singer, writer, director and they'd do anything to pay the bills, get attention or die trying. To them, it would be a tip-off in exchange for cash or a tweet that made them look like a big-shot in their home town: '@imthenextpacino With Zander Leith and he's on the booze man #PARTEEEEEEEBABEEE'.

To Zander, it would be a shit-storm of publicity that would take days to cancel out with denials and staged shots of him surfing or hanging out at a juice bar. It was all such bullshit, but it was a small price to pay for this life. At least, that's what he told himself when he was sober. In rare moments of drunken clarity, he wasn't so sure.

Everyone who was anyone was here. Wes Lomax's influence and status demanded it. And just for tonight, they'd all pretend that at least three-quarters of the people in the room weren't so twisted with jealousy they'd strangle Lomax in a second for a fraction of what he had.

Shit, he needed a drink.

Zander worked the room. A kiss for Wes's latest girlfriend, an up-and-coming Chinese action star who was famously double-jointed. He shook hands with producers. Nodded to directors. Schmoozed the money guys. Everyone got acknowledged and validated, their egos suitably stroked, while he made sure they could all see that the whole rehab thing was a blip and the movie star was back.

Spotting a few allies, he worked his way over to a group in

the corner. Don Michael Domas, star of *Call Me*, the sitcom that had inherited the *Friends* audience and managed to hold it for the last decade. Lee Vandan, male model, who earned half the rate of the female supermodels but let it pile up in the bank while he lived in a beach shack near Zuma and spent every day on the waves. Josh Wilson, writer, who'd polished the scripts of half the best action movies of the last year and didn't care that he didn't get billing, so his name was barely known outside the hallowed ring fence of Hollywood. All that mattered was that it was on the speed dial of the money guys on the inside.

The three of them cheered and shook hands when Zander rolled up. Always a loner, these were the guys he considered the closest thing to friends. They'd hang out at the beach. Catch a beer. Watch a game. They didn't share their problems or worries, but that worked out just fine for them – that's what $500-an-hour therapists were for.

An old J. Arthur Rank-style gong summoned them through for dinner. Nice touch.

More handshaking as Zander worked his way to the table at the front and centre of the room. Wes was already there and greeted him with open arms.

'You look great, son, really great.'

'Thanks, Wes. Feeling good, man.'

Shit, he needed a drink.

The meal passed in a flurry of camaraderie and bonhomie, the perfect facade of appreciation for a man who'd survived forty years in the most cut-throat industry on earth. Silent clips of his movies ran on a loop against the white wall behind the stage. For Zander, it was like watching a reel of his life. It was an unusual situation, an actor who worked almost exclusively for one studio, but it had been the perfect arrangement for them and Zander had never had any wish to diversify. Wes understood him. Loved him, even. Although, he was under no illusions – even now, Wes would fire his ass if he damaged the bottom line.

When the last of the dessert dishes were removed from the tables, the lights dimmed slightly and the event manager gave Zander a prearranged nod.

As he stood up from the table and made his way towards the stage, the perfectly calibrated sound system gave a burst of the theme tune for the Dunhill movies. The crowd applauded as they all turned to watch the action.

Zander reached the podium, the music faded, and he instinctively took charge of the crowd.

Shit, he really needed a drink.

'Ladies and gentlemen, thank you so much for being here tonight to honour a man who is one of the greatest producers we have ever known, one of the greatest visionaries our industry has ever had, one of the greatest inspirations to a generation of film-makers.'

The mandatory applause was swift and rapturous. There were many more Wes Lomax plaudits that a compère less discreet than Zander could have added. One of the greatest shaggers who ever lived. One of the most ruthless bastards to anyone who ever crossed him. One of the biggest egos that ever swaggered to his place on the Walk of Fame.

But it was Zander who was speaking. So he simply ended with 'A man who is, for me, the greatest friend. Ladies and gentlemen, I give you Wes Lomax.'

Three hours with a Pilates instructor and a quick fuck in the limo on the way there had given Wes the flexibility and energy to bound up the stairs like a man half his age. The two men embraced before Zander returned to his seat, the guests now on their feet giving a standing ovation to Lomax the Conqueror.

Wes thanked the thousand-strong audience, then launched into a monologue that recounted his career in humble yet glorious terms. His speechwriter had done a stellar job after being given the brief: 'I want them to know how fucking brilliant I am without coming off as an asshole.'

As it rolled on and on, Zander tried not to be distracted by the bottle of red wine that sat on the table in front of him. Just one glass. Just one.

'And that brings me to perhaps the most wonderful movies I have ever produced, the Dunhill series.'

More applause.

'And an actor I want to make special mention of here tonight, Zander Leith.'

Suddenly Wes trumped the 1964 Rioja as Zander knew instinctively what was happening. To the outside world, Wes was thanking an actor for a couple of decades of loyal service. The truth was a little more pragmatic. Wes was protecting his investment. He was letting the world know that Zander was still on top. Making sure they all knew that the tarnish of his spell in rehab had been repolished up to a perfect shine that would carry the Dunhill franchise on for many more years.

Zander watched Wes push his preprepared script to one side and switch to improvisation.

'When I met Zander back in 1990, I was of course only sixteen . . .'

The glitterati laughed on cue.

'But even then I knew this guy was something special. The story of how we met has been told a thousand times, but hey . . . indulge me.'

Murmurs of encouragement reached the stage.

'I was golfing in Scotland – man, it rains over there – and I found a script.'

Zander's throat suddenly felt like sandpaper as the memories collided with the desperate need for . . . Shit, he really needed a drink.

It was a struggle to maintain a relaxed demeanour and casual smile when all he really wanted to do was go. Taking the bottle with him.

'A really special script.' Wes was on a roll now.

Zander was sliding into hell. He was back there. Back then.

Davie slid into the booth of the cafe. Opposite Zander, Mirren budged over to give him room.

'Listen, Mirren, I need that stuff you wrote.'

Mirren's guard went up instantly. Face flushed. Fear obvious. 'Why?'

'It doesn't matter. Look, just give me it, OK? I promise it's cool.'

'Have you gone to the police?'

Davie was horrified. 'Don't be so fucking daft. OK, look, there's this guy staying in the hotel. A movie guy. I want to give it to him.'

The noise of Zander slamming the table made everyone turn to look at the three slightly dishevelled teenagers, two of whom had been sat there all morning nursing two cans of Coke – an unusual sight in St Andrews, a city of students who unpacked their clothes, books and Daddy's trust fund when they arrived.

'Fuck off, Davie. Don't be so stupid. I told you, you should have burned that stuff,' Zander hissed to Mirren.

'I was going to, but I . . . I . . .'

'Zander, for Christ's sake, shut it. Leave her alone. Look, mate, I know you don't want to hear this, but we're fucked. What are we gonna do? Stay here forever? We have no money, nowhere to go, and I dunno about you, but I'm fucking sick of living like this.'

Zander couldn't argue with the last point. They'd managed to find casual jobs – Zander and Mirren in bars and Davie in the kitchen of the St Andrews Grand, the most prestigious hotel on the east coast. But even three wages combined was barely enough to cover rent on the bedsit they shared, Mirren in the single bed, Zander and Davie in second-hand sleeping bags on the floor. Food was an occasional luxury, and every-thing else was out of the question.

'No one can see that, Davie. It's way too risky. What if someone realizes . . . ? What if it gets out? When we get back to the flat, I'm getting rid of it. We'll find another way.'

Davie had looked crestfallen as Mirren lifted her eyes from the Coke can and spoke for the first time. 'Zander's right. I shouldn't have shoved it in my backpack. Stupid. Forget about it, Davie.'

Zander had been so furious that he'd missed the look he later realized had been exchanged between them. Mirren was telling Davie where it was. Where to look.

'Aw, fuck youse, then. I need to get back to work.'

But he hadn't. Davie'd gone to the bedsit, got the rough, short draft of a story from Mirren's backpack. Forty thousand words. Not long enough to be a novel, but long enough to tell a story that was horrific to all of them. But Davie knew that to someone else it would be something different. There was an opportunity here. And right now it was the only one they had.

Davie had gone back to the hotel, promised a room-service waitress a date if he let her take the next order to the Lomax room, delivered Wes's blue steaks with a side order of Scottish noir.

It was a stunt that had been tried in a thousand variations, but this time Davie got lucky. When he wheeled the trolley into the room, Wes shouted for his companion to bring his wallet so he could tip the waiter. Davie had almost lost his train of thought as a girl who looked about seventeen, huge tits and totally naked, strutted out of the bedroom.

'Ten dollars or ten minutes with her?' Wes had joked, to a furious glare from the girl.

Later, much later, Davie had told them that Wes had roared with laughter and slapped his own thigh. 'Come sit here, baby, and I'll make it all better.'

Davie was momentarily forgotten as the girl crossed the room and did as she was bid, giving him time to slide the manuscript from under the tablecloth and leave it on the coffee table beside him. Wes never noticed, given that he was already busy sucking the tit of his hostile girlfriend.

Davie never did get the ten quid. But they got a lot more than that.

Zander snapped back to the present, caught up with Wes's abbreviated, edited version of events.

'The minute I read it, I knew it was something special. It took a few days, but when I tracked down the kids behind it, I spotted a young guy who had a shit attitude and nothing to say for himself.'

Zander automatically bowed in deference as the spellbound audience joined in the joke, the glittering masses completely unaware of just how true it was.

'So let me get this straight,' Wes had said a few days later, after a call to the number scribbled on the front of the script had summoned them to his room at the Grand. 'You wrote it, but you three are – what, partners?'

His tone was playful. Mocking.

Mirren had nodded and looked at Zander with eyes that begged him to go along with this. Her desperation had been the only thing that had got him there in the first place. He'd resisted. Raged. Tried to punch out that wee bastard Davie. Until Mirren had stopped him.

'Zander, no! Jesus, what's wrong with you?' Then calmer, 'Zander, I know you don't want to do this. Neither do I. Why would I want to put this out there? But we have nothing else. Davie is right. We have to do it. Please, Zander. For me. Please?'

Now he was standing in front of this American, feeling like he was twelve and trying to suppress the urge to kick the fuck out of the headmaster's desk.

'OK, so here's what I think. I'll go with the whole partnership deal thing. Your writing is something, little lady. How'd you come up with the storyline?'

Mirren hesitated. 'Just . . . dark imagination, I s'pose.'

'Well, honey, I might like to buy me some of that.'

Zander clenched his fists, desperate to deck the patronizing prick.

'And you –' he turned to Davie, '– what you did took some balls. I like that.'

Davie nodded eagerly, desperate to get to the bit where Wes would say something that would remove them from the misery of their existence.

'But you, boy. You're part of this deal too,' he told Zander.

'I'm not. I want nothing to do with it.'

'Would ya listen to this? He wants nothing to do with it,' Wes roared, turning the knob way past patronizing.

Davie and Mirren grimaced uncomfortably as Wes waved his cigar around for dramatic effect.

'OK, well, here's the deal. Acting we can teach. But you are Cal in this script. You're that kid that fought back. You're exactly how I imagine him. I can see it.'

Score one for accuracy, Mr Lomax.

'So the deal is this. You're in or there's no deal. End of story.'

A month later, they were all in Hollywood. Low budget, shot on two cameras, a haunting, harrowing tale of violence that was so authentic it could be replicated on any night in any city across the world. Two and a half years later, they picked up an Oscar for their movie, The Brutal Circle.

Somewhere along the line, Wes took Zander under his wing. Protected him, developed an influence that sat somewhere between boss and benefactor. It had worked for them.

At the time, Zander had been grateful because, quite frankly, it was all he had left after his two best friends had sold him out to the only bidder.

Disloyal bastards.

'We've worked together for twenty years now and, Zander, I owe you my thanks.'

Zander stood, nodded and then raised his hands to applaud the man on the stage. The thousand people around him followed his lead.

They allowed Wes to sum up his speech and clapped him off the stage. Zander hugged him as he passed, then summoned every shred of acting talent he possessed to endure the next hour with gregarious charm. Halfway through, he surreptitiously texted Leandro with instructions to come collect him. As soon as was respectfully allowed, he made the standard Hollywood excuse.

'Gotta go, guys, early call in the morning.'

It wasn't a lie. And it made Wes beam with pleasure. 'Glad you're taking care of yourself, son,' he told him as he shook his hand.

It took another half an hour to work his way back out of the room, pressing flesh and air-kissing where expected and auspiciously wise.

When he made it to the door, he inhaled a lungful of cool Beverly Hills air.

Shit, he really needed a drink.

Leandro drew to a halt in front of him and Zander reached for the door, just as a hand tapped his shoulder.

'Hey, leaving so soon?' Cindy purred.

'Erm, yeah. Early call.' Man, she was beautiful. Zander had a sudden urge to lick Jack Daniel's from every single inch of her body. Slowly. Carefully. With an erection that would take all night to die.

'So, still making the offer that you're all mine?'

Her voice was on the same come-on level as dropping her dress to the floor and lying on the bonnet of the car wearing nothing but heels and a smile.

In a previous life, Zander would have enjoyed the experience. Taken her up on the offer. Every synapse of his brain was now screaming, 'Go on, hurry up, right now. What the hell are you waiting for?'

But . . . man, this was excruciating. It was a one-way street that only ended badly. He knew this. She'd be back at his apartment. They'd party. A threesome with Jack Daniel's and then a few hours later, Hollie would be dragging him into the shower to sober him up and checking he'd used a condom so she didn't have to flag up a paternity risk to the lawyers.

What a mess. What a crap-storm of a mess.

'Sorry, honey, but I really do have to go. I wish I didn't.'

He made it sound like regret, not rejection, then leaned over and kissed her on the cheek. Paps got some shots off, but he wasn't worried. He didn't have his tongue down her throat, and anyway, there was no law against kissing a stunning girl.

She slipped her number in his pocket as she whispered goodbye and then waved as he jumped in the car and drove off.

Inside the vehicle, she was already forgotten.

'All right, Romeo?' To Hollie's amusement, Zander actually jumped.

'What are you doing here? Leandro, dude, I expected better.' His tone was half joking and Leandro replied with a helpless shrug.

'She called me and told me to pick her up on the way. I ain't saying no to her.'

'That's because I sign your cheques, Leandro,' Hollie added, with a wink he caught in his rear-view mirror. 'Just remember that, dude.'

'Oh, I do. Lost bad tonight. Any chance of a raise?'

Hollie responded by raising the barrier that separated the front from the back of the limo, crowding out Leandro's chuckles.

'So what, babysitting me now?' Zander asked her.

'You don't pay me enough to hang out with you,' Hollie said, her smile softening the blow.

'So that means there's a problem.'

'Good-looking *and* smart,' Hollie replied.

'What's up? Another drug test?'

'Yup, but not yours. The super in your building called tonight. Apparently there's a teenager lying on your doorstep sleeping. I pay him a hundred a week to call me before he calls the cops.'

'Good to know.'

Years of acting saved him from giving anything away, but he desperately wanted to punch out someone at that clinic. What the fuck was going on with their security?

'He described her and I'm no Charlie's Angel, but it sounds like Chloe. He said a car service dropped her off. Of course it did. Kid's in rehab, yet she can still summon a car. Gotta love LA.' She sighed. 'Anyway, we're either going to have to take her back to rehab again or to her mother's house. I don't know what shit went down with you two, but, Zander, I really think her family should deal with this. It's not your problem. We can drop her over there. They live in the Colony and I've got the address.

'So what's it to be? Rehab or Mirren McLean? You decide.'

Zander closed his eyes. Gently. So his head didn't hurt even more.

Shit, he really needed a drink.

34.

'Daddy's Gone' – Glasvegas

Glasgow, 1988

The nylon seam on her baby-doll was making her itch and leaving red welts under her arm, but Marilyn wasn't changing it. No way. He'd be here any minute and it was his favourite – baby pink, so sheer you could see her nipples through it – and the little furry knickers matched perfectly. Not that they'd be on long. Three pairs he'd ripped off. Just as well they were only a couple of quid a time or he'd be paying for them. He saw her all right with cash, but that wasn't the point.

Pushing her feet into pink mules, she stood up and checked out the view in the full-length mirror that was stuck onto the teak wardrobe. Not bad for thirty-five. The negligee hid the stretch marks and the few pounds she'd put on over Christmas. Her tits, creamy and huge, spilled over the top, just the way he liked them. The back view was OK too – no landslide on the arse yet.

The top of her dressing table was littered with bottles and jars, and not just to cover the ring marks that had been on this crap piece of furniture when she'd bought it down the charity shop. This wasn't how she'd ever thought she would end up living. Potential. She'd always had potential. There wasn't another girl in school that even came close to looking as good as she did. There was nothing she couldn't have done. London. Hollywood. New York. And men with money were easy to find. All she had to do was hang out at the casino and they'd be round her like flies round shit. Made it all the more stupid that she was the one who got caught out. Some American in the oil industry, swore he'd had the snip. One weekend in the Excelsior Hotel at Glasgow Airport, a couple of hundred quid in her handbag at the end of the night. Not that she'd asked for it. That wasn't her thing. It was a gift. A present for a good time had by all. Nine months later, the second part of the present arrived.

If she'd realized she was pregnant before she was five months along, she would have done something about it, but hey. Too late. It happened. It just shouldn't have happened to her.

A quick spray of Dior Poison between her tits, a slick of lip gloss and she was ready.

Grabbing the pink silk robe from the bed, she headed downstairs, careful not to put her glass heels anywhere near the broken steps. This house was a shithole, but what could she do? Her bloke had been promising to do something about it for years and she knew he would eventually. She knew better than to nag. And besides, when he visited, there wasn't much time for talking. The very thought made her stomach swirl and her clit tingle.

'Do you want something to eat?' Mirren looked at her expectantly, waiting for an answer.

'Nah, I'll get something later.'

Sometimes her honey phoned the takeaway for a special fried rice when they were done shagging. Didn't want to spoil her appetite just in case.

'You sure? I could make something?'

Marilyn took a bottle of lemonade out of the fridge and banged the door shut. 'I said no.'

What was wrong with that girl? There had to have been a mix-up at the hospital. There was no way that kid belonged to her. Look at her, sitting at the kitchen table, all bloody sanctimonious. What a waste it was. If she made a bit of an effort, she wouldn't be bad-looking. Instead, she pulled her hair back, no make-up, and always had her head stuck in a bloody book.

What kind of life was that? The girl was never going to get anywhere unless she smartened up her act and found someone who could take her away from this shit life. And not one of those boys she hung out with. Screw one of them, fine, but always be looking over his shoulder to see if something better was coming up the road.

The girl should just be grateful that her honey looked out for them, bunged them some extra cash every now and then, and one day she knew he'd make good on his promise to give her a different life from this pathetic existence.

The lemonade fizzed as she added the vodka and then took a sip. She didn't drink a lot. Just a wee sundowner to loosen her up a little.

'Mum, I—'

The sound of the front door opening interrupted whatever the girl was about to say. Didn't matter. Her head was already back down in her book by the time Marilyn made it to the door.

Showtime.

She saw his grin widen as he spotted that her nipples had grown hard. That's what he did to her. Giggling, she let him pull her up the stairs, but they didn't even get as far as the bedroom. He bent her over the top stair and tore the pink knickers off her again.

There was a loud bang and for a second she thought it was another stair cracking, but no. It was the banging of the front door. That bloody girl. Off in a mood again. She was going to have to cop on to the fact that no one liked misery. And if she was going to escape it, then there was only one way to do it.

Marilyn McLean smiled and gasped as her honey demonstrated her point.

35.

'Tinseltown In the Rain' – The Blue Nile

OK, so now what? Sitting cross-legged on the bed in her hotel room, notepad out, Sarah logged into her laptop. Tapping into the hotel's Wi-Fi, she launched the internet, then opened the top three celebrity tracking websites. She put Davie, Zander and Mirren's names into all three. Nothing current. The last sighting of Mirren had been days ago. Someone had posted a picture of Zander Leith leaving Wes Lomax's party, and a couple of grainy shots of him in the back seat of a car entering the studio yesterday. And Davie Johnston seemed to spend his life screaming at paparazzi and being abused at Lakers games.

No help at all. Where were they today?

She tried Twitter, Facebook and Instagram, running searches on all three stars. Again, nothing that could help her today, but hell, some girls didn't hold back on the things they were offering to do to Zander Leith. And they didn't hold back on what a douche Davie was either. Douche. Sarah said the word out loud. It wasn't in her usual vernacular, but it certainly made a point.

One of her legs started to go dead, so she shook it out.

Come on, there had to be more than this. There was no way she was coming here and hitting a wall on the first day.

Minibar, water, think.

All she had to do was get in front of one of them and see their face when she asked them about their lives in Glasgow. Repeated requests for interviews had all been knocked back; there was no mention of any press conferences or junkets she could hijack, so she had to come up with another plan.

So far all she had was a vague notion that she could find out their addresses and doorstep them, but there was absolutely no doubt that these three would have impenetrable security in place to stop fans trying the same thing.

Another search, still nothing.

Determined to crack this, she picked up the phone and punched in a direct dial to the one person who might be able to help.

Ed McCallum picked up on the second ring.

'Mighty leader, how are you this evening? No life, so still at the office, I see.'

He laughed. 'I have a life. There's a bag of charlie in front of me and I'm waiting for three hookers I ordered an hour ago.'

'Then I'll call the NHS and tell them to send medical assistance urgently. It'll be too late by the time they get there, but at least you'll die happy and you'll know I tried to help.'

'Bless you. So how's the holiday? Sunning yourself on a lilo?'

'Absolutely.'

'So where are you?'

'Erm, I'm in—' Sarah listened as he interrupted her with

a hacking cough. Twenty Benson & Hedges a day for forty years had left their mark.

She waited till he was done before deciding to change track slightly. 'OK, so before your lungs give up, I need a favour.'

'Shoot.'

'Say I was in . . . oh, I don't know, LA?' she drawled.

The guttural sound he made was somewhere between a laugh and a cough.

'And I wanted some help in tracking down a celebrity. Off the record. Not on company time. Purely out of interest.'

'I understand,' he played along.

'How would I go about that?'

'You wouldn't. You'd get your arse back here and get back to your proper job,' he told her.

'And if I was really stubborn and stuck to the contractually bound eligibility that states I'm allowed some bloody holiday time, would you have any other suggestions?' she teased.

Another cough/laugh. Sounded like he was the one who needed the holiday.

'You would phone the LA press agency we use and tell them that your incredibly magnanimous editor had given you free rein to use them to help you along. Whatever they charge, I'm docking it out of your wages.'

'Thanks, Ed. You're amazing.'

'I know.'

'And if you're still alive after the whole charlie and hooker episode, I'll bring you back a present. Want a Hollywood sign for your desk?'

'Don't know how I've managed to survive without one,' he told her brusquely, before hanging up.

Sarah punched the air, then sourced the telephone number for the bureau and called. Someone called Gemma answered.

'Hi, Gemma. This is Sarah McKenzie from the *Daily Scot*. I'm looking for a little help. I'm trying to set up interviews with Zander Leith, Davie Johnston or Mirren McLean . . .'

'They won't see you. They're all on lockdown. Nothing until the next round of junkets.'

'Yes, I get that. But look, do you have any visibility of where they'll be, where they hang out? I just want to get in front of one of them.'

Gemma sounded entirely bored on the other end of the line. 'OK, hang on, what did you say your name was? Sarah McKenzie?'

'Yep, from the *Daily Scot*.'

'OK, I'll just need to call them and verify. Hang on.'

Sarah was left on hold for what seemed like ages. She was on the point of hanging up when Gemma came back on the line.

'OK, Mr McCallum said we're good to go and no expense spared.'

Sarah's fist clenched as she mouthed a silent 'Yes!' followed by, 'That's what I like to hear.'

The open chequebook had obviously piqued Gemma's interest too. 'Is this, like, something big you're working on?'

It was the obvious question. There was no way they'd want to miss anything worthwhile on any of these three.

'Nope, just background stuff. I want to talk to them for a

tourism campaign we're launching back home. You know, home-grown Scottish stars, big profile over here . . .'

Sarah could practically hear Gemma yawning. 'Cool. OK, so let me see . . .'

Tapping of keyboard keys ensued.

'Nothing in the pipeline for Mirren McLean. She's in pre-production on the next movie about that Scottish dude. No engagements. Her kid is in rehab, though, so you might get lucky there. Life Reborn in Malibu.'

Sarah already knew that. Nothing she'd been told yet was new – all of it freely available on the internet.

'Zander Leith . . . man, he's hot. OK, again, in production. Nothing released about his schedule. But I know he surfs at Venice and Zuma. You any good with a board?'

'Only if it's ironing.'

Gemma didn't get the joke and Sarah's hopes were diminishing by the second. She was actually going to have to get out there and physically hunt them down.

'And Davie Johnston, OK, so he's got his thing tonight.'

'His thing?'

'Yeah, some anniversary thing with Jenny Rico. Can't believe she's married to him. Thought he was cute, but turns out he's a real d—'

'Douche, yeah, I heard,' Sarah replied. She totally belonged here. Totally.

'Let me look at the release that came in from his PR. OK, so, like, here's what's happening. According to this, like, totally lame crap, "Despite his recent troubles, Mr Johnston and his wife are fully supporting each other and he's so happy to be celebrating the landmark event with his wife and closest friends at Soho House on Saturday evening." That's, like, tonight.'

Sarah's elation dipped. 'That's members only, isn't it?'

'Yeah.'

'OK, so, Gemma, I'd really, really like to get in there tonight. Is there a way to make it happen?'

A hesitation, then a slightly reluctant 'I'm a member, so I can sign you in, but I'd, like, totally have to be out of there by eight. You're on the drinks and I like champagne.'

'Done!'

'OK, I'll meet ya at reception at seven.'

'Gemma, I think I love you.'

'Yeah, I love me too,' the other reporter laughed.

At seven thirty, Sarah was beginning to get nervous. No Gemma. It happened. How many times had she cancelled plans because she got called out on a story or caught up on something in the office? Adrenalin and optimism were making her heart race just a little faster than normal. OK, a lot faster.

'Heyyyyyyy!'

Success. It could only be Gemma from the LA bureau. Grinning, and trying not to make it obvious that she was totally scoping out the new arrival, Sarah scanned her from head to toe. Long blonde hair extensions, 120 pounds, perfect nose, perfect teeth, incredible make-up and dressed like she was about to go to the VIP box at a rock concert. Impossibly tight pencil skirt, a killer silver chainmail top, bangles all the way up one arm and a Chanel bag. This was seriously high maintenance for, let's face it, a day at the office. Even if the office was an exclusive LA club frequented by people she normally only watched while munching overpriced popcorn at the cinema.

Sarah followed Gemma into the elevator which took them skyward, to a room with the most breathtaking view Sarah had ever encountered.

At the bar, they both ordered champagne, and as she handed over her credit card, Sarah said a silent prayer that the bill would be less than the cost of the flight over.

'OK, so I totally can't stay long,' Gemma told her, all the while her eyes fleeting across the room, checking out faces. There was obviously nothing that grabbed her attention because her gaze returned to Sarah. 'So, a tourism thing, right? That's, like, awesome.'

Sarah nodded, suppressing the urge to bite. Curing cancer was awesome. Space travel was awesome. Her lie? Not even on the awesome scale.

'You working on anything exciting just now?' Change the subject, act friendly but clueless. She didn't want Gemma getting any kind of a whiff of a story.

'Yeah, that's totally why I need to head off. I'm on this, like, really cool human-interest thing. Have you heard of Pete Barry?'

Sarah nodded. He was an action star. Did martial-arts films where the bad guys always had prison tattoos and the good guys only killed twenty people an hour in the name of justice. He'd married a former child star just after her sixteenth birthday, with the permission of her mother, of course. They all belonged to some religious cult with a head office on a ship that was parked off the Californian coast.

'Yeah, apparently the wackos have given them a baby as a wedding gift. Weird, huh?'

No, not really, Sarah wanted to say. Compared to, like, aliens landing. Or superheroes. Or the fact that last week she was trudging through the wet streets of Glasgow and now she was sitting in an exclusive club on Sunset Boulevard attempting to stalk an A-list star. Not weird at all.

'So, like, anyway, I have to go.' Gemma was up off her chair and did a whole huggy air-kiss thing.

Sarah experienced an unfamiliar palpitation of panic. She was going to be left here? She covered it up with a brilliant smile and an attempt at confidence.

'Oh. Right. Well, let's hope he shows up.'

Gemma looked perplexed. 'He'll show, don't worry. Give it an hour or so and he'll be here.'

An hour. As soon as Gemma was out of sight, she turned to the barman. 'Hey, can I have a Diet Coke, please?'

In an hour she would be face to face with Davie Johnston and she was going to have to be sharp, because there was only going to be one winner.

36.

'Stay' – Rihanna (ft. Mikky Ekko)

'Hey, are you ready?'

Jenny was leaning against the door frame, the halogen lights in his personal closet-cum-chill room bouncing off the sequins on her silver Marchesa one-shoulder sheath. He swung round in the leather chair, struck by the contradictions in this scene.

This room contained three walls of designer clothes, a state-of-the-art computer system, a marble bath that had been imported in one piece from a quarry in Italy. In total, that lot cost more than most people made in a lifetime, the stuff dreams were made of.

In the doorway, one of the most beautiful women in the world, his wife, a gorgeous, funny, warm star who was both smart and successful.

He was about to go to a party, a celebration of ten years of marriage that appeared to the outside world to be a true love match.

When he was a kid growing up in Glasgow, he'd have given anything to have this life. Anything at all. He had more than he could ever wish for – except happiness. He had everything, including, he realized, a large dose of self-pity, but he was utterly miserable. Scared. Anxious. This was different from the old days, even the darkest ones, when it seemed like life had gone to shit, because at least then he had optimism. Or maybe it was hope. Either way, being at rock bottom was a whole lot easier when he had nothing to lose.

Now it could be everything. The career. The family. And if the reporter who had been up harassing his mother didn't give up, he could lose – what, his liberty?

He got up and grabbed his jacket from the hanger on the front of one of the mirrored panels that allowed him to check out his appearance in 360 degrees. The last few weeks of worry, combined with skipping his normal muscle-building regime, had left him looking even trimmer than usual. It suited him. In fact, he'd never looked better. Yep, irony was the gift that just kept on giving.

Engine running, the limo was waiting for them in their huge circular drive, its gleaming bodywork illuminated by the beauty of the fountain that shot jets of water and rays of white light into the night sky.

Davie had long since stopped noticing it.

They climbed into the car, and Jenny automatically reached for the bottle of Dom Pérignon Rosé 2002 – always her drink of choice.

'Soho House, Mr Johnston?' the driver checked.

'Indeed.'

The private members' club had been the obvious venue for tonight's celebration. Over on Sunset Boulevard in West Hollywood, it was like a tiny British colony in LA, a crowd of UK talent, writers and industry insiders. The only downside was that a reciprocal arrangement with the media haven Soho House in London made it a bit of a regular haunt with British journos, but they knew that inside the club they had to keep it discreet and off the record.

Glass in hand, he turned to her.

'Cheers,' he said. 'Ten years.'

She returned the gesture. 'Cheers.'

After they had both taken a long sip. Davie placed his glass on the top shelf of the inbuilt minibar.

'And I know our actual anniversary isn't until Thursday, but I wanted to give you this tonight.' From the hip pocket of his jacket he pulled a small navy leather box, with an instantly recognizable crest on the front. Jenny let out an audible whistle.

'So far I like,' she told him. Harry Winston even topped Dom Pérignon on her list of favourite brands.

The box opened like window shutters, both sides folding back to reveal a blue suede interior. Nestled in the middle was a stunning circle of diamonds.

'It's an eternity ring.'

'I see that,' she purred, as he slid it onto the third finger of her left hand, where it nestled like it had always belonged beside her engagement ring and wedding ring. So it should. He'd had it designed to complement the other two. The inch between Jenny's knuckles was now some of the most impressive real estate in Beverly Hills.

'Until a few weeks ago I'd have said it hadn't been a bad ride,' he told her, holding her gaze as he leaned his head back against the cream leather upholstery. 'But I guess the last couple of weeks have blown that theory.'

She didn't reply. He took that as encouragement to go on. 'We'll get through this, though, Jenny. It's just a bad patch. We'll get past it.'

Perhaps some of that teenage optimism was still in there after all. Maybe this was the wake-up call they needed. Perhaps they could get their marriage back on track, ditch the lesbian lover, reconnect with the kids. Maybe in the long term he'd look back on this as a pivotal point in his life, when he realized he was on the wrong path and the gods of karma gave him a nudge back in the right direction.

'Davie, are you on crack?'

Her forehead muscles that still had the power of movement puckered very slightly in the middle, his only clue that she didn't agree.

'We haven't got a chance. Nothing. It's over for us.'

An involuntary choking cough prevented him from answering for a few moments. 'So what the fuck are we doing here, then? We're on our way to celebrate our tenth anniversary, for Christ's sake.'

'Yeah, because it's been arranged for months and I'm not cancelling because I don't want it to look like I'm a disloyal jerk who is deserting you when the chips are down.'

'So tonight is – what, pity?' he raged.

'If that's how you want to see it, then, yeah.' She sat back, almost wearily taking another sip of her champagne. 'Come on, Davie, we're not going to ride off into the sunset together and we both know it.'

'What about the kids? Don't you owe it to them to give us another shot?'

The palms of her hands curved into a fist as the brow re-furrowed. 'Don't you dare play the kids card.'

Davie bristled as her tone lowered to something resembling deadly. 'Tell me anything about them. Anything. Favourite colour. Best friends. Favourite movie. Anything at all.'

It was a cheap shot but effective.

'I love them,' he offered weakly.

'You love no one, Davie. Not even yourself.'

Wow. Just wow. That one got him right in the solar plexus. Speech eluded him. Thankfully, the outburst seemed to have deflated Jenny's fury.

'Look, Davie, I'm not abandoning you,' she said, conciliatory now. 'I'm going to stick by you, carry on the way we've been until you decide otherwise. I'm here for you now and will be for as long as you need me. We're still family and nothing is going to change that, OK?'

Maybe he'd done something right after all to evoke such fierce loyalty. Just a shame that right now it was tussling for supremacy with sadness and regret. He should have tried harder to make it work. Made different decisions. Pulled it back. Despite what she said, maybe there was a glimmer of hope. Just a glimmer. An uncharitable thought flashed through his mind and he instantly batted it away. If it got out that he'd returned the ring, the gossip columns would kill him.

An eye-squeezing pain behind his forehead thudded as they drew up at their destination, entering the underground car park of Soho House. It was one of the perks of the establishment. A private entrance, no paps. However, that didn't stop him automatically playing the part that he'd crafted and maintained for the last decade.

'Stay where you are, mate. I've got this,' he told the driver, before stepping out of his side of the car and going round to open the door for his wife.

Jenny took his hand, then unfurled her breathtaking body until she stood beside him. They moved into the reception area, then took the elevator to the penthouse, a stunning space, decorated in a classic vintage style, with a 360-degree view of Los Angeles.

As the doors opened, Jenny turned her Julia Roberts smile on full beam for the waiting photographer. They'd agreed to let US Weekly get ten minutes of access for $50,000, as long as the images didn't look staged and the Johnstons were given full photo approval.

Camera and phone use was prohibited in Soho House, so they were confident that these would be the only images to hit the public domain.

Carla, the event planner whom Jenny used for everything from a picnic to a black-tie charity ball, joined them and walked them through to the private dining area. As they entered, suitably late, everyone was already seated, but they put down their glasses of Ruinart Blanc de Blancs, rose to their feet and clapped them through. It had been planned a small affair. Intimate. Thirty of their closest friends and one lesbian lover.

At the top of the table, they kissed, sending the applause volume up a notch. Davie held the gold velvet chair out for Jenny to sit, then headed to the matching chair at the other end of the long, polished mahogany table.

It was almost medieval in its symbolism. The king and queen at either end of the table, and in the middle, the lackeys and jesters. And, he noted, not a single noble knight in attendance. Fuckers. The hairs on the back of his neck began to tremble as he scanned the faces along either side of the table. His agent, Al, of course, with his twenty-five-year-old wife, Mel, a razor-sharp scriptwriter whose satirical comedy about internet dating, *Click Me Up*, was killing it in the ratings. There was no doubt she'd used Al to break into the business, but to her credit, her talent was keeping her there.

There were Jenny's co-stars, her director, producer, friends. On his side? No one was there. The stars of his reality shows hadn't shown. He'd made every one of those assholes and yet they weren't here. The judging panel from *American Stars*, all of them on $5 million a season, hadn't forked out the cost of a limo and a gift he didn't need and come along to celebrate his fucked-up happiness. He'd worked with them for almost fifteen years. Now he'd been cut from the show, they'd developed amnesia. The seats that should be occupied by names that beamed into the nation's living rooms every week were taken by suits he only recognized because somewhere along the line he'd added them to his payroll. Three corporate lawyers from CSA. Greer Ness, his personal lawyer, and his wife, Tanya. Jesus Christ, even Al's secretary was there.

The pain in his head was working its way south to his chest now, squeezing it, making sweat pop from his pores as the act of breathing stopped being an automatic function.

No one was here. No one who mattered.

The waiter, who looked like he'd stepped out of an Abercrombie & Fitch ad, responded to his signal instantly.

'A large Macallan and ice.'

'Coming right up, Mr Johnston.'

Was it his imagination or did even that come over like a sneer?

As soon as the drink arrived, he downed it in one go and asked for another, ignoring the wary, uncomfortable glances of those around him. What did they matter anyway? Booze had never been his thing, but that one was for medicinal purposes. His heart rate slowed a little. The sweating stopped. Tonight was a show and he just had to get to the final curtain. He raised his hand and ordered a repeat prescription.

The waiter got the message and kept them coming through the meal. By the time dessert was served, Davie was wondering why he didn't drink more. All those years of treating his body like a temple didn't give him the buzz he was getting right at this minute.

The marketing genius that lived in his soul immediately summed it up. Whisky. Makes the world seem like a better place when it's all gone to crap.

The thought made him laugh, freaking out the guests at his end of the table even more. These jerks were on his payroll and yet they were looking at their watches, wondering when they could get away with leaving.

'Ladies and gentlemen, I'd like to say a few words.' At the popular end of the table, Darcy Jay was on her feet, one hand on Jenny's arm and a glass of champagne in the other.

'Really? You think?' Davie asked, instantly inciting glares of scorn from Al and Jenny, and one of defiance from Darcy.

'OK, go ahead. Everyone, please give your attention to my wife's . . .' He paused and everyone in the room stopped breathing. This was Hollywood. Every single person there probably knew the truth, yet he'd be a pariah if he said it out loud. Long live the act of pretending. '. . . best friend.'

Every other pair of shoulders in the room relaxed just a little.

'Thank you, Davie.' Darcy smiled sweetly at him, before looking around at the other faces there. 'Thank you all for coming. I'd just like to thank Jenny and Davie for inviting us all here tonight to share their joy.'

Murmurs of approval and a handclap from one of the more eager-looking guests. It took Davie a moment to place him. He wanted to rest his head on the table when he realized it was Cyril, his business manager. Oh dear God, they'd been so stuck for invitees that his accountant was here. This had better be tax-deductible.

'I've known them both for many years now and I can honestly say that they're the most special couple I've ever met: warm, loving, incredible –' Darcy was speaking in plural, but looking only at Jenny, '– and they deserve a lifetime of happiness and the kind of love that only a true soulmate can bring.'

She was still looking at Jenny. Jesus, she'd be as well sinking to her knees and screwing her right there in front of everyone.

As the guests clapped, Davie muttered, 'Another Macallan, please,' and got to his feet.

'Darcy, thank you. Your con-con-contribution to our marriage can never be underestimated.' The slight slurring added a subtle hint of menace, sending every pair of shoulders back to the standard position for acute apprehension.

'I'd just like to say thank you all for coming. Welcome to this surprisingly *unstarry* occasion. But how lovely to see so many people who've come here all the way from my payroll.'

Silence.

'Oops, British humour, American silence. Tough room.'

They still didn't laugh.

A sudden realization hit him as he swayed unsteadily on his feet. They wanted him to fuck up. He could tell. Not one person in this room gave a toss about him. They were waiting for him to fail, to hand the win to Darcy, to call timeout and give up.

Well, he wasn't going to. No way.

He looked at Jenny and he knew that he wanted her. Had to keep her. Couldn't make it easy for her to go. She'd loved him once – he really believed that. If he was losing his dignity, his career and his life, he was gonna fight to keep her. She hadn't left him. She was here tonight. She had his back. That was all stuff they could build on, right? They weren't like some celebrity couples, banking on two C-listers making one A-lister. They were both stars, even if his shine was a little tarnished at the moment.

'And I just wanted to say one thing. Jenny, like everyone else, we've had our . . . *differences* over the course of our lives together. But I love you, baby. And I'm going to do everything in my power to make sure that we're back here in ten years' time, celebrating our twentieth anniversary. In Hollywood years, that's, like, a century. Over the last two decades I've produced some of the biggest hits on TV. But my proudest productions are my co-productions with you – our gorgeous children. They mean the world to me. And let me tell you, and everyone here, that nothing – and I mean *nothing* – is ever going to come between us. Forever, baby. Ten years, eight letters, three words. I love you.'

He raised his glass and the rest of the room followed, all pretending not to think they'd just listened to the biggest pile of reality-show-level crap, all aware that the devoted wife's beaming grin stopped before reaching her eyes.

This was a power play, and fuelled by Macallan, he was under the delusion that he was up on the scoreboard.

After dinner, Al and Mel were the first to leave, Al shaking his hand and leaning towards him to envelop him in a hug.

To an observer, it looked like a gesture of love and friendship. Thankfully no one was close enough to hear the parting shot Al whispered in Davie's ear.

'Go home, Davie – before you give me another fuck-up to deal with.'

'No worries, Al. No worries. Everything under control.'

The trickle became a tsunami that cleared the room in what seemed like no more than a few moments, until just he, Jenny and Darcy remained.

'Good speech, Davie,' Darcy told him.

'You mean that?'

'No.'

He smiled at the predictability of it.

'I'm gonna get my wife back.'

Jenny's irritation was all over her beautiful face. 'You know I'm right here? Listening to you? You're a mess, Davie. Go home. The kids are at Darcy's with a sitter. Not that you'd know that. We're gonna go back and hang there tonight.'

'Ooooooooh, cosy.' OK, so granted he was being a little

juvenile, but hell, he had to have some fun tonight. After all, he wouldn't get change out of $30,000.

'Another Macallan, please,' he shouted to no one in particular.

Jenny couldn't hide her disgust as she strutted past him. 'You're a fuck-up, Davie. And you're lucky I'm sticking around. Go home. I'll send the car back for you.'

'Yep, I'm a lucky guy,' he agreed, to the sound of the door closing.

Hauling himself to his feet, he pushed away the empty Macallan glass, grabbed three partially full glasses of champagne, emptied them into one glass and wandered through to the bar area.

It was pretty quiet. Just a few bodies at a couple of tables. No one stayed out late in Hollywood unless they were hustling, on the clock or falling off the wagon. Anyone who was working had an early call time in the morning, and the rest were in AA, NA or GA and knew that the later they were out, the more chance they had of surrendering to whatever vice claimed them.

He climbed onto a stool and ordered a drink, just as a thud on his back sent him reeling forward, almost giving him a spontaneous nose job without the comfort of anaesthetic.

'What the . . . ?'

'Davie, you're getting slow.'

The voice came from Greer Ness, the head of the law firm that had looked after Davie's interests since he was a fledgling star clutching an Oscar that was way out of his league.

Greer was the epitome of the term 'Masters of the

Universe'. Early sixties, distinguished grey hair, impeccably cut and swept back, a torso that came with the shoulders of a linebacker, courtesy of a lifetime of working out and the complement of good tailoring.

'Not slow, just generous. Don't wanna make an old man feel bad.'

Greer laughed. But of course he would. A lot of money over a lot of years earned a few notches on the sycophant scale, even for a lawyer of Greer's standing. Several Macallans didn't obscure the sad truth that if Davie's life was going tits-up, the one person who would benefit would be the guy with the broad shoulders who would take his generous cut while attempting to minimize the damage.

'You OK, buddy?'

'Dandy. Drink?'

'No, you're fine. The car's waiting.'

'Am I being billed for it?'

'You are.'

As Greer grinned, Davie realized that if he squinted, Greer looked like the better-built brother of Michael Douglas. The thought, as well as the conversation, amused him.

'Then make it quick.'

'Jenny.'

'My wife.'

'Correct. Glad you're up to speed. There's a problem.'

'The fact that she's probably right now sitting on the face of another chick?'

'If only that was the only problem,' Greer said, his demeanour solemn for the first time.

'OK, I'll play along. What could be worse than that right now?'

'She's divorcing you, Davie.'

Well, there was a statement to end the banter.

'What? No way. She's not, man. I don't know where you're getting your information from, but you're wrong. Look, we're not perfect and there's a few issues, but she told me tonight she's sticking around.'

'She isn't, Davie. My source is impeccable. She's serving papers on Friday.'

For a moment the information stunned him into silence, until the confusion won out.

'Friday? But why . . . ?'

'Because your actual anniversary falls on Thursday.'

The realization was brutal. How could he not have realized? Ten years. California divorce laws aside, their prenup was on a sliding scale, ultimately allocating her $10 million should their marriage last more than 10 years. It made no differentiation if it was twenty-five years or ten years and one day.

She was playing him for money. Well, hello, New Low Point.

'I'm sorry for bringing this to you now, buddy, but I just got a call with a heads-up and we don't have time to waste here. What do you want me to do, Davie?'

Davie drained the glass and set it on the bar. 'File on Wednesday. Late. So she doesn't find out until Thursday.'

'You sure?'

'I'm sure.'

'It's done. You gonna be OK here? I can drop you or call you a cab?'

Davie shook his head. Right now, the last place he wanted to go was home. Top of his to-do list, he decided, was to head to the Sunset Marquis, call a number he knew on the way there and then spend the night with the six accommodating but expensive women who would be waiting there for him. He might even charge the bill to that bitch Darcy.

'A gin and tonic, please.'

For a moment the voice flitted around in his brain before Davie realized what was unusual about it. Glasgow. Shit, how many drinks had he put away?

He glanced to his right to see the owner of the voice claim the seat at the end of the bar.

'Hey. There's an accent I haven't heard for a long time. Glasgow, right?'

Many years in LA had given his voice a transatlantic twang, but suddenly his accent transformed to pure west coast Scotland.

'Yep. I'm originally from Ayr, but I moved to Glasgow a few years ago,' she replied, flicking back one sleek sheet of auburn hair.

'Well, of all the bars . . .' Corny, but hey, he was a half-wasted, soon-to-be-divorced, hot mess.

As the barman placed her drink in front of her, she thanked him, then took a sip, making no effort whatsoever to continue the conversation.

He liked that. Even in his current category of holy fuck-up, a girl on her own in a bar at night would normally be giving him her best come-on. Not a hooker, then. No wedding ring, so not waiting for her husband. And she was wearing black tailored trousers, stiletto ankle boots and a green shirt, buttoned above the tits. Too conservatively dressed to be on reality TV.

'Where in Glasgow?'

'City centre. Park Circus.'

Davie remembered it. On the couple of times he'd been back to Glasgow in the early days, he'd stayed in the new Hilton, right on the edge of the M8 motorway, looking over to the west of the city and the Park area, famed for its stunning crescents of nineteenth-century townhouses. Back then, that was where the power people lived: lawyers, politicians, people who were successful in theatre and arts. He presumed that hadn't changed much, despite the fact that this chick didn't obviously fit into any of those categories.

'So what are you doing in LA?'

She shrugged. 'Just, ugh, boring stuff. Work. Don't remind me.'

'OK, well, I won't remind you about work if you don't remind me that I'm having a shit day. So, pleased to meet you, Park Circus.' He leaned towards her, battling to keep his balance. 'I'm Davie.'

Her smile was real cute as she returned the introduction. 'I'm Sarah. Pleased to meet you.'

37.

'Every Breath You Take' – the Police

Mirren watched her sleeping girl, watched the rise and fall of her chest, watched her eyes twitch as a dream or a nightmare took control of her reflexes.

Chloe's hair felt soft and silky to the touch as Mirren stroked it back from her face. When Chloe was a little girl, Mirren would come home late from work and sit on her bed, sometimes for hours, just listening to her breathe. How had she gone from that angelic little creature to this angry young woman who created such chaos and pain? When exactly had Mirren lost her baby and gained an addict? And why had Chloe decided that the person she hated most on this earth was her mother?

Night after sleepless night told her that there were too many answers. And none that had an easy fix. The rebellion had started in Chloe's early teens, with demands for sleepovers, late nights, money and an eighteen-year-old boyfriend who was given too much freedom, too much money and too much access to everything LA had to offer.

And then Jordan Lang had come along, that piece of scum

who'd inherited his father's drive and used it for nothing but getting hooked up and high.

Even before she'd taken care of that situation, Chloe's obsession with him had worried her.

She'd seen it before. The waiting by the phone for him to ring. The jumping to attention when he demanded it. The submission to his every whim and demand. He clicked his fingers, Chloe jumped. And Mirren wasn't going to let that continue. Her daughter was better than that. Way, way better.

She'd had to find a way to stop it and she had. Any mother would have done what she'd done, wouldn't they? Wouldn't they?

Chloe stirred, shivered, and Mirren pulled her thick cashmere blanket up a little higher and tucked it around her daughter's shoulders.

Keeping her here had been the right thing to do. She owed whoever had sent Chloe home a sincere thank you. The limo driver had drawn up to the gates of the Colony, asked security to alert Mirren and then handed over her daughter without waiting to make formal introductions. Whoever was behind it had her gratitude. She also owed Judge Hamilton a huge thanks for taking the time to hear her lawyers' appeal in private, and giving them a seventy-two-hour reprieve before taking her back to Life Reborn.

Not that much progress had been made since she came home. Chloe had been alternating between sleeping and screaming since she got here, and the doctor and nurse that Mirren had installed in the next room were struggling to get any kind of balance or clarity. But at least Mirren knew where she was, knew that she didn't have to worry about her fleeing the clinic and ending up stoned, jailed or worse.

How many times were they going to go through this? And how many times was Mirren going to wonder at the irony that she could buy almost anything on earth that she wanted, use her power, influence and cash to make almost anything happen, but she couldn't fix her daughter?

When she left Chloe's room, she knocked on the next door, alerting the nurse that she was leaving. My God, how things changed. She'd grown up in a tiny terraced house that was the same square footage as her closet, yet her daughter was growing up in a home where she had her own self-contained wing, with a small kitchen, lounge and two guest rooms, which currently hosted medical professionals called in to look after the eighteen-year-old who had everything but a contented soul.

Mirren's bare feet padded against the marble floor as she headed for the kitchen. There, she put the kettle on the stove and prepared a teapot. It was a habit from her youth that had never died. A pot of tea, two teabags, left to stew until it was just the right colour, before being poured and then diluted with milk. None of this herbal tea nonsense.

The only concession she made was that she no longer took two sugars. She'd learned when she arrived here that sugar was on the toxicity horror list somewhere between crack and high-grade plutonium.

Her drink was fully prepared before she even acknowledged Jack, sitting at the table in the corner of the room. The kitchen turret had been a feature she'd added on after they bought the house from the estate of a writer who had made his money in the early studio days and invested it in the early 1940s, when he bought a plot owned by Rhoda May Rindge, who was reluctantly selling off land along her magnificent beachfront. Decades later, Mirren liked to think it had brought him comfort, when he died alone but happy, sitting on a chair on his deck, looking out over the ocean.

If that bore no resemblance to the reality of how it happened, she didn't want to know.

'Hey,' she said, sliding into one end of the huge semi-circular booth.

'Hey. How is she?'

'Sleeping.'

Jack looked like he should be doing the same. His pallor was grey, and there were thick black circles under his eyes. His pale blue T-shirt was an old one Mirren recognized from his days playing football in the garden with Logan. The thought made her smile, even though their silence went on for just a few moments past comfortable.

'Have you found out how she got home yet?'

Mirren shook her head. 'No. The car service wouldn't say who hired them. And she was so wasted, I doubt if *she* even knows. Does it matter?'

Jack contemplated the bottle of vitamin water in front of him. He'd started drinking that just a few months ago. Around the same time as the trendy clothes crept in and the manscaping started, all of it deodorized by a strong whiff of Eau de Midlife Crisis.

'Guess not. Just want to make sure she didn't come to any harm. Y'know . . .'

The pain was etched all over his face and suddenly Mirren

had an inkling as to what was going on with him. It was all too much. All of it. The wife who was working long hours making movies, the son who became an overnight sensation and was now on the road for most of the year, but most of all, the daughter whom he couldn't help, the one who was putting herself in danger and rebelling against them with such ferocity it split her heart in two. Chloe had always been Jack's little girl, the princess who would run to him the moment he came home, whose face lit up when he entered the room. The last time he saw her, she spat in his face.

The leap from being deserted by a young adult he adored to having an affair with a young woman of almost the same age wasn't one that required a stunt team. A psychologist would have a field day with him. Lou would tell her it was all shit, but Mirren couldn't help feeling there was something to it.

And now, as he sat there looking haunted by guilt and fear, her heart melted just a little. He wasn't the type of guy to cope with this kind of emotional trauma. How long had he been falling apart, and why had she never noticed?

She reached out and put her hand over his.

'It'll be OK, Jack. We'll keep getting her the help that she needs and sooner or later it'll sink in.'

'Do you think so?'

'All we can do is hope.'

'And what about us, Mir? Any hope left for us?'

She took a moment to answer, determined not to seem glib or insincere.

'I think so. I think there has to be.'

'I'm so sorry. You know that, don't you?'

It seemed uncharitable to point out that he hadn't looked particularly repentant when his girlfriend was straddling him in a bath only a few nights ago.

He moved over to her side of the cream leather booth and lifted his hand to the side of her face, traced a line down her cheek with his index finger. Mirren fought an almost overwhelming urge to slap it away. She didn't want him touching her, feeling her, putting hands on her after they'd been . . .

She shuddered.

'It's OK, honey. I'm sorry. I'm so sorry, Mir. Forgive me. Please forgive me.'

He'd pulled her head towards his chest and he was stroking her hair, whispering her name.

A hand cupped under her chin and raised her lips to his and he kissed her: soft, tender, like she was made of glass and he was terrified that she would break.

She desperately wanted to pull away, but wasn't this a test? Hadn't she told him to come home, to try to make it work? If she was going to keep punishing him, this would never work. She had to try. Had to find a way to move on.

'I want you, baby. Oh God, Mirren, I need you.'

Is that what he said to *her*? Did he whisper that before he fucked her? Before Mercedes took his dick in her mouth?

He stood up and pulled her towards him, then lifted her up so that her legs went round his waist like they'd done a thousand times before. They moved as one to the island in the middle of the room. There, he sat her on the edge of the marble.

'The door, Jack, lock the door.'

In two strides he'd done as she asked, and then he was back, gently pushing her body backwards until she was lying against the cold stone, then easing down her yoga pants.

'You are so fucking beautiful.'

Mirren squeezed her eyes tight shut, blocking out the voice, forcing her mind to take her somewhere else.

Still gently, slowly, he pushed her legs apart and then went down, placing butterfly kisses along the inside of her thighs, licking, teasing, until the urge to fight left her and she started to welcome the sensation.

His tongue flicked against her clit, then pulled back to circle it, then flick, then circle . . . His hands kneading her inner thighs now, while hers went under her vest until they reached her nipples and she replicated the movements down below.

God, she'd missed this. Missed the feeling of lips, skin, of being turned on . . . but this was different. She didn't want to do this with him.

With one last moment of suction on her clitoris, Jack pulled back, and she squinted her eyes open to see him stretch up and undo his zip.

The urge to resist was back now, excruciating dread at the thought of his cock going inside her, the same cock that had entered someone else only a few days ago. She couldn't. Just couldn't. She didn't want it near her, not touching her, not spilling its juices into her body. The thought repulsed her, fighting with the delicious sensations that still lingered.

'No, Jack,' she whispered. 'Not tonight. Not that.'

His horrified expression told her that he instantly got it, yet the dick in his hand remained hard and uncompromising.

She couldn't do this. She couldn't. It wasn't the right time.

But if she didn't, what would happen? Would he leave? Go back to Mercedes? Leave her children to deal with a divorce? Hadn't Chloe already been through enough?

And yet . . .

She couldn't even contemplate making love. Right now, it was gone. Dead. But she had to try, had to make him think she was into him, could be his wife again. In every way.

There was only one way to do this. It couldn't be Jack. Had to be someone else.

And there had only ever been one other.

Suddenly her body was here, but her head was somewhere else. With someone else.

'Watch me, Jack. Watch . . .'

Again, he understood. It was a game they used to play when they were younger, after Logan, when they hadn't got around to sorting out birth control but wanted to be careful not to add a new addition to the family.

Jack took a step back, his hand undulating now, pulling his cock, the end of it engorged and desperate to get to work.

Eyes still closed, Mirren felt between her legs, her fingertips moving past the narrow strip of pubic hair, slipping inside, finding the nub that had already been teased and tenderized.

She began to massage it, her muscles responding by sending bolts of tingling tightness to her ass and stomach.

She heard a groan as Jack, standing a foot or so back, watched every stroke, listened to every moan, his jerking becoming faster now, more demanding.

Closing her eyes for the last time, Mirren concentrated on her own pleasure, on her body, on the feeling, on the scene that was in her head, the voice that went with it, the one that wasn't quite real but was saying everything she wanted to hear. The voice from more than twenty years ago.

'*You're beautiful. Gorgeous. Incredible. I've waited for this for so long. So, so long.*'

He was looking at her now with eyes that pierced her heart, making it race, making her nipples even harder and kicking off a wave of ecstasy that started deep inside her and was now spreading, permeating every hot, tight inch of her body.

'I'm going to come, Mir. Fuck, I'm going to come.' The voice was unrecognizable, somewhere off in the distance, drowned out by the one that was filling her head, bringing her closer and closer to . . .

'Fuck! Oh yes, oh hell, yes . . .' In the distance again, drowned out by . . .

The scream took her by surprise, so thick and guttural that it was almost a howl of pain, of delicious, burning, blissful agony that came, and came, and came, so that even the feeling of hot liquid soaking her body couldn't detract from the intensity of the orgasm.

When she eventually opened her eyes, Jack was slouched against the wall, head back, his limp dick dangling over the open waistband of his jeans.

For a moment Mirren didn't want to move, determined to savour every moment of . . . No, it was gone. He was gone. The voice in her head, the feelings that he gave her, the things he was saying, all gone and she could weep with longing to have them back.

The noise of Jack's zip was enough to set the first ambush of shame in motion. For the first time in her life, she'd made love to her husband while thinking about someone else. And not just anyone. Him. Oh my God, where had that come from?

She couldn't make eye contact with Jack, not that it mattered. He leaned over, kissed her softly. 'I love you, babe. And I'll never screw up again, I promise. I swear.'

No reply was forthcoming.

'I'm just gonna grab a quick shower, then head to bed. You coming up? I want to hold you, babe. All night.'

Mirren nodded. 'In a minute. Let me just get cleaned up.'

He kissed her again and then waited until she had climbed off the kitchen island and grabbed a towel from the pile in the linen cupboard, before opening the door and heading upstairs.

Wrapping the towel around her, Mirren went in the opposite direction, out the back door, down the path that dissected the garden, and then stopped at the cabana that stood at the edge of her property. Inside, she dropped the towel and pulled on a swimsuit, before following the path to the sands and then crossing the short distance to the ocean. It was freezing against her feet, knees, hips as she entered, and only when she was submerged up to her neck did her body's thermostat kick in and adjust to the waters, making her shivers stop and the goosebumps disappear. Mirren lay back and floated, letting the salt water soothe her aching head, her tense shoulders, and clean the remains of her husband from her body.

If only she could float on. Just drift. Keep going until she reached somewhere that didn't come with uncertainty and pain and worry.

Somewhere he was.

The thought made her spring to her feet, only her toes reaching the seabed. Her thighs fought against the receding tide as she waded to shore. In the cabana, she showered the salt off her body, then grabbed two fresh towels, wrapping one in a turban round her head and fashioning a makeshift toga with the other. Back in the house, she locked the back door, then headed upstairs, turning left at the half-landing where the stairs split in two different directions. The right-hand staircase led to their 2,000-square-foot master suite. The left one travelled somewhere far more important. At the open door leading to Chloe's room, she paused and watched as the night nurse smoothed out Chloe's blanket once more.

Mirren liked this woman, a steely German who made no concession to the fact that Mirren paid the bills.

'Please do not be waking her up. Only just got her back to sleep.'

'She was awake?' The guilt hit her like a sucker punch, right in the gut, winding her. Her baby had wakened and she'd been downstairs, screwing on the kitchen island. What the hell kind of mother was she?

'Indeed. She opened her eyes for a few moments. She was mumbling. Difficult to make out exactly what she was saying. She was asking for someone.'

'Me? Was she asking for me?'

'No, I think not. It didn't sound like "Mom". Sounded like something else. Something I have never heard before. Like Ander. Sander. Yes, Sander. That was it.'

Mirren's heart stopped. Just stopped. Suddenly she was back in the past once again.

Her mind flipped back to the call from Davie. At the time,

it had been unsettling, but in the midst of her life disintegrating, she'd filed it away and chosen to ignore it.

But this?

There was no ignoring this.

Her daughter was asking for someone, and with an inevitability that made her bristle with utter horror, she knew it was Zander Leith.

Zander Leith.

Why the hell was Chloe asking for Zander Leith?

She had to know. Had to get to the truth.

Since the second they were born, Mirren had known that there were no lengths she would not go to in order to protect her children from the past.

With a gut-wrenching blend of fear and panic, Mirren knew that theory was about to be tested.

38.

'When We Are Together' – Texas

So much for the impenetrability of the A-list star. Sarah knew she'd been wildly optimistic in hoping that she'd actually manage to speak to Davie Johnston, but there he was, sitting at the bar, utterly pissed, feeling mighty sorry for himself, desperate to unload on a complete stranger.

The biggest surprise was that she almost felt sorry for him. The revelation made her rethink her plan to go straight for the jugular, catch him off guard – in, out, leave the battlefield, don't stop for casualties. Move on to Zander Leith. No, it would clearly be better to go soft on this one, at least initially.

'My turn to buy you a drink,' she said. 'You sound like you need it.'

'Man, your voice is fucking fabulous. I think I'm homesick. Which is really weird because I haven't been homesick in twenty years.'

Sarah waited until the barman had refilled both glasses. 'Honestly? All that time and you've never wanted to go back?'

Davie laughed. 'Honestly? I never wanted to come here in the first place. I applied for a house in Cumbernauld, but it was full, so I came here,' he joked.

Sarah's cackle came from deep inside. Cute. Surprisingly cute.

Davie shook his head, smiling. 'Turned out to be a good move. I like the sun. Like the business. Too much good stuff here.'

It seemed churlish to point out that the man who was professing to have a great life looked like one of the saddest people she'd ever met. How bizarre to think that only a few days ago, she'd been chatting to his mother. A small part of her wanted to tell him, to give him something comforting and familiar to cheer him up. A really small part. Every other instinct was telling her that the fact he was off balance was her best chance to milk him for information. Crisis, conflict and chaos were the three best friends of the journalist.

'So you know who I am, right?' he asked her.

How to play it? Dumb and hopeful, or switched on and unimpressed? There was no contest.

'Sure. *American Stars* is shown on some obscure channel in the UK. Seems like quite a big deal over here.'

That would do for now. Stroke his ego a little, but no need to mention that she was fully aware of his status as a US powerhouse. Or should that be 'former US powerhouse, now generally referred to as "douche" '?

When he'd asked her earlier what she was doing in town, he'd taken her brush-off too easily, so he obviously didn't much care about anyone else. It was his world; everyone else just lived in it.

'Not so much of a big deal anymore,' he said, shaking his head woefully.

Oh dear Lord, the drama. This guy was acting with all the pathos of a leading man in a daytime soap.

'Having a bad week?'

'Bad month. You haven't heard?'

It was tempting to come clean, but what would be the point? The shutters would come down and there would be nothing to be gained. Instead, she shook her head.

Davie raised his glass to her. 'Well, congratulations. You must be the only person in the free world who hasn't heard that my life came back and bit me on the ass.'

'So what happened?'

He drained his drink, then gestured to the barman for a refill.

'*American Stars* ditched me. The world thinks I'm an asshole. My wife thinks I'm a dick. That just about sums it up.'

Sarah thought for a moment. 'And your friends?'

He swayed towards her. 'Dunno. You're my new best friend. What do you think?'

Oh bugger, he was flirting. Seriously giving her come-on signs and flashing green lights.

This wasn't in the plan. Or perhaps it was, given that the only plan she had was to wing it and hope that something great came up.

She realized that he was waiting for an answer to his question.

'I don't know. So far I think you're a pretty nice guy. You're the first person I've met here, so I don't have much to base it on,' she replied, careful to stay on the friendly side of flirtation, confident she could handle this. How many times had she had to manage drunk guys for the sake of a story back home? Too many to count.

'Do you wanna get out of here? Go somewhere else?'

Here we go, Sarah realized.

'Depends.'

Davie's eyebrows raised with surprise. Obviously not used to any form of resistance, then. Not surprising. He was great-looking, rich and famous. And even in his pissed state, there was definitely something endearing about him.

'On what?' he asked, his amusement clear.

'Well, here's the thing. I have a boyfriend back home. He's really big and he could kill you with his thumbs.'

'Ouch.'

'Indeed. So if you're looking for anything . . . intimate . . . then I'm not that person. But if you want to hang out, grab something to eat, then I'm up for that.'

Behind the bar, the barman had been polishing the same glass for ten minutes, utterly engrossed in the conversation. Even the bits that were in such a strong accent he couldn't quite understand them. He made a mental note to watch *Braveheart* again.

Davie contemplated his answer for so long she thought she'd blown it. Shit. Too cold? Too frosty? Making sure he wasn't viewing this as a hook-up was crucial, but at the same time she wanted the meeting to continue. Needed it to. Already in her head she began to work out a plan B. If he blew her off now, she could phone his assistant in the morning, go the official route, even mention that she'd spoken to Davie the night before. Plan C, track his next event. Show up. Hope for a second shot at this.

'With his thumbs?'

'Absolutely.'

'What about if I just take you for more beers and maybe a burger?'

'Then he might be mildly miffed, but he'll probably let you live.'

'OK. Might have some fries as well. May as well make it worth it.'

The barman was still staring. Still polishing the same glass. Still enjoying the conversation. Sarah, to her surprise, was too.

Davie slid off his seat, more by design than accident, but only just.

When he stood up, Sarah realized that he was actually slightly smaller than he looked on TV. Maybe five feet ten – about the same height as she was in her four-inch heels.

'Can you see if my car is down at the door, buddy? Let them know I'm on the way down.'

Sarah didn't miss the irony. Last week, she met this guy's mother in what was, in effect, a soup kitchen. This week, it was limos in LA. In terms of wealth divide, she'd just crossed the Grand Canyon of material goods.

Davie spoke to the driver as they climbed into the car. Actually, reclined into the car would be a better description. The interior was white leather; an unopened bottle of champagne was cooling in the ice bucket, two glasses sitting between the bucket and a selection of individually wrapped chocolates. It was a far cry from the Glasgow Underground, her normal mode of transport.

'So, tell me what I'm missing.'

'Missing about what?'

'Glasgow.'

'What do you want to know?'

'Dunno. Just talk. Just want to listen.'

His reaction took Sarah completely by surprise. He'd done nothing but talk about himself all night, his conversation veering between self-love and self-pity, telling her how great he was and then telling her how other people in the business thought he was great too. Or used to.

'OK, well, there's the Royal Concert Hall, which is really beautiful. Especially at Christmas, when the ballet comes. It's good to make a night of it, to go see the lights at George Square and walk round to the Concert Hall. And—'

'Are you sure you won't sleep with me?'

His words were a little slurred as he spoke, while spilling champagne as he attempted to refill his glass.

'Positive. Look, it's fine if you want to drop me off. I understand completely.'

'No, 's'OK. But I may ask you again. Lots of times. Is that OK?'

Sarah laughed. 'Sure. Just as long as you don't expect a different answer.'

'Fair nuff. Just wondering, though – is there, like, a scale?'

'A what?'

'A scale. With your boyfriend, the one who's going to kill me with his thumbs. So, like, if we just kiss, will that be, say, a mild concussion? A blow job – broken wrist? If there's a scale, it might be worth weighing up my options. I've a high tolerance to pain.'

'No, I think it's a strict "touching equals death" policy.' Sarah struggled to suppress her laughter and remain deadpan.

This guy, even in his state, was really funny and surprisingly hard to dislike.

'Ah well, then. He sounds a bit uncompromising. I definitely think you should dump him.'

'I'll take that on board. Thanks for the advice. I'll give it serious thought.'

'OK. Now, don't take this the wrong way, but I need you to get down.'

'Where?'

'Under the eyeline of the window. And then I'm going to put a blanket over you. We're just about to pull up at my house and I'm guessing a whole big scumbag pool of paps will be there.'

Whoa, his house? This wasn't in plans A, B or C. Sarah looked out of the window and realized they'd left the city behind. This street was treelined, winding, with an occasional set of huge gates punctuating high walls and lengths of dense bushes.

'I thought you said we were going to grab something to eat?'

'Sandra—'

'Sarah.'

'Sorry, Sarah. Look, I promise it's not shady. It's just that things are a bit complicated and I can't get papped on the night of my wedding anniversary having an In-N-Out burger with another woman. My cook does a great burger. I promise. Now please duck.'

'But the windows are tinted.'

'Sometimes the flashes still catch shapes. Don't wanna take any chances.'

'Shit,' Sarah spluttered, as she slid down onto the floor, only to be immediately plunged into darkness by a black fur throw she'd noticed on the rear-window shelf earlier.

It blocked out the flashes, but it did nothing to stop the noise.

'Davie, is your career over? Put the window down. Talk to us, man!'

'Jenny, are you in there? Are you still sleeping with him, Jenny?'

'Put the windows down! Two minutes! Just two minutes! A few words.'

The car had stopped now. Sarah presumed they were waiting for the gates to open. The noise was like a wall of sound, unrelenting, heckling. And still she could pick out phrases, shouts, aggression peppering almost every demand.

'C'mon, Davie, you're fucked. We all know it. Wanna apologize to your fans?'

'Do you know your wife is fucking someone else?'

'Are you suing his ass, Jenny?'

'Say something, Jen. C'mon, just a quick vid. Cut him loose, man. He's washed up.'

As the temperature rose under the heat of the blanket, Sarah realized that her fists were clenched and her heart was beating out of her chest. This lot made her look like Mother Teresa in the ruthless stakes. She could handle aggression, could handle abuse – God knows she'd had enough of it in her years at the *Daily Scot* – but to have this every time you left and returned to your house? That had to wear you down.

The car moved off again, the sound of the mob receded, and suddenly she could breathe again.

'You OK?' Davie asked, as he flicked the blanket off and she slid back up onto the seat.

'Yeah, fine. That lot were a bit hostile. Not fans, I take it.'

Davie shrugged. 'They're just looking for a pay cheque. The more they piss me off, the better their chances of getting a reaction. One snap of me losing the plot can earn them thousands. Sometimes hundreds of thousands.'

Sarah knew this already, but chose not to share that information right now. Getting kicked out of a limo, forced to walk back down the driveway and then scale a twenty-foot gate in front of dozens of vultures with cameras didn't appeal. Tonight was becoming a bit like an out-of-control train and she was fairly desperate not to derail it in a way that would lead to global public humiliation.

When the car finally came to a halt between a stunning fountain and the front door, she hesitated before climbing out.

'Can they see us? Long lenses?'

He shook his head. 'Nope. It's completely screened by those trees.'

Reassured, she climbed out when the driver opened the door, and followed Davie through another door, this time the one at the entrance to the house, helpfully held open by a stunning blonde female in a black sparkly minidress and eight-inch heels.

'This is Ivanka. My housekeeper. Great burgers.'

'Very pleased to meet you,' Ivanka replied in a thick accent with a tone that suggested she was anything but.

Wow, the hallway was breathtaking, like something out of a 1940s movie set. A cream marble floor, with cream walls that glistened all the way up to the double-height vaulted ceiling. A sweeping split staircase in dark wood. Huge portraits of Davie and Jenny Johnston and the children lining the curved walls.

The sight made her freeze, ask the obvious.

'Davie, won't your wife be pissed off that you've brought some strange female home?'

'Are you strange?' he replied. In a bizarre flash of recognition, Sarah had a mental image of an old movie. Yes, she was Liza Minnelli. He was Dudley Moore. This was *Arthur*.

'That wasn't actually my point.'

He walked ahead, compelling her to follow. 'My wife won't give a flying fuck. Right. Ivanka, burgers for two, please. Heavy on the mayo. And tomorrow, deny all knowledge of feeding me carbohydrates.'

'Yes, Mr Johnston.'

He was still walking; she was still following, through into a den area that had two huge semicircular leather sofas and a gigantic TV screen on the wall.

A bottle of scotch was liberated from the bar in the corner and Davie poured them both an inch of honey-coloured liquid, then knocked his back in one go.

This guy was seriously messed up.

'Can I ask you something?'

'Shoot.'

'Do you bring a lot of women back here? I mean, I'm not trying to freak you out, but I wouldn't think it was the safest thing to do.'

'Nope.'

'No, it isn't, or no, you don't?' Jesus, Arthur was back.

'Both. You're the first chick I've ever brought back here and that's because you're right – it's not safe.'

'So why did you bring me here?'

For a moment Sarah thought he hadn't heard because he just stared straight ahead. No movement. Frozen.

'Because you made me laugh. Because I didn't want to come home alone. Because my life's already shit and can't really get any worse. Unless your boyfriend with the thumbs turns up.'

The attempt to inject a bit of levity didn't disguise the painful truth of his other reasons. Sympathy flared again. This guy had everything. Everything. Yet in just a few hours Sarah had realized that he was one of the unhappiest people she'd ever met.

Ivanka teetered through on her heels, carrying a tray with two laden plates. Burgers. Salads. Sauces. The smell made Sarah's stomach flip straight to starving.

By the colour of Davie's face, it had a very different effect on him.

'Back in a minute,' he said, wobbling to his feet and heading back out in the direction they'd come in.

Sarah waited a few minutes for him to return. Nothing. She took a bite of her burger. It seemed rude to start without him, but she was starving. Another bite. Then another. Soon it was gone and she was still sitting there, unsure as to what to do.

OK, options. She could go look for him, but what if she set off alarms? Or went into his kids' rooms? Or fell over his wife? It seemed unwise to give the temperamental housekeeper a chance to stab her and claim she thought it was a house invasion.

On the other hand, she was a reporter. Snooping was what she did. Getting to the truth. Finding out facts. But . . . this was so, so out of her league. What the hell was she doing here? Not that she was an expert on A-list celebrity lives, but she had a fair guess that he was going to freak out when he discovered who she was. Shit.

OK, she could explain. There had been no lies. Just a few omissions of the truth. Couldn't blame her, really. And he was so wasted that even if she told him the truth, he probably wouldn't absorb it. Lying wasn't an option, though. He could Google her name and in twenty seconds he'd have links to every feature she'd ever written.

Weariness and that last whisky crept up on her, so she lay back, kicked off her boots and curled up, pulling a throw off the back of the sofa.

It was no use. She had to tell him. He'd probably freak out, but she could handle a bit of flak.

How bad could it be?

39.

'The Honeythief' – Hipsway

Glasgow, 1988

If anyone ever decided to make a soundtrack of her life, they could just forget all the melodic stuff and set the story to the thudding of a headboard against a wall.

Mirren sat at the kitchen table, trying to concentrate on the preparation for her English Higher. Did George Orwell write his classics to the sound of his mother shagging her boyfriend upstairs? Did Anaïs Nin come up with her best work while listening to her mother begging him to go harder, faster?

God, she'd do anything to get out of here. Anything. The minute her exams were finished, she was packing up and looking for a job and a flat-share. Didn't matter where – as long as it was out of earshot of her mother's whimpers. Not that Marilyn would notice, and if she did, she'd probably be glad. She'd no doubt pull on her favourite pink baby-doll and move the shagging from the bedroom to the couch. Urgh, the thought made her shudder.

The words she needed to get down for her essay got blocked by irritation, so she pushed it to one side and pulled the black

A4 notebook out of her schoolbag. Where Mirren went, it followed, and it documented everything. Her day at school. The disaster of the perm that had made her look like she'd had a fight with a Flymo. Her thoughts on everything from music to books to the rank shiteness of The Hit Man and Her. Although, after a few cans of Diamond White, it wasn't that bad.

And of course she wrote about personal stuff too. About what it felt like when he touched her. How she hated to say goodbye. How Zander and Davie were the ones who made her laugh whether her mother was ignoring her or swinging from a chandelier.

Urgh, another horrible mental image. She picked up the pen and wrote the title.

The Headboard.

'Whit's that yer writing there, then?'

The mug of tea next to her left hand almost went flying when she jumped.

Her mother's sex god wandered into the kitchen wearing just a towel round his waist. Mirren resisted the urge to vomit.

'Homework.' Deadpan. No eye contact. It was bad enough that she'd had to listen to him for years, didn't mean she had to like him.

In fact, ambivalence was slowly turning into a deep dislike. Ambivalence. There was a word to factor into her next essay.

Arse. There was another one. Noun. A man who thinks he's in any way attractive when he's actually a repulsive prick. Once upon a time, she thought he was OK, but not now. The one-liners she used to think were hilarious now seemed corny. The chat that was once inclusive and entertaining now bordered on creepy.

It was becoming difficult to conceal her hostility, especially because it upset her mother. That was always a bonus.

'Ooh, check you, Miss Prim and Proper. Gonna be too good for us soon. Leave all us plebs behind, will ye?'

Mirren ignored him, just kept her head down. Kept on writing. He'd wander off again. He always did. All mouth and no trousers. Prick.

'Think ye could teach me a thing or two, then?'

He was behind her now, carrying two cans of Tennent's he'd just taken out of the fridge.

'Oh, I bet you could.'

Still talking. Why was he still talking? And why did he sound so . . . weird? He was almost whispering now. She stared straight ahead. Frozen. Not taking the bait.

'And I bet I could teach you a thing or two as well.'

The stink of beer and fags filled her nostrils as she realized he was leaning down behind her, his head almost resting on her shoulder.

'Yer ma said yer shagging now. Found a condom in yer bag. Shame that. Who is it? Some spotty wee nyaff that spurts his stuff before he's even got yer bra aff?'

Mirren's teeth clenched together. Shit, her mum knew. She should have been more careful. Although, it obviously didn't bother her because she'd never mentioned it. Not a word.

Nothing new there. It would be more surprising if she cared.

And why was he still here? Talking shite? He must have had too many beers and now he was doing that thing where he thought he was the dog's bollocks. Arse.

Still she said nothing. It was the best way. He'd realize she wasn't biting and he'd get bored and go back upstairs to the baby-doll queen.

'That's not what you need, girl. You need a real man.'

His breath was even stronger now that he was only inches from her ear. He was leaning against her shoulder, his towel touching her and making her stomach turn.

'This is what you need, doll. This right here.'

There was a moistness on her neck, a movement, a . . . Oh my God, he was licking her neck. And his . . . Oh fuck.

It took a moment for her brain to catch up, and when it did, her chair flew back as she leaped to her feet. The towel was on the floor and he was standing there, his erect dick protruding in front of him.

Her horrified reaction didn't make an iota of difference. If anything, his smile became wider, his leer more pronounced.

'Aw, don't be like that. It'd be the best you ever had. C'mon here and let me show you what—'

Instinctively, with no real idea what she was doing, Mirren fumbled for something on the table that she could use to stop this. When she found it, her only instinct was to throw, sending hot tea splattering over him, the walls, the floor . . .

'Ya wee bitch!'

She was terrified, raging, frozen – utterly unable to scream or shout. And what would happen if she did? Her mother would come running down the stairs and she would take one look at the scene in front of her and somehow it would be Mirren's fault. The realization made her voice kick in.

'Get away from me,' she hissed. 'Or the next time I'll make sure the tea is boiling.'

His face went even redder as he reached over, picked up

his towel from the table, and wrapped it back round his waist.

His face was right up against hers now, nose to nose. 'Aye, you do that. And I'll kill you and I'll kill her. And don't ever doubt it.'

'What the hell is going on here?'

Her mother's voice was shrill behind her. Mirren couldn't look. Didn't have to. She knew Mum would be wearing her short black silk kimono that she'd bought with the coupons out of her fag packets. Her hair would be tousled and her lipstick long gone. And the smell of sex would still be on her body.

His words were light and jovial. 'Nothing at all, love. Your Mirren just being a bit clumsy, dropped her tea. I was just telling her to be more careful.'

'Well, you needn't think I'm cleaning that up,' Marilyn said. 'Don't know what's going on with you these days. Too much time with your head in those books.'

How stupid could her mother be? How could she not notice the ice in the atmosphere? Not even question why her daughter was shaking as she faced off against a half-naked man twice her age? Just Mirren's fault for being so clumsy.

But then, Mirren expected nothing more. If that was the ending of a book, she'd have predicted it perfectly.

The glare of warning was still in his eyes as he walked past her. His expression said supremacy. Triumph. Right now, she had never hated anyone more.

'There's a mop in the boiler cupboard,' Marilyn told her, before giving a playful yelp as he reached round her and grabbed her arse, pulling her towards him and kissing her hard on the mouth. Marilyn's arms went round his neck, the belt of her kimono loosening and letting the silk part to reveal half of her large, white pendulous breasts and the red lace of her knickers. Mirren forced her eyes away, but too late to miss seeing her grab his hand and, still giggling, lead him back upstairs.

'Come on, then. Think we've got some, erm, talking to do,' Marilyn teased him.

He didn't give Mirren a backwards glance as he followed her mother, his dick leading all the way.

Mirren scanned the scene in front of her, the puddle on the floor, the soaked textbooks, the removal of the last tiny shreds of respect she'd had for her mother.

The sooner she got out of here, the better. It had to happen. The second her exams were over, she was out.

In the meantime, she made a promise to herself that this would never be allowed to happen again.

And if it did, she'd be ready with a lot more than a mug of lukewarm tea.

40.

'A Girl Like You'
– Edwyn Collins

It was the train going past that woke him. The noise, holy shit, the noise. Thud. Thud. Thud. His eyeballs were rattling with every beat, the pain like a pressure cooker, squeezing his head tighter, tighter, until he decided death would have been a mercy.

The train crashed straight into Davie's forehead as he pushed himself up, desperate for water to lubricate the sand that seemed to have been blasted against the inside walls of his mouth and throat.

The pain. Holy shit, the pain.

Crushing. Crucifying. If he was a horse, they'd have no option but to shoot him.

How the fuck did alcoholics do it?

Fumbling, he eventually located the knob on his bedside table and twisted it just slightly, altering the transparency on his windows from blackout to light enough to see, not so light his eyeballs would explode.

The room was too hot. Or maybe too cold. His receptors

294

were too busy screaming with pain to relay specific information.

Random strands of thought were bursting into his consciousness. Information. Last night. Jenny. Lawyer. His grey matter fought to join the dots. Divorce. The bitch was divorcing him. He was in her cross hairs, she had lined up the lawyers, and they'd fire her bullets just as soon as they'd passed the ten-year threshold. Unbelievable. Detaching from the trashed brand, saving her own skin. Congratulations, kiddies, today is brought to you by the letter 'f' – for 'fucking marvellous'. He had to think. Had to deal with it. Needed to consider what to do, not just pull off a knee-jerk reaction. And yes, going over to her girlfriend's house and throwing a brick through her Venetian windows fell into that category, much as – should he ever recover his motor skills – it would be tempting.

Carefully, so as not to cause his body to slide into shock, he got out of bed and stumbled to the bathroom. He stood to pee, his body angle forwards, so his head rested against the cool of one of the $1,000 tiles that lined the wall behind the granite urinal.

Granite. Cost $50,000. To pee. This was all sorts of messed up.

Bladder drained, he let his trousers fall to the floor, kicked his Schiesser briefs down to join them, then peeled off his socks and shirt and added them to the pile of last night's detritus. A shower was an ask too far, so he took the thick black cashmere robe from the back of the door and pulled it on, then slowly, carefully, gritting his teeth with every step, he headed downstairs.

In the kitchen, Ivanka had her back to him, throwing a concoction of carrots, wheatgrass, lemon and papaya into the blender for his morning juice.

Too late, he realized that his brain hadn't thought through the next stage in the process. The screaming blades of the machine made tears prick his eyes. This was what hell felt like.

'Mr Johnston, good morning,' she said, her brusque, heavy accent and over-Botoxed face making her seem disapproving of his very presence.

Apparently, great food and loyalty were included in the pay grade, smiles and warmth extra.

'Juice? And spinach omelette?'

'Juice. Just juice. Thanks.'

'Very well.'

Still disapproving. Jeez, cut a dying guy a break.

'And your friend is out having coffee on the terrace.'

It took a moment, a long moment, before it registered. Even longer before it made any sense. The pixelated memory eventually formed a shape he vaguely recognized. A girl. Scottish. Cute. Long copper-coloured hair. At the bar.

Oh mother of God, what had he done? And why was she still in his house?

This wasn't the kind of shit he normally pulled. He was way too careful for this. No drugs. No booze. No fucking strangers. And definitely, absolutely no one in his house whom he didn't completely trust. That's why he'd been able to stay afloat and prosper in this business for so long. And for what? For it all to go to rat shit anyway.

The anxiety and irritation morphed nicely into paranoia.

Hell, she could be anyone. And what had she done while he was asleep? Had a tour of the house? Rifled through his office? Planted a microphone or, worse, a fricking camera somewhere?

'Ivanka, can you call security and have them arrange a bug sweep of the house today?'

Only the Juvéderm in her lips stopped them from pursing in a defiant gesture of 'I told you so'. If she wasn't such a great cook, he'd definitely fire her ass.

Grabbing the brown juice from the breakfast bar, he slung on a pair of Sama sunglasses that were lying on the counter next to the door to the terrace.

OK. Here's the plan. Go out, be nice, be apologetic, get rid of her without making her hate you so much she'll sell a story to the paps or put it all over Facebook.

He locked on to her before she noticed him coming. Sitting in the huge, all-weather wicker-style chair, her knees were pulled up to her chest, her eyes closed, head back, letting the sun radiate on her face. Even in his chronically debilitated state, he could see the contradictions. Number one, she was in LA but she was sunbathing. Not the most popular pastime here, for fear of skin cancer or – and sadly this was the ultimate fear – wrinkles. Number two, in the last thirty seconds his mind had built her up to be a crazy, a hooker or a slut, yet she wasn't naked. What did it say that in his all-new, decimated life, that was considered a bonus?

'Hi. I'm Davie.' Open with disarming humour, then gently work up to 'Please leave before I call a SWAT team.'

The coffee mug she held, balanced on top of her knees, splashed as she instinctively jumped. OK, so stalker/stranger now had second-degree burns. Smooth start to the evacuation. He saw then that she was wearing the same green shirt as the night before, but her trousers appeared to be missing, revealing her white cotton boy shorts. Cute.

'Sorry, I didn't mean to scare you.'

'No, no, it's fine. My fault. I was dreaming – didn't hear you coming. And hi, I'm Sarah.'

'I remembered that bit.'

'Did you?' she asked, smiling, one eyebrow raised. Wow, fully functioning eyebrows. Another anomaly.

'Well, almost,' he admitted sheepishly.

Sarah gestured to her coffee mug. 'Your housekeeper made me coffee, but she didn't look thrilled. Should I have asked her to taste it first?'

His laughter made his head pound again. Son of a bitch.

'Probably,' he winced. 'Sorry, head feels like I've had hair gel administered with a baseball bat.'

'That bad?'

'Actually, worse.'

The hangover may have taken control of his senses, but he still noticed that her smile was gorgeous. Not a pageant grin. It was friendlier than that. Warm. And it reached her eyes, making them crinkle at the sides. The whole green eyes, deep auburn hair, freckles across the nose combo was unusual here, and so strikingly different from Jenny's and Vala's exotic Latin vibe. But this girl was gorgeous in a quirky, naturally pretty way.

It was only when the noise of the coffee mug being placed on the table in front of them broke the silence did he realize a few moments had passed.

'So,' she broke the pause in the conversation first, 'have you worked out how you're going to make me leave without offending me yet?'

'Why would I—'

'Because that's exactly what you should do,' she interjected. 'I could be anyone. I could be a mad stalker who's been watching your every move for months and now I'm in your house.'

'Thanks. I'd just managed to put the lid back on my can of paranoid worms. So are you a mad stalker?'

'Yep.'

He groaned, but she cut him off with 'But not yours. I'm Ryan Gosling's stalker. *The Notebook* gets me every time. I think I should have his babies.'

Cute and funny. Suddenly, the urge to get rid of her wasn't as strong as the urge to just sit here for the rest of the day talking to her. Looking at her made him want to smile.

'I know his manager – I'll pass on the offer if you like?'

'Oh my God, that would be amazing. And it'll stop me killing you and writing Ryan's name in your blood. Another bonus. Sorry, too far?'

He took a sip of juice and then stopped to consider if it was going to stage a return.

Nope, it was staying down. Great. He might make it without adding throwing up to his list of recent public humiliations.

'Definitely too far,' he assured her, realizing that made her grin even wider, the familiarity kicking in a flashback from last night. She'd made him laugh. A lot. And God knows right now he could do with a laugh.

'I hope you don't mind me asking, but will your kids be back anytime soon? It's just, well, you know. It's probably not appropriate for them to see me here.'

What did it say about his fatherhood skills that the thought hadn't even crossed his mind? The fact that she'd mentioned it made him add thoughtful to the list of pretty, cute, funny and Ryan Gosling's stalker.

'No, they're at work. They're in a show here. *Family Three*.'

'And they work Saturdays?' she asked doubtfully.

'Sometimes. Four days a week, that's the deal.'

'Wow. In the old days, it was only the poor who sent their children out to work.'

'It's not exactly . . .' he started to defend himself, then stopped. What did it matter if she was making a judgement? She was probably right. They'd probably completely fucked up the kids. Macaulay Culkin. Britney Spears. Lindsay Lohan. It's not like being a child star had a great rep for turning out stable and balanced individuals. 'Whatever,' he finished with a dismissive wave of his disgusting yet nutritional morning juice.

'Sorry,' she said.

'For what?'

'For sounding like a judgemental knob there. It's none of my business.'

'That's OK. So, erm, what is your business? Other than stalking Ryan.'

The mood changed instantly, as her facial expression flicked from open and warm to something else. Apprehension?

She put her feet on the ground and sat up straight, clasping her hands on her naked thighs.

'OK, look,' she started hesitantly, 'this might freak you out a bit . . .'

'More than the image of you writing my name in blood?'

'Definitely.'

'Smashing,' he replied.

His sarcasm was momentarily distracted by her thighs. They were gorgeous. White. Muscular. And the hair that had been straight and sleek last night was wavy now, that messed-up, just-out-of-bed way. Why was he thinking this right now? Concentrate. Priorities. Back to words.

'My name is Sarah McKenzie.'

Even in his befuddled state, it set off bells of recognition that made him want to hold his head until the vibrations stopped.

'You're trying to remember where you've heard that name before?'

He could only nod.

'I work for the *Daily Scot*. A few weeks ago, I called to ask if I could interview you. Your people blew me off.'

There were no words. He simply rocked forward and let his head fall onto the glass tabletop. Then he groaned. Really loudly. Until she resumed speaking.

'I'm sorry. I know I'm probably the last person you want to be with right now. Except your wife. You told me last night that she thinks you're a dick . . .'

Another groan.

She continued, 'But I promise that nothing you told me up until now will be on the record. I promise. It would be unethical, anyway, given that you were utterly wasted.'

301

He left his head on the table. The coolness was helping douse the flames of the Seventh Circle of Hell.

A reporter. In his house. One that was already after a story. A story about back home. It was like inviting in a serial killer and asking him to sharpen the steak knives. Think, Davie, think. He had to play this right. Had to make sure that he didn't mess this up, because if she ever got to the truth . . . Oh no, he was definitely going to vomit.

'I'm sorry. I thought about lying, but you could have Googled me in a split second and found out who I really was, so there was no point. Look, I'm not trying to do a hatchet job, or make your life tough. I just wanted to interview you about your family back home. I, erm, I met your mum. She's lovely.'

This revelation seemed to give his spinal column the motivation it needed to propel his body upwards again. His expression made it clear this wasn't great news.

'You're the one who visited her on the bus?'

Sarah nodded, her top teeth visible as they chewed her bottom lip. That's what guilt looked like. His heart started to mirror the thudding in his head as – against his every screaming instinct – he knew he had to probe further, picking off a scab to reveal the poison of his old life.

'And what is it you want to know?'

Her shoulders shrugged. 'I'm just doing a lifestyle piece and I'd like to know more about you when you were younger. More about your family and how they felt about you leaving. What your success means to them now.'

'No plural,' he interrupted sharply. 'No "them". It's just me and my mum.'

'Sorry. I knew that already. It was just a slip of the tongue.'

He wanted to believe her. Lifestyle piece. Innocent. Harmless. But he was realistic. There was no way she was going to come all the way over here for a story their PR people and a photographer could rustle up in ten minutes. Yes, his mum is thrilled; no, he hasn't lost touch with his roots; and of course they're still as close as ever.

He wasn't buying it.

And besides, she was a reporter, not a magazine journo. Reporters looked for stories, dug for dirt. And there was enough of that in his past to fill a quarry.

The original conversation he'd had with his assistant, Jorja, played back in his mind.

'*We've had an interview request from a journalist called Sarah McKenzie at the* Daily Scot. *I know you love to keep your profile up in the UK, so shall I set up a date? She wants the focus to be your life back in Scotland, growing up with Zander Leith and Mirren McLean. Oh, and she said something really weird, something about wanting to meet the families the three of you left behind.*'

The three of you. Why link them together now, two decades after the event, when they'd had absolutely no connection in all that time?

For the last twenty years of his life he'd wondered what it would feel like if the ghosts came back to haunt him. Now he knew. Sickening. Terrifying. He was almost thankful for the physical distraction of the hangover.

But he'd been around enough to know that he had to act like he had nothing to worry about, because the minute she sniffed fear, she would know for sure she was on to something.

He just had to hope that she was fishing, that this was simply curiosity based on absolutely no evidence whatsoever.

Just as his addled mind attempted to formulate some kind of workable strategy, the French doors opened.

Like a Russian superhero in steel-spiked heels and a pencil skirt that gave her steps a ten-inch span, Ivanka appeared thrusting a phone towards him. 'It's Al. Urgent.'

The fear of 'urgent' was outweighed by the relief of 'interruption'.

He got up and casually padded a few metres across the perfect lawn, out of earshot of his houseguest.

'Hey, man, what's happening?'

'Jenny. She's going on *The Brianna Nicole Show* on Wednesday night. Anything we should be worried about?'

Where to start? Number one, she was divorcing him. Number two, she was going to take millions. Number three, the last shred of his credibility would be gone because even those who had a suspicion that he wasn't Satan's spawn would convict him without a trial because they'd figure that's why Jenny left him. Number four, *The Brianna Nicole Show* was the only talk show that actually went out live, and had an average audience of five million a night. This was all sorts of bad. Not that she'd say anything on *Brianna*. Oh no. The new series of *Streets of Power* was on the horizon so this was purely a business appearance and she'd gloss over any personal stuff. Besides, the most crucial element of the plan was that she kept the facade of a happy marriage going until at least Thursday, their actual anniversary. Then she'd file on Friday and go with one of two game plans. She'd either keep the divorce proceedings quiet until the current storm had passed, then in a few months they'd announce that they'd decided to split, were best friends, and wanted nothing but happiness for the other, or game plan 2: she'd make it public immediately, go to the press, use it for publicity and explain the suddenness by saying she'd discovered some terrible secret about him that she couldn't possibly share with the world because he was the father of her children. His money was on the latter. And given his current popularity rating, the global public would right now believe that he was second only to that bloke that ran North Korea in the evil stakes.

Think, Davie, think. One problem at a time. Put the journo to one side for a second and deal with problem number two. Multitask. Play the game. Turn it to your advantage. There had to be something to be saved from this, a way to spin it to help him out. He slipped into sports mode, coaching himself to move forward, go for a win. Get back in the game, Davie. Come on, son, get back in the game.

'Nope, nothing to worry about. But I'm just thinking, Al. How about we make this one special? Call the producer at *Brianna*. Tell her to expect another guest. And tell her we want to make it a surprise for Jenny. TV gold. Special moment. All that stuff. And if she even dares to hesitate about me going on, tell her neither Jenny nor I will be back. End of story.'

He hung up, walked back to the terrace and placed the phone down gently on the table, concerned that another loud noise may well tip him over the edge.

Right, back to the other trifling issue – the fact that he had somehow managed to acquire a tabloid journalist as a houseguest, one who could destroy what little life he had left.

There were two ways to play this. He could rage at the fact she omitted to mention her occupation and banish her from the premises, throwing out phrases along the lines of having her run out of town. Or he could use his considerable charm, keep her onside and give her what she wanted to know while keeping her away from anything that could cause him further damage. Or worse.

The former was his first instinct; the latter made more sense.

'Sorry about that. So, what were you saying?'

Sarah held her hands up in a surrender position. 'Look, you've every right to be pissed off, and I'm sorry. But I would still like to work on a piece with you. You have a big fan base back in Scotland and it would be a brilliant coup for me to get a personal interview with you. You know, "local boy made good" stuff.'

She was lying. They both knew it. And they both knew that he wasn't going to agree to what she wanted. But for now, he had to get a break to think. And to get some pain-killers for his aching head.

Right on cue, a shooting pain right across his forehead made him visibly shudder.

'Are you OK?'

'Yeah, sure. Just the after-effects of too many refreshments. The last time I got wasted – I mean proper wasted – I think I was about sixteen.'

The eyes crinkled, the bashful expression made an appearance as he went for the full-scale charm offensive. It seemed to work.

'Was that back in Glasgow? What happened?'

Wow, he walked right into that one.

'Look, I'll tell you all about it, I promise. But can we take a rain check right now? Can we continue this when my bloodstream isn't eighty per cent Macallan?'

'Sure.' An edge of incredulity crept into her voice. She was clearly surprised he'd come down on the side of cooperation. Score one for the hung-over douche.

'Great,' he said, using every ounce of physical and mental strength to switch into Davie Personality Johnston mode. Pull it back, son. 'So where are you staying?'

'Le Parc Suite, off Melrose.'

'OK. So how about I come pick you up one day this week, take you for lunch and we'll talk? We'll put the interview together, maybe arrange a few pics?'

'That would be . . . great. Amazing.' He could tell it wasn't the reaction she'd expected. Good.

'Then it's a deal. But if you don't mind, I need to go now. Can I trust your promise that everything you've heard up until now will stay confidential?'

'Absolutely.'

Either she was a brilliant liar or she was telling the truth.

'Thanks, Sarah.' He stood up, bringing the conversation to a full stop with a tone that said 'warmth and trust' instead of the more accurate 'fear and horror'.

'I'm gonna hit the shower. Ivanka will show you out.'

'Will she have me killed on the way?'

'Not today. She doesn't do hits at the weekend.'

'Good to know.'

He checked his watch. 'And if you go now, you might make Bouchon for lunch. I've heard it's Ryan's favourite.'

This time her smile was genuine. 'My day just got even better. Thanks, Davie.'

'No problem.' As he held open the door for her to pass him on the way to the waiting cab, there was a definite tug of regret. In a different world, he could like this chick. But hey, nothing was ever that simple. This had to be closed down and he'd have to find a way to make sure that happened.

But first, time to play a little chess with his bitch of a wife.

And it was his move.

41.

'Iron Sky' – Paolo Nutini

Filming had overrun by hours and Zander desperately wanted it to be done. They'd been on set for twelve hours, and for ten of them he had been suspended in a harness that was cutting off circulation to his ass.

Yep, he was living the dream.

When Axl Chang, the director, finally called 'Cut,' he would have cried with relief if it were not for the fact that he was still in character as Dunhill, and the British spy would never succumb to weakness or weeping.

Dunhill did saving the world from evil forces. He did not do cramp in one leg and serious impingement of his genital area.

The crane creaked as he was lowered to the ground and Hollie immediately materialized beside him.

'How do you do that?' he asked wearily.

'Do what?'

'Just appear like that.'

'It's a gift. OK, so I know you're tired, but you had meetings tonight and I've managed to shift all of them except one.' Hollie flicked through emails and texts on her iPad as she spoke.

Zander held up his hands to let the stunt team unclip him and set him free. Only when his nethers were liberated did he reply.

'Which one?'

'Adrianna Guilloti. Their head of marketing has flown in from New York and he's on the red-eye back out tonight, so I couldn't move it. You're meeting him at eight p.m. at Shutters. I switched it from the Chateau so that he's closer to the airport and you're closer to home. Give you more time to impress him.' Hollie rounded off the barb with a playful nudge. 'Woo, Mr Leith. Woo him. To the tune of a million bucks if you do it right.'

Adrianna Guilloti was a major emerging player in the men's fashion world. More classic than Tom Ford, edgier than Dolce & Gabbana, they were gaining serious market share in the high-end sector. They'd already put together a proposal with the business managers and now they wanted a meeting with Zander to seal the deal. 'One on one, no suits' had been their official request.

Zander ran his fingers through his hair, breaking the bond on the gel that had held it meticulously in place all day, then sat on a prop box while the make-up assistant removed the last trace of foundation and mascara from his face.

'Hollie, I'll love you forever if you get me out of it. Seriously.'

'You'd better love me forever anyway, and no, I can't. Look, they're on course for world domination, and despite the fact that they've seen pictures of you sprawled in a gutter, they still want to talk about an endorsement deal. It's a huge one. I'd be remiss in my duties if I didn't make you go, so get it together and do your fricking job.'

The make-up assistant froze, mouth agape.

Hollie looked up from her iPad. 'What? Too much?'

Zander shook his head, his expression rueful. 'I thought this town was supposed to be full of sycophants who did nothing but suck up to the talent? How do I replace you with one of those?'

'An Adrianna Guilloti suit is hanging in your dressing room, you have less than five minutes to change, your car is already outside, and it's available to take you straight home afterwards, where there's a salad and protein shake in the fridge, both your favourites, and I've left a couple of DVD screeners on your coffee table. Still wanna fire me?'

'Yes. But I won't. Need to keep Americans in jobs. Doing my bit for the economy.'

Hollie's laughter followed him along the corridor, and she was still smiling as she walked with him to the limo ten minutes later.

'So how are you really doing?' she asked, searching his face for clues. 'Wes wants you to meet a shrink. The one he uses. Which probably means you'll be cured of the longing to drink but be suddenly desperate to have threesomes with young aspiring actresses who'll do anything for a break.'

Her words were flippant, but Zander was still stuck on the first part. 'I'm not seeing another shrink, Holls. Can you make it go away?' He wasn't even annoyed, more somewhere between weary and quietly resistant.

'You sure?'

'I'm sure.'

There was no way he was going down that road again. Every therapist he'd ever known had kicked off by attempting to take him back to his childhood, and if there was anything that was absolutely sure to make him want to drink, it was there.

Right there.

Sitting between a fucked-up father, a devout mother and a desperation to escape the burden of both.

'OK, I'll see what I can do. And I'm just saying, there's an AA meeting on at Venice Recovery Center tonight, ten p.m.'

'You do keep trying, don't you?' Zander said.

'Only because you pay me to,' she replied, only able to say that because they both knew it wasn't true.

It was a different car tonight – no Leandro to keep him company and no drinks in the minibar. Hollie had done her job. Almost. He took a flask out of his sock and threw back some neat vodka. Grey Goose. Just one for the road. One. He'd been sober for days and this wasn't letting anyone down. Not really. It wasn't as if he was going to get wasted. Even as he tried to justify it to himself, he knew he was being a dick. How could he have had such focus and determination only a couple of days ago and now it had gone to shit?

Travel time came in at way over an hour thanks to killer traffic all the way along the 10, so the rest of it was gone by the time he got to Shutters On the Beach, a stunning, elegant five-star hotel on the sands of Santa Monica, with an awesome view of the famous Ferris wheel at the end of the pier. The maître d' showed him to a table on the terrace with a panoramic view of the ocean. A beautiful thirty-something woman sat waiting, drumming her steel-coloured fingernails on the table. As soon as she saw him, the transition was remarkable – from stern irritation to wide smile in a split second. If this broad didn't make it in fashion, she'd have a future in acting.

So they were both in the land of make-believe. She was pretending she was happy to be there, and he was pretending to be sober.

'Adrianna Guilloti. Pleased to meet you.' There was a slight, sexy trace of a Latin or European accent.

'Zander Leith. And apologies. I thought I was meeting your head of marketing tonight.'

'You were. I've sent him on to the airport and I must leave here shortly to go join him.'

Zander waved away the menus that were being offered by an obviously star-struck waitress and ordered drinks. A martini for her, a soda water for him.

It gave him time to weigh up what was going on here. Damn, his brain wasn't kicking in as quickly as it would if it hadn't taken a car ride that was sponsored by Grey Goose.

Hollie had briefed him on the company months ago and he tried to remember what he knew about the boss. She was self-made. Half Italian. Or Spanish. Based in New York, had some major-bucks investors, and their brand was beginning to make real headway in the market.

As he stared at the woman responsible, he could see why. Sure, she was beautiful. Long, sleek black hair that was straight from the *Pocahontas* costume department, cheekbones you could ski off, dark red lips that clashed against her hazel eyes. But it was her style that stood out most. A man's suit jacket, exquisitely tailored in deep grey, with a white shirt left open just low enough to expose a couple of inches of rich caramel cleavage. A matching skirt, cut below the knee, but tight enough for the highly trained eye to spot the tiny bumps of her stocking clips.

It might have been the vodka, but right then he was fairly sure that she was the most breathtaking sight he'd ever seen.

She didn't even make a polite pretence about checking her watch. Rolex President in rose gold, he noticed, while detecting the unmistakable aroma of Chanel No. 5 and serious cash.

'Forgive me for being direct, Mr Leith, but I don't have long. I just wanted to meet you and give you an opportunity to reassure me that my investment will be a wise one.'

OK, so she was straight to the point. Direct. He could handle that.

'I have no doubt that your endorsement will benefit my brand and I think we could have a mutually profitable partnership, but you see, I have become troubled by nightmares . . .'

Her warm smile and ambient tone made it clear they weren't of the ghoulish kind.

'And in those nightmares a very wonderful actor is punching someone while wearing an Adrianna Guilloti suit.'

Either Zander or the Grey Goose decided to play. It was unclear which.

'So, red carpets, editorials, publicity shots – all good. Fights and anything that could lead to your clothes being accessorized with handcuffs – all bad.'

Her throaty chuckle made something in his groin area stir.

'Yes, exactly. I think we understand each other.'

'Great. I'm sure I can match up to your expectations,' Zander told her, eyes crinkling, thinking she'd played this game before. Hard-ass. Professional. With just a large hint of so damn sexy.

'That's good to hear. Now, again, forgive me, but I must go catch my flight.' She stood up and offered her hand.

He took it and kissed it, a gesture that would be cheesy if performed by any other guy. When accompanied by his standard mischievous expression, Zander Leith could pull it off.

Half the restaurant blatantly watched her go; the other half pretended not to while resolving to up their grooming schedule. And that was saying something in this part of town.

How much did he want to go after her? Persuade her to stay. He'd just netted a deal that would be worth $1 million this year and yet that was being kicked out of the park by the fact that he desperately wanted to know more about that irresistible creature.

Long ago, a shrink had told him he had an issue with short-term gratification and taught him some cognitive behavioural therapy to deal with it. He took a deep breath and attempted some CBT in the hope of derailing the urge to go after her, attempt to seduce her and no doubt make a colossal fuck-up that would end with him being dropped from the deal and seeking solace in the bottom of a bottle of Jack. Calm. Focused. Early call tomorrow. Calm. Focused. Early call tomorrow.

'Can I have the check, please?'

'The lady already took care of it, Mr Leith.'

Pure class. Man, she was killing him. Another time, he told himself. Another time.

The urge to party hadn't quite left him, so he decided to walk home. Hollie would kill him for going anywhere on foot without security, but the need to be outside was as irresistible as it was compelling.

He texted the driver to let him go, slipped out of the French doors leading onto the boardwalk, kept his head down, removing his tie and jacket as he went. As soon as he reached the sands, he pulled off his shoes and socks, rolled up his sleeves. His $5,000 suit had suddenly become beachwear.

Now he was a silhouette. Not famous. Not a star. To the few people who lay around the sands in the darkness, he was just another guy strolling along the edge of the water.

In the distance, the flickering lights of a plane rose from LAX. It was too soon to be the red-eye to New York, but it still resurrected the image of Adrianna Guilloti in his head. There was someone who had it together. Knew what she wanted. Had he ever really felt like that? There had never been a plan or a purpose. It was all just action and reaction, moving along, dealing with the days and getting into shit at night. Short-term pleasure. Long-term chaos.

What could he offer someone like Adrianna Guilloti? Yeah, there was the money and his face on a billboard, but what else? Would she come bail him out when he got messed up? Forgive him when he fell off the wagon and was papped falling out of Lix with some half-naked babe from a reality show?

Zander Leith had never had a grown-up relationship in his life. He'd moved from movie to movie, location to location, picking up three-month flings here and there, usually with models who spent the majority of their lives in different time zones.

And when he wasn't screwing up his sex life, he was a wasted mess, reacting to paparazzi-baiting, biting back and giving them exactly what they wanted – an out-of-control tosser whose car-crash actions made sellable footage.

The faint whiff of marijuana and the sound of music playing along the boardwalk alerted him to the fact that he had crossed the threshold from Santa Monica to Venice.

He thought of cutting across the sands, heading up Rose and going to the 10 p.m. AA meeting. He should. He really should. Maybe it was time to sort himself out. Stop running. Make commitments. That thought, rather than the sea breeze, made him shiver. Besides, last time he'd gone, the room was half full of people who had no problems with alcohol, just a problem getting a role in Hollywood. They were just there for the networking.

Hello, my name is Chad and I'm an alcoholic. I also did three years in acting class and I don't mind doing full-frontal nudity.

Still, right now, he didn't feel any more together than they were.

There had to be something seriously wrong with a guy who could shake on a million-dollar-deal and still feel like he had nothing worthwhile in his life, and worse, found it difficult to summon a reason to fix it.

Ruling out the detour to the AA meeting, Zander walked

another few hundred yards, then cut across the sands to his apartment block, speeding up now, decision made. Moral dilemma solved. AA could wait. Right now, at home, a Jack and Coke had his name on it. Just one. Maybe two. For all he knew, there could be ten hours in the harness again tomorrow and that would be a killer with a hangover. Not that he hadn't done it before. That was the secret. Enough to stay loose, not too much to fall over or slur. He'd managed to live the last two decades of his life mildly drunk, and with the delusion of the veteran alcoholic, he was fairly sure no one knew.

He let himself in the front door and climbed the stairs to his apartment. Halfway up, a sudden wave of dread hit him. Please God, don't let Chloe be there again. He'd already dealt with that too many times and he had no desire for a replay.

The anxiety rose as he turned the corner, only for the trepidation to switch to confusion.

The first thing he noticed were the grey jeans and the leather boots. Then the black hoodie, with red curls escaping from the inside edges of the hood.

Shit. Seriously? Again?

'Chloe, come on, you can't—'

The rise of her head cut him dead.

'Hey, Zander,' she said. The voice hadn't changed. The decades rewound like the reels of a slot machine in reverse. Mirren was staring at him with the steely eyes that haunted his sleep.

'I think it's time to have a conversation about your relationship with my daughter.'

42.

'Stay Away' – Nirvana

'You'd better come in,' Zander told her, clearly rattled.

So he should be. The hour she'd sat waiting had been a tortuous internal wrangle between dread, confusion and sheer bloody fury.

How fucking dare he? He was a grown man, and Chloe was . . . She was a child. Deep down. Underneath all that attitude and bravado.

He was the last person she wanted to see right now. As if Jack's affair and Chloe's addictions weren't enough to deal with, now she was forced to face the man who'd made it oh so clear he never wanted to see her face ever again. Not that she blamed him. They'd done too much, hurt too deep. Their past was water under the bridge that could still drown them at any moment and they all knew it. That was why she hadn't returned Davie's calls. That was why she'd scrupulously avoided running into Zander Leith for the last twenty years. She hadn't watched his movies. She'd turned her head away from the billboards. She'd switched off talk shows the minute he walked out, stage left, arms open, ready to hug Jay Leno,

319

Jimmy Kimmel, Chelsea Handler. And yet now, looking at his face, that beautiful face, she just wanted to touch him.

Or kill him.

It was hard to say.

He held open the door of his apartment and let her pass. Always the gentleman. Always had been. If she'd had to imagine where he lived, this would be exactly it, she realized as she scanned the room. Wooden floors. White walls. Doors that opened to a balcony overlooking the ocean. Simple. Basic. A few months before, she'd accidentally come across pictures of Davie's mansion in an architectural magazine, and it was so over-the-top, ostentatious and lavish. Exactly Davie. Loud, extrovert, making a statement. Zander was the opposite end of the 'look at me' scale.

'Why here?' she asked, crossing the room to the balcony doors and looking out onto the ocean, the waves illuminated by the lights along the boardwalk. She got the desire to be near the water; she understood the lack of material stuff, but the location?

'Why here?' she repeated. 'Why not Malibu?'

There was a long pause and she almost turned round to look at him, but she couldn't. Not yet. She didn't trust herself not to crumble. The whole time she'd sat out on his landing she'd been preparing her speech. Ranting. Raving. Drilling him for the truth. Now, she just wanted silence, a breather to adjust to the seismic shift and the explosion of feelings the last five minutes had caused.

'I like the noise,' he said. Of course. He'd be miserable somewhere quiet. Cut off from the world. Up in the Colony, the only activity was the occasional delivery or gardener firing up a lawnmower. Here, even with the doors shut, there was music, voices, activity in the distance. That's exactly the life Zander would choose. For a second she was sad she hadn't made the same choices.

Behind her, she could hear a cupboard opening, the clink of glasses, the sigh of someone who didn't want to be in this moment.

'Drink?' he said, drawing up beside her, a glass of Jack Daniels in each hand. Reluctantly she took it. This wasn't a social call, yet not one second of it was going as she'd imagined.

They both stood and stared into the darkness. Several moments passed before either found words.

'Is she OK?' Zander asked, almost a whisper.

Mirren's rage kicked in again. 'Why do you care? What's my daughter got to do with you?'

He ran his fingers through his wavy hair, still exactly the same style that he'd had for his whole life. It was like a snapshot of their past.

'I met her in rehab,' he said, as if that should make everything perfectly clear.

'Oh, for Christ's sake. Of course you did. In this world, that makes complete sense.'

The bitterness and fury were impossible to conceal.

'So what is this, then? She's eighteen years old, Zander.' Saying his name jolted her into silence.

'I know what age she is. There's nothing you need to worry about here, Mirren. We're friends. That's it. Nothing more.'

'Of course you are.' Even as she was saying it, she didn't believe it, and yet she had to, because she couldn't go there.

Couldn't contemplate it. Couldn't open her mind to the fucked-up consequences and implications of that.

'Mirren, let me tell you about it. I promise—'

She cut him dead. 'You can promise me nothing, Zander. Addicts don't keep promises.' She thrust the glass into his hand, realizing it was trembling as much as hers.

'I have to go. I can't stay here.'

'I know.'

'But I'm warning you, Zander. Begging you. Stay away from my girl. Stay. Away.'

He nodded his head. Silent. That was Zander Leith all over. Always had been. A man of few words. Deep. Nothing on the surface. Davie always said . . . Davie. The thought made her stop at the door, turn round.

'Davie called me, left a message. Some journalist from the *Daily Scot* wants to talk to him about our families back home.'

'I know. She called me too. I brushed her off. Davie will do the same.'

'You sure?'

'Yeah. He's far too smart to let her anywhere near him.'

'I hope you're right.' She took a few steps into the hall. 'Goodbye, Zander. Please don't ever talk to my daughter again.'

With that she started walking and didn't stop until she reached the car, her head screaming with potential scenarios, all of them too painful to bear.

Two addicts. Both in her orbit. If they crashed together, the meteor shower would wipe out her world.

The speedometer didn't pass sixty as she drove home, coastline all the way, right along the PCH. Thoughts collided in her head, images, scenarios. Was this all her fault? Had she failed Chloe? Was her daughter about to become another victim of her catastrophic past?

No. She wouldn't let it happen. She'd do what she had to do. Get Chloe back into rehab. Get her straight. Work with her. Rebuild their relationship. And perhaps when she was in a good place again, she might even tell her. The truth always comes to the surface. Maybe she should be the one to bring it there before anyone else did.

As she slowed down to approach the entrance to the estate, the guard spotted her and raised the barrier and waved her through, her speed increasing but only into the twenties. She was in no hurry to get home.

With a heavy heart, she slung a left into her driveway, so different from the beach property she'd just left.

The thought made her stomach churn.

It was his voice she heard first as she opened the car door.

'Mirren! Mirren. Oh thank God, Mirren. I think she's sick. Really sick.'

Her legs refused to move; her brain struggled to process. 'What do you mean, sick?'

'She got drugs, Mir. Must have had them stashed in her room. She took them and . . .' Jack was wailing now, standing on the lawn, his expression one of sheer terror.

Nothing was making sense. Jack. The noise. Coming up behind her. The blue light. On. Off. On. The bang of a door.

'Excuse me, ma'am, we're coming through.'

Two medics, running past her, and now she was chasing them, going after them, running, screaming.

'Noooooooooo!'

43.

'Crazy' – Gnarls Barkley

For a long time Zander didn't move. Couldn't. Just nothing there. This is what the day after a bottle of Jack Daniel's felt like: the nausea, the crashing agony in his head, the fear, the anger, all bubbling on a wave of dread.

Yet Mirren had only left five minutes ago.

He threw open the balcony doors to try to relieve the claustrophobia that was suddenly making the walls creak towards him. And the itch. The itch was back and his skin was starting to feel like it was crawling. Only one thing medicated that pain. There was no coke in the house. In the distance, he could hear music and he knew that a score was only five minutes away, in any one of two or three bars within a few hundred yards.

He grabbed his jacket, fumbled for his wallet, opened it and . . . empty.

No money. Just a note.

'Sorry, don't hate me. I've taken your cash in case, well, you know. If you need anything, call me. Love, Hxx'

Aaaargh!

The itch was seeping out of his pores now, moving from

under the skin to the top of it, searching, probing, demanding to be satisfied.

One line. Just one line. He did a calculation in his head. Next drug test was Monday. Today was Tuesday. There was a slim chance it would still be in his system, but he didn't care. He didn't care. Shit, he did care.

He couldn't face that again. The disappointment in Wes's face. The sadness in Hollie's. This was the moment the counsellors talked about. Yes or no. In or out.

A shred of sense somewhere deep in the survival synapse of his mind told him it could only be out and he knew that wasn't going to be possible if he stayed here. His resolve might last an hour. Maybe two. But he knew himself well enough.

He had to get away from here or he was going back to a cloud in Colombia and that could only end badly.

The idea came out of nowhere, shaped up in his mind, and instantly, he evaluated the pros and dismissed the cons.

No contest.

The number was answered on the second ring. 'Good evening, Mr Leith. How can I help you?'

'I need to go to New York. Tonight. Can you organize a jet at Van Nuys?'

'Of course, Mr Leith. Do you have your security code and password there?'

He rhymed both off, one from the card in his wallet and the other from memory.

'Your code and password have been accepted, Mr Leith. How many passengers will there be?'

'Just one.'

'Yes, sir. And when do you wish to leave?'

'Soon as possible.'

Now. Right now. Before he did something incredibly stupid. Yep, what did it say about his life that this was the most *sensible* plan he could come up with?

'Certainly, Mr Leith. OK, let me just check . . . Sir, I've got the flight company on the other line. They have a Challenger 605 on standby and it can be ready for you in one hour. Is there anything else I can do for you this evening?'

'Can you send a car to my house? Twenty minutes? And arrange a car into Manhattan at the other end?'

'Certainly, Mr Leith.'

'Great, thanks.'

What had his therapist said? Go after another buzz. Find a high that didn't come from any kind of chemical or alcohol. Disrupt the desperation for coke by focusing on something else. Exercise. Love. Sex. Travel.

Tick number four and hold the other three on standby.

Packing took less than ten minutes as he threw a couple of T-shirts, a pair of jeans, socks and a shirt into a bag. Despite a high-profile underwear campaign in the early days, he preferred to go commando.

Travelling clothes next. He exchanged the trousers of the Guilloti suit for black jeans, but kept on the white shirt and jacket. With a pair of Armani black leather boots, it worked. Not that fashion was his thing, but he wanted to look pass-able. Put together. Nothing like a druggie desperate to hoover up a large pile of fine white powder.

It was only an hour and a half later, as the LA lights grew

smaller and disappeared, that he realized he'd omitted one vital call.

He speed-dialled the number.

'Oh God, tell me it's not handcuffs or a dead body. Anything else I can deal with,' was her opening line.

It felt good to laugh. There hadn't been enough of that lately.

'You might want to rethink that statement after this conversation.'

Hollie played along. 'OK, hostage situation, you've joined a terrorist cell, the discovery of an evil twin. Other than that I'm good. What's that noise in the background? Are you in a car? I warned Leandro to let me know if you called him. Tell him he's fired.'

'Not a car, and Leandro's in the clear. I'm on a plane.'

'I hadn't even got onto mode of transport yet! Crap, dammit. Oh God, I'm scared to ask. Please tell me this is a wind-up. Damn, why can't I work for Matt Damon? He's like the most scandal-free guy ever. It would be fricking heaven. What plane, Zander? I swear I'm calling Damon's office in the morning.'

'I need to go to New York.'

'No, you don't, Zander. What you need is to get yourself to set in the morning. What you need is to make a movie. What you need—'

'OK, OK, I get it.'

'So you'll turn around?'

'No.'

'Shit.'

'Sorry. Look, Holls, it was really close. It was this or the dark side,' he said, using Hollie's code for drug-dealer central.

There was a pause on the other end of the line as she digested this.

'So the fact that you're on a private plane, heading for New York, spending a hundred thousand dollars is actually a best-case scenario?'

'Absolutely.'

'I'm sure Matt Damon's number will be in the book.'

'He won't love you like I do.'

'Well, hello, Flattery, I've been expecting you.'

'I'm sorry to leave you with the crap . . .'

'No you're not.'

'But can you clear this with the studio?'

A strangled exhalation of irritation was her initial reply, then, 'OK, I'll call Axl in the morning, but don't blame me if he goes Jackie Chan on your ass.'

'You'll protect me,' he joked.

'I'll help him,' she replied. 'Look, it shouldn't be a deal-breaker. You were only scheduled for a couple of hours in the morning for blocking. We'll get a stand-in. I'll tape it, go through it with you later.'

'Thanks, Hollie. I really mean that.'

'I know you do. Can I ask why you're going to New York?'

Zander laughed. 'Oops, sorry, captain says we're about to hit turbulence.'

'But—'

'Sorry, Holls, phones need to go off.' The last thing he heard as he pressed the red button on his cell was something about 'asshole' and 'calling Matt Damon'.

Call disconnected, he threw the phone on the white leather sofa, poured a glass of Jack Daniel's from the bar.

'Mr Leith, I could have got that for you.'

The male steward materialized from behind the curtain in front of the lounge area. Tall, impeccably groomed, a young Richard Gere, who'd probably been on ten casting calls that day before doing the night shift on the jet.

Zander was glad it wasn't a stewardess. Over the years there had been many flights, and while the majority of the stewardesses were the epitome of professionalism, there had been a few who were more than happy to join in the party. Good times, but not for tonight. Tonight he needed something entirely different.

'That's OK. Listen, I'm just gonna take this back with me and get some shut-eye. Can you give me a shout when we're half an hour out?'

'Will do. There's a call button on the bedside table if you need anything.'

'Thanks, mate.'

The bedroom was small but luxurious, big enough for a double bed and some room to walk around it. The bedding was cream silk, with Frette sheets, perfectly arranged gold jacquard shams and booster pillows. Zander kicked off his boots, took off his shirt and, JD in hand, lay back and switched on the TV using the remote that was on the bedside. The guys on TMZ were pounding on some NFL player who'd been caught in a strip club while his very pregnant wife headed to the maternity suite. The next item showed Davie Johnston heading through the gates of his mansion, while his wife and her co-star Darcy Jay disappeared behind Darcy's front door. The innuendo of the chat made sure the implication was clear, without anything actually being said.

Harvey Levin, the TMZ chief, was, as he liked to remind everyone, a lawyer.

As the attention switched to a brawl at LAX between a snapper and Lex Callaghan's mother, the hilarity ramped right up. Mrs Callaghan was in possession of a fierce right hook. They were still discussing it, to the sound of the *Rocky* soundtrack, when Zander fell asleep, missing the rest of the show.

At exactly thirty minutes until landing at Teterboro Airport, young Richard Gere woke him with an egg-white omelette, fruit, juice and coffee. The airline kept a record of his preferences.

In the washroom, he showered, shaved and pulled his jeans back on, this time going for a white Prada T-shirt. It would look OK under the Guilloti jacket. Aviator shades on, he headed down the stairs to the car that was waiting on the runway as requested.

Eight a.m. and morning traffic into Manhattan was flowing surprisingly freely. Perfect.

He'd already looked up the address on his iPhone and gave it to the driver. Fifth Avenue. On the adjacent block to Trump Tower.

The driver flicked on the hazards while he pulled over to let Zander out at the door to the building. The doorman, a sixtyish guy in a grey uniform, had opened it before he even got there.

'Good morning, sir. Can I help? Oh. Mr Leith. I watched the Dunhill *Triple Jeopardy* only last night. Great movie. Wife's certainly a fan.'

'Great to hear.' Zander paused, aware of how this situation

would go, exactly as it had done a million times before. The expression on the doorman's face said it all. 'Do you have a piece of paper?' Zander added.

'Indeed.' He sprinted over to his desk and came back with an A4 sheet of paper and a pen. Zander took both.

'What's your wife's name?'

'Janice. Janice Crane.'

Zander scribbled something on the paper. 'OK, got a camera phone?'

The doorman pulled a smartphone from his pocket as Zander held the paper up in front of him.

'OK, go for it.'

Sixty seconds later, one unsuspecting Queens housewife would be shopping in the frozen-food aisle of her grocery store when a photo would come through from her husband, a selfie of him and Zander Leith, her favourite actor, holding up a sign saying, 'Good morning, Janice.'

Her life would be complete. Her husband would get laid tonight.

Meanwhile, back on Fifth Avenue, George the doorman was having one of the best starts to his day ever, and that was saying something for a guy who had worked Manhattan doors since he was a teenager.

With a grip that was as fierce as it was enthusiastic, he shook Zander's hand. Only when he was done did he release it and rewind to the fact that Zander Leith was there for a reason.

'Sorry, Mr Leith, how can I help you this morning? And whoever you're here to see, please don't mention this or I'll be out on the hot-dog stands by the end of the week,' he said with a twinkle in his eye.

'Don't worry, George – your secret's safe. I'm actually here to see—'

His words were interrupted by the buzzing of the door, and he didn't even have to look up to see who was there. For once in his messed-up life, this was actually playing out like the movies.

'Darn it!' George sprinted to the door, his face flushing at his very obvious lapse in his duties.

The new arrival didn't notice. Her gaze was fixed on Zander's, watching him stand there, leaning casually against the reception desk, as if this was an everyday occurrence.

He was watching her too. Her jet-black hair gleamed and her oversized YSL dark glasses cut out the winter sun, her eight-inch, steel-heeled stilettos and leather skirt a sharp contrast to the cream cashmere swing coat and the grey Hermès Birkin she carried in the crook of her arm.

This was a *Vogue* editorial shot come to life.

'Good morning,' she said, with all the confidence of someone who expected things like this to happen in her life.

'Good morning,' he replied. 'I was in the neighbour-hood . . .'

That one got a laugh, and if it was possible, as she threw back her head, she became even more beautiful than before.

'But how did you know I'd be here today? And this early?'

'Because you've been out of the office for a couple of days and you seem to me to be the kind of lady who would make sure she caught up with anything she'd missed while she was away. Educated guess. And a bit of wild optimism.'

Adrianna Guilloti laughed again, walking towards him now.

'And you got here by . . . ?'

'Challenger 605. And I say that to be factual, not to act like a dickhead.'

'I appreciate that,' she assured him, pulling off her gloves, one finger at a time, completely unaware of just how fucking sexy that was. Zander was experiencing a familiar stirring in the crotch area. Hell, even George had a boner and that didn't happen often without a little help from a small blue pill.

They were toe to toe now. Face to face.

'And since you seem to have all the answers this morning, how exactly did you envisage the rest of this day?'

Zander smiled and shrugged. 'I hadn't got that far. I figured I'd do the legwork and leave the rest up to you.'

George, the epitome of discretion, looked away as Adrianna lifted her face and brought it even closer, closer still, until their lips were only millimetres apart. Then she paused, like an adder contemplating her prey.

Her prey moved first. Zander's hand touched her neck, lightly to begin with, before coming up higher and framing her face. Then he pulled her mouth to his, their lips almost still as they touched and held there, before moving, in perfect synchronicity.

After way too long to be anything less than a promise of something more, Zander gently pulled back.

'So what now?'

Adrianna's stare and the rise at the corner of her mouth were almost a challenge.

'That's up to you. Where are you staying?'

He hadn't even got that far. But then, it wasn't a tough question. He looked over to George.

'Bud, can you call the Carlyle and tell them I'm on my way?'

'Of course I can. Consider it done.'

'Does that work for you?' he asked Adrianna, with absolute confidence that it did.

She shrugged nonchalantly. 'I can live with it.'

He kissed her again, both of them laughing.

'Then we should go.' One hand rested lightly on the back of Adrianna's coat as they headed to the door; the other was outstretched as Zander passed his new acquaintance.

'George, good to meet you.' The two men shook hands.

'And great to meet you too,' George replied, once again flaunting the grip of a well-oiled vice.

With his other hand, George opened the door and then watched the surreal sight of Zander Leith and Adrianna Guilloti climbing into a limo.

Only when they were out of sight did the realities of the situation kick in. George went behind his reception desk, pressed rewind on the security camera and scrubbed the last thirty minutes of footage.

Mrs Guilloti's husband owned the building and George wouldn't want to be around if evidence of this morning's activities fell into his hands.

Even as he scrubbed the tape, George knew that it could cost him his job. Hell, it could cost him his legs. But hey, he'd have a happy wife and a lifetime of telling his grandkids about the morning he met Zander Leith.

44.

'No Mean City' – Maggie Bell

Glasgow, 1988

'Have you washed your hands, Davie?' Zander's mum asked, just as she'd done before every meal he'd had at her house since before he could talk.

'Aye, Mrs Leith. Twice,' he said, face pure innocence.

Zander booted him under the table, and shoulders shaking, they both buried their faces in their clasped hands as Mrs Leith moved on to stage two of the pre-dinner ritual.

'Dear Father, bless this food we are about to receive, knowing that we take it with thanks and gratitude to the Lord Jesus Christ, your son, who has given us the fruits of his bounty . . .'

Davie fought not to giggle again. The fruits of his bounty? It was gammon steak and chips. The only fruit here was the pineapple rings she fished out of a can and plonked on the gammon before she took it out of the grill.

'. . . and forgive us for the sins we have committed. Oh Lord, grant us the power to serve You, in Jesus's name, Amen.'

'Amen.' The word echoed around the table.

'Right, boys, tuck in before I claim the lot. I'm starving and nothing's safe.'

Davie grinned as Jono repeated his oft-used banter, but he noticed Zander didn't. It was no secret that his mate hated his dad, but Davie found it hard to feel the same. Mr Leith was always a right laugh, even if half the scheme was terrified of him. Davie preferred to keep onside, amuse him, avoid rocking the boat. So while Zander sat in silence, barely raising his eyes from the table, Davie kept everyone entertained with a steady stream of stories and gossip. He liked doing that. Taking something that happened and adding bits on until it was a blinding story that bore little resemblance to the truth. What did it matter? It gave everyone a chuckle. And he liked that Jono always gave him the time of day – gave him a wee idea of what it must feel like to have a dad.

'More peas, Davie?'

'No thanks, Mrs Leith. I'm allergic to vegetables. Bad for ma health.'

Zander's dad laughed again, but Zander just gave him that look, the one that said, 'Shut the fuck up, ya diddy.' It wasn't exactly a newsflash. Davie winked at him, just to wind him up even more.

The first crash was so loud that Davie's initial thought was that a car had smashed through the front of the house. That had happened up at number 1 on the end, when the ice-cream van had mounted the kerb and gone straight through their new double glazing. The police and an ambulance were called, but only after every kid in the street had filled their pockets, hats and jumpers with every piece of confectionery they could loot from the back of the van. The irony was that they'd only put the double glazing in so that the kids wouldn't hear the ice-cream van.

Now, startled by the noise, three of them jumped to their feet, only Zander's dad staying perfectly still. Even the second bang, just as loud as the first, didn't make him move. Later, Davie would decide that he'd known what was coming, was prepared for it.

His mum used to talk about 'time standing still', but he never really knew what that meant until that moment. They just stood there, frozen, not saying a word, and then suddenly the door burst open and three men charged in, all of them wearing balaclavas and tooled up. Davie might have peed himself just a little.

Zander's mum was screaming now, but Jono was still sitting there, saying nothing, not moving. What was the point? There were three of them and they were fucking gorillas. Gorillas carrying fuck-off big knives, and a baseball bat that had huge nails hammered through the end, so it looked deadly.

He definitely peed his pants at the sight of that.

Only then did he notice that Zander had run in front of his mother and was holding the bread knife that had been on the table just seconds ago. Mrs Leith had her eyes shut, praying now, lips moving but nothing coming out.

Always in touch with his emotions, Davie was quick to realize that he now qualified as being fucking terrified. This wasn't good.

One of the balaclavas had gone round the back of Zander's dad now, grabbed his hair and pulled it back, while Balaclava Two punched him square in the mouth. Still Jono didn't react. Man, he had balls of steel.

Balaclava Three watched the action and only when Jono's head had been returned to something approaching a normal position did he speak.

'Where is it, Jono?'

'Don't know what you're talking about.'

Bang. Another punch. This time teeth came flying out and blood splattered all over the table. All Davie could think was that it looked like he'd put tomato sauce on his gammon steak. Oh God, they were all going to die. Frantic, he eyed the door. He could make it. He was fast. Nippy.

'Don't even think about it, son.'

Apparently Balaclava Three practised mind reading when he wasn't studying effective methods of intimidation and torture.

He was going to die. And he hadn't even said goodbye to his mum. Tears sprang to the back of his eyes and he fought to stop them falling.

Zander's dad's face looked like mash now, blood dripping from his mouth, his nose, his forehead.

'Last chance, Jono. And, son –' he was talking to Zander now, '– don't get any ideas about that blade you're holding, because if it comes anywhere near me or my men, I'll take it off you and your ma will be wearing it as an earring. Do you understand me?'

Zander didn't reply, his eyes blazing, his knuckles white around the sheath of the knife.

'Last chance, Jono, then these fine boys will be having liver for dinner. Yours. Uncooked.'

The balaclava laughed, and that made him even scarier than when he was just being generally mental and deadly.

338

One of the sidekicks pulled Jono's hand onto the dining table and held the knife above it. Then slowly he brought the blade down, to the left of his thumb, then the next finger, then the next, a thud between each digit as the point of the blade hit the table. Faster. Faster. He repeated it one side to the other, then back, then again, then back, the noise matched only by the battering thuds of Davie's heart.

'Where is it, Jono? Where is it? Where is it?'

He was speaking faster now, keeping time with the twisted game of chicken that was going on at the table.

'Where is it?'

'Aaaaargh, ya fucker!' Jono screamed, as the blade punctured his middle finger, impaling it on the table.

'That's yer wanking hand fucked, then,' the boss said, apparently amused at his own joke.

'Keep going,' he ordered his co-psycho.

The thudding started again, between the fingers, faster, faster . . .

'Aaaaaargh.' Index finger this time, blood spurting everywhere.

'Holy Mary, mother of God, pray for us sinners . . .'

Behind Zander, his mum had turned up the volume and was rocking back and forward, eyes shut, as if she'd cut herself off from reality altogether.

Davie wished he could do the same.

Thud, thud . . . Over and over again, until all five fingers had been impaled and released a spurt of thick red liquid. Davie wanted to vomit. Right there. Right now. This was the most horrific thing he could ever imagine.

'Get the boy.'

His imagination screamed and went into the foetal position.

One of the balaclavas turned from Jono and weighed up the options. The teenager with the knife in his hand, or the one with the rapidly spreading damp patch on the front of his grey stay-press trousers?

No contest.

'No. No. No,' Davie whimpered, moving backwards until he was flush against the Formica unit. All he could look at was the knife, the one that was coming towards his face, at his neck now, the tip pressing against his skin, piercing it, a trickle of blood, a scream that he didn't even realize was his.

'Da, tell him. Tell him now!' Zander was pointing his weapon straight at his dad now, his face twisted with rage.

'OK, ya cunt!' Jono yelled, stopping the balaclava before the nick became a decapitation.

Davie's relief was instant, mixed with an urge to go over there and do Jono's other hand himself. What the fuck had taken him so long to intervene? The sadistic bastard.

'Lovely. We're all playing nice now,' the boss psycho announced. 'So. Ten seconds and then we start that all again. Where is it, Jono?'

'It's not here.'

'I don't think you have the hang of this question-and-answer thing. I didn't ask where it wasn't. I asked where it was.'

Jono spat a huge ball of bloody goo onto the table. Davie's urge to vomit rose again.

'I'll take you to it.'

The chief psycho laughed. 'Now, why didn't you say that in the first place, when you still had two hands to wipe your arse?'

His buddies reacted to his signal, pulling Jono up from the table, snapping handcuffs onto his bleeding hands. Jono reverted to stony silence, obviously determined not to give them the satisfaction of his pain. Davie resisted the urge to boot him in the baws as they dragged him within kicking distance, then past him and out of the room. They were gone as fast as they'd arrived.

Only then did Davie wonder where the police were. Surely to Christ someone would have called them, let them know that three psychos had just stormed the house at the end of the terrace, the one with the statue of Our Lady in the garden and the font of holy water at the side of the front door?

But even as the question ricocheted round his brain, he knew the answer. No one around here would call the police, because the only thing more terrifying than three tooled-up maniacs on the rampage was the thought of what Jono Leith would do to you if he found out you'd brought the police to his splintered door.

'You OK?' The voice was distant, vague.

'Davie! Are you OK?'

It was Zander, shouting at him now, while he guided his mother to a chair and supported her as she sat down. Her eyes were still closed, her mouth still repeating the same prayer as she rocked back and forward. 'Hail Mary, full of grace, the Lord is with thee . . .'

Davie's legs gave way and he collapsed onto the floor. 'I'm OK. I am. What the fuck was that?'

Zander was on his knees in front of his mum now, holding her, trying to stop the movement.

'Billy McColl,' he answered. It was all he had to say. Billy

McColl. *The biggest drug dealer on this side of Glasgow, an old pal of Zander's dad. Obviously the friendship had hit a stumbling block. But why the balaclavas if everyone except him knew who they were? Then Davie remembered the camera at Zander's front door. The laughs they'd had when it had been installed, right up until Davie had flashed his willy at it and Zander's mum had dragged him down to the chapel and forced him to confess. The priest had made him repeat the story three times. Old guy must have been hard of hearing.*

'Jesus, Zander, he'll kill him. He will.'

Zander pulled his mum even tighter, forcing her to stay still while he stroked her hair, shushed her, cradled her like a baby.

'I fucking hope he does.'

45.

'Drunk In Love' – Beyoncé (ft. Jay Z)

His car was parked right outside the building, but even that was too far away. Zander opened the nearest door and watched as she stepped in, the curve of her ass magnificent as she slid onto the leather seat. By the time he got round to the other side, his hard-on was pressing against the inside of his fly, desperate for release. Not yet. Patience. He jumped in and saw she wasn't playing to the same rules of restraint. Her skirt was already up to her creamy thighs, her stockings straining, her right hand inside the delicate lace of her panties.

He made a cursory glance to check that the divider was blocking the driver's view. Spectator sports weren't his thing. At least not with her. He wanted her all to himself.

As soon as he was beside her, she removed her hand from her panties and thrust her fingers into his mouth. He could taste her. Wanted her. And forget patience, it had to be now. Adrianna was on the same page and calling the shots. Climbing on top of him, she straddled him, the deep plunge of her cleavage in his face, forcing him to inhale her musky scent, her nipples straining through the sheer fabric of her silk blouse, demanding attention. He started to unbutton her shirt; she stopped him. His hand crept downwards, pulled the lace to one side; she grabbed his wrist, blocked him again.

He groaned. This was excruciating. Desperate. He needed her now.

Suddenly the car drew to a halt and in his peripheral vision he saw a concierge approach.

Laughing, he flipped her to the side, enjoying her defiant yelp. Just in time, she pulled her hemline back down, flicked her hair, recovered her poise, smile wide as the concierge opened the door.

'Good morning, Mr Leith. Welcome back to the Carlyle.'

The Carlyle. Zander's favourite New York hotel. Sometimes called the Palace of Secrets, it was trusted for its discretion by JFK, Marilyn Monroe, Elizabeth Taylor, Princess Diana and a galaxy of other stars over the years. There was a long-standing rumour that there was a secret underground tunnel that allowed its illustrious guests to arrive and leave in absolute privacy. Zander was happy using the front door, especially this morning, when haste was at the top of his agenda.

Wordlessly, not touching, they headed inside, turned left to the elevators, where another concierge was waiting. Zander let Adrianna go in first, but she paused halfway, so he was forced to pass her. As he did, she grabbed the lapel of his jacket and positioned him so that he was leaning against the rear wall facing her, her back to the uniformed gentleman.

'Central Park View Suite, please,' Zander told him, then turned all his attention to Adrianna. Not that he had any choice. She'd already grabbed his hand, sliding it into the waistband of her skirt, then down, until his fingers could feel her wetness.

They ascended thirty-three floors, and as the doors pinged open, the concierge kept his gaze discreetly averted, allowing Zander to withdraw, recover.

'Thank you,' Zander said to the concierge, who replied with a wry smile as the door slid shut.

There were only a few steps to the suite door. There, Zander's body was pressed hard on hers, pushing her against the wood, her hand down, squeezing his balls until he managed to open the mechanism with his key card. Door open, they fell inside, before Adrianna strutted to the window, forcing him to follow, bringing the landscape of Manhattan into their world.

There, she placed both hands wide on the glass as his arms wrapped around her, his breath against the back of her neck, licking her, tasting her. His solid erection pushed into her back, his hands found her nipples, tracing a slow, excruciatingly teasing line round them, then squeezing, hard enough to make her gasp. Adrianna's head fell to one side and she groaned, then twisted round to the sofa on her right, gliding downwards so she was positioned over the arm of it, her ass in the air, waiting for him.

Zander knew what was expected and swiftly obliged. He dropped to his knees, slid her skirt up to reveal her flawless, taut buttocks. Her legs wide apart now, he slipped between them, as she tore off her panties, allowing his tongue to explore her cheeks. Slowly, tasting every drop of her, he moved downwards, until he found her clit, circled it, teased, then entered her, making her pant, scream, beg him to go deeper, until . . .

'Stop!' she demanded, then reached back, grabbed his hair,

pulled him up while she spun round to face him. 'I don't want your tongue. I want your cock.'

Zander smiled, happy to relinquish control, every one of his senses white hot and ready to explode.

Deftly, Adrianna freed his throbbing penis, pushing his jeans downwards. Sitting on the arm of the sofa now, she lifted her legs, spread them wide again, pulled him into her, guided his cock inside her. One leg clasped round him, then the other, holding him in a vice of pure desire. He rode her, pummelled hard against her, watching the ecstatic curves of her beautiful face.

'Bed!' she gasped. He obeyed, swiftly kicking off his boots and jeans. Wearing no socks today had been an inspired move. Her arms snaked round his neck, allowing him to carry her through to the king-size bed, still inside her, her mouth biting down on his until it drew blood.

As he placed her down on the bed, she slid her legs over his shoulders, so that he could get deeper, further, faster. In only seconds, he felt her pussy clamp down on him, her body buckle, her eyes shut and her hands grasp the white bed linen.

'I'm coming.' Her voice was pure sex.

Deeper, further, faster.

'I'm coming. Like. Never. Before,' she screamed, shuddered, lost control.

Zander fought not to come with her. Not yet. Too soon to let this ecstasy end.

He slowed, switched to tender movements, but as soon as Adrianna's orgasm had subsided, she snatched back control and switched it up again.

Seizing the power and displaying the suppleness and

strength of a gymnast, she moved from under him, pulled him down and then climbed on top, straddling him, pulling him inside her. Skirt still round her waist, the new position finally giving him the opportunity to tear open her blouse, revealing a black plunge bra, over-plump, flawless, natural breasts. Using every perfectly formed ab muscle to raise his torso, he sucked her nipples through the lace, then flicked it open, letting her breasts spill out.

The muscles in her tight thighs clenched as she lifted and lowered onto him, time after time, until he knew he couldn't stand it much longer, would have to come, but no . . .

Not yet. Still too soon. A rapid movement, a lift, he flipped her onto the bed and parted her legs, then twisted round so he could go down there, lick her, taste her, his face buried in her pussy.

'I want to taste you too,' she murmured, manoeuvring under him, taking him in her mouth, scratching her nails down his back as they both lost themselves in the classic sixty-nine, sucking, biting, sweating, shuddering until they both came, hard, fast, loud, together this time, both of them drinking from the other.

Eventually, spent, Zander collapsed beside her, face to face now. 'You are the most beautiful woman I've ever seen,' he told her truthfully.

'I am,' she said, her eyes a blazing contrast to her smile.

'And an incredible fuck,' he added, laughing.

'I'm that too,' she agreed, kissing him, softly this time. 'And if you lie right there I'll show you all the other things I can do too.'

Zander didn't object.

46.

'All I Wanna Do' – Sheryl Crow

There was no denying that elements of the last couple of days had been highly indulgent, given that she was here for only a week and it was work, not pleasure.

Although, Sarah preferred to look at it as assembling the tools for the job and then conducting research.

One tool in particular definitely topped the nice scale.

On Monday morning, when she'd gone online, there had been loads of cars at the hire company that were perfectly adequate and in budget. A basic Ford Focus had seemed like the best bet. Economical. Functional. Absolutely fine. But like a legion of Brits who had gone before her, the minute she got to the pickup point and spotted the bright red convertible Mustang, she'd been unable to resist driving it away.

Sod the cost. Even if it was just for ten minutes, she was going to drive down Santa Monica Boulevard with Sheryl Crow blaring on the radio. The stellar altitude here had definitely done something to her sense of extravagance. Or perhaps it was spending the night in a house that wouldn't leave change from $40 million. She'd checked the cost on Google.

Anyway, the car might cost as much as a brick in Davie Johnston's mammoth estate, but she'd still felt a little light-hearted recklessness when she drove it out of the car-hire lot.

It was a treat. And not something she did very often. Spending wasn't one of the things that gave her a particular thrill. She was more functional and pragmatic. Her salary at the *Daily Scot* left her comfortable enough to pay half of all their bills. Simon had argued at first, pointing out that his name was on the mortgage because he'd bought the flat years before, so she'd told him to look at it as rent. They'd get around to changing the title deeds if they ever made things more permanent, but in the meantime, it was only right that she contributed to the roof over her head.

As for the other expenses, clothes had never particularly interested her. As long as she had smart outfits for work and a few decent looks for going out, she was happy. Shoes were functional and she'd never seen the point of the designer bag or statement jewellery. Low maintenance, Simon called her. She was never quite sure if that was a compliment or an insult, but he'd definitely have revised his view if he could have seen her cruising behind the wheel of her flash sports car.

Somehow what – in her opinion – qualified someone as being a pretentious arse in Glasgow seemed perfectly normal here. Wearing sunglasses indoors. Carrying small dogs around like accessories. Or worse, as she'd seen several times a day, tall, leggy, gorgeous women wandering around on the arms of little old men. Either they were a financial catch or there was a trend for taking Grandad out for the day.

After picking up the car, she'd headed straight for the

Grove, the shopping centre just off West 3rd Street on the outskirts of West Hollywood. There had been dozens of paparazzi shots of Davie hanging out here and she wanted to suss it out. Perfectly manicured lawns, a fountain with water jets that danced in perfect time to music. She watched as it switched from the swing of Dean Martin to Kool & the Gang's 'Celebration'. There were even Picassos on the wall at the valet parking reception area. This was like a cross between a gallery and a theme park for adults who liked to splash their cash.

Abercrombie & Fitch, J. Crew, Nordstrom, Barneys New York, Kiehl's – suddenly, she was tempted to stay and kill the credit cards, then stop at the Cheesecake Factory for lunch. At least she'd get a travel feature out of it.

But no.

That wasn't why she was here. Focus. Back to business. One more stop, at AT&T on 3rd Street, Santa Monica to pick up a US pay-as-you-go phone.

Calls, texts, photos. That was all she'd need. Before she even left the car park, she'd texted Davie with her new number, not entirely sure that the number he'd given her when she left the afternoon before was genuine and not the contact details for some pizza place in South Central. And even if it was his number, there was every chance he'd block her the minute he got the text.

To her surprise, the reply had been almost instant.

'Great. Enjoy your day. Speak soon. Glad we met. P.S. Still alive? Ivanka looks guilty.'

She hastily tapped out an answer.

'Only just. At court fighting restraining order requested

by Gosling security. Doesn't he realize that when he meets me, he'll love me?'

She'd pondered the weekend's activities as she cruised around the streets of Beverly Hills.

Davie Johnston had been nothing like she'd expected. Completely poles away from her preconceptions. Top of the list had been aloof, unapproachable, arrogant, suave and – given his recent exploits – a real nasty piece of work. But somehow he'd been . . . She struggled to find the words. Messed-up. Lonely. Funny. Kind of sweet. And there was a desperation around him that was so palpable she could almost touch it. If that's what fame got you, you could keep it.

The revelation about her identity had clearly rattled him, but he'd recovered well. Normally she prided herself on being able to suss out what someone was thinking before they knew themselves, but Davie was more inscrutable. Probably came with living in a city that revolved around people pretending to be someone else.

It was just difficult to know if it was her job or the fact that she wanted to rake into his past that had him more on edge, so she'd immediately back-pedalled and gone for the whole 'lifestyle interview' line. Soft start. Break it in gently. Don't shut it down until she'd had at least some chance to dig around, to find out if there was anything to her hunch that there was a story here.

Convinced she'd blown it, it had been a real surprise when he'd agreed to see her again, but what did it mean? Nothing to hide? Something to hide? Or he was still drunk from the night before and not quite in control of his faculties?

Whatever the outcome, her job there was done for the moment.

Switching focus, she'd spent the rest of Monday and all of Tuesday hitting the phones, Facebook, Twitter, Instagram, gossip sites, and the celebrity hangouts the internet told her were frequented by Mirren McLean and Zander Leith.

She'd had no luck tracking either so far. Their press people were giving her the standard 'no interview' line, and the agencies had no engagements flagged for either of them this weekend. Zander had started shooting on a new movie, and the soonest Mirren appeared on the radar was next month, when she was speaking at the Writers Guild on Doheny, in Beverly Hills. She needed another plan. Something a bit more radical.

After going back online this morning and coming up blank again on the celebrity tracking websites, she realized she'd been making the assumption that the stars would be protected by gated estates like Davie's, but what if they weren't?

It had only taken her ten minutes online to find out that Mirren stayed in Malibu Colony, and another five to learn that, legally, the beach on which the most expensive real estate in America sat was actually public and there were a couple of access points that could let her walk along it. After a thrilling jaunt up the Pacific Coast Highway, she parked the red fun-mobile on Malibu Road and climbed over a small wall down onto the beach below. As long as she stayed below the tideline, she was on public property. Google Earth had been no use – it seemed like street view was blocked for this area. However, she'd managed to find a brilliant app that pinpointed the access points to the sands. Once there, she simply walked along, her neck permanently crooked as she stared up at the incredible homes and balconies just feet above her. There wasn't a person in sight. In fact, it was almost eerily deserted. One, hang on, two people walking their dogs along the whole mile or so of beach and one maid cleaning a glass veranda. On a thirty-minute stroll from one end of the Colony to the other, they were the only people she saw.

Bizarre.

Back in the car, she headed south again, back the way that she'd come. This time, going straight ahead instead of slinging a left onto the 66, she stayed on the PCH as it curved left at Santa Monica Pier; then she flipped right onto Lincoln. God bless satnav.

When she reached Rose Avenue, she turned right, then pulled into a parking space on the street just after the junction with Pacific. From there it was a sixty-second walk to the beachfront, where she turned left and headed along the boardwalk until she reached the address she'd jotted on the piece of paper in her pocket.

Zander's address had been impossible to find online, so she'd put a call in to her new best friend Gemma at the press agency. And Gemma was right when she said that you'd never guess Zander Leith lived there. It was just like all the other blocks within view. Nice. Impressive even. Right on the beach, and hey, everything looked better in the sunshine. But it was 12 miles and tens of millions of dollars away from Davie Johnston's home.

Night and day.

And why?

Two guys from the same street, both thousands of miles away from home and they'd chosen lifestyles that were at opposite ends of the ostentation scale.

Already, Zander intrigued her. For weeks she'd read everything she could find on him and yet she still felt like she knew nothing about him other than that he drank too much, did drugs, had occasional anger issues and had dated some of the most beautiful women in the world, each one of whom was, it would seem, politely returned to singledom after a relationship that lasted no more than three months.

This guy had issues. But why? His mother? His father?

Had to be his father.

No one disappears into thin air – not someone with a lifestyle like Jono Leith.

Sarah headed back to the car, determination reinvigorated. There was a story here. It was already Wednesday, she only had a few more days here, and right now her only lead was Davie Johnston.

She pulled out her new phone and texted him again. 'Hey, still on for a catch up this week? From the future Mrs Gosling xx.'

No reply.

Bugger, perhaps she'd gone too far. Too keen. OK, no more texting. There was a little cafe at the corner of Rose, right on the beach, and she stopped there for a cold beer and a few minutes to think. This could be intoxicating, this life. It was obvious why people came here and then never went home again. Glasgow in the cold, dark nights or LA with the year-round sunshine and outdoor lifestyle?

Three laughing girls on roller skates sped past her, delivering the answer.

Sunshine every time. And if this was some weird episode of *Location, Location, Location* with Kirstie and Phil showing her the three homes she'd visited, the choice would be easy.

She'd take Zander's. Davie's was so huge it was quite frankly terrifying. Mirren's was scarily quiet, the atmosphere almost rarefied. But here, she could live. She could breathe. There were people around, and the ocean would never be the same two days running. This would do. Her little red sports car and a condo on the beach. Sold to the lady in the sunglasses bought for twenty-five quid at Glasgow Airport.

Back at the hotel, a room-service burger and a nap later, she decided it wasn't a bad day's work. Progress. Her FitFlops were not much closer to a story, but at least she could probably wing a piece about the differing lifestyles of the three conquering heroes.

There was a slight delay before the TV responded to the instruction from the remote and switched to Channel 14. A talk show called *The Brianna Nicole Show* had been trailing an interview with Jenny Rico all week and she was curious to see the illusive Mrs Johnston. According to the TV guide she'd just picked up at reception, *The Brianna Nicole Show* was filmed live in front of a studio audience and went out at 11 p.m.

Sarah chided herself at the missed opportunity. If she'd known that, she'd have tried to wangle a ticket for tonight's show.

Damn.

The ring of her phone interrupted her irritation. For a moment her hopes climbed. Davie calling her back? Setting an interview time? It was almost a disappointment when she realized it was the UK phone and Simon's photograph was flashing on the screen.

Accept Facetime?

She pressed the green button.

'Hey, lovely, you're up early,' she told him, spotting that he was already in the office and it was only 7 a.m.

'Got a case to prepare and couldn't sleep, so I thought I'd just come in early.'

It was so familiar. The man was the only person who worked even more hours than she did. He was obsessive. Dedicated. Committed. Sitting in a boardwalk cafe on Venice Beach in the middle of the day would be his idea of hell. Even when they went away, it was strictly first-class, five-star resorts, where he always had Wi-Fi and could call the office whenever he wanted. Which he did.

People depended on him, he'd tell her after he'd spent three hours on the phone to an opposing counsel.

There was no arguing with his logic. In Scots law, the SCCRC was the last hope for the innocent, the last chance to play the system for the guilty. Only last month, Simon had managed to prove that a man who'd been in prison for fourteen years for murdering his wife was innocent. Absolutely innocent. New advances in DNA had pinpointed the presence of someone else at the murder scene, someone who was also now inside, serving life for killing two other women.

The man cried when he walked free. His children, grown now, had taken him home.

That was the work that Simon did. And if it made him an obsessive, sometimes cold, occasionally irritable and controlling workaholic, then that was a trade-off worth making.

'How's La La Land?'

'Warm,' she replied, laughing. 'And beautiful. I feel like I'm living in an episode of . . . of . . . What was that show you used to watch? The one with Jeremy Piven.'

'*Entourage*.'

'That's it. I'm in an episode of *Entourage*. Without the drugs or the strippers, but there's still time.'

She could see him moving stuff around on his desk and shuffling papers as he spoke.

'I called you on Sunday afternoon, but it just rang out,' he told her.

'Yeah, sorry. I noticed the missed call, but by that time it was midnight and I didn't want to call you back in case you were asleep. I must have had the phone on silent without realizing. I thought it was probably better to stick to texting so that I didn't interrupt anything important.'

White lie. Yes, it was on silent, but that had been because she was at Davie Johnston's house having coffee on his terrace and thought a call from her boyfriend might be a distraction from the matters at hand. And since then, she'd just stuck to a couple of daily texts because she was distracted by the hunt for Mirren and Zander. Now she felt a tug of remorse for her crapness in the girlfriend stakes and made an attempt to compensate for it.

'This time difference is an awkward one. I'll call you in the morning, though. It'll be about eight a.m. here, so that's four o' clock your time.'

He hesitated before answering. Typical Simon. Every answer measured and considered. 'Can't do. I'm at a reception in the Blythswood Hotel. Something to do with the Commonwealth Games regeneration programme. Invitation from the Lord Provost.'

'Well, you'd better show up, then,' she teased.

He didn't bite. On the mute TV in front of her, the titles were rolling for the start of *The Brianna Nicole Show*. A picture of Davie's wife, Jenny, flashed onto the screen, followed by one of the actor Lex Callaghan. Small world. He was the Clansman, Mirren McLean's hero. Looking at him, Sarah could see why. His face was so perfect it looked like it had been carved from stone in the image of some Greek god. The cheekbones, the jawline, the perfect teeth, all of it sitting on a frame that oozed masculinity. There was a reason every one of those movies made in excess of $100 million and he was it.

Third on the bill was a rapper who'd just launched a new clothing line that was fashioned entirely from white leather in honour of his decision to follow the teachings of Kabbalah.

Just another night in LA, then.

'Look, tell you what, why don't you call me when it's good for you?' she said, olive branch firmly extended in the hope of lightening his mood.

'OK, will do.'

'Goodnight, then. Love you.'

'Love you too.'

A little tense, not their most adoring phone call, but Sarah wasn't unduly concerned. In fact, if she was being entirely honest, his attitude irked her. If he was off abroad, working on a case that was important to him, she'd support him unconditionally. OK, so this wasn't saving an innocent man from a miscarriage of justice, but it was her job and it mattered to her. And if he couldn't muster up enthusiasm and support, he could at least avoid going the petulance route.

Sod it.

Sipping the beer she'd liberated from the minibar, she turned up the volume on the TV and watched, transfixed. Back home, she had absolutely no interest in the celebrity world. She didn't watch the soaps, couldn't care less about reality shows and, other than the famous names she met in the course of her work, had little interest in people in the public eye. But this lot were strangely fascinating. Shinier. Brighter. Wackier.

The rapper was on first. Fifteen minutes, including commercials, of talk about his new calling, punctuated by rants about how his new clothing line was ordained by God. Fair enough. Sarah added 'crazier' to her list of adjectives.

Lex Callaghan was up next, talking about the next movie, the perfect balance of promotion, self-deprecation and amusing anecdotes. He was definitely a pro. By the time he shook hands with Brianna and headed stage left, Sarah was already looking up the UK release date for the movie.

'And now, ladies and gentlemen, give it up for Jenny Rico!' The crowd went wild and the camera panned to the left, then paused as one of the most beautiful women Sarah had ever seen came out from behind the set panel. Jenny's show wasn't on British TV, or perhaps it was, but Sarah so rarely turned the television on she'd never caught it.

Photographs in magazines did her no justice. Even the L'Oréal ads didn't capture how truly breathtaking she was. Not just the face. The body too. The way she walked. The breasts that had a life of their own. She was wearing a red bodycon dress, with a low plunge at the top, revealing a cleavage that didn't stop. The hemline reached mid-calf, giving her a Jessica Rabbit wiggle that made Sarah realize that when it came to comparisons, this woman was a different species altogether.

'Jenny!' the host welcomed her, kissing her on both cheeks, then standing back to allow her to savour the audience's applause, responding with a wave of thanks.

'You pay them to do that,' she told Brianna bashfully when they eventually stopped.

Cue a chorus of hilarity off camera.

Wow, she had them eating out of her hands and she'd barely said a word.

They were clearly not strangers, as Brianna launched into an easy chat, talking about Jenny's show (going great – highest rated on her network, new series starting next week), her new cosmetic contract (very honoured to be asked, a dream come true), her superstar children (yes, they're so happy and balanced, and she was truly blessed). Either the beer was off or this woman was making Jenny slightly nauseous. Bland didn't even begin to cover it. Davie Johnston – for whatever faults he might have, and there were undoubtedly plenty – was funny and sharp and irreverent. His wife was calling it in, saying all the right things, lapping up the appreciation, but she had nothing to say. Nothing new here. Please move along.

The image of her with Davie just didn't gel. These two didn't match as a couple. There was no fit.

'And we have to ask . . .' Brianna's voice took on a more serious tone. 'Your husband, Davie, has been a long-time friend of the show and he's had a bit of a rough time lately. How's he doing?'

Only because Sarah was transfixed by her face did she notice the tiny pulse of irritation on the side of her forehead and the slightest furrow of her brow. Two tiny movements, almost indiscernible, but pretty conclusive proof that this wasn't in the script.

'He's doing great,' Sarah said, out loud.

'He's doing great,' Jenny echoed.

Sarah thrust her beer into the air in celebration of her prediction skills. 'Slam dunk.'

'You know, our hearts go out to Sky Nixon and her family, and we're praying that she'll get well soon.'

There was a very definite punctuation on the end of that sentence, making it clear that was the end of the comment.

Brianna was already way ahead of her. 'And I hear you had an extra-special celebration this past weekend.'

Obviously delighted to change the subject, Jenny switched a gear up to tease and flirtation.

'We did! We had an incredible party for our tenth anniversary.'

'Thanks for the invitation,' Brianna joked.

'You didn't get one? That's my PA fired, then,' Jenny shot back.

It was the first thing of any wit she'd said all night.

361

'Actually, it doesn't matter because I'm sure I'll get the opportunity to congratulate you both in person right here...'

Another involuntary flinch, puzzlement this time, maybe a shade of fear. Whatever was about to happen, Jenny knew nothing about it.

'Ladies and gentlemen, Davie Johnston!'

The camera swung back to the entrance point in the set and Davie stuck his head round it. Either the studio applause guys were doing a great job or the audience were just in a generous mood, but the reaction was fairly impressive. Not on the same scale as Jenny's rapturous welcome, but encouraging enough.

Sarah was surprised to find herself smiling as he walked on, head slightly bowed, eyes up, like a naughty kid caught with his hand in the reality cookie jar. There was definitely something endearing about him. Her promised chat with him couldn't come quickly enough. She was desperate to get this interview in the bag, desperate to speak to him, to fish, probe, to get to whatever it was that made this guy such a hot mess of issues. Desperate to get to the truth. And sure that Davie was going to be the one to deliver it. If there was anything there, she'd be the one to crack him. She was sure of it.

Out of nowhere a chair materialized next to Jenny while Brianna greeted Davie with a double handshake.

As he sat down, giving a salute of thanks to the audience, Sarah caught Jenny's body language. Ouch. Defensive. Stiff. Furious. The set of her jaw belying an almost simmering rage. Chick might be a good actress, but the loving wife wasn't her best performance.

Davie sat down, put his hand over his wife's and gave her a beaming smile.

The tiny delay in her reaction gave her feelings away again. This was a brilliant starting place for the interview. So, Davie, tell me exactly why your wife hates you so much? If she could kick off with that, it might throw him enough to let her burrow under his other issues. It was a process she'd perfected over years spent watching cop interviews and court cross-examinations.

'So, Davie,' Brianna said, 'I believe you've got a little present for our darling Jenny?'

The audience burst into applause again, as Davie reached in his pocket and pulled out a ring box. They had no idea it was the same ring box that he'd presented to her in a limo just a few nights before.

He opened it to a gasp from the crowd as the camera zoomed in on the glistening ring of diamonds. 'It's an eternity ring,' he announced to his wife, the one who was trying desperately to smile through gritted veneers. Ninety-nine per cent of the population would buy it. Sarah didn't.

He took it out of the box and slid it onto the third finger of her left hand, where it nestled beside a rock the size of a cola cube.

'She gets one for the other hand in another ten years,' he joked. 'But in the meantime, we've got another announcement. Tomorrow we're renewing our vows. We're setting sail at sunset and we'll recommit to each other, just as we did ten years ago tomorrow.'

Was it Sarah's imagination or did he emphasize the 'tomorrow'?

But hang on. Tomorrow? No, no, no. She'd hoped to interview him tomorrow. Or the next day. He'd definitely said this week and that only left tomorrow, Friday or Saturday.

'And another honeymoon?' Brianna asked.

'Absolutely,' Davie replied. 'In fact, we might set sail and just keep on going . . .'

Sarah's beer bottle froze halfway to her lips. Damn. Shit. Bugger.

Her interview just got torpedoed and sunk.

47.

'Love Will Tear Us Apart' – Joy Division

Glasgow, 1989

Everyone knew he did it. Everyone knew he was guilty. Everyone talked about how Jono Leith had killed Billy McColl and Jono Leith fucking loved it.

Zander watched as his dad sauntered from the car towards their block, walking with the swagger he'd developed to cover up the limp caused by Billy McColl's men using his left leg as a trampoline. It wouldn't happen again. Billy was dead, and just in case any of his crew got delusions of power and felt like making a name with a spot of violent retribution, Jono came permanently team-handed – two huge guys, one in front, one behind, another two waiting in the front seats of the Rover.

Jono Leith had definitely moved up a league, and Zander had never hated him more.

Two months. That was all the time it had taken to bypass small-time hood and manoeuvre straight to the big league, do not pass go, keep the get-out-of-jail card handy.

The details were sketchy. It's not as if they were reported in the Daily Record *or the* Daily Scot. *All Zander knew was what he'd seen, and everything else was patched together from overheard conversations and rumour.*

The night Billy McColl and his men had dragged his dad out of here had been the longest of his life. His mum had shot out of the house straight to the chapel to pray with Father Cooney for Jono's soul.

Mirren had come over, joined Davie at the table and they'd sat there, saying nothing. Two bottles of Irn-Bru and a packet of chocolate digestives had seen them through the night. The call came at 5 a.m. Jono was in the hospital but alive.

Alive.

Fucker.

Multiple fractures – four fingers, three ribs, one leg. Concussion, cigarette burns to the forearms, three missing toenails, and wounds requiring a total of 124 stitches. None of it fatal. McColl was clearly in a charitable mood, the cops said, sniggering at their own joke. Zander, sitting on a chair beside the hospital bed, said nothing. He didn't blame them. To them, Jono Leith was scum. He didn't feel inclined to contradict them.

A drug deal gone bad, they said. McColl brought smack up from Liverpool, agreed a keeper's fee with Jono to store it for him. Instead, Jono had sold it on, pocketed ten grand and failed to inform the rightful owner until he came looking for it. Supply and demand gone wrong somewhere along the line.

Billy expressed his displeasure, taking it out on Jono's bones. Not for a minute did he think the gallus wee bastard would come back for him. That wasn't how it worked. That wasn't the chain of command, the rule of hierarchy.

Apparently, no one told Jono. A week later, he dressed in a delivery uniform he'd stolen from the washing line of a post-office driver, took a gun he'd been storing for an Edinburgh hitman under the struts of Zander's bed, limped into Billy McColl's snooker club early in the morning, straight into the office, and shot him through the forehead.

To no one's surprise, twelve people in the club at the same time didn't see a thing.

What happened next was textbook gangland promotion 101.

Jono had contacted Liverpool, done a deal to take over the route, paid for the next consignment with Billy McColl's ten grand and bought himself into the game. No more bank jobs and security raids. Drugs were the future. The collection of hoods he'd called his associates were now his employees, all swapping intermittent windfalls for a salary. It was a win-win situation.

Meanwhile, everyone, police included, knew he'd done it. Unsurprisingly, in the absence of forensic evidence or eye-witnesses, they hadn't bust a gut to get a conviction. Billy McColl was no loss to society. And besides, they had the measure of Jono Leith and for now, they were prepared to give him some rope and hope he'd hang himself.

Instead, Zander knew, he'd become even more unbearable than before. Back then, he'd thought he was some big-time gangster – now, he pretty much was. To his mum's devastation, Jono no longer even pretended to care about her.

Almost twenty years of devotion and suffering and he'd repaid her by telling her she'd been a millstone round his neck since the day he met her and proceeded to leather her until she begged God for mercy. Zander had found her broken on the outside and inside. This time she had healed, at least on the surface. Next time she might not. Zander knew the day of reckoning was coming – he just needed to get everything in place first. Had to make sure his mother would be taken care of, make sure nothing could go wrong. There could be no coming back from what he was going to do. But it would be worth it.

As he watched the prick get closer, his stomach knotted just a little tighter. Oh yes, it would definitely be worth it. He wouldn't fear the day he'd find his mother dead. Or have to listen to her crying over the loss of the beast she still loved.

That was the hardest part. His mother still loved Jono Leith.

And that was why he knew that she was upstairs right now, tears streaming down her face, as she watched her husband walk past her front door and into the home of the woman he'd been shagging for the last ten years. The lover who put him first, above herself, above God, above her daughter, Mirren.

As always, Marilyn McLean welcomed Jono in.

48.

'True' – Spandau Ballet

Jenny Rico was a vision in white, her dark waves floating behind her as she held on to the mast of the yacht and arched her back, giving the photographer a stunning silhouette against the sunset.

The Newport Beach Yacht Club, forty-five minutes south of LAX, wasn't a millionaire's playground; it was a billionaire's playground. No matter how big your yacht was, there was a bigger one right behind it. Many times over the years Davie had considered adding a boat to his collection of toys, but – ever sensible – he'd been dissuaded by the old adage that a boat owner is only happy twice in his life: the day he buys the boat and the day he sells it.

Now, in white pants and a white shirt, open at the neck, sleeves rolled up, feet bare, he stood in the background, staring out to sea. It was a breathtaking shot. One that would run on the front covers and centre spreads of every celebrity magazine and melt the hearts of romantics all over the country. Only when the photographer had moved on to set up the next image did Davie approach his wife. Hopefully she'd calmed down. Taken it on the chin. Accepted that she'd tried to pull a fast one and got royally outmanoeuvred. Game over, let's shake hands and be friends.

'You cunt,' she hissed.

Hold the friends.

'My bad,' he agreed, smiling for anyone watching, while speaking quietly so they couldn't be overheard by the photographer or any of the three assistants who were floating around the set. 'I'm a terrible guy for trying to save our marriage while giving you incredible publicity at the same time.'

'Don't you dare suggest that this is for me. This is all about you. All about making you look like husband of the year. I should have told you to fuck off.'

'You should. But then you'd have lost all this lovely publicity and looked like a tit at the same time.'

Jenny wore the scowl of a woman who was at a photo shoot that had been put together in hours, pretending that she was about to renew her vows with a husband she would quite happily drown.

He knew he'd dodged an expensive bullet, but this wasn't giving him any pleasure. Before all this, he and Jenny had rubbed along quite happily, she with her life, he with his. Back then, they both had the same goals – build careers, make millions, keep their personal lives on the down low so that they could continue to milk the family image and brand.

'Oh Jesus Christ, a minister. You actually brought in a minister.'

'Al's idea,' he told her. 'One of his assistants. Got ordained on the internet.'

'I'm losing the will to live. Fucking joke,' she spat.

There was no doubt it was ridiculous, but it was all about

survival. He still didn't have a plan or a strategy to get himself back on top. This was firefighting. Keeping the wolves at bay. He'd read a poll on the internet that morning that put him as the third most unpopular Hollywood movie star, behind Mel Gibson and Tom Cruise. Third most unpopular. Shia LaBeouf was fourth. When you lose a popularity contest to Shia LaBeouf, it's time to give up and go home.

'Last shot, Davie,' the photographer told him cheerily. They were standing in the bow of the boat now, in a pose so corny it looked as though Celine Dion could appear at any moment and burst into a chorus of 'My Heart Will Go On'.

'OK, Jenny, face to me. Great. Gorgeous. To each other. With love. Amazing. Spectacular. OK, I think that's a wrap. I'll have these emailed over to Al by nine a.m. tomorrow.'

Davie did a quick calculation. Al would have the deals brokered with the celebrity mags by the close of play, so these images would be on the newsstands by Monday. Job done. Short-term publicity win, and when she realized he'd filed, she'd have to keep quiet otherwise she'd look like a queen bitch. In a few months, when his popularity had climbed back up from somewhere around the earth's core, they could announce that they'd amicably split.

Her phone rang just as she was about to follow the rest of the camera crew off the boat. The cataclysmic fury that crossed her face told him that it was her lawyer breaking the news.

'You've filed? You cunt,' she repeated with such vehemence that Davie bypassed reason and went straight to stringent defence.

'You're absolutely right. I should have just let you file tomorrow and fuck me out of millions.'

She didn't even have the decency to look repentant. That wound him up even more. 'Really, did you think I wouldn't hear about it? Come on, love. You should have known better.' Oh, shit. He'd gone too smug. Cool, smart and powerful equals good. Smug equals dickhead.

This was all of her own doing, but it was no big surprise that she wasn't thrilled. Jenny was oozing fury now. Tonight she should have been lying in bed with her lover, planning how they were going to spend one of the biggest divorce payments in history.

'I hate you,' Jenny hissed.

'I think you'll find you've covered that point already.'

Wise enough to know that this wouldn't end well, he decided to bring it down a notch.

'Look, Jen, I never intended to file, until I heard about your shit plan. The way I see it, we can let the divorce stuff rumble on while we give it another go and hopefully make it work in time to call off the lawyers, or we can keep this quiet for now, then announce in a few months that we've separated amicably. That gives me time to sort out all the other stuff that's going on.'

'Go fuck yourself.'

They might have to work on that 'amicably' bit.

'Look, Jen, come on. Work with me here. I've got the boat for twenty-four hours. Want to hang out? Get something to eat? See if we can resolve this?'

'Are you nuts?' she rounded on him. Then, in a voice that

dripped malice, 'Set sail and do me a favour – don't come back.'

Really? Was this how it was going to be now? The new landscape of his life? Suddenly Davie was weary. Bone-weary.

When she flounced off, he didn't bother saying a word. She was gone. It was over. Done. He was left alone, on a yacht, on Newport Beach, feeling like shit. He cracked open a beer. Then another. Then pulled out his phone ready to call . . . No one. There was not a single person in the world he wanted to speak to. What did that say about his life?

Sighing, he speed-dialled number one. To his surprise, it was answered on the first ring.

'Hey, Mum,' he said. 'Just thought I'd phone and see how you're doing.'

There was silence on the other end of the phone.

'What's happened?'

'Nothing. Why?'

'Because you haven't called me first in twenty years.'

'I have!'

'No, you haven't, son.'

With a crashing dent to his soul, he realized she was right. He was a selfish bastard.

'I'm fine, Mum, honest. I just wanted to see if . . . maybe you want to come over for a couple of weeks? The kids would like to see you.'

'And you?'

'Me too, Mum. I'd like that.'

'Then I'll come,' she said, completely matter of fact, as if it was the kind of thing they did on a regular basis. That was his mum. No fuss. No drama. Just a good, stoic heart and total loyalty. Yes, she'd moan about the size of the house, the amount of time the kids spent at work and the food that was in the industrial-size fridge, but if her son wanted her there, then that's where she'd be.

'How did you get on with that lassie? The one from the *Daily Scot*?'

'Yeah, fine. She's actually here now. I saw her the other day and I'll be talking to her again this week.'

Another pause. 'You know, son, you don't have to do anything you don't want to do. Since you were a wee boy I've been telling you to slow down, look around you, but you were too busy going places. Your dad was the same.'

That surprised him. It was the first time he could ever remember her mentioning him. Ever. He'd always just been that mythical figure out there somewhere, the guy who'd left before he was born, who never got mentioned because it made his mum flinch with pain.

'My dad?'

'Look, son, I have to go.' She was flustered now. Obviously trying to recover from her slip of the tongue.

'Hang on, Mum. My dad. Tell me something else about him.'

The pause was so long he thought she'd hung up.

'He didn't know what was important, son. Treated everyone around him like they didn't matter. No one around him told him what he needed to hear. Nothing real. Sometimes I worry you're making the same mistakes.'

This time she really was gone, leaving him holding the phone, staring into space.

What the hell was all that about? She wasn't stupid. She

watched TV; she read the papers. She even had a computer now and had been indoctrinated into the world of Google. It was a fair bet that she'd heard what was going on with him, and yet she'd never mention it directly. In her world, it just wasn't done that way. He was a grown man now. Had to make his own way, and she wouldn't dent his west of Scotland male pride by interfering.

He lay down on one of the sunloungers in the middle of the deck. His mum was right. No one around him. Nothing real. Hell, how long had it been that way? And why had he never stopped to question it?

Closing his eyes, he had a mental image. Him, Mirren, Zander – squeezed into the hut, knocking back a bottle of cider while Mirren played some crap music. But they were laughing. Really laughing. Like when your guts ache and you don't think there will ever be anything as funny as this again.

For him, there never was.

Another image. Sarah McKenzie, sitting on his terrace. There was a connection there. Something real. Wasn't there? Or maybe he was just losing the plot. Perhaps so. But right now, the thought of going home depressed him. The thought of staying on this boat all night alone depressed him even more. There was nowhere to go. No one to see.

It was her or Shia LaBeouf. He chose her.

49.

'Sky Blue and Black' – Jackson Browne

The beep was steady, still, repetitive, yet instead of being irritating, it felt like it was the only thing keeping the seconds ticking by, the only thing keeping the world turning.

If it stopped, it was over.

Done.

Cedars-Sinai was a well-oiled machine when it came to saving lives, but it couldn't work miracles. River Phoenix was pronounced dead here. Frank Sinatra too. And there was no way her daughter's name was being added to the list.

No way.

Chloe. Stupid, stupid Chloe.

They'd brought her in, pumped her stomach, then – ironically – doped her up in the hope that putting her into a medically induced coma would help her body recover. The doctors were cautiously optimistic, but apparently the next twenty-four hours were crucial. The scans showed normal brain activity, the heart was working fine, but nothing was certain after such a major seizure.

Every cliché had already gone through Mirren's mind.

She'd take her daughter's place in a heartbeat. She'd give up everything just to make her girl well. There was no deal with the devil she wouldn't make. But clichés weren't going to help. Prayers might, but it was a long time since Mirren had believed in any kind of God.

Beep. Beep. Beep.

Logan was on his way back from Brazil. Vancouver. Toronto. Mirren had lost track. But he had a three-day hiatus and had hired a jet to get him home to his sister. His life was truly extraordinary – a seventeen-year-old with the finances to summon a jet, yet one who cared enough about his family to rush to his sister when she was ill. It gave her hope. That kind of goodness was in Chloe too; it had just been suffocated by too many years of chaos and crack.

Mirren's head fell onto the white blanket, just inches away from the hand that clung on to Chloe's as if by just touching her she could pass on the will to live, the strength to fight.

She'd sent Jack home and, quite frankly, didn't care if it was the right thing to do or not. They'd spent the first ten hours facing each other, saying little, their communication halted by guilt and self-accusations. If only she hadn't gone out. If only she'd stayed by Chloe's side. If only her daughter didn't hate her fucking guts.

But she did. And there was nowhere to hide from that.

Beep. Beep. Beep.

She moved her head onto the top of her arms and tried to clear her mind, but it wasn't working. A flashback from the past was replaying in her head in full technicolor. She desperately wanted to switch it off, make it go, but it wasn't budging. She was in another room, another time. She was standing in front of Jordan Lang and she was holding a gun. And she was making the mistake that would end with her little girl lying in this bed now, a year later.

The noise of the heart monitor subsided, replaced by the scene in her head and the sound of her own voice . . .

'You have no fucking idea what I would do. You have no fucking idea what I am. And if you knew what I'd done before, trust me, you'd be sitting there in a river of your own piss.

'You got my daughter high, you filmed her having sex, and now you're blackmailing her. Trust me, right now there is nothing I won't do to protect her from you. Nothing. But please, please test me. Because I'll say you attacked me, I'll say it was self-defence, and I'll have forgotten all about it before they've finished picking your brains out of the carpet.'

There was no blood left in his face now that the mental image had caused all functions to shut down except the one that was creating a real risk he would shit himself.

He knew how it worked. His father was one of the biggest producers in the industry. He knew how palms got greased, stories got changed and laws were bent to accommodate the powerful.

'Now give me the phone.'

'It's there,' he said, gesturing to the bedside cabinet to the right. 'Are you gonna shoot me if I reach for it?'

'Maybe. But I'll definitely shoot you if you don't.'

Tentatively, all pretence of having the upper hand now long gone, he reached over, picked up a gold BlackBerry from behind a pile of Xbox games.

'Find the text you sent Chloe and put it on the screen so I can see it. Don't press play.'

A few clicks of the thumb, then he chucked it to the end of the bed so that it was within her reaching distance. Her stomach lurched when she saw the screen. It was almost enough to make her index finger involuntarily jerk on the trigger.

'Are there any other copies? Did you send it to anyone else?'

'No.'

'If I find out you're lying, you know I'll be back. And it won't end well for you.'

'I swear, no one else. Swear to God.'

This was why she had no belief in religion.

Picking up the phone with her gun-free hand, she slid it into the Chanel.

'Not to sound clichéd, but you're going to leave LA.'

'No fucking way.'

Mirren carried on as if he hadn't even spoken. 'You're going to take the cash and you're going to leave. And you're not coming back. I've got a meeting with your father tomorrow and I'm going to show him this.'

'No, no, no. You can't.' Suddenly the twenty-one-year-old who had been so full of attitude and defiance just ten minutes ago was a little boy again, begging her not to go to Daddy.

Mirren ignored it.

'Oh, I can. And I'm going to tell him the consequences of you coming near my daughter again. I've known your dad a long time now. He'll do the right thing. If I don't kill you, he'll turn you in himself.'

His face told her she was right. Kent Lang might be one of the most powerful men in Hollywood, but he had a reputation as being a decent guy, someone who was passionate about justice, who made it his mission to expose atrocities in Darfur, to remind the world about the horrors of World War II, to highlight the plight of Haitian refugees. She was fairly sure he'd quickly come around to defending the rights of a seventeen-year-old girl who was being blackmailed over a sex tape by his scum of a spawn. There was no way he'd let his son drag all of their lives into the gutter.

'I'll call here later and I'll expect to hear that you're gone. Don't call, don't write. Understood?'

'Understood.' His voice was a little shaky.

She slipped the gun in her purse and backed out of the door. The lift down was shared with six Japanese tourists who talked incessantly all the way. She didn't crumble.

Crossing the lobby, a woman pushed a buggy towards her, a little girl in a pink hat giggling at the world. Still she didn't crumble.

Down the stairs to the underground car park. Into her car. Past the guard at the barrier. All the way to Lou's house on Beverly Drive. Still she held it together.

Lou opened the door. 'Oh, honey . . .' she said, with love and concern.

Mirren crumbled. Sobbed on the doorstep where she fell. Cried until Lou eventually stopped holding her, managed to get her back onto her feet and supported her through to the lounge, where she talked and cried until it was dark, until she was strong enough to put a smile on her face, go home and take care of her daughter.

She'd visited Kent Lang the following day at his Holmby Hills estate and told him what happened. Everything. He'd fully supported her, thanked her for not going to the police and making it public, assured her that he'd see to it that his *son caused her family no further problems. And she'd felt relief. It was over.*

Beep. Beep. Beep.

The memory left her and she was back in Cedars-Sinai, holding her daughter's hand, crippled by the knowledge that the relief she'd felt all those months ago had been misplaced.

Looking back, Kent Lang had been almost right. Almost. She hadn't counted on the three scumballs in the room knowing who she was, and one of them being lucid enough to tell Chloe that her mother had visited her boyfriend right before he disappeared.

There had been rage, tears, accusations, all of which had finally settled down and merged into good old-fashioned hatred.

Mirren never told her about the tape or the demand for money. She wasn't going to allow that shadow over Chloe's life, didn't want to burden her with anxiety that there could be another copy and that her humiliation could become entertainment for the sick masses. Mirren would shoulder that one.

But now, she wondered if she'd done the right thing. Chloe hadn't been able to draw a line under it and move on. Instead, the longing for Jordan and the determination to punish her mother had made her habit spiral out of control, no matter what Mirren did for her, no matter how many gutters she dragged her out of.

Maybe it was time to tell her the truth. Let her take accountability. Let her heart break so that she could then heal. And maybe, just maybe they'd find a way back from this.

The twitch of the hand that lay under hers made her head

snap up. It was very slight. If she hadn't been so still, she'd never have noticed it, but now it was enough to make her heart soar. This was Chloe telling her something. It wasn't too late to fix this. They'd get through it. She'd explain. Chloe would get it and they'd figure out how to move forward.

She sat bolt upright, looked at her daughter's beautiful face, leaned over, put a hand out to stroke her hair. But . . . Chloe's head moved the other way, fell to the side. Mirren didn't understand. Couldn't work out what was happening.

Until the sound of the monitor changed.

Beeeeeeeeeeeeeeeeeep.

50.

'Secret Garden' – Bruce Springsteen

Thirty-six hours with Adrianna Guilloti and Zander realized that no drug had ever made him this high. No booze had ever blown his mind the way she did. They hadn't left the suite since they'd burst through the door a day and a half ago. They'd been having sex for at least half of that, and Zander was somewhere close to love by the time he finally responded to Hollie's fifty-eighth text, informing him that a jet would be waiting at Teterboro at 10 p.m. to get him back to LA. Persistence was definitely one of her sterling qualities. He called down to reception and asked them to set up transport to the airport. Minimal travel time. He didn't want to waste a minute that he could be here, even though they'd now reached the anticlimax, the crushing comedown after the exquisite, adrenalin-rushing high.

The New York sky outside was already fading to black as Adrianna dressed by the light of only the bedside lamp and prepared to leave. Now Zander lay in bed, cigarette in one hand, the other arm behind his head as he watched her retrieve her underwear from the Louis XV chair in the corner.

'You're pretty incredible.'

Adrianna threw back her head, laughing, like a model on a Cover Girl advert. 'Ah, you tell me so many things I already know.'

Couldn't beat confidence.

'So how are we going to make this work, then?' Zander exhaled, his naked torso resting into its perfect, beautiful form of toned muscle and sinew.

Her expression told him immediately that she knew what he meant, and that her answer wasn't going to match up to his hopes.

'Oh, Zander, my darling,' she purred, walking towards him, wearing only a black lace thong, a matching half-cup balconette bra, suspenders attached to 5-denier silk stockings, her feet already in black Manolo Blahnik stilettos. 'This has been an encounter that I will truly never forget. But that's what it was. An encounter. My husband will indulge my little indiscretions as long as they're frivolous and brief, but he is far too jealous to let it go any further.'

Stop. Rewind. Husband? It might have been an idea to have researched that before flying 3,000 miles to do the whole Romeo thing. He never, ever touched anyone else's wife. Never. That wasn't who he was. Damn. He didn't have many morals, but that was one of the few. What a tit, he chided himself. Yet he was an idiot with a dick that was red and swollen from the best sex he'd ever known. Sometimes morals definitely had their drawbacks.

'Oh, you didn't know about my husband?' Adrianna asked, registering his surprise.

'No.'

'Then perhaps that is something you should investigate

before you have dreams of another encounter. I am in LA next week. I can spend an hour, maybe two with you, perhaps play around a little.'

'Play around?' he said, with a smile, as she crawled onto the bed, straddled his legs and worked her way upwards until his erect dick was once again waiting for her. Clearly, his cock didn't do morals.

She bent down, took it between her tits, holding them together as she pushed down, pulled back, her tongue darting out to lick the tip on the downward motions. There was an explosive groan as he came, shooting into mid-air, Adrianna having already pulled back so that she avoided spoiling the recently applied make-up on her beautiful face.

The news of the husband had been a blow, but if he was going to be rejected, then this was definitely some way to go.

Once fully dressed, she returned to the bed and kissed him on the lips. 'I'm glad our deal came with this unexpected bonus,' she said, their noses touching, her voice tinged with amusement, her movements belying a definite hesitation to bring the weekend to a close.

Eventually, she pulled away, and then she was gone, and he was still lying there, naked, exhausted and just a little bit sad. A husband. Hadn't seen that one coming at all.

The buzz of his phone interrupted his mental slump.

A text.

'On way to airport yet? Don't make me hunt you down.'

Shaking his head, he pushed off the bed. Man, he felt like he'd just done a full-contact stunt fight scene. Everything ached. The thought that a couple of shots of JD and a gram of coke would take the edge off it crossed his mind and he swatted it away. He wasn't going there. Couldn't. There would be drug tests this week, and anyway, didn't the million-dollar endorsement, with the sexiest, horniest woman he'd ever known, come with a condition that he stayed straight?

Lifting the phone again, he let reception know he'd be checking out in half an hour. Twenty-eight minutes later, showered, dressed and black D&G aviators covering the shadows under his eyes, he registered a flash as he climbed into the limo. A pap, across the street. Zander just hoped he was on a general recon and not there because he'd heard a rumour about a movie star and a married fashion mogul.

No point worrying about it. It was what it was, and challenging the guy would only make it seem like he was covering up something huge. Far better to ignore it and hope that – like most pictures that got taken – it came to nothing.

By the time he stepped out of the car and headed for the West 30th Street helipad, he'd completely forgotten about it.

Nine minutes later, he touched down at Teterboro Airport and headed to the waiting jet.

The muscles in his ass hurt as he climbed the stairs. At the top, young Richard Gere was waiting for him with a hot towel.

'Good to see you, buddy,' Zander said, shaking his hand and taking the towel. 'Can you add a Jack Daniel's on ice to that?'

'No, he bloody can't,' came the reply from the lady sitting just inside, on the white leather sofa closest to the door.

'I meant an orange juice,' Zander quick-fired, as he leaned

down and kissed her on the cheek, laughing when she ignored his 'Evening, lovely.'

'Has anyone ever pointed out that you really have issues with impulse control?'

'Yep, my PA. But I don't listen to her, as I suspect she's overly judgemental.'

'Judgemental, my ass,' Hollie shut him down. 'I swear to God you're going to give me a heart attack.'

'I'm sorry, Holls. I am.'

'No you're fricking not,' she said, smoothing back the brunette hair that was pulled into a low ponytail. She was channelling the Bond-girl look – black leather trousers, black polo-neck sweater, gold chain round the waist.

'I am, I swear. So, how many people have I pissed off?' he asked, tossing his jacket onto a chair and slouching down on the opposite sofa, where young Richard Gere was already waiting with a large glass of chilled juice.

'Wes isn't chuffed, but that's because he's fairly sure you went on a bender and are at this very moment lying in a pool of your own bodily fluids in a Tijuanan jail.'

'That was last weekend,' Zander deadpanned.

'Axl managed to work without you yesterday and today. I told him that you weren't there because your doctor instructed you to rest your chaffed inner thighs.'

'I have chaffed inner thighs?'

'Yes. It was the harness. Not sure Axl believed me, but the set doc is screaming about failings in health and safety, and dangle times, and . . . urgh, it's a whole big chaffing mess caused by thighs that are not even fricking chaffed.'

Zander was too much of a gentleman to point out that they probably were now.

'So. Adrianna Guilloti.'

'How did you know that?'

'Deduction. I've met her. I'm straight and I'd still screw her all the way to New York and back.'

She took his silence as confirmation and proceeded. 'You know she's married . . .'

'I do now. I didn't on Tuesday.'

'. . . to Carlton Farnsworth?'

That caught him off guard.

'The real-estate guy? But . . . but . . .'

'I think "Holy shit" is the expression you're looking for.'

They'd never met, but Zander knew who Carlton Farnsworth was. He had come across him when he was researching a role a few years ago about a Wall Street mogul gone rogue. Farnsworth was a self-made man. Construction. Stocks. Hedge funds. Now wealthy beyond belief. No criminal record. More ruthless than Trump. More intense than Shvo. Shadier than any of the big names. He owned a large percentage of Queens, Brooklyn and several statement properties in New York. There had been many rumours over the years concerning cement boots and dirty money, but nothing that had ever stood up in court.

'She kept her own name when they married, but they've been together forever. They're, like, a major power couple. Always in the press. Nothing in there set off an alarm in your brain?'

'I'm not sure the brain was engaged,' he admitted ruefully. Shit. Carlton Farnsworth. The one time he breaks the 'no married women' rule, he does it with Carlton Farnsworth's wife. A few hours ago, the 3,000 miles between New York and LA seemed way too far. Now, suddenly, it didn't seem far enough.

'Hang on,' Hollie said, staring at him. 'I just want to capture the exact expression on your face so that when you piss me off, I can conjure this up and gloat.'

Zander laughed and knocked back the orange juice. Fuck it. What's done was done. Over. A great – what was it Adrianna called it – encounter, no need for a second act. The thought didn't break his heart, but it sure made the world seem like a less exciting place.

'So anyway, much as it's lovely to see you, to what do I owe the pleasure?' he asked, as they moved over to their chairs and clipped in their seatbelts in response to the announcement that they were about to start taxiing.

Hollie shrugged. 'I didn't know where you were, didn't know if it was gonna get messy, so I thought I'd better come over in case I had to drag you out of a crack den or identify your body,' she said breezily. 'So I flew here yesterday – first class, thank you very much . . .'

'You're welcome,' Zander replied.

'And spent the night in the Plaza – again, thank you . . .'

'No problem.'

'And you treated me to a night at the theatre – *Jersey Boys* – and a new Chanel clutch. Oh, and these pants. You're really very generous. I don't think Matt Damon could match it.'

'I try. You're worth it.'

The jet picked up speed and they both closed their eyes

as the nose of the plane rose, pushing them slightly back into their chairs.

'So anyway, spill. What was she like? Worth spending the rest of your life without kneecaps?' Hollie asked, lifting a cup of coffee from the tray that young Richard Gere was now holding in front of her.

No answer.

'Zander?'

No answer.

'Zander?' she repeated.

Still nothing.

51.

'Come Fly With Me' – Frank Sinatra

Nothing. Just a tiny snuffle of sleep. Hollie rolled her eyes, then checked her watch, making a quick calculation. Six hours until landing. And given the state of Zander's under-eye luggage, he'd probably be out until touchdown.

'Anything else I can do for you?' young Richard Gere asked.

'N— Erm, actually, what age are you?'

'Twenty-three,' he replied, clearly a little puzzled.

Another calculation. Nope, he broke her ten-year rule.

'Ah, born a year too late. Thanks but I'm fine.'

'Are you absolutely sure?' YRG wasn't giving up that easily. This broad was gorgeous. And it did get boring when there was nothing to do around here. That's why he preferred the rock stars to the business clients – groupies, liquor and he was frequently invited to join the party. Actors were usually the worst. Completely self-obsessed. One guy he'd seen in a dozen movies once asked if he could have a different air supply from the journalists who were riding up back. Another made a weekly trip to see the daughter that no one knew he had, accompanied by the mistress who sang songs to him while they had sex. And then there was the squeaky-clean actor-turned-politician who insisted the two secretaries who never left his side were Harvard graduates. Perhaps they were. But the minute the jet left the ground, they stripped naked and stayed that way for the whole flight, both of them sporting the kind of body hair that hadn't been seen since the 1970s. Huge full bushes. Underarm frizz. The three of them would then head for the bedroom, only emerging when the wheels hit the ground.

Before YRG had left his home town, determined to make it as a movie star, he'd reckoned Hollywood had a pretty twisted side. Now he knew just how twisted it was, nothing surprised him. But hey, as long as they were all consenting adults, what was the harm? And if there was a little something in it for him, all the better.

This wasn't the job he'd aspired to, but until Spielberg came calling, it would do just fine. He gave his sexiest movie-role-audition grin to the woman in the hot black leather pants, but she still didn't bite. Shame.

Hollie knew exactly what he was thinking and it wasn't that she wasn't tempted, but she had a strict 'no more than ten years younger' policy. Bloody scruples – no wonder they were the first thing to go when anyone got success. They didn't half spoil the party.

'Thanks, but I'm good.'

As soon as he'd gone back through the privacy curtain, Hollie stood up and opened the overhead locker at the front of the fuselage. She'd taken this jet enough times with Zander to know where the supplies were kept. Extracting a blanket, she opened it and spread it across her boss, who now had his head lolling to one side, a tiny droplet of drool crystallizing at the corner of his mouth. If his fans could see him now.

Settling back down, she pulled her laptop out of her bag and got to work on emails, firing automatic responses back to the ones she could answer, prioritizing the ones that she'd need to consult with Zander on. There were no major surprises. His schedule for the next week was there. Invitations to several events. An analysis of fan activity from the administrator of his official fan clubs on Facebook and Twitter. Then there were the usual fishing requests from tabloids and TV entertainment shows. Could Zander comment on the rumour that he was dating Cameron Diaz? Was it true that he visited Hawaii last weekend with Jennifer Lawrence? Did he care to answer the accusations that he was being difficult on the Dunhill set and that there were rising tensions between him and Axl Chang? Did he wish to challenge their source who claimed Mr Leith had pec implants and was planning to have a facelift after shooting concluded? All bollocks, all replied to with a swift and firm 'Story denied, categorically untrue.'

Not a single whiff of a rumour about New York or Adrianna Guilloti. Thank God. He was sailing closer to the wind than ever with this one. She fancied his chances of surviving a crack den in Compton more than his odds of surviving crossing Carlton Farnsworth. Fool. And yet – she glanced over at him, still sound asleep – he was a lovable fool.

As long as Zander wanted her, she'd never be Matt Damon's, she thought with a smile. A dozen more emails were filed, answered or categorized before she got to the final one. Sarah McKenzie. The name was familiar. A quick scan and she realized why. This was the Scottish journo who had requested an interview a few weeks before. She'd forwarded it on to Zander, but he'd answered with an unequivocal no. It had stuck in her mind because he'd been unusually snappy about it. Wasn't like him. But then, he was just out of rehab and not in the best place.

Emails done, she updated his calendar, ordered his meal choices for the week, all of them delivered in airtight, temperature-regulated dishes to the set, planned his workout schedule, dermatologist visit, and set a meeting with Guilloti's people for the first fitting for his suits for awards season. It was still a couple of months away, but that's how long the process took. Only when all that was done did she take out a book, a thriller by Denise Mina. She'd started reading Scottish thrillers when she first went to work for Zander and now she was addicted.

Twenty minutes from landing, after a blissful few hours, she turned the last page and woke up Zander. The shadowed, exhausted man who got on the plane was gone, replaced by bright eyes, a cute wink and a voice that was on the sexy side of twenty Marlboros a day.

'Morning,' he murmured. 'Did the earth move for you?'

'You wish. Orange juice there, your vitamins are on the table, coffee and toast coming up.'

'I love you.'

'You should.'

The night was dark when they landed, and as they descended the steps, Leandro was parked on the tarmac waiting for them.

Zander was happy to fly commercial when time constraints allowed, but there was no denying this was a kick-ass way to travel.

Leandro held the door open for Hollie, who was balancing her cream Birkin – last year's Christmas present – an iPad and several shopping bags from Fifth Avenue stores. Zander decided it was safer not to ask.

'I'll drop you first and then head on home,' Hollie told him.

'Are you sure? I don't mind swinging by your place first.' Hollie's Marina del Rey condo was a ten-minute drive from his home. When she first started working for him, she'd lived in the Valley, but they'd jointly decided that his life would benefit from having the person who ran it, sorted it and kept it out of the gutter living nearby.

'Nope, it's fine. Because if I get dropped first, you'll get home, there will be some dire emergency and I'll have to come over, and then sleep deprivation and a large dose of PMT will kick in and I'll want to kill someone.'

'I can't think why you're single. Really. Not a clue.' Zander shrugged, face a picture of innocence.

'Because I work for you,' she blasted. 'I have no life. None. This is like permanent charity work. I do it for the cause. Isn't that right, Leandro?'

In the front, Leandro nodded. 'Absolutely. Whereas I do it for the money. Sorry, Mr L, no offence.'

'None taken.'

They cleared Van Nuys Airport and sailed right through to the 405, heading south.

This was his favourite hour in LA. Quiet traffic, night

people, none of the stresses of the day. Right now, he wanted to tell Leandro to take a detour, head down Sunset, maybe stop at a club, grab a beer, but he knew if he even suggested it, Hollie would take him out. Sometimes it was difficult to say who was the boss in this relationship. In fact, scrub that – it was perfectly clear. Hollie trumped him every time.

The faint sounds of Blake Shelton came from the speakers and Zander reached over and turned up the volume. 'Mine Would Be You'. One of his favourite songs. About someone sharing the best times of their life with the person they loved.

Perhaps it was time he thought about getting his shit together. The weekend had been incredible, but for what? For Adrianna to go back to her husband and for him to go home to an empty apartment? Maybe now that he was clean, he should give the relationship thing a try.

Go for a bit of normality. Maybe even take some time off and think about travelling, maybe Nashville, somewhere south, just somewhere he could get away from the spotlight and take time to re-evaluate, live a life with no drama for a while.

'Mr L, looks like we have a tail. Same car has been behind us since we left the airport.'

Hollie stretched round, peered through the glass.

'Doesn't look like a pap. Not their style. One driver. Woman. So I think we can safely say your friend in New York hasn't sent a hit squad. Yet.'

Zander didn't even bother turning round. If the tail was still there by the time they hit Venice, he'd flag up security and they'd drive straight to the cop shop. Standard procedure if he felt there was any threat. Which he didn't. Probably just coincidence. Or a lone pap who got lucky – loads of them were women these days. Some had great covers too. Strolled into clubs and restaurants looking like they were there to party and as soon as they got up close, the cameras came out.

'So who is she?' Hollie asked herself out loud. 'Definitely haven't seen her before. Weird car for a pap. Not exactly low profile. Zander, do you know anyone who drives a red Mustang convertible?'

Nope. Nothing.

'OK, let's see where it goes. Leandro, head for home, but don't turn off Lincoln until I say.'

Hollie grabbed her iPhone, held it near the back window and used the camera function to zoom in on the licence plate.

She called the studio's head of security and put it on loudspeaker.

'John, Hollie Callan. But then you probably already knew that because you've inserted some tracking chip in my ass.'

'We only do that for very special clients, so yes, you're right. What's the boy wonder done now?'

'I heard that,' Zander shouted in, laughing. 'You know I have a gun?'

Hollie pulled it back to business. 'Listen, we have a tail and I'm texting you a licence plate. Red convertible. Female driver. Just want to make sure it's nothing sinister. We're about fifteen minutes out of Venice. Can you call me back?'

'No problem. Don't turn off Lincoln until you hear from me.'

'Already done. This ain't my first rodeo. But then the chip in my ass told you that.'

It took him less than five.

'Rental. Female. Sarah McKenzie. Mean anything to either of you?'

Hollie nodded. 'Yep, British journalist. Been trying to get facetime with Zander for a few weeks. Why the hell is she here? Bit of a drastic leap for an interview.'

'Want me to send over some guys to watch the building?'

'Nah, it's fine. One chick on her own. I can take her. With or without the boy wonder.'

John laughed. 'I don't doubt it. OK, call me back if you change your mind. You know where I am.'

Hollie hung up. 'OK, let's wait till we hit Lincoln, then give her the benefit of the doubt for a while. If she hasn't backed off by then, I'll call the cops and have them intercept her. They can't charge her with anything, but it'll keep her out of the way for a while. At least long enough to get you home and out of sight. I should get danger money for this shit.'

Hollie swept round onto her knees and watched as the red convertible continued to follow. The privacy glass meant the journo chick wouldn't see that they'd spotted her. Good. Better that way.

The car lurched to the side as Leandro turned it onto Lincoln and Hollie tapped in the private number for the Venice Police Department. Most local PD stations had them now, strictly for high-profile risks only. Wouldn't do for a deranged stalker to take out a celebrity in the neighbour-hood. Wouldn't be good for business.

Four minutes.

Come on, lady, disappear.

Two minutes.

Last chance, doll.

Hollie's finger was about to press connect when she saw their pursuer lift a cell phone to her ear. Chat. Smile. Chat.

Must be a guy, Hollie decided.

Another smile, another chat, then . . . Yes!

The red car signalled right, slowed down and then did a U-turn, heading back up the way it had come. If that chick ever got bored with the newspaper industry, there would be a job for her in stunts.

52.

'I Knew You Were Waiting'
– Aretha Franklin and George Michael

'Hey. So I hear congratulations are in order,' she said, her tone light, before he'd even had a chance to kick off with hello.

Davie was suddenly too exhausted to even go with a shred of pretence.

'On the record or off?'

'Off.'

'OK, so perhaps everything isn't exactly as it seems. Look, what are you doing tonight?'

'Oh, you know. Just driving. Stalking Ryan Gosling through the streets of Santa Monica. I think I'll ask him to marry me here. Lovely setting.'

She was crazy. In a good way. In a way that made him want her here right now.

'Sounds like a plan. Look, let's do the interview tonight.'

'Really?' She sounded surprised, with just an edge of wariness.

'Yeah. OK, let me think. Head to the Parker Hotel down on Ocean Avenue. I'll send a chopper.'

Pause.

'As in a bike with unnaturally large handlebars?'

'Cute. But no. The Parker has a helipad. The chopper will be there within the hour.'

It took one phone call to his private concierge to arrange, and only when he'd hung up did he take pause to wonder what the fuck he was doing and why.

For seventy-five minutes and fifty seconds he had no idea why he'd done it. For the last ten seconds, as she strutted up the gangway, eyes squinting to see him in the semi-darkness, he knew exactly why.

He wanted to impress her. Distract her. Keep her onside. Know her better.

However, his alarms bells were screaming. Connection or not, this girl was the most dangerous that he'd ever met. In one night she'd managed to get into his house, learn his secrets and manipulate him into another meeting. Up until a couple of hours ago, he'd been intending to blow her off, or keep her waiting so long that she gave up. Or perhaps feed her a manufactured story in the hope that she'd skip back to Scotland, pleased with being sprinkled with the stardust in Tinseltown.

Even to him, he sounded like a dick. When had that happened? When had he gone to sleep a decent, normal, eager-to-please kid and woken up a complete dick?

Now, as she strutted towards him in a white scoop-neck T-shirt that was falling off one shoulder, a pair of white capri pants and silver flip-flops, he realized that it would be so easy not to care about her story or her motivations. He'd have to be guarded. Watch what he said. But maybe it was time for a bit of reality, and if that meant playing with fire, so be it. He'd already been well and truly burned.

'Good evening,' he greeted her, suddenly aware that he was still dressed like he was going to a wedding. Probably time to pull on some jeans. He held out a hand to support her as she jumped into the boat.

'Hi. So, am I gatecrashing your second honeymoon?'

He laughed. 'I deserved that. But no. My wife has gone to . . . Actually, I don't know where she's gone. Lift your top.'

'What?'

'Lift your top.'

Her hands went onto her hips and her chin rose in defiance, while her tone kept it light, almost daring. Wow, she was a mass of contradictions. 'Sorry, but I need to know someone way better than this before nudity becomes part of the relationship.'

'Cute. I just want to check there's no tape. Leave your phone on the table there too.'

He could see that she was considering this before complying.

'It's that or nothing – up to you.'

'You don't trust me?'

He pressed the button to raise the anchor.

'Absolutely not.'

She shrugged, threw her phone on the table and pulled her top over her head to reveal a white sports bra.

'Satisfied?'

'Absolutely.'

'Grab a seat,' he told her. 'There's champagne on ice. Brought it for my wife. Turns out she wasn't in the mood. Who knew?'

'I'm more of a beer kinda girl,' she replied. 'Sorry. No class.'

Davie reached into the cooler behind him, pulled out a Bud and handed it over, thinking that refusing $500-a-bottle champagne was the classiest thing he'd ever heard. He took a beer for himself too, then jumped off deck, untied the mooring rope and jumped back on, then pressed the button to retract the anchor. Engine burring, he slowly reversed the boat away from the slip, turned and headed forwards with more confidence in his boating abilities than he had in his personal judgement skills. He had been sailing since he landed in LA. One of the things about growing up on an estate in a densely populated city is that it gives you a craving for the countryside or the shore. He chose the latter.

'Is it OK to go out in this at night?' she asked, looking just a little disconcerted.

'Sure. Criminals do it all the time. That way, no one sees them dump the bodies.'

'You're a riot,' she said, no trace of fear now.

· They drank beer and made small talk for an hour as he navigated out of the harbour into the Pacific, then turned north, following the coastline.

Eventually, just north of Santa Monica, he dropped anchor and headed for the sunlounger next to her. He sat on the edge of it, facing her as he spoke.

'Can I be honest?'

'Uh-oh. That's never a good sign,' she said, her smile utterly disarming.

Man, she was good.

'I don't know what you want from me,' he said. 'So I'd like you to tell me. And if I believe you, I'll help you.'

Even as he said it, he was holding his breath. She couldn't know. No one did. This had to be all innocently motivated – a completely frivolous piece and she'd just used it to get a freebie holiday.

'I want to know what it was like, back then,' she started hesitantly. 'I want to know about your life growing up in Glasgow. About what made you come here, what shaped you. I want to know about your family.'

They both knew that she wasn't telling the whole truth yet, but it was a start. OK, he could do this. Talk. Just talk. Give her enough. Stop when it got to the bit that could never be shared.

'OK, but here's the deal. I'll decide later what's on the record and off.'

She thought about that for a moment and he could see that she realized there was no option. Better to have something to build on than nothing at all.

'Deal,' she agreed.

'Where do you want to start?' he asked, unbuttoning his shirt. He tossed it to one side and pulled on a sweatshirt. The temperature had dropped now. Low fifties. He pulled a thick fur blanket out from underneath the seat panel and handed it over to her.

She gazed at the sky for a few moments, thinking. Then, 'Tell me about your first proper girlfriend.'

Straight to the heart. Bullseye with the first arrow.

'I was sixteen.'

'Late developer.'

'I was.'

'OK, so tell me about the first time you fell in love.'

'Ah, same girl.'

'Really?'

What did it matter now? He could move the goalposts later. Right now, he just wanted to talk.

'There's only ever been one.'

'What, you mean before your wife?'

'No,' he answered honestly. 'I've only been in love once.'

'How long were you together?'

He thought about that for a moment. 'About six years.'

'So what went wrong?'

He shrugged. 'Things. Stuff. People.'

Gently, clearly careful not to say or do anything that would stop this revelation ball from rolling, she pressed on.

'And where is she now?'

There was a pause. A long pause. He couldn't say it. In twenty years he'd never looked back, never brought it up or discussed it. It was like the door had been closed and nothing could open it again.

But now, he wanted to. It was time. Reality, his mum said. He needed some reality.

'She's over there somewhere,' he said, pointing north towards the lights of Malibu. 'The only person I've ever loved is Mirren McLean.'

53.

Silence

Glasgow, 1989

Mirren could smell the booze as soon as he spoke.

'Well, look at Little Miss Swot. Head in the books like some smart wee cunt that thinks she's too good for the rest of us.'

Mirren kept her head down. No smart-arse retort. No eye contact. Nothing to provoke him. If she'd learned one thing having Jono Leith as such a malevolent presence in their home for all these years, it was that challenging him never ended well. The odd slap. The push. The blistering verbal abuse. After the tea incident last year, he'd never tried anything else sexually inappropriate, but she always felt threatened. Vulnerable.

If she spent the rest of her life working on it, she still wouldn't have time to count all the ways she despised him.

Or all the ways she despised her mother.

How could Marilyn live like that? Life dedicated to a vile prick, one whose wife lived just a few houses away? It had been bad enough when Jono just came here a couple of nights a week and she had to listen to them banging all night, but now he'd moved in full-time it was so much worse. She just wished Billy McColl had killed the bastard instead of the other way round.

But no. He was here, and his egotistical shite had ascended to a whole new level. How could her mother find this man attractive? Now he was spinning her a line about buying them a big fuck-off house in Milngavie and treating her to a BMW. It was all pish. Would never happen. In the posh suburbs, Jono Leith would be shit on their shoe, someone treated with contempt for being the scum that he was. Here, however, he was king of the hill, looked up to, feared, and even – among the smack-addled imbeciles – respected and admired.

It all made Mirren sick. But it wouldn't be for much longer. There was another life out there for her. She wasn't naive enough to think that she could go live in a garret somewhere and pen the next classic, but she had dreams and a vague plan. Work, live somewhere safe, write in her spare time. Maybe a novel. Maybe the short stories she'd been writing for years. It didn't matter. The very process of putting the words down on paper were a release, an escape from reality. It soothed her. Comforted her. When she wrote about Davie, it made their love real. Indelible. When she wrote about her fears and pain, it allowed her to put it in a box, to release it from her soul. When she wrote about Jono Leith, it allowed her to imagine all the ways she wanted to slowly, tortuously eviscerate him.

'Not speaking to Uncle Jono?'

Shit, he was still there. Mirren didn't look up. There was no point. It didn't matter what she said – it would be wrong. Her body stiffened as it waited for the blow. Last week, the slap to

407

the back of her head had been so hard her face had bounced off the table, causing her nose to bleed like a river.

When Marilyn appeared and saw the damage, she was almost apologetic. 'Oh, she's always getting those,' she told Jono. 'Watch you don't get blood on that new shirt, sweet pea. Mirren, put your head back and make sure you clean that up when it stops.'

With that she'd disappeared out to the local pub, hand in hand with her grinning lover.

Mirren wanted to vomit. The same sensation she was getting now as she realized that he wasn't leaving her alone.

He swaggered across the kitchen, his repulsive leer twisting his features to a whole new level of ugly. With creeping anxiety, she felt his fingers go into her hair, twisting strands of her curls tighter and tighter until . . . he yanked back her head, forcing her to look up at his sneering face.

'Too good for me, are you? Too fucking prissy. You know what you need?'

All bets were off. It was one thing keeping quiet to avoid provoking him, but he was not going to lay a finger on her without her fighting back with everything she had.

'Don't you fucking dare touch me!' she spat, her right hand flailing upwards, trying to catch the face that was just out of reach. Her left hand reached round, tried to grab the hand that was holding the back of her head like a vice. Unwittingly, she'd left no protection for the front of her body. He took the opportunity, ripping the top of her T-shirt as he pushed his hand down inside it, under the cotton fabric of her bra, and grabbed her breast.

The realization of what he was doing made Mirren's whole

body rear and buckle, sending her chair skidding out from under her and the table flying across the room as she kicked out.

She roared with physical pain and mental anguish as she fell, Jono still holding his grip on her hair. Flailing, punching out, twisting every bit of her body . . . but none of it helped. He was too heavy for her, his force too strong.

He was on top of her now, straddling her, pinning her hips to the floor. Chunks of her hair were ripped out as he pulled his hand round and changed his grip, his hand over her mouth, stopping her from screaming any more, while forcing her to look at him, to watch his face as he . . .

Oh God, no.

No.

His fingers were fumbling with his belt, then his button. Then his zip came down. Then he was pushing down the waistband of her leggings.

No! She wasn't going to let him. He couldn't . . .

Inside her head, there was a roar as she felt him pushing inside her. Oh no. No. No.

Still punching, still trying to buck him off her and all it was doing was making him smile more until . . .

He was laughing now. Laughing as he pummelled against her, watching her face, loving every moment. Faster. Faster. Faster . . . Until he came, spurting his poison into her body, infecting her with every seed of his evil.

Mirren died inside.

Nothing left.

Nothing.

Her body flopped, defeated, as her soul shut down, desperate to protect itself from the horror.

There was nothing left to feel. Her body was numb, her brain blank, her heart broken.

Nothing left.

Just a shell. A violated, broken shell.

Lying in a pool of sweat, blood and his toxic semen, Mirren begged her body to respond to her, to get up, to fight back, even now. It was too late to stop the horror, but there was still time to make him pay. If only she could move, rise above him, scream, shout, kill. But he was still there, on top of her, smug satisfaction all over his red, sweating face.

'Not too fucking good for us now, are you? And don't go running that smart mouth off to your mother. I'll tell her you begged me. Daft cow will believe it.'

'Will she, Jono?' The whisper was laden with sadness.

Mirren twisted her head and saw her mother standing there like a tragic figure in her baby-doll nightie, black mascara tears streaming down her face. The distraction gave Mirren the split second that she needed to push him off her, to jump to her feet, sprint to the door.

And she ran.

Mirren ran to Davie.

54.

'Just the Way You Are' – Bruno Mars

The only person he'd ever loved was Mirren McLean? She hadn't seen that coming.

Sarah pulled the blanket tighter around her shoulders and took another sip of beer while she thought this through. It had crossed her mind that there might have been a romantic attachment in that trio, but she'd thought it was more likely that it had been between Mirren and Zander. No offence to Davie, but teenagers were shallow. And while Davie was a good-looking guy, Zander Leith had always had the aesthetics that made millions of women all over the world put him at the top of their shag list. In a direct competition between the teenage Zander and the teenage Davie, Sarah had no doubt that Zander would be the one getting off with girls outside their local disco.

She had to ask: 'Mirren and Zander never had a thing?'

Davie, over on the other lounger, staring towards the lights of Marina del Rey, Santa Monica and Malibu, shook his head. 'Nope. They had a different vibe. More of a brother-sister thing.'

'Why do you think that was?'

Sarah watched his reaction. Over the years she'd inter-viewed hundreds of people – victims, bereaved, criminals, lawyers, witnesses – and the one thing that was true of them all was that sometimes the truth was not in what they said but in how they reacted. Now she saw the classic signs of stress, concealment and fabrication in Davie. A flinch. A glance to the lower right. The nervous jerk of fingers running through hair. The pause. Then looking her straight in the eye. OK, so she was going to get a version of the truth. Not the whole truth, not a lie, somewhere in between.

'I suppose it's because they related to each other. Neither had a particularly settled home life. They both had challenges. Maybe similar ones. They were close. Really close. But Mirren and I were the couple.'

'Did Zander mind that? She was gorgeous, wasn't she?'

Davie smiled, and Sarah saw the nostalgia and sadness in his face.

'So beautiful. I don't know if you've seen the pictures of her daughter, Chloe . . . ?'

Sarah nodded. 'Yeah.'

'Well, Mirren looked exactly like that. I couldn't believe she chose me. I was nothing compared to her. Yet she was my first, and she chose me to be hers. And no, Zander didn't mind. He was our mate, and relationships weren't his thing. He was more of a loner. Deep.'

That jolted a question about what he'd told her.

'You said that they both had challenges. What did you mean?'

Davie shrugged, and Sarah saw the reflex clench of his jaw, slight purse of his lips. He couldn't say. Wouldn't say.

OK, so there was the line. It was no surprise when he answered, 'You'll have to ask them that, I guess.'

'I tried. Neither of them will see me.'

That didn't seem to come as a surprise to him. 'It was a long time ago. Not everyone wants to go back to the past. Look at the lives we have now. Zander's a star; Mirren is brilliant; I'm on a yacht with a super-hot chick . . .'

The charm was lowered from cheese level thanks to the tongue that Sarah knew was firmly in his cheek.

'Super hot,' she agreed, grinning. It was a much-needed relief of the tension. Set the comfort level back to bearable for him. Probe a little deeper now. Easy. Gentle. Don't scare him off.

'And yet you don't see each other now?'

'Sure we do.' He was blustering. Spinning. 'We bump into each other at events and shit like that.'

'But you're not friends.'

'No.'

'Why?'

Another flicker of – what? Anger? Irritation? Sadness?

'Like I said, our lives have changed. They're different. We're different. People grow out of each other and I guess that's what happened to us.'

Sarah stared at the moon above her. It was obvious he was lying, but she wasn't going to press because she didn't want him to clam up and . . . well, something else. It took a few moments to bubble to the surface of her psyche. She felt sorry for him. How ridiculous was that?

There he was, this big-shot star with his $40-million estate and his glittering life. And OK, so his career had hit a bit of a speed bump, but aside from that and a troubled marriage, he was pretty blessed. And yet right now the sadness leached out of his every pore. He looked so crushed, so vulnerable, so . . . All she wanted to do was go over there, put her arms around him and hold him. Christ, what was in this beer? This wasn't her. She was hard-arse. Ruthless. On a mission. But still . . . One side of her psyche was getting mighty infuriated with her apparent lack of ability to come up with answers, until her emotional grey matter finally 'fessed up the answer. She had known Davie Johnston for only a few days, but she liked him. Really liked him. He was arrogant, and totally messed up, yet there was just something about him that touched her.

Jesus, how did that happen? And how did she make it stop?

As if the Gods of Great Timing were paying attention, her phone rang, utterly breaking the spell of the moment.

She thought about ignoring it, but Simon would only keep ringing back until he got her, and if he didn't, he'd worry, kick into action. The last thing she needed was the LAPD breaking down her hotel-room door.

Davie gestured her to answer it. 'Want me to go?'

'No, it's fine,' she answered, picking up the phone and accepting the call. Davie disappeared anyway, down into the bowels of the boat, obviously trying to be considerate of her privacy.

'Hi.'

'Hi, darling. How's things? Left me for a movie star yet?'

It was a dry dig, yet Sarah couldn't help the twinge of guilt that rippled through her. She dismissed it immediately.

Ridiculous. OK, so she was on a boat on the ocean in the most romantic setting on earth, and yes, to her surprise, she was feeling a nugget of something resembling care for the person she was with. But that was it. Nothing more. Yet somehow she knew that if that information was relayed, Simon may see it slightly differently and jump to ludicrous, wildly inaccurate conclusions.

'Not yet. Still looking. They all have this thing called security. Totally gets in the way. What are you up to?'

'Just heading into the office. Case to prepare.'

'Simon, do you ever give it a break? It's – what? – six o' clock in the morning and you're already on the work treadmill.'

Her outburst took her by complete surprise. Why did that seem strange to her? If she was at home, then chances are that 6 a.m in the morning would play out the same way for her too. OK, so she might not be on the way into the office, but she would be up doing research, catching up with the overnight news, planning her next story. Other than holidays, their lives were completely dedicated to work. Priorities: work, then each other, then everything else in life.

Wasn't that the wrong way round? And why was she only realizing this now? What was it about this week that was causing her to question it? Clearly, she'd been in LA too long. The heat. The glitz. The glamour. It was absolutely fake, shallow, and there was undoubtedly an undercurrent of darkness keeping the whole lot afloat, and yet there was something resoundingly optimistic here. Something inspiring. Positive. Like everyone was pushing to get on board and have the life of their dreams. She'd spent so many years enmeshed in violence and crime and the very worst of humanity that it was a relief to take a deep breath of warm air and experience a different life.

Oh bollocks. Sarah put the beer down on the nearby table. There must be something in it that was making her lose the plot.

Right. Back to Simon. Her boyfriend. Her partner in life. Home.

He sounded a little distracted as he answered her, but at least his tone was lighter than it had been the last couple of times they'd spoken. 'I know, honey, but we're going to court on this case next week. A murder charge. Not sure we've got enough to prove his innocence yet, but we're close. So where are you? Sounds really peaceful.'

'Oh, I'm just . . . catching up with some work. On the roof terrace at the hotel. There are lights, so I can see what I'm doing. Was just getting a bit claustrophobic in the room, so I thought I'd come up here for a bit of fresh air.'

'Sounds idyllic,' he whistled. 'Too bloody idyllic. You are still coming back to me, aren't you?'

'Absolutely. Just might dig a pool in the garden while you're at work next week. And employ a waiter to bring me champagne every hour. As long as I can do that, I'll be back.'

'A pool? There's a pool at the club.'

He hadn't been listening to her, she realized, picturing exactly what he was doing. He'd have the phone under his ear, briefcase in front of him at the kitchen table. It would be almost completely covered with case notes and he'd be sifting through them, slipping the ones he required into the case. Then he'd close it, roll his shirt sleeves down, clip on cufflinks and pull his jacket from the back of the door, slipping it on, juggling the phone from one ear to the other.

'You're right. I'll just go to the pool at the club. Look, I won't keep you – I can tell you're busy. Good luck today.'

'Thanks. You too. Only two more days and you'll be home. Love you.'

And he was gone. Charging out through the door, into the car and away to save the legal world from yet another travesty of justice.

Only when she reached over to put the phone back on the table did she realize that Davie had returned, clutching two more bottles of beer.

'You lied to him. Do that often?' he asked, not accusing but curious.

'No. Never, in fact. I tend to be a pretty straight-up kind of person, but he's been a bit . . .' Sarah paused to find the right word, '. . . miffed lately. Didn't want me to come here. I don't think he can decide if he misses me or is still pissed off that I came. I just didn't want him to freak out and get all weird about the fact that I'm on a boat with some other guy. He knows it's work, but it would still make him uncomfortable.'

Taking the beer he offered to her, she sat back down on the lounger, facing him this time, their knees just a few inches apart.

'Should it?'

'No, of course not. There's nothing to be uncom—' Sarah stopped. Their eyes were locked; her stomach was flipping, her mouth suddenly too dry to speak. 'What?' she managed weakly. It was pointless. She knew. They both did. This had never happened to her before. Never. She didn't do uncontrollable urges and rash impulses, but right now something deep inside was almost hypnotically drawn to him. Wanted him.

'I want to kiss you,' he said. 'But my judgement has been a bit off lately, so I just need to check.' His voice was low, filled with utter longing and speaking directly to the reflexes that were controlling every single one of her erogenous zones. 'If I do lean over and kiss you, are you going to knock me out?'

'Off the record?' she whispered, suddenly struggling for air.

'Off the record,' he answered.

'No.'

Slowly, gently, Davie Johnston got up from his lounger and joined her on hers. Then, their eyes still locked, he lifted one hand and traced a line across her eyebrow and down her cheek, round her jawline then back, down the side of her neck and along her bare shoulder, her blanket falling away, her senses acutely aware that she was crossing a line. A big line. And yet absolutely nothing could stop her.

She could smell him now. Rich, natural, with just a hint of beer. His breath was on her and then . . . his taste. Lips, soft. She opened her mouth to his and realized that it wasn't enough. She wanted more. Her hands came up to his neck and then into his hair, holding him to her. Her tongue traced his teeth as she fell back, pulling him on top of her.

The panic came out of nowhere and rose from somewhere in her stomach, suffocating her lungs. She couldn't breathe. Couldn't breathe. Had to stop . . .

'Davie, I can't. I just can't.'

His head snapped up so that he was facing her, obviously confused.

'I'm sorry,' she said, slipping out from underneath him. 'I can't do this. I shouldn't have. I've never . . . God, I'm so sorry.' The crushed expression on his face was devastating. Then she could see his jaw clench, his eyes close, his shoulders slump.

'What do you want from me?' he asked.

Nothing, she wanted to say. Just you. The internal wrangling started again. A voice in her head, the cynical hack, telling her to get a grip. Emotions didn't run her show; her head did. And come on, who was she kidding? He was Davie Johnston. He pulled this stuff all the time and she'd fallen for it. She was about to fuck up her whole life for a guy who probably wouldn't remember her next week. That couldn't happen. She couldn't let it.

She came to a decision, reached round to her back pocket, pulled out a piece of paper, unfolded it and placed it on the table between them. Not a word was spoken, until, 'That's Zander McLean's dad, Jono Leith. And your mum. Not sure who the other two are, but I was hoping you could help me.'

Still he said nothing. She took that as a sign to continue.

'He went missing years ago, a couple of years before you, Zander and Mirren came to LA. From what I can gather, he was a career criminal who pissed off a lot of people. Perhaps that's why he vanished. Zander has never spoken about it and I've no reason to think he'll start now. So if you're asking me what I want from you? I want you to tell me the truth about what happened to Jono Leith.'

55.

'Nothing' – The Script

Zander led the way into the apartment; Hollie followed him. 'Just got to check your voicemails and look for any signs of eighteen-year-old wasted chicks. That OK?'

'Sure,' Zander replied. 'Wanna stay for a beer?' He caught her furious reaction and hastily offered an alternative. 'I mean a coffee?'

'Tempting, but I'll pass. I want my bed, my DVR, five episodes of *Scandal* and I want to lie in private stroking my shiny new Chanel purse.'

While Zander hit the shower, she made a quick check of his voicemails, put his phone and iPad on charge and headed for the door.

She was out and halfway down the stairs when she heard his phone ringing. Damn. She thought about going back in, but . . . hey, she was his PA, not his mother. It could be Adrianna Guilloti calling to have phone sex while her husband was in the tub. And that was one thing Hollie didn't need to hear.

Still ringing. Aaaargh. It went against every instinct to leave it, but it was midnight, she was tired, and . . .

It stopped. And since Zander was in the shower, it was highly improbable that he had answered it, so that must mean they'd given up.

Excellent. A call at this time of night only meant bad news, strippers or drugs. The whole Adrianna Guilloti incident aside, she really felt they were turning a corner. All she had to do was keep his life as ordered and disciplined as possible, while making it interesting enough to stop him getting bored. Most importantly, no drama. No stress. No heartache. So whoever it was on the phone could take a hike.

Zander Leith was closed for drama.

56.

'She' – Elvis Costello

Why were they pulling her away? Why? That was her girl there. They were saying things she didn't understand. Using words she didn't know. Gone, they said. Gone.

No. She wasn't gone. She was right there. In front of her.

Beeeeeeep. Stop that fucking machine. Mirren spun round, raised her leg and booted it against the wall. It cracked, fell; the cable jerked, pulling the clip off her baby's finger.

Her baby.

Oh God, her baby.

She was gone.

'Mrs Gore! Mrs Gore, please.' A nurse had her arms around her, trying to calm her. What the hell was she doing? Why was she talking to her when she should be over there, helping Chloe. Chloe. Oh God, Chloe.

Mirren fell to her knees and screamed until nothing else came out except tears, choking fucking evil tears.

Rewind. Take it back. Change the dialogue. This wasn't real. It couldn't be. She couldn't be on the floor when Chloe was there, in front of her, not breathing.

No. She was her mother. She could change this. Make her come back.

Pushing the nurse away, she climbed onto the bed, slipped an arm under Chloe's head and gently pushed her hair back with her other hand. 'It's OK, baby, Mom's here. I'm here, honey. Don't worry.'

Cold. Why did Chloe feel cold?

Leaning over, her face touching Chloe's, cheeks wet with tears. Her breath would bring her back. If she just lay there, kept her warm, made her heart beat for them both, it would be fine. It would be fine. It would be fine. It had to be fine.

The nurse was watching her now, pity written all over her face.

'Help her, please help her.' A whimper now. 'Oh, Chloe, no. Please no.'

Her head fell against the pillow now, her lips touching Chloe's cheek, their hair, same colour, same curls, meshed together so she didn't know where hers stopped and Chloe's started.

They were one person. One person, with only one heartbeat.

And that's how they stayed.

For the longest time.

Until the nurse was gone, and only the light of Chloe's bedside lamp still shone in the silence.

Sometime later, Mirren had no idea how long, the nurse returned.

'Mrs Gore,' she said softly, 'can we call anyone for you? We have a room you can sit in . . .'

'I want to stay here. I'm not leaving her.' Mirren didn't recognize the voice. It was hers but different. Tragic. Broken. It was who she was now. The mother of a dead child.

'That's fine. Stay as long as you need.'

Until the end of time, Mirren wanted to say. This was her child and she wasn't leaving her. Not ever.

When the nurse had left, Mirren kissed Chloe on the cheek, like she'd done every night of her childhood. Every night. She'd watch her sleep for a few moments and then kiss her cheek. 'Goodnight, my darling. I love you.'

Tonight, she added, 'Sleep for now, my love. I'll get Daddy.'

Jack. She had to tell him.

Hands trembling, she rifled in her bag, found it, dialled. It only rang twice.

'Jack . . .' she blurted.

'Oh, hi, Mirren.' Not Jack. Oh God, not Jack. 'How's Chloe doing? Jack said he, like, totally overreacted last night when she was unwell. And he's still real shaken up. So is she feeling better? Hang on, I'll get him. Jack, honey, that's your ex-wife on the phone.'

The smug victory in Mercedes Dance's voice was unmistakable. So Jack had gone running back to her. When the going got tough, the spineless ran for cover. Mirren wanted to tell her it didn't matter. It didn't hurt. No one won. Because now that her daughter was dead, no one would ever win again.

She hung up. Dialled Lou. Straight to voicemail. Hung up again.

Now the aching had started. Aching for someone to be with her, for someone to tell her it was a dream, a nightmare.

She dialled again. The number she'd found in Chloe's phone, saved, swore she'd never use.

He answered after five rings. 'Zander, it's Mirren. I'm with Chloe. Zander, my baby is dead.'

And he roared.

57.

'Clown' – Emeli Sandé

What was it they said? Your life could only change when you hit rock bottom? Gets worse before it gets better?

Well, Davie decided, he must be due for a mighty big slice of paradise.

For a second there he thought he had it. Sarah. How had that happened? He'd known her for a few days and yet she was making him feel things he hadn't felt for a long time. Too long.

When was the last time he'd actually wanted to make love to someone? Not a quick bang or an opportunist blow job. Even lust in the early days with Jenny hadn't been like this. That was all about physical connections, aesthetics, two driven people on the same path. But this? This was a real, heartfelt, meaningful connection and it had taken him by complete surprise.

Almost as much of a surprise as the stunt she'd just pulled.

Talk about a boot in the bollocks. He'd envisaged a night under the blanket, in the peace of the ocean, talking, loving. Shit, he was starting to sound like a Movie of the Week on Lifetime.

One with a tragic ending.

He'd been played. Absolutely played. And the only thing that made him more pissed off than being played was the fact that he'd walked into it with his defences down. Twenty years of self-preservation, of convincing himself that he had all he ever needed, only for this girl to change his mind.

And now this. All his nightmares, all his regrets began right there on that piece of paper.

To his surprise, he felt the sensation of his left eye twitch. Christ, that hadn't happened for years. Since he was a teenager. A kid, hanging out with Zander and Mirren, lying on the messed-up floor of his hut, listening to the Sunday-night chart show while smoking Embassy Regal and laughing until it hurt.

A few years later it would hurt more than he could ever have known.

His heart thudded out of his chest and he had a sudden urge to jump. Swim. Just keep going until the currents decided his fate.

She knew she was on to something and she wasn't letting go.

How many movies had he seen where this happened? Where the suspect was cornered, confronted with the evidence and forced to spill the details? Three choices: reveal the truth, push her overboard, plead ignorance.

The first option was out of the question, because this wasn't just his secret; it belonged to all of them.

The second was tempting.

But it would have to be the third. He'd never been much

of an actor, but now he was about to have a starring role. Scene 1, Take 1, the part of 'Innocent Man'.

'Yeah, that's Jono's dad,' he said. 'And our mums.'

'Our mums?' Sarah asked, sounding puzzled.

OK, so he'd given away some information that she didn't have before.

'Yeah, Zander's mum, Mirren's mum, Jono, my mum.' He pointed as he went. Three women, a brunette, and two blondes, all in plush black coats, all looking like they'd rather be anywhere than there. The only hint of a smile was on Jono Leith, standing in a smart suit, well tailored. Davie remembered it. He'd bought it from Cecil Gee in Glasgow. Cost £500 and he never stopped telling everyone that. He'd worn it to his last court appearance and then Zander's grandmother's funeral – about two weeks before . . . before . . .

Drums of fear playing in his head blocked the thought.

Meanwhile, Sarah was staring at the image. 'I knew one of them was Maggie Leith, and I knew one was your mum, but I had the other down as a sister, and I had her and Maggie the other way round,' she said, pointing to the two women on Jono's left. Davie watched her brow furrow as she caught the obvious implication. Marilyn McLean was holding Jono's hand, making it seem like they were the couple, while Zander's mum stood slightly apart, disjointed from the group.

There was something else. Something there that didn't seem right. He just couldn't get his mind to focus on what it was.

Breaking off, he headed to the wheel, snapped on the engine and steered the boat round in the direction of the shore, making it clear that for him the discussion was over.

Sarah followed him, unwilling to let it go.

'You still haven't told me what happened.'

Davie shrugged. 'I don't know,' he lied, hoping only one of them knew that. 'Jono was always going off, getting banged up, having affairs. Last I heard, the rumour was that he met some *Playboy* girl in London, moved there. He's probably in an Essex nursing home right now, telling the rest of the patients stories about his life as a big-time gangster in Glasgow.'

She stayed silent for a few seconds, arms wrapped around herself either for protection or heat. Davie wasn't sure he cared which.

'So was that it?' he said eventually. He had two motives. One, to get her off the subject of Jono, and two, to try to reclaim a shred of honesty from her. 'That's what all this was about? You wanted to know about Jono, so you pretended you wanted me?'

Sarah's head reeled up. 'No! It wasn't just . . . Look, I like you.'

The laughter came from a dark place at the pit of his stomach. How many girls had he said that to? How many times had he palmed one-night stands off with the same line?

Listen, I really like you, babe. I'll call ya.

He never did.

'Stop! We have nothing else to say to each other. When we dock, get off the boat, don't call me, don't contact me, and if you're going to write about me, you'd better make sure your facts are correct and you've got great lawyers. Understand?'

'Davie, I'm sorry. I didn't mean this to turn out this way. This has never happened to me before. I . . .'

Christ, she was priceless. She was still trying to cover herself, play the innocent. This time he wasn't buying. Not only had he sussed her out, but he'd realized something even more significant – she knew nothing. Nothing at all. Because if she did, she'd be using it now to try to get more information out of him. All she had to go on was that Jono wasn't around anymore. That was it. And if the police couldn't solve that mystery all those years ago, she wasn't going to be able to do it now.

All he had to do was stay away from her and this would go away.

And he could do that.

Couldn't he?

58.

'Signed, Sealed, Delivered (I'm Yours)'
– Stevie Wonder

Sleep wasn't an option. Neither was sitting down. Or reading a book. Or – oh dear God – calling home.

Apparently, the only available choices were lying on the bed staring at the ceiling or . . . Actually, it was a one-choice deal.

What the hell had she done? And even worse, what had she almost done?

Never in her life had she even considered being unfaithful. She wasn't that person. She was the one who made informed decisions, reported on the chaos in other people's lives, and yet if that one blast of panic hadn't overtaken her, she'd have had sex with Davie Johnston.

And even now, hours later, she still wasn't sure that she didn't regret stopping.

She was done here. It was over. Enough of the stalking. Time to face the reality of the situation. She wasn't going to get anything from these people. Even if she met Zander Leith and Mirren McLean over pancakes at IHOP, they weren't going to tell her anything. And she couldn't go near Davie again. Her face burned at the thought of him. He must think she was a major bitch, and she didn't blame him. Nor did she understand why the thought of him hating her made her stomach flip. Time to go home, before she lost more than just her integrity and her savings.

Her ticket was booked for the day after tomorrow, but she would bring it forward a day. Time to get home.

Standing up, she scanned the room for the oversized rugby shirt she wore in bed. Not that she'd sleep, but she wanted out of these clothes. He'd touched them. And she'd let him.

Spotting the shirt hanging on the back of the door, she crossed the room, reached up to get it and then jumped back with a yelp as there was a knock on the door.

Sarah froze.

Unless Simon had crossed the Atlantic and made his way here, there was no one who should be knocking on her door at 3 a.m.

The temptation to ignore it was excruciating. That's what she should do. Creep back to the bed, go under the duvet, go to sleep.

So why was she leaning over, looking through the spyhole and then opening the door?

Davie didn't move, just stared at her, both of them frozen, until, 'I need you.'

His words, his voice so low it was difficult to hear it over the thudding in her chest.

One step back and the decision was made.

His hands went to the side of her face, cupping it as

431

they moved towards the bed, a well-aimed back-kick closing the door.

Her groan was involuntary and came from somewhere deep inside as his hand gently pushed up her T-shirt and unzipped the front fastening of her sports bra. And then he was down there, a line of kisses taking his mouth to her breast and he was circling her nipple with his tongue, then sucking, slowly, tenderly, pulling a line of intoxicating desire up from deep inside her.

Then he drew back. 'Are you OK? Are you sure?'

Sarah answered by pulling him back down to her, kissing him, her tongue locking with his, dancing, inviting him to go further.

Their clothes seemed to melt away, unsure as to who was removing them, discarding them, revealing another part of each other. Allowing the other to see, touch, feel. He caressed her like she was made of glass. Sarah knew she should be self-conscious, torn, conflicted, but all she felt was a need to have him and the pure, unadulterated bliss of his touch.

Sex with Simon was energetic and satisfying, but this was a different level. How could that be? Making love with her long-term partner seemed impersonal, almost perfunctory, yet being with this man she'd only known for a few days was giving her a rush she'd never known.

He waited for her, came when she did, watching her face as she called out his name.

Afterwards, they lay silent, his head on her belly. Sarah stroked his hair, unsure what to say, all the doubts returning. She now knew what incredible sex felt like. Mind-blowing sex. Sex that you never wanted to end.

But this was wrong. And stupid.

What the hell was she playing at? He was the source of a story. The biggest story of her career, the one that could be a game-changer, and she'd just had sex with him. It went against every principle she'd ever had. And yet it had been inevitable. From the moment he stood at the door she'd never wanted anything more. Not even the scoop of a lifetime.

But now, hormones out of the equation, the doubts took over. He was so used to women throwing themselves at him. And hadn't she made it so easy? He hadn't even had to ask twice before her clothes were off and she was letting him in. What a pushover. What the hell had happened to her since she came here? One-night stands weren't her thing, and neither was cheating on her boyfriend. Another wave of guilt came crashing down. Simon. He was a good guy. Decent. And now she'd betrayed him.

'I think you're amazing,' Davie whispered, raising his head off her stomach and kissing a line down to her pubic hair. Then his tongue went searching, probing . . .

She reached down and brought his head up, bringing his lips to hers, kissing him softly, then letting him go.

Wordlessly, she slipped out of bed, suddenly conscious of her nudity.

She gathered her clothes, covering her body, all the inhibitions that had been missing in action earlier now firmly in control. She hastily pulled on her jeans and T-shirt, not even bothering with her bra while he watched her, wordlessly, her blanket pulled across his pelvic area, but his carved torso and gorgeous face still on display.

How had this happened? She had a boyfriend. She was a

professional. She was here for a story. She was not here to have the best sex of her life with a guy she barely knew. She'd lost herself there for a moment. Blame the heat or the moonlight or whatever. But she didn't do drama and treachery. She was a good person. Time to rewind the clock, reclaim her dignity.

The whole time she was running this internal dialogue, he was watching her, studying her.

'Are you OK?' he asked.

She shook her head, fully dressed now, but still flustered. 'I shouldn't have done that. I'm on a story. I have a boyfriend.' Somehow repeating the argument that had been in her head only moments before reinforced her resolve.

Time to move on. A blip. It was a blip.

'OK,' he said softly. 'But I don't feel the same.'

Oh damn, he looked hurt. Not the vulnerable face again. It crashed through her defences and she felt a desperate longing to hold him. She had to get him out of here before she capitulated again.

'I don't believe I'm saying this, but . . .' Mr Confident, Mr All-Singing Showbiz was struggling to find the words. 'I thought – man, I've never said this before and meant it – but I thought there was something there.'

No, don't do this. Don't make it worse.

She was desperate to agree with him. Yes, there was. There is. But how could she?

Pull it back, Sarah, she told herself. Get it together. Be realistic. Was she going to stay here and what? Be Davie Johnston's girlfriend? Of course not. This wasn't real. It was a fantasy, a crazy moment of lost inhibitions. If Davie was a normal guy, then maybe there could be something. But he wasn't. This guy was a self-confessed shagger, in a hopelessly confused situation, and the only outcome for her if she carried on down this road was pain.

'I'm going to go for a shower,' she told him gently. 'I'm sorry. I think you should leave.'

59.

'Pray' – Take That

Case closed. Court adjourned. As Davie sat in the back of the cab on the way home, he realized that nothing that had happened to him in the last few weeks even came close to how this felt.

And considering he'd pretty much lost his entire life, that was saying something.

There was just something about her. Something that . . . grabbed him.

She obviously didn't feel the same.

The sun was rising over his estate as he reached the gates, and a couple of paparazzi sleeping on the sidewalk sprang into action. These guys really needed to get a life.

May as well make it worth their while. He flipped them the V-sign and their flashbulbs popped like strobes.

That would be on every online celebrity site by lunchtime, all of them with a sensationalist headline and a team of experts quoting information from 'inside sources' to have an informed debate as to whether or not he'd lost the plot. They would conclude that he had. He wasn't sure he disagreed.

Back in the house, he headed for the shower, dropping his clothes across the room on the way there.

No sign of Jenny – obviously staying with Darcy. And if she was there, the kids were probably there too.

So yet again he was here. Alone. Karma was a bitch and she was dishing it out to him.

Had it all been just one big set-up? Was this another Lana Delasso? A game that ended with 'Loser' at the end of his name?

Going there had felt like a risk, and had taken more bottle than standing in front of the press hounds begging for forgiveness. Making love to her had been amazing, but she couldn't wait to get rid of him afterwards.

He wasn't going to hang around for that kind of rejection twice.

Done. Gone. Lesson learned.

Out of the shower, he headed for bed, naked, and crashed down on the duvet. Fuck it, he was staying here all day tomorrow. Maybe all week.

The clock beside his bed said six thirty when he drifted off to sleep. It said eleven thirty when he woke up, and eleven thirty-five when the thoughts that were floating around in his head settled into some kind of understandable form.

Sarah. Last night. Rejected him. But rewind. Before that. On the boat. He wanted her. And then . . .

The picture. There was something wrong with the picture. He studied a snapshot of the image in his mind.

Maggie Leith. Marilyn McLean, holding hands with Jono. Ena Johnston, his mum, on the other side. The other side. The hand. There was a hand curling round the back of her neck, so that only the fingertips were visible in the photograph.

In his whole life, he'd never once seen any man touch his mother.

So why was she allowing Jono Leith to hold her like she belonged to him?

60.

'Hymn to Her' – Pretenders

Zander stood in the doorway for a moment, his legs locked, unable to move, to do anything but just look at her, head bowed, her hand still clasping Chloe's.

From here it looked like they were both sleeping. Chloe, so peaceful, with no sign of the sullen frown or the angry glare that he'd become so familiar with.

She'd been such a sweet kid. Angry. Wild. But under all that, he could relate to the troubled soul that lay beneath. There didn't even have to be a reason for it. Sure, his early life hadn't been great, but that didn't mean he had any more right to be a fuck-up than anyone else. Chloe's idyllic childhood didn't mean she had any less.

Eventually, he found the strength in his legs to move forward, to touch Mirren's shoulder. As her face turned up to his, he flinched at the utter agony that seeped from every pore.

'I'm so sorry,' he whispered. Kneeling down, he silently wrapped his arms around her and let her fall into him. Still her right hand didn't leave her girl.

Zander felt the vibrations of her shaking body and knew

that no matter how tightly he held her, they would never stop.

He knew because they'd been here before. Mirren. In unbearable pain. Zander. Feeling partly responsible.

If only he'd taken Chloe under his wing more. If only he'd got her more help. If only he'd understood how badly this would end.

If only they'd never met and Mirren McLean hadn't been raped by his father, hadn't written the script, they hadn't made it a movie that changed their lives.

If only. If only they hadn't disappeared from each other's lives for twenty years. But it had been too much for him. He couldn't handle the fact that their new lives had been built on evil. His father's evil.

'I tried, Zander, but I couldn't help her. I couldn't make her stop.'

'Shhhhh.' He stroked her hair, listened to her sobs, acknowledging the pain he was feeling and understanding that hers was a million times worse. In his peripheral vision, he saw a nurse hover at the door and then leave.

Her face against his shoulder, tears soaking his T-shirt, Mirren's voice was a choked whimper. 'I don't know what to do now. Don't know how to breathe without her here.'

Still stroking her hair, Zander murmured soothing words for a long, long time. Until the light outside was no longer, until the tears were dry and they sat there in silence, clinging to each other, saying nothing at all.

'I'll stay here with you for as long as you need, but we have to let the nurses work now, Mir. Let me take you home. I'll stay with you there too. I won't leave you, I promise.'

Eventually, she nodded, and supporting her like a child, he helped her to her feet. Zander reached out and gently traced his finger across Chloe's cheek. 'Goodnight, beautiful girl,' he murmured softly.

Beside him, Mirren leaned over and kissed her girl again. More tears now, the silence of her pain making his head roar.

'I love you, Chloe. I'm so, so sorry I didn't save you.' Mirren leaned down, until her cheek touched her daughter's and stayed there, until he gently lifted her away.

They'd only gone two steps when her legs buckled. With the reactions of a sober man, he caught her, swept her up and carried her to his car. There, he took a blanket from the trunk, wrapped her in it and placed her in the passenger seat, holding her hand until they reached the gates of the Colony. The security guard waved them through. At the house, he lifted her again, carried her into the empty building, the hall littered with the debris of the earlier emergency call-out. A mask. Gloves. A discarded blanket. Mirren just stared straight ahead, as if in a trance, swollen eyes wide open. To his right, he spotted a lounge area with a sofa, took her through there and laid her down, kneeling on the floor beside her. This is what he should have done years ago. Taken care of her. Cosseted her. Stayed with her until the pain healed.

'Mirren, is there someone I can call? Tell me who you need.'

'Just Chloe,' she whispered, shivering now, despite the humid heat of the night. Acting instinctively, he climbed onto the sofa beside her, his arms around her, her head resting on his chest.

'It's so unfair, Zander,' she said, her voice monotone, numb. 'Why was it my girl? Why did God take Chloe and yet he let a bitch like Marilyn live?'

61.

Silent Scream

Glasgow, 1989

Davie's back door was closed but unlocked as always – no one would break into a house on the same block as Jono Leith. Mirren burst into the kitchen, but it was empty. She searched upstairs, but no one was there either. There was music in the bathroom. His mum. She always took her transistor radio in there while she was having a bath.

Where was he? Where was he when she needed him?

The hut.

Bolting outside, she ran to the end of the path, every bone in her body aching, blood dripping from her head, her nose, from between her legs.

When she burst through the door, Davie jumped up, thrust the cigarette in his hand behind his back, looking guilty. Eighteen years old, working down the local pub behind the bar, and he still hadn't told his mother he smoked.

There was a momentary flash of relief. 'Bugger, I thought you were my mum there. I nearly . . .' The realization. The blood on her face. The torn clothes. The matted hair. The red streaks on her bare legs.

Another voice. Zander. Lying on the floor to her right. 'What the fuck?' He was on his feet now, but Davie got to her first. Her Davie.

'What happened? Who did this?' She buried her head in his shoulder. 'Mirren, who? Who was it? I'll fucking kill him. Who did it?' He was screaming at her now, shocking her with his vehemence. Davie was the fun guy, the non-confrontational, easy-going one who didn't have a temper, didn't get angry, and now his eyes were blazing, face full of anguish.

'It was Jono,' Zander said, a statement, not a question.

'Was it?' Davie wailed, his eyes seeking answers in hers. 'Was it Jono?'

The involuntary sob, a guttural cry from her throat was all the answer he needed, and suddenly he was gone, barging out of the hut, Zander running with him.

'Leave it, Davie. I'll get him. I'll get him,' Zander shouted. Davie didn't stop, kept running, Mirren now tearing after them both.

This wasn't what she meant to happen. Davie wouldn't have the strength to go against Jono Leith, but Zander . . . Oh God, Zander did. This wasn't what she'd wanted. Either Davie would end up dead or Zander would end up in jail and it would be all her fault.

'Stop, please stop.'

Davie reached the door first, kicked it open with a force she never knew he possessed, but then reeled backwards as Zander caught his jumper, swung him round, pushing him down to the ground and running in first.

'He's mine, Davie. Go home. Go fucking home.'

Zander disappeared into the hallway, but Davie was back on his feet now, charging after him. Pain ripping her insides apart, Mirren was too slow to stop him. She could only follow as they stormed down the hall. At the end, she could see Zander burst open the kitchen door and then freeze. Jono must be there. Must be waiting for him. With what? A knife? A gun?

Oh God, she'd caused this. Whatever happened now would be all her fault.

In front of her, Davie reached Zander and mirrored his reaction. Sudden brake. Completely still. Running on pure adrenalin, it took a split second to reach them, another to push through where they were standing, another for her to make sense of the scene.

Sitting on a chair at the table, her mother. But it wasn't a Marilyn she recognized. This one had black tramlines running down her face from her eyes to her jaw, her hair dishevelled, blonde tendrils escaping from the ponytail she always wore because Jono liked it. But it was the spatter that took Mirren's breath away. Her mother sat there, not moving, face blank, covered in drops and dashes of red blood, all over her face, her hair, her neck and . . . Oh no. Mirren couldn't bear to look, yet she couldn't turn her head away. One shoelace-thin strap of her mother's baby-doll had snapped, the fabric dropped to reveal a huge white breast, smeared with blood, her mother making no effort to cover it up, as if completely oblivious.

Mirren's eyes followed Marilyn's dead stare, downwards, to her right, where Jono Leith lay on the floor, a knife sticking out of his chest, a pool of deep red liquid still moving, spreading around him. His chest didn't rise. It didn't fall.

Mirren pushed past Davie and Zander and rushed towards her mother, but still staring at Jono, Marilyn wordlessly put a hand up to stop her.

'Mum?' Mirren gasped. No answer.

'Mum?' she tried again. Then, ignoring the lack of response, went on, her voice soft, tender, 'I can't believe you did that for me.'

Marilyn finally turned to look at her, eyes still dead, her actions almost robotic.

'I didn't do it for you,' she said in a voice devoid of emotion. 'I did it because he wanted you instead of me. I did it for me.'

'No,' Mirren wailed, tears falling. 'No, Mum, say that's not it. Say . . .'

Davie's arms were around her now, and for the first time he spoke to Marilyn. 'You fucking bitch,' he spat. Marilyn didn't react. Zander did.

'Look, what are we going to do here? We can't leave him, can't phone the police. This will kill my ma,' he told them, the irony of his statement escaping him, before he suddenly realized the call wasn't his. 'Mirren, I'm so sorry. Do you want us to phone the police? Whatever you want. Anything.'

'No!' Mirren knew instinctively that couldn't happen, grasped the implications immediately. He'd raped her, but he was dead. The thought of her mother being taken away, of having to relive this every day in the eyes of other people, to have them pointing, talking. And then there would be a trial. Evidence.

No. She didn't want any of that. All she wanted was to get away from here and to forget.

'Davie, help me,' she begged.

Davie was always the fastest thinker of them all, the sharpest, the one with the ideas, and he didn't let her down.

'Oh fuck, we're going to get jailed for this. But, Mirren, you stay here and get this place cleaned up, get her in a bath,' he said, gesturing to Marilyn. Then back to Mirren, 'Are you OK? Do you think you can do this?'

'I think so. I can do it.' The second sentence was stronger than the first, like she'd made up her mind, found some inner resolve.

'OK,' he said, opening the under-sink cupboards and taking out kitchen roll, bleach, cleaning fluids, then grabbing a mop and bucket from the floor-to-ceiling boiler cupboard.

'There you go – do what you can. Me and Zander will come back and help you.'

'Where are you going?'

Davie was one step ahead. 'Zander, you grab his feet. I'll get his arms. Let's get rid of this cunt.'

62.

'Home' – Michael Bublé

Glasgow, 2013

Sarah almost hoped he wasn't home. She just needed time. Space to think. And somehow, fourteen hours, alone, on an aeroplane, just hadn't been enough. Her brain felt numb, wasn't kicking in when she really, really needed it to. How was she going to explain why she'd suddenly arrived back a day early? How was she going to explain it? Really sorry, I had sex with a movie star, then thought I'd better come home because my life has somehow become one big lie? Or hey, Simon, missed you so much – except for that pesky couple of hours that I was naked on top of a guy I travelled thousands of miles to investigate.

Oh, and yep, I did decimate both my personal and professional ethics in one fell swoop. Two for the price of one. Yay me.

How low did that make her feel? Of course she had to tell him about Davie, and she would, just as soon as they had some time on their own together. But right now, she couldn't bear to hurt him. He was in the middle of a huge case, and she knew that she had to wait until that finished. There was enough on her conscience – she couldn't add risking a cataclysmic upheaval in a lawyer's life that could possibly affect the outcome of someone's trial. Bad enough that she'd risked everything they'd had together. Destroyed it.

The thought of not telling him, of carrying on like nothing had happened had crossed her mind, but she'd dismissed it. That wasn't her. Sarah didn't do lies – at least not in her personal life – and she didn't do duplicity. Honesty was the only way. And if it cost her Simon, then that was her own fault.

Besides, in her heart she knew it was over. If she truly belonged with Simon, she'd never have cheated on him, never have let Davie touch her.

The thought made her wince. Davie. It made her stomach queasy every time she pictured his face. Hurt. Furious. He'd walked out without another word. Not that she blamed him. What a royal screw-up the whole LA thing had turned out to be. She was left thousands of pounds out of pocket and had come home with no evidence, no progress, just a broken relationship and a pain in her gut every time she thought back to how she'd behaved. That was karma for you.

The taxi pulled up outside the flat and she was suddenly desperate for her own bed, her own home, milk in her tea that tasted normal.

Looking up, she could see that there was a light on in Simon's office. No surprise there. Perhaps if they'd dedicated as much time to each other as they did to their jobs, it wouldn't have come to this. Not that this was in any way his fault. It was all on her.

As she opened the door, it struck her that this was like one of those clichéd scenes in a movie when someone arrives home early and catches their partner in bed with their lover.

Not Simon's style. Absolutely not. Simon was all about truth and justice and fairness. Cheating wasn't in his personality. But then, until last week she'd have said the same about herself.

Leaving her suitcase behind the front door, she wearily climbed the stairs, psyching herself up to be cheery and normal and the returning loving girlfriend. Just one night of sleep, she promised herself, then she'd face up to the situation.

The higher she got, the more snippets she could hear of Simon's voice. He must be on the phone. Bit late, but it wasn't unusual for him to talk to clients well into the night. If she was in luck, it would be a long call and she'd be asleep by the time he was done. Nausea swirled between her stomach and her throat. Oh God, this was awful. Awful. In a moment she realized she could back out, take a cab to a hotel. Why hadn't she thought of that? It was exactly what she should have done. She could go now; he didn't have to know that she'd even been . . .

What was that?

The tinkle of laughter? A woman's voice.

They were in Simon's study, so it must be someone from the office. His intern perhaps?

The door was open a few inches, and as she got closer, she could see the top of his head, sitting in his chair, facing his computer. It was so funny she almost laughed. He was on a conference call. No clichéd discovery. He wasn't having an affair and she wasn't about to walk in and see him having sex with his secretary, his intern or the next-door neighbour.

The thick gold carpet muffled the sound of the door opening, so much so that he didn't even have a chance to turn round.

Which probably wasn't a bad thing.

Because as Sarah entered the room, she realized he was absolutely alone. He was absolutely sitting in his office chair. And he absolutely had his trousers at his ankles and his dick in his hand.

'Oh my God, Simon.'

The voice wasn't hers.

It came from the screen, where Pippa, his best mate's girlfriend, was on her knees, naked, and frozen, a large purple dildo vibrating like a jackhammer as she squeezed it between her tits.

'Simon . . .' Pippa repeated, her voice tight with horror.

'Yes, darling. Yes.'

He was wanking faster now. Sarah couldn't bear to look.

Oh, the irony. Via the wonders of Facetime or Skype or whatever screen-to-screen service they were using for their mutual gratification, Pippa was probably miles away and was staring at Sarah, yet Simon was so close she could slap the back of his head and he had no idea.

'Simon!'

The tone of her voice finally registered in the part of his brain that recognized a potential problem, and he paused, mid-tug.

'Look behind you,' Pippa told him, dropping the dildo. It continued to vibrate.

In excruciating slow motion, Simon turned his head and saw her standing there.

'Fuck.'

Sarah had no words. Instead she smiled. And waved.

'Honey, I'm home,' she told him deadpan, before turning and heading back to the door. Half an hour later, she checked into the Hotel du Vin on Great Western Road. More expensive than she could afford, but the newspaper had a corporate deal and she knew that Ed wouldn't mind her using it.

Almost twenty-four hours later, she was still in bed. Fourteen hours of sleep, interspersed with several hours of thinking.

Pushing back the white duvet, she padded across the room and pulled a bottle of beer from the minibar. She didn't bother with the glass. It drove Simon mad when she drank from the bottle. Past tense. She'd blocked his number, so she had no idea if he was trying to contact her, and no clue as to where he was. Right now, that was fine.

The fleeting anger was gone, pushed out of the way by the knowledge that to hold this against him would make her a hypocrite. If anything, she'd done worse. As far as she knew, he'd only fucked Pippa on screen – that had to rate below the exchange of bodily fluids. If there was an infidelity score sheet, she was currently top of the leader board.

There were decisions to be made. She'd have to move out, find a place of her own, sort out her life, but she wasn't due back at work until tomorrow and right now she just needed to get past the jet lag and get her head back together.

She was so deep in thought she almost missed the buzz

of her phone, only catching it a second before it would have switched to voicemail.

'Sarah?' Rob – Simon's best friend – sounding, if she wasn't mistaken, slightly pissed.

'Sarah, is that you?' Cancel the last guess – make that *very* pissed.

'Hey, Rob, are you OK?' she asked. Oh God, Rob. She should have checked on him, tried to find out if he knew about his girlfriend and his mate's screen connection.

'He's been shagging Pippa. I've suspected for ages and she's just confessed. Said it's been going on for weeks. Fucking weeks.' He knew. And suddenly Simon knocked her off top place on the infidelity chart. An ongoing fling definitely trumped a one-night stand.

'I know, Rob. I'm sorry.'

'Can I come over? I'm coming over.'

'Rob, no. Don't. Thanks. I'm not at the house. I'll meet you at the weekend, but I just got back and—'

'I'd kill the bastard but I'd never hack prison.'

'I know, Rob.'

'You know you should have gone out with me?'

Sarah laughed for the first time since she'd touched down in Scotland. 'You're right. But look, I have to go. Rob, I'll call you.'

They both knew she wouldn't.

After cracking the top off the beer bottle, she headed back to the bed, just her thigh-length white jumper and cream slouch socks protecting her from the chill.

She crawled back in, picked up the remote control and

flicked to the hotel movie channels. Comedies. Thrillers. Family. Classics. Porn.

If she wanted the latter, she could just Skype home.

She went for Classics. There must be a movie in there that she wanted to see. It took a few moments to scroll through the hundreds of options beginning with A. Nothing. Then to the Bs. She was almost at the end when her finger jumped off the button.

The Brutal Circle (1991).

Their movie. Sarah had watched it back in college – maybe eight years ago – and remembered being absolutely gripped by it. But that was the last thing she needed right now. A dark, mildly terrifying thriller about . . . about . . . she couldn't quite remember. Something about a young girl and an older man. Didn't matter. This wasn't the time for darkness and harrowing storylines. The part of her brain craving comfort ordered her to switch it off. Turn over to the Comedy Channel. There must be a *Friends* episode on somewhere.

Yet, somehow, the rest of her wasn't responding. The titles rolled. Glasgow. A young Zander Leith – wow, he was young – swaggered across a concrete square of wasteland, surrounded by four rows of terraced houses. As he passes a house in the middle of the terrace, he spots a young girl, about fourteen, sitting on a bench outside the front door. In front of her, a young boy, around the same age, floppy hair, cute grin. Zander wanders over in time for him to hear Davie Johnston ask her, '*So why are you out here, then?*'

The girl took another puff on her cigarette, dead eyes looking downwards.

'Because she's in there with a bloke and I don't like hearing them.'

This took Davie's and Zander's characters by surprise. 'So every night you sit out here . . . ?'

'In there with a bloke,' the girl repeated.

Sarah couldn't move, could barely breathe. The minutes passed; the light on the TV flickered as the images changed; her beer went flat in the bottle she gripped in her hands.

Two hours later, she knew. Knew the whole story. It had been right there all along.

Her mind buzzed as facts whirled around, falling into place, making her heart ache for Mirren's tragic neglect and the brutality she faced in the end, for Zander's harrowing upbringing of violence and fear, and for Davie, the sweet young thing who tried to keep it all together, put patches on the pain.

It was all there.

She had her story.

63.

Screams

Glasgow, 1989

Jono Leith was so fucking heavy. How could he weigh this much?

Davie's breathing was fast and gasping as he staggered a few feet, then placed the weight down. 'Hang on, hang on. Can't get a good grip. Give me a minute.'

Zander showed no expression, just gave Davie the break that he needed.

He was freaking out inside. Freaking out. A dead body. He'd never seen a dead body before, let alone touched one. The blood. And Jono, so white, no colour left in his face or body. Like he was made of chalk.

They'd had the sense to roll the body in a polythene sheet before moving it. Jono had acted all flash when he'd called in the decorators to have Marilyn's kitchen painted. Aubergine. Apparently it was the in colour. Now the cover sheet they'd left behind was being put to a very different use. And they'd needed it. The stuff coming out of him . . . Urgh, Davie didn't even want to think about it. He was so light-headed. Couldn't breathe.

Davie stared at the hut in his garden, trying to work out the distance. Mirren lived in the middle house in the block, Zander at one end, Davie at the other. They just had to get it across two gardens, then past his window to the hut.

And they had to do it all without being seen. That meant staying close to the walls, dragging the body under the eyeline of the windows: commando crawl, pull, commando crawl, pull. There were access gaps between each garden so the bin men could get in to collect the black plastic bags that nestled inside steel cages outside every back door.

Well, now they were definitely throwing out a piece of rubbish.

The Macalisters on the other side weren't a problem. They both worked the night shift down at the frozen chicken plant. But his mum was always saying that old Mrs McWilliam, between Davie and Mirren, had the surveillance skills of a bloody telescope. He checked his watch. Almost eight. They'd just have to hope that she was so engrossed in Coronation Street that she didn't notice a polythene-wrapped corpse being dragged past her window. Commando crawl, pull. Commando crawl, pull.

This was mental. Pure mental. They were bound to get caught, jailed, and they hadn't even done anything wrong. Mirren's mum was a fucking fruit loop and they were going to get the blame. But what else could they do? Heart racing, hands shaking, there was no other choice. He tried not to look at Jono, not to think of the lump he was carrying as a real person, because if he did, he'd lose it. Freak out. A glance at

Zander told him nothing about how his mate was doing. He couldn't even begin to imagine how that would feel – carrying your own dad. Dead. Blood oozing under the polythene so that now it looked like a packet of steak you'd pick up from the supermarket.

Davie turned to the side and vomited, retching until there was nothing left to come up. Stomach empty, he closed his eyes, took a deep breath and forced some air back into his lungs.

'You OK?' Zander asked. 'I'll take the blame for this, Davie. Go home. I swear I'll never say you helped. I'll tell them it was me.'

Davie shook his head. How many times had Zander said he wished his dad was dead? Too many. But saying it was one thing, seeing it was another. He wasn't going to bail out and leave them to deal with this now. They stuck together. It's what they did.

'OK, let's go,' he told Zander, once again heaving his half of the body up, waiting until his pal had done the same. They got a fair distance this time. Fast and small steps now that they were no longer crossing someone else's garden.

One last semi-sprint and they burst through the hut door, hurtling the body between them, jumping at the bang as it hit the floor. Looking at each other, they slid down the walls, sweating, breathing hard.

'How did this happen?' Davie sighed, not really a question, not expecting an answer. He could feel the tears sitting at the back of his eyes, waiting to fall, and he pushed them away.

Zander reached into the hole in the floor, the one made all those years ago by a stray fag, and felt around, then pulled out a bottle of vodka he always kept there, took a slug and rested his head back against the wall. Both of them were filthy, their clothes matted with blood and dirt, their faces streaked where sweat had smeared the dust.

'It's weird. I hate him. Have always hated him. But now I just feel nothing,' Zander said quietly. 'Not even glad he's dead. Just nothing.' He knocked back another inch of vodka.

Davie's guts twisted again, but he knew there was nothing left to throw up.

'So what's the plan?' Zander said.

Davie nodded towards the hole from which Zander had pulled his vodka. 'There. We lift more of the floor, bury him underneath. No one can see us if we stay inside.'

'You've got to be fucking kidding,' Zander said, one hand running through his hair. 'We're putting my dead da under your hut?'

'Got a better idea?' Davie challenged him.

Zander paused, thought for a moment. 'No.'

'So we take up that half of the floor,' Davie said, pointing in the direction of the hole, 'and dig deeper, put the soil on this half. Then when we're done, just fill it with the soil again. Then tomorrow morning, I'll go to B&Q. Not the one in Darnley. Another one. Further away. Just to be sure. And I'll get some concrete, the ready-made stuff. I'll put a layer of concrete over the ground and then put the wooden floor back down. Look,' he finished wearily, 'it's all I've got.'

More vodka before Zander wiped his mouth with the back of his hand and then pushed himself up. 'Then we'd better start. I'll get a shovel from my garden and take the first shift. I meant what I said, pal. I'll do this.'

Davie shook his head. 'Naw. I'm in.'

Hours later, they were back on the half of the wooden floor that they hadn't ripped up, Jono no longer there, buried under the freshly replaced soil next to them. For once, Davie reached over, took the vodka bottle and took a slug. The reaction was instant. It didn't even get as far as his stomach before his mouth rejected it, spraying it across the wall.

'Christ, how can you drink that stuff?' he asked.

Exhausted, head resting on his knees, Zander didn't reply for a long time. Davie was beginning to wonder if he'd fallen asleep when he eventually croaked, 'Thanks, Davie. I mean it.'

Davie smiled sadly. 'Just hope we get away with it. Don't fancy Barlinnie.'

He wasn't joking. HMP Barlinnie stood like a grey fortress overlooking the city, a warning that it was up there, waiting for the mad, the bad and the evil.

'If anyone had seen us, we'd have known by now,' Zander murmured, a layer of hope sitting over a tone that blended confidence with desperation.

He was almost right.

The Macalisters were both at work, as hoped, so their house lay empty. Old Mrs McWilliam had missed Coronation Street, but only because she'd had a fish supper for tea and the massive intake of food had made her doze off in front of her four-bar electric fire.

There were no dog-walkers in the woods behind them, no kids loitering around where they shouldn't be, no police keeping an eye on Jono Leith's territory using covert surveillance. None of that.

Just Davie's mum, standing well back from the window,

wearing a thick fleece dressing gown, cigarette in hand. The noise of Mirren running around the house looking for Davie had momentarily distracted her from the book she was reading in the bath. Sidney Sheldon. He was her favourite.

She'd climbed out, opened the bathroom window, saw the state of Mirren as she'd flown out of the hut a few moments later, her boy and Zander in tow.

Then later, she'd seen the boys carry something into the hut.

It wasn't difficult to work out what had happened – some of her guesswork slightly off base, some of it spot on.

But the thing they'd dragged into the hut? She knew. Of course she knew.

For four hours she'd stood there, watching the light shine from the tiny opaque window, listening to the sound of gravel, soil, digging.

But at no point did she go there. That wasn't her job. Her job was to watch, oversee, look for danger coming, protect those she loved, keep their secrets.

Hadn't she been doing that for years?

This was just one more secret to add to the list.

And Ena Johnston would die before she gave it up.

64.

'Over the Rainbow'
– Eva Cassidy

Mirren knew that the Hollywood glitterati would turn out in force for Chloe's funeral. That's what happened here. Just another place to be seen, another opportunity to network. In a town that hated death unless it was at the hands of an action hero and earned over $100 million at the box office, they turned up, wearing black, even though it drained the complexion.

She couldn't bear it. Not today. So she'd insisted on family and close friends, invitation only, no more than twenty people, only those whom she trusted.

The ceremony was to be on the beach outside her home, to scatter the ashes of her girl in the place she'd loved more than anywhere else growing up. Mirren would sit on the deck night after night, watching her fearless twelve-year-old hit the waves in the sunset. Now she would always be there, in the ocean, her breath in every wave that crashed to the shore.

And no black or formality. Mirren was in a white flowing shirt, over jeans, her feet bare, her red hair flowing down her back. Everyone else was similarly casual. The rebel in Chloe would have loved that.

'You ready, honey?' Lou's arm was tight around her shoulders, passing support and love by osmosis.

Mirren nodded. What else was there to do? Keep going.

'Mom, are you OK?'

Keep going for her boy. Her gorgeous, six-foot, beautiful boy.

If there had been one blessing of the last fortnight, it was that he'd been here with her, arriving the day after Chloe died, the two of them clinging together in their grief. Some nights Mirren coped; other nights he was the parent, holding her, comforting her, promising her that they'd get through this.

Mirren took Logan's hand and let him lead her down through the house. Ahead of them, Lou was on her cell, the breeze from the sea carrying her words back to Mirren.

'And let me tell you something. Stop. Turn around. Go home. I don't care if you're at the fricking gate. I don't care if you're attached to him by fricking handcuffs, string or an invisible fricking force field. Turn around and go home. If that prick is too insensitive to see that you shouldn't be here, then you'll have to be the grown-up.'

Pause.

'Don't tempt me, doll. Because if you're here, I'll make sure that the photos I have in my desk drawer of you and an ageing reality star – a *female* ageing reality star – go viral. You know who I mean. Hell, I might send them viral anyway, just for fun.'

Lou snapped her phone shut and turned, jumping when

she saw Mirren right behind her. 'Oh, babe, I'm so sorry. Did you hear all that?'

Mirren nodded. 'It's fine. Mercedes?'

'Ah, so smart, my friend,' Lou replied with a warm smile. 'Unfortunately, Jack's slut, not so much. On the way up, she had a thing with Lana Delasso. It'll be interesting to see if she repeats it on the way down.'

Mirren shook her head. 'Don't, Lou. Let Jack have this one.'

Right on cue, Jack walked in the door, his face ashen, looking ten years older than he ever had before. He wasn't doing well.

Logan greeted his dad coolly. For her son's sake, she'd find a civil way to make this work, but there was no going back for them.

The truth was that Jack couldn't cope with reality. All these years he'd been away, she'd taken care of everything. She'd shielded him from the worst of their problems and hadn't minded when he'd headed off to a new location and left her to deal with things. When he'd finally had to face Chloe's illness, he'd reacted by seeking solace and escape with Mercedes. Anything to protect himself from a pain he couldn't handle.

Mirren would never regret marrying him. In hindsight she could see that there was blame with her too. Was he a rebound after Davie? Maybe. But it was security she craved. A normal home. She'd needed an anchor and, back then, she thought Jack was it. If she hadn't been so determined to make it last, she would have realized long before now that the anchor had no grip on shifting sands.

To her left, she heard Lou pick up the phone and speak again. 'OK, you can come in. But you've got Mirren to thank for it. Remember that.'

'Sometimes I wonder why we're friends,' Lou said, taking Mirren's hand now, while Logan took the other, and together the three of them headed out to the sands.

A couple of Chloe's friends were there. A few of Jack's buddies. To the left of the arch of white flowers that Mirren had constructed as a permanent memorial to her daughter, Zander stood, his cream shirt softly billowing in the sea breeze. Beside him, Lex Callaghan and his wife, Cara, looking beautiful in a floor-length blush maxi with ruby flowers in her hair.

Jack took charge, always the producer, thanking everyone for coming, then wistfully, choking back his emotions, recalling Chloe's life, from the time that she was his little princess until she hit her teens and onwards. They didn't mention her troubles. They'd agreed there was no point. That's not who their Chloe was. She was their angel, their love – the person she became when she did drugs was a stranger to them.

So they'd celebrate the good, let go of the bad. Wasn't that what she'd been doing her whole life?

Her tears fell as they cast the ashes, silent tears. This wasn't a time to indulge her pain. Her son needed her to be stronger than that. Later, as the sun set, she stood alone.

Jack and Mercedes back under whatever rock they'd crawled from. Lou and Logan inside having hot chocolate in the kitchen. Their friends all travelling home, all heartbroken, but already healing, moving on. It was all anyone could do.

'Hey,' he called. He'd always been one of few words.

'Hey.' In the distance, a lone surfer was a silhouette against the dipping sun and Mirren watched as he moved with such grace it was as if he belonged to the sea. Just like Chloe now.

'I've missed you,' she said softly when he arrived.

Zander nodded. 'I missed you. And I don't just mean the last couple of days.'

Mirren got it instantly because she felt the same. She smiled. 'Talk to me, Zander. About anything. Just talk,' she asked him, the emotion catching in her throat, raw and aching from days of grief.

He picked up a pebble and with a flick of the wrist cast it into the ocean. They both watched as it bounced several times before disappearing. They'd practised that at the local reservoir for hours when they were kids.

'I just couldn't handle the reminders,' he confessed. 'Couldn't handle the fact that something so shameful, so horrific, had changed our lives, brought us so much. Didn't seem right. I was already drinking, already messed up. Couldn't handle the anger. At you and Davie for creating a permanent reminder, at Jono, at my mum . . .'

'I get it all, Zander. I struggled with it too, but then I decided that Jono owed me. Owed me a new life. And I took it.'

He nodded, cast another skimming stone.

'I get that. We just handled it in different ways, I guess. No right, no wrong. Although maybe I was too young and stupid to see that at the time. And then it just seemed too late.'

'Where is she now?'

'Who?'

'Your mum.'

'Gone. Cancer. Two weeks after we won the Oscar. She'd moved to a convent in Ireland. They took care of her to the end.'

'Oh, Zander, I'm so sorry.'

He shrugged, not because he didn't care, but because it was done.

'She'd never have lasted without Jono anyway. She loved him. God knows why, but she did.'

Neither of them spoke for a while, sat on the sands, both with their own thoughts. Finally Mirren broke the silence.

'She's still around, you know. Marilyn. Went down to Liverpool, met the guy Jono was buying the drugs from. Married him. As far as I know, they're still together. She sent a photograph a few weeks ago to my office. Still looks the same, hanging on to the arm of this tall, imposing-looking guy, scar on one cheek. It was always the danger that attracted her. Turned her on. I sent the photo back. Not interested. She gave up her rights to my life a long time ago.'

'So why do you think she got back in touch?'

Mirren shrugged. In the light of dusk, her skin was almost alabaster white, a stark contrast to the dark circles underneath her eyes.

'Money. Fame. A free holiday in LA. She said she'd been up at Manny Murphy's funeral in Glasgow, so maybe being back there threw up memories. Could be anything. But Marilyn's only interested in what's in it for her, so it's a fair bet it wasn't because she was pining for her daughter or desperate to see her grandchildren. Grandchild, now. Only one.'

The sadness was almost unbearable.

Zander put his arm around her, held her close.

'Just one day at a time,' he murmured softly. 'And if you want me to, I'll stick around to help you.'

65.

'Let Her Go' – Passenger

When the buzzer from the gate rang, Davie was standing right next to it and automatically pressed the intercom button. His mum must have cleared baggage reclaim quickly. Normally he'd have gone in the limo to collect her, but he'd taken the kids down to the beach for an hour. It wasn't much, but it was a start. Lots of things had caused the shift in his view of parenting responsibilities. All the shit that had happened to him, Jenny's behaviour, the fact that the divorce was filed, under absolute confidentiality, and if it went to war, he wanted to show that he was making a real effort to be a dad. Not because he thought it looked good, but because he wanted to. Turned out Bella and Bray were really good kids. No thanks to him.

But he was determined to make the change because he was beginning to get it now. He got what it meant to be present, to be a parent. It was written all over every one of the images of Mirren's stricken face, plastered all over the celebrity mags in the days after Chloe died.

He was devastated for her. It was like it wasn't real. Nothing, he knew more than anyone, was real here. It was all just another titillating drama for the magazines and entertainment shows to feed on. He'd wanted to go to her. Of course he had. Desperately. But the last thing he wanted to do to Mirren McLean was cause her more pain, drag her back there. They'd tried to make it work. Back in the early days, when they first got here, they'd tried to act like before, to love each other, protect what they had. But the shadows were too dark.

Zander had disowned them, disgusted that they'd coerced him into using the story. That left just the two of them in this shiny new world. It should have been fun, exciting, thrilling, but all they saw when they woke up every morning, when they looked at each other, even when they closed their eyes, was that night.

In the end, it was too much. They were in love, but they were killing each other one memory at a time.

So they'd said goodbye, agreed never to speak again, never to meet. And he'd missed her every single day. Not today's Mirren – the successful, strong, accomplished Mirren. He'd missed the girl he adored, who'd cried when they made love for the first time, and who'd left him believing that perhaps real love only happened once.

'Hi, this is Sarah McKenzie. I'd . . . I'd like to speak to Davie Johnston.'

Leaning against the sink, Davie closed his eyes. Brilliant. Great. Just what he needed today.

He was tempted to ignore it, tell her to piss off, but he knew that it would eat away at him. Why was she there? Had she discovered something? Back to ambush him? Ready to go public with some combination of fact and fiction?

God knows he didn't need this right now, and Mirren definitely didn't.

Apprehension rising, he pressed the buzzer to open the gate and then headed to the front door. Ivanka was at the store and he was suddenly aware that he was on his own. No time to call a friend. No time to plan a defence. No time to go change out of his surfing T-shirt and board shorts. No time to prepare his heart and make it promise not to make an arse of him again. That lesson had been learned.

By the time the front-door buzzer rang, he was right there. Wordlessly, he opened the door and let her follow him back into the kitchen. His preference would have been to talk on the doorstep, but he was savvy enough to know that she could have let a photographer in and they could be out there, waiting in the gardens, ready to capture his reaction to anything she said.

'So what shall we start with?' he asked her, pulling out a stool at the breakfast bar and gesturing for her to do the same. 'Do you want to just ask me what you need to know, or do you want to fuck me first to make sure I'm nice and vulnerable and then maybe you'll get better answers?'

Harsh. And she reacted with a physical jolt. It took her a moment to answer as she climbed up onto the stool, her face flushed with – what? Heat? Embarrassment? Anger?

Even in his state of heightened anxiety, he could see that she looked different. Her hair was loose, in messy copper waves that reached down past her shoulders. Her eyes were bright, the green even deeper than before, almost a perfect match for the string of jade that hung round her neck, making a plain white vest and denim shorts seem edgy rather than just casual. No make-up, just a soft sheen on her lips.

'I deserved that,' she nodded, her hands clasped in front of her, nails painted dark grey.

'I know.' He wasn't letting her off the hook. Not until he knew why she was here. Another fishing expedition? Another interrogation?

'I know everything,' she said, her voice low and calm, which was the exact opposite of the emotions that swept over him. Speech wouldn't come, so he listened, watching as she pulled that bloody picture out of her pocket once again.

'Jono Leith was seeing Marilyn McLean. That's why they look like husband and wife here in the photograph. He was her lover. He attacked Mirren. Raped her, maybe. One of you killed him. In the movie, Zander takes the blame, but I'm not sure that's true.'

It had always been a risk, to make the movie of their story, but what choice did they have? Stay on the run, no money, no qualifications, no future? Or try to do something, anything to grasp for a better life?

No contest.

Mirren's account of what happened that night, the story she'd written, the one that he'd slipped in front of Wes Lomax at the St Andrews hotel, had been a faithful account of the truth. When they'd adapted it for the screen, there'd been some changes. Wes felt that Zander – brooding, handsome Zander – should be the fall guy, break the heart of every girl in the audience. They'd agreed, glad to have injected some fiction into a plot that they claimed had come entirely from the depths of Mirren's imagination.

At the time, they'd waited. Waited for someone in Scotland to watch the movie and put two and two together. Waited for Jono's body to be somehow found. Waited for it all to come crashing down.

But none of that happened.

What they hadn't realized was that almost nobody cared. Those who did were glad Jono was gone and most people believed the story that he'd gone off with Marilyn.

Marilyn wasn't going to tell anyone any different.

Zander's mum believed that story, and much as she loved him, she thanked God that she didn't have to live with the daily shame of watching the man she'd taken vows with in front of God commit adultery with the woman two doors along. God may forgive him, but she never would.

The criminal community shut down, convinced that Jono's disappearance involved cement boots, the River Clyde and payback for shafting and killing Billy McColl.

And the police? They were just happy to be shot of one more specimen of law-breaking scum. They put more effort into finding a lost cat than they put into locating the disappearing Mr Leith.

'So, what? What now?' Davie asked, neither confirming nor denying, frantically scrambling in his head for some way to make it out of this intact.

'Nothing.'

He could deny, get his lawyers on it, file an injunction . . . What did she say?

'Pardon?'

'Nothing. I'm doing nothing.'

It was so absurd he laughed. 'So let me get this straight.

You *think* you've stumbled onto a huge story that would set you up for life, one that you could milk to death – newspapers, TV, maybe even a book – and you're not going to run it?'

'No.'

'Not even in the *Daily Scot*?' His arms were wide now, gesturing disbelief.

'No. I don't work there anymore. I quit. And even if I hadn't, I still wouldn't run it. There's no evidence. No corroboration. Mirren has been through enough and . . .' He could see she was struggling to find the words. 'Maybe Jono Leith is no loss to the world.'

That took the wind out of his pissed-off, overanxious sails. Instant deflation.

It was almost as if saying all that, getting it all off her shoulders, made her sit up a little straighter. He noticed that her jaw jutted out slightly and he wasn't sure if it was defiance or pride, or just a determination to stay strong and remain unemotional. Reading her had clearly never been his strong point.

'I quit my job, quit Scotland, moved here a week ago. I'm going to be working out of the LA bureau. Travel and lifestyle stuff for the whole group, not celebrity gossip, so you don't have to worry.'

'The boyfriend?' Crap, why was he asking? Why? What did he care, he thought – while suddenly caring immensely.

'Gone. Long story. Actually, not that long. He met someone.'

'*He* met someone?'

For the longest time she didn't speak. Just stared. Not a sound except for the beat of his heart.

'And so did I,' she whispered, her eyes locked on his.

For the first time he heard a break in her voice as emotion caught in the back of her throat, as she watched, waited for him to speak. Nothing came. The fear was still there. Was this a set-up? Another sting?

Silence. More silence.

'So, OK . . .' she said, clearing her throat, 'I'm going to go. I just wanted you to know in case you were worrying, or . . . scared. There's no need to be. It's done.'

He so wanted to believe her. Wanted to pick her up, swing her round, scream with relief and then . . . but no. Not yet. Not until he was sure and the knot in his stomach had time to fully unravel.

'Where are you staying?' he managed to shout, as she reached the doorway.

His question made her pause, turn round, and for the first time she grinned, almost shyly.

'Same place as last time. When you're ready, come and get me.'

Davie was still laughing as the noise of her car faded into the distance, crossing over with another, more familiar engine getting closer. He met his mother at the door and took her coat.

'Someone looks happy, son. It's good to see you.'

'Good to see you too, Mum,' he told her, meaning it.

'But I don't know why you booked me in first class. You know I don't mind being in the normal seats. Waste of money, so it is. Why would anyone pay thousands of pounds for just a few hours in a comfier chair?'

'You're worth it. I'll send a private jet next time. Totally freak you out.'

That one got him a punch in the arm. 'Don't you dare. Oh dear Lord, I'd be affronted. I could buy a new soup bus with what they charge for one flight.'

They were moving through to the kitchen, his arm around her, so glad he'd persuaded her to come. 'The kids are dying to see you,' he told her. 'We're having dinner here tonight. I told them you'd make a Scottish speciality. Don't know where you're going to get steak pie and chips at this time in LA.'

'Don't you worry, son. You could put me in a desert and I'd still manage to rustle that up. Right, a nice cup of tea, I think. I brought my own teabags and some caramel wafers. I know how you—'

Her carefree chat stopped, and as Davie pulled his head out of the fridge, he realized why. The photo. The one Sarah had left. Still on the breakfast bar. And now his mum was staring at it, and it had stolen her words, and slapped her face until it was frozen.

Oh God.

'Mum?' he asked, over with her now, his arm around her again, hoping she could feel his love, desperate to ask the question that had been bothering him since the night he first saw it. Eventually, he realized that she couldn't speak, and decided he had nothing to lose.

'Mum . . .' he began, feeling more terrified than he'd ever been in his life, 'was Jono Leith my dad?'

66.

'Lego House' – Ed Sheeran

It was a perfect California sunset. The rays of light popped from every ripple of the ocean, their colour changing from white to burnt orange as they caught the reflection of the red rays of the sun slowly disappearing into the horizon.

On the Malibu beach in front of her home, Mirren and Zander sat on the sands, Mirren cross-legged, in black denim shorts and a grey tank, forty but looking no more than thirty. It was strange, Zander thought. In the last couple of weeks she seemed to have turned back the hands of time.

In the days after the funeral, they'd talked, twenty years' worth of conversations crammed into hour after hour of talking, crying, healing and even laughing. How could that be? Such a terrible time and yet there had been moments of light in there, brief but just enough to give them the strength to keep going.

During that time she'd told him that for years she'd lain awake at night listening for Chloe, searching the streets for her when she didn't come home, panicking that she'd die in her sleep when she came home high or wasted.

Now, sleep still often eluded her, but only because she was

sitting on her deck, watching the waves, having conversations with her girl out there in the ocean.

How he wished he'd been there for her.

He'd been so angry when they'd first moved here, so disgusted that they'd pushed him to make the movie, so scared of the demons that it would raise in him. And raise they did. Twenty years of addiction and chaos.

He hadn't been fit to love or to care for anyone. But as she told him repeatedly, he was here now. And that was all that mattered. They loved each other. Always had. Not in a romantic way, but as brother and sister, family, bonded over two sets of fucked-up DNA that had almost destroyed them both.

Almost.

'Heard from Jack?' he asked her, rolling up the sleeves on his white shirt, then shaking sand grains off his jeans.

Mirren nodded. 'He pops in every couple of days, has a coffee. Says he might go on the road with Logan for a week next month. Mercedes doesn't seem to be objecting. Think having an affair with someone might be a bit different from being their full-time partner,' she said, just a hint of a smile playing on her lips. Who could blame her? 'Especially now that she's six months pregnant.'

'Do you think it's Jack's? I heard there's some uncertainty. Charles Power's wife has cited Mercedes in their divorce.'

Power was the actor Mercedes had starred with in Jack's last movie.

Mirren flicked a stray strand of hair from the side of her face and shrugged sadly. 'I have no idea. Jack's problem. Not mine anymore.'

'How's Logan taking it?'

'Losing Chloe is breaking his heart. Our divorce isn't. He says he hears from his dad more now than he's ever done. I'm glad. Anyway, enough about me. How are you doing?' she asked, nudging his leg with her toe.

'OK. I think. Mostly. The filming is keeping me straight, and your friend Lou has threatened to send Carlton Farnsworth pictures of me with his wife if I fall off the wagon again. I've no idea if they really exist,' he said, smiling, 'but I'm not taking any chances.'

'It wouldn't surprise me in the least. That woman knows everything,' Mirren said, ramping up the feasibility factor.

'Yeah, you've got to love her. But listen, Mir, you know I won't go back there. I wouldn't do that to you. And I wouldn't do that to Chloe. She deserves better. She deserves me to stay clean for her. And I will, I promise. So please don't think you ever have to worry.'

'I know,' she said, her quiet confidence in him radiating between them. He'd made the promise to himself the night Chloe died. It was over. The drink. The drugs. He was completely clean for the first time in years and it felt . . . strange. Not great yet. Not even good. But he knew that if he went down that road again, Mirren would be devastated and he wouldn't do that to her. She deserved better.

'And what about the delectable Adrianna?' she asked. 'Did you see her again?'

'Are you kidding me? Nope. I'll save my scenes of dodging death for situations that have a stunt double.'

To anyone wandering past, surfboard under their arm or walking their dog along the Malibu shore, it would look like any two old friends, comfortable with each other, glad to be there.

'Are you sure that you're ready to do this?' Zander asked. They both knew what he meant. Mirren turned to look back at the gap between her house and the one next door.

'Too late if I'm not,' she said, raising her hand in greeting.

Zander followed her gaze and saw Davie Johnston walk towards them. His stomach clenched, then relaxed. It was he who had left Davie behind, cut him dead, and he'd give anything to change that now. But would Mirren? He'd never seen a love like theirs before. Solid. Complete. Both sure that it would last forever. Maybe their lives would have been better if it had. It was Jono's legacy. The bastard was dead and yet his actions still had consequences.

As Davie reached them, they could tell he was nervous. His left eye flickered the way it had done in times of stress since he was a toddler. That, right there and then, made Zander get up, throw his arms around him and hug him. Holding him so tightly that both of them struggled to breathe. Judging by the way it was reciprocated, Davie felt the same.

'Whenever you boys are done . . .' Mirren said warmly. At once they were fourteen again, and they fell on her, making her scream with laughter.

Those casual bystanders would now assume that they were three adult members of the same family. Had to be.

Only when they got their breath back did they all stop to look at each other properly.

'Thanks,' Davie said, 'for inviting me over. You've no idea what it means . . .' He stopped, his voice suddenly breaking.

'We do,' Mirren told him. 'Zander and I have been back in touch for a few weeks . . .'

'I'm so sorry about Chloe, Mir.'

'Thanks, and yeah, that brought us back. But it didn't feel right without you. So we thought, if it's OK with you, maybe we could give it another try. Be in each other's lives. Just friends,' she said, reassuring him of where they all stood.

'God, I'd love that,' Davie said at once, and Zander could see the pain that was still there.

'But there's stuff I need to tell you both first. There was a journalist trying to contact us a while back . . .'

'Yeah, she called me,' Mirren confirmed.

'I told her you were too smart to let her anywhere near you,' Zander said confidently.

The awkward pause told them he was wrong.

'It's a long story, but she worked out the truth. Or at least what she thinks is the truth. But it's not going any further. She still doesn't know where Jono is, had no proof of what happened, nothing to go on. And even if she did, I believe her when she says she wouldn't use it.'

'Why?'

'Because . . . because I trust her. And she's quit her job. And come here.'

The three of them took a moment to digest this. 'Are you sure, Davie?'

'Yeah. I really am. Danger over. Trust me.'

'We always did,' Mirren answered truthfully.

Another pause. 'Is he still there?' Zander asked, each word excruciating to spit out.

Davie picked up a stone and threw it at the shoreline,

making it skim across the surface exactly as Zander had done a few weeks before.

'Yeah. I was talking to my mum about it last week. Turns out she knew all along. Saw us that night. So she's never moved house, never will, just stayed there all this time protecting me. Protecting all of us. I own the house now, bought it for her years ago because she insisted on staying there. Now I know why. She was worried someone might move the hut. She had to watch over it. Look, this isn't perfect, but we've lived with it this long and we'll just have to go on, trust that it will be OK.'

'Might be easier now that we're in each other's lives again,' Mirren told them, and Zander gave in to his urge to throw his arm around her and give her a hug. She was the strongest woman he'd ever known. They'd be fine. It took him a moment to recognize the emotion, and eventually he realized it was confidence. Confidence in the future. For the first time in perhaps his whole life, he felt sure that everything was going to be OK.

'How is your mum?' he asked Davie, noticing for the first time that they were dressed the same: both in shirts, his white, Davie's pale blue, both in the same shade of jeans, both in bare feet. There was a synergy to it. Sitting on either side of Mirren, they looked like bookends.

'Yeah, she's good. But I have to tell you something else. And I'm sorry, Zander – so sorry if this hurts you.'

'Oh bugger, and it was all going so well,' Zander murmured, trying to ease the sudden tension with a joke.

'She told me that . . . that . . . Oh fuck. Right. The reason that we stayed where we stayed? The reason that she never found someone else to share her life with, the reason that she was so fucking stoic and strong and she never complained . . .'

'Was?' Zander asked, fairly sure the answer wasn't going to be something trite and amusing.

Davie's lips were moving, but he could barely hear his own words. 'Jono was my dad too. We're brothers, Zander.'

For a moment Zander couldn't decipher what he'd said. Brothers? How could that be? But then, why would it not? Loyalty was never Jono's strong point, but control was. It would be totally in character for him to make someone pregnant, then arrange for them to be close by so he could keep an eye on things. Suddenly Zander remembered the presents for Davie's birthday, Christmas – Walkmans, computer games, brilliant stuff, all overly generous for a neighbour's kid. Zander hadn't given it a second thought back then. Now he did and it all made perfect sense.

'Mate, say something,' Davie begged. 'I just need to know whether or not to start running.'

Typical Davie – defusing everything with a nervous laugh.

And it always worked. Zander held out his hand – to his brother.

'All I can say is you might have got the brains, but thank God I got the looks.'

Epilogue

'Sunshine On Leith' – the Proclaimers

Los Angeles, 2 March 2014

Helicopters circled the skies above the Dolby Theatre, just high enough so as not to breach the no-fly zone, which would interfere with the sound systems of the eighty-two film crews that lined the red carpet below. The presenters in their tuxedos and ballgowns put as much effort into their appearance as the stars whom they tried to corral into their spaces for a sixty-second sound bite.

The Oscars were late this year, delayed by a week so they didn't clash with the 2014 Winter Olympics. No one minded. It gave the beautiful people another seven days of sweating, pummelling, injecting and plucking themselves to perfection.

Davie Johnston was the first to arrive, co-presenting with Ellen DeGeneres. The thing with someone like Davie was that you could never keep him down for long. As long as he was making money for this town, he was good for business. And he was. His latest production, *Beauty and the Beats*, had been a monster hit, knocking Lana Delasso's show out of the number-three slot. Poor Lana – overtaken by a show with a shit title. He'd pondered changing it, but the network had loved it so he had let them run with it. You had to know when to pick your battles. Lana had lost hers. The cameras had followed her to Brazil, where she got ass implants, then married the doctor who'd inserted them. To her horror, one of them had ruptured, so she was now lopsided, and the doctor had released a sex tape, pocketed the cash and scarpered back to Rio de Janeiro. Davie had of course sympathized with her . . . but only in public. In private, he'd sent her a picture of Kim Kardashian's butt and a $50 voucher for a Beverly Hills plastic surgeon.

Even that story hadn't knocked the other reality-TV scandal off the front pages. Sky Nixon, aided by her mother, Rainbow, had been caught attempting to blackmail a New York politician after a sordid threesome involving Sky and her mother. Turns out Daddy was filming the whole thing via a hidden camera in the chandelier. Rainbow was most furious because she said she had the worst angles. Anyone who'd, rightfully, doubted Davie now believed he was innocent. He wasn't going to try to convince them otherwise.

Davie waved over at his soon-to-be-ex wife. Jenny Rico and Darcy Jay were officially a couple now, both blissfully happy and sharing parenting of the kids with Davie. Rumour had it he was in a new relationship, but this time around, he said he was keeping it all to himself. Although one Scottish reporter did have the exclusive.

Mirren McLean was the next to step out of the limo. Dressed in a blush Dior sheath, overlaid with hand-sewn crystals, her hair swept back like a Roman goddess, she looked absolutely stunning. She was nominated for Best

Screenplay, Best Director and Best Movie tonight for the last Clansman. She was the favourite to win all three, despite saying that not even the triple win would come close to the joy she felt on launching Chloe's Care, a drop-in centre for teens with substance issues.

Right behind her was Lex Callaghan and his beautiful wife, Cara, dressed in vintage Chanel. All three greeted each other with genuine warmth and the cameras went wild, especially when they posed one either side of Lex. It was an image that would flood the media around the world the next day. Pure Hollywood. Lucky guy.

Jack Gore wandered over. Single again, it had smashed the headlines when Mercedes Dance had taken a DNA test that proved within a margin of 99.9 per cent that Jack Gore was not the father. Mirren posed happily with him. The official line was that they remained great friends for the sake of their son, Logan, who was currently on tour with his band and selling out 50,000-seat stadiums across Europe.

And finally, last to arrive, as only the stragglers on the red carpet remained, was Zander Leith. And boy, was he worth waiting for. Dressed in a Guilloti tux, flecks of grey hair at the temples, he had never looked more dashing. On his arm, his assistant, Hollie, looking like a curvy babe and beaming with confidence. There had been rumours that their relationship was more than professional. Neither party would confirm or deny.

Four hours, fifty-seven minutes later, Mirren McLean took to the stage, graciously received her Oscar for Best Original Screenplay and smiled. It was unusual for a sequel to win it, but the box office agreed that it was the best of a brilliant series.

'I'd like to dedicate this to my daughter, Chloe. The world was a brighter place when she was in it and I will never stop missing her every moment of every day.'

The cameras panned to the audience. Nicole Kidman. Jennifer Garner. Gossip columnist Lou Cole. Tears running down their cheeks.

'I'd like to thank my son, Logan, for being just the coolest, best-looking guy on earth.' Laughter through the tears now.

'And finally, I'd like to thank my other family. The one I chose for myself. This is also for Davie Johnston and Zander Leith.'

And the applause thundered on.

Acknowledgements

From Ross

To the three wonderful women in my life, Brianna, my mum Isabel, and sister Elaine. You all know how much you mean to me.

Jim, Hollie, Euan and all the brilliant Ross and King Clans.

To those people who believed in me from back in the day . . .

Roddy Hood, Eric Simpson, Richard Park, Rod Natkiel.

For inspiration, Paul Cooney, Jack McLaughlin, Sheila Duffy.

The gang of brothers led by my brother from another mother, Allan Stewart, Paul Coia, Gary Hely, Lance Tankard, Julian Stone, Jim Piddock, Kenny MacKenzie and Adrian Woolfe.

Those who've 'managed' me, Jan Kennedy, Jill Shirley and David Meehan.

For making work a better place, Emma Gormley, Sue Walton, Neil Thompson, Helen Warner, Steve Gee, Dan Brown, Donald Martin and Duncan Leven.

I miss you, Hal Fishman and Jeremy Beadle.

For being great pals, Gary Barlow, Lorraine Kelly, Sue Barker and Julie McGarvey

Sarah Cairns and all the staff at the Mandarin Oriental, Hyde Park, London. I'm a 'Fan'.

To YOU reading now for supporting my career in radio, TV, theatre, film and now in print!

From Shari

My life is blessed with three incredible guys. John Low and our small blokes are everything.

Deadlines would never have been met without the friendship (and unpaid chauffeur services) of some very special people: Jan and Paul Johnston, Lyndsay Macalister and Neil Wilson, Pauline and Kevin Feeney, Gillian Miller and Barry Murphy and my irrepressibly spectacular step-daughter, Gemma Low.

To the sisterhood, Frankie, Janice, Linda, Wendy, Pamela, Isobel, Sylvia, Mitch, Carmen, Lennox, Emma, Hazel, Doreen, Mel and Fairy Crean.

And the menfolk, Gary Bock & Mike Bitner

To Cyril and Lilian McWilliam, Brian and Kate Rodden, John and Lynne Wilson, Diane and Billy McLean

To my family – Sadie, Rosina and all the Hills, the Murphys, the Lows, the LeCombers and the branches that make our very large tree.

To the unflappable Rebecca Ritchie at Curtis Brown, and Eloise Wood at Macmillan

Thank you once again to the journalists, booksellers and bloggers and readers who have shown stellar support over the years.

And from us both . . .

As always, a million thanks to our agent, the fabulous Sheila Crowley, who championed Shari King from the start.

And to the utterly magnificent Wayne Brookes for his enthusiasm and belief. We heart you. We do.

xxxx

Special Note

This novel is pure fiction, although we have included some famous names, places, events and used artistic license to change a few details along the way.

In 1993, the Oscar for Best Original Screenplay was won by Neil Jordan for the outstanding *The Crying Game*.

Our fictional hero, Davie, does not of course have rivalry with the very real and very successful Ryan Seacrest.

Similarly, he has never met Simon Cowell.

And we're fairly sure that even if our characters existed, Gerry Butler and Ewan McGregor would still win more column inches.

Love,
Shari King xx